AFTER

THE PRESIDENT

DISAPPEARED

A NOVEL

by

Rodger Christopherson

intercept777@centurylink.net

Other books by the author
A Little Bit of Anarchy
Out of the Fire Mist
Monkey in a Tree
Beverly Hills Women
Three Weeks Until Tomorrow
Illusions
Beyond Heaven and Hell – non fiction
Health - non fiction
Origins & Meaning -- non fiction
Circles in the Sand - Poetry

This is a true story. It either happened, will happen or is happening this very minute in some parallel universe. Anything is possible.

NIGHT FLIGHT

Minutes off the runway at 3am in the morning and into level flight, the head attendant on board the later-day Air Force One, placed three well-cooked eggs, five sausage links and three slices of toast in front of the President of the United States.

"Well, that's more like it," the President said as he lifted up one egg with his fingers and looked under it. Then he began to eat in his typical egregious manner, regardless of the fact that none of the others in his diplomatic entourage had their food as yet, especially his wife.

"Good," he said to her as the second attentdant finally set her own dish down, pointing to his plate with his fork. By then his second egg had already disappeared, along with his toast and a link of sausage. One by one the other members of the party were then served and began to eat also. Gratefully so, because they knew that if they had been forced to watch the president much longer they would have completely lost their own appetites. The First Lady, on the other hand, was becoming embarassed. Her husband's behavior had begun slipping lately and seemed to be getting worse. Actually right after he took office a year and a half ago for his second term. But whenever she had asked the president's personal physician about it, he had simply shrugged and told her not to worry. So, okay, she had decided, but it still bothered her. Not so much for what he might be going through, however. She had long ago stopped caring about that. It was what the rest of the world might think and how it might reflect on her. But for now, so what, she assured herself as he began talking again. She was getting off the plane in Hawaii in just a few short hours and he would be on his own for the rest of the trip without her.

"Okay," the president said at last, with his mouth still half full. "I'm glad you could all make the trip."

3

On it went, as the president finally finished chewing and continued. He talked as the first lady ate her breakfast and went on through the breakfasts of all the other members of the group and through their second cup of coffee. Eventually, however, the ordeal came to an end as the Chief Executive burped loudly, unsnapped his seat belt and stood up.

"I'll have more to say on that when I get back," he stated as he pushed past his wife and headed for the restroom.

Jack Briggs, reluctant, newly appointed nuclear-arms advisor, watched him closely, studying the hidden tension in the aging face that belied the bullying bluster manifested in his behavior. Quite frankly, the man appeared more than a little harried.

"Damn," he said under his breath as he turned and watched the president proceed to his destination, push open the lavatory door and go in.

"Damn," said Sam Birnstead, the Secretary of the Navy, verbalizing Jack's thoughts as he came across the aisle and sat down beside Jack.

"This is going to be a long trip," the older man stated. A big man man with a strong face and a manner of addressing things that Jack had admired from the first time they had met.

"Certainly looks like it," Jack stated in agreement.

"Anyway. How's your wife doing? Heard she had some complications."

"Yes," Jack replied. "Nearly lost the baby. The Doctor put her on complete bed rest until the end."

"Not the best of times to be on a trip."

"Especially on this plane with a dozen countries ready to blow us out of the sky."

"Probably more. How come you accepted your appointment?"

"Damned if I know. But this is it. Once we're back, I'm done. How about you?"

"Well, it's probably hopeless but I keep thinking maybe there's still something that can be done to get the international situation under control."

"Isn't that what this trip is all about?"

Sam scanned Jack's face before he replied, realizing that there was no way Jack could have known the truth before hand.

"Not really," he answered. "His intent is to provoke the Japanese into attacking China, pure and simple," he said bluntly.

Jack looked back at him. Their eyes locked for an instant. Was Sam being serious?

"I'm serious," Sam assured him. "The man has completely jumped the track."

"How so?"

"Well, he used to be just a fundamentalist's fundamentalist who simply thought he had a direct link to God. That's why he ran for President to begin with. But lately he has begun to think its all one sided and that God is not listening to him anymore in return. That he has been rejected for not doing enough to save the world."

"Save the world? Him?"

"Yeah. How about that?"

"And he thinks he has a divine mission and he's failing? How?"

"Well," Sam said with a shrug. "One thing he seems to be very concerned about is that it's been over thirty five years since the turn of the century and Christ has not reappeared for the second coming. Then, since Christ hasn't shown up, the Judgement has not been performed, the wicked have not been purged and the righteous have not been lofted up to heaven."

The idea was so ludicrous Jack almost laughed but checked himself and let the impact of it sink in.

"I hope you're not going to tell me that he really thinks there's something he can do about it," he replied.

"I'm afraid he does. He thinks the planet needs a world-wide holocaust in order to get God's attention and bring about the Tribulation and the Rapture."

Jack shut his eyes and sat there for nearly half a minute before responding.

"So he's trying to get the Japanese to bomb China and precipitate a world wide conflict? Is that what this is all about. Is that why we are on the way to Japan?"

Sam nodded, "I know. Pretty damned horrific, isn't it?"

"And with two and a half more years in office. What if he can make it happen?"

"That's the thing that really keeps me awake at night."

They sat there without speaking further as Jack tried to absorb the immensity of what was finally beginning to make some sense. George W. Bush had gone down in history as the most inept president ever to take office. The one who had been on the verge of sending civilization back to the dark ages. But that was nearly three decades earlier. In the meantime God had not purged the wicked from the face of the earth. They had multiplied instead and overwhelming evil deeds were becoming the order of the day. And, once again driven by fear, the political pendulum in America had swung wildly to the right. Only considerably further this time as Stanley Drukus had stepped forward to capitalize on the public's obsessive apprehension and put himself in the White House, obviously now, to personally guide humanity back onto the path of righeousness. It was a horror story of immense proportions that went on and on and guess what? Here Jack was, on board a plane with a lunatic, heading off into the unknown, a strong sense of foreboding growing inside.

"Well, I think I'll go in the back and get some rest," Sam said at last as he got up. Then he looked back at the lavatory where the subject of their conversation was still locked away behind the door after at least fifteen minutes, made a face and shrugged.

"Talk to you later," Jack said and nodded his concensus. Then he also took a glance down the aisle. He was not the only one. By then that closed door had become the subtle subject of conversation in the cabin area for those farthest from the first lady. One member of the group even quietly suggested to his neighbor that perhaps the President was constipated.

By then, however, the First Lady was having difficulty hiding her own concern and growing embarrassment. *What now*? she asked herself. What was that damned fool doing back there? Couldn't he hear the snickering? Didn't he have any pride at all? What was she supposed to do? Good grief. He could have at least waited until after they got to Hawaii to do something this stupid.

Finally, for lack of alternatives, she got up and went down the aisle where she tapped softly on the door, trying to ignore all the eyes that were on her. There was no response. Quite puzzled, she knocked louder. Then again. Finally, looking back, she happened to catch Jack's eye and gave him a helpless stare, completely at a loss as to how to deal with the situation. Quite tempted to pretend he didn't understand and turn away, Jack at last felt sorry for her and left his own seat. At her side, his even louder raps were also to no avail.

"Stanley," the First Lady finally said in shrill iritation and pounded some more.

With the entire staff now viewing the ongoing scene, Jack

rattled the door quite severely. Then he spoke to the stewardess who finally found a key that fit the lock from the outside.

"Please," he said, as he motioned for her to proceed.

Dutifully, she opened the door a small amount and stepped back so the President's wife could look in, which she quickly did. After a brief moment the First Lady withdrew her head and stared at Jack with the strangest, most bewildering expression he had ever seen in his life.

Jack then pulled the door open the remainder of the way and peered into the tiny room himself. It was completely vacant. President Drukus was not inside.

A rather strange joke to be playing on everyone, Jack said to himself, uncertain as to what might have actually happened. Especially since the president was much too vain a person to be playing practical jokes on anyone. And certainly not on himself. Well, perhaps he had somehow gone back to the galley for some reason. But, if so, how had he managed to leave the lavatory without anyone noticing, since it was in clear view of half the passengers? And why had he taken the trouble to somehow lock the door behind him, if that were even possible without a key. Either way, it would have been a rather strange thing to do. Especially for the President. But the matter was soon out of Jack's hands. The lead Secret Service agent had already been alerted down in the lower cabin.

What was going on, he demanded when he arrived at the lavatory, then listened impatiently as the First Lady became agitated, angry and unable to explain.

"I don't think we have a serious problem," he stated quite authoritatively, however, placating her to the best of his ability, encouraging her to retake her seat and relax.

"Obviously, he has to be on the plane somewhere. We'll track him down soon enough. He's probably conducting some kind of improv security exercise with the help of an unspecified flight crew member," he told her with assurance.

I damn well hope so, she said to herself, conceeding. Thank god he hadn't just gone in there and died in front of all these people with his pants down. How horribly undignified that would have been and with that a search was conducted. It proceeded though the airplane, into the cockpit and finally into the baggage compartments below. After some forty five minutes of conjecture, intensive search and an even more thorough second search, only one thing seemed clear. Impossible as it sounded, the only conclusion that could be drawn was that the President was no longer on board the world's most secure aircraft.

MISSING

Back on the ground at Camp David two hours later, Air Force One was wheeled into its private hangar and the immense metal doors securely locked behind it before anyone was allowed to disembark. With the passengers on orders to stand by, all baggage, food supplies, cartons, containers and any other item of any size not bolted to the airframe was removed and thoroughly searched by base Military Police personnel for clues or body parts, as was the empty aircraft once again. By now the sun was full up and the new business day had begun in the nation's capital, but the whereabouts of the President was still a complete mystery. So was that of the Secretary of Commerce and the Secretary of the Navy with whom Jack had just shared some time. Also very unusual, the Camp David base commander, General Max and his second in command, Colonel Barnes, had not reported for duty that morning either, and were now over three hours late.

While this had been going on, other members of the Presidential group attempted to locate the Chief of Staff, who had remained behind on the trip. He, too, had not arrived at his office. Nor was he at home at that moment.

"He's probably still out jogging around the park," his wife explained matter of factly to the staff member who had called. What was the problem? Except when it was raining, he did it everyday.

"Or, he could have stopped for coffee at that small cafe nearby. The Donut Shack, I think it's called. Sometimes he does that after he runs. Must have. His car keys and briefcase are still here on the kitchen table where he always leaves them when he goes to the park. Of course.... I'll have him call you the minute he gets back. Before he gets in the shower."

"Would you believe it?" another staff member said. "She's off to Palm Springs."

"Who?"

"The Vice President. Who else?"

"Again? I thought she just got back. Or maybe that was Tahiti. Whatever. Get her on the phone."

"Jesus. Why does she keep doing that? I thought VPs were supposed to spend some time in Washington."

"She claims it's in the nation's best interest to keep as much physical distance between herself and the President as possible, in

8

case the President's security net is ever penetrated."

"Right!"

"What does that mean?"

"Well, you know how Drukus hates women. He's never forgiven the party for forcing her on him and he's damned well not going to acknowledge her any more than he has to, even though she is in the subservient position. The thought of having her in the Oval Office in case he is ever incapacitated must drive him nuts. But that's besides the point. The nation can't be left leaderless. We need to reach her. Who are you talking to?"

"The cognizant secret service agent. They're checking now. You know, I bet part of the problem is all the bad names he called her after that time he patted her on the butt in public and she stiffed him. Just a minute. What...? She's playing golf with a group of women's rights advocates and has left explicit instructions that she is absolutely not to be disturbed. Even if a terrorist blew up the White House. Really? She said that? Wow. But have you actually seen her in the last couple of hours?"

"No, sir. I have not," said the voice on the other end of the line. "But that was what was on her calender and her escort vehicle picked her up early, so I can only assume....."

"Assume, hell. Get out there or get over there, or whatever. But find her. This is an emergency."

"Well, okay. Yes, Sir. I'll do my best, Sir," he said. "But you know how she is. If she gets offended she'll trash my career for sure.... Yes, Sir. Thank you Sir."

The same was true of the Secretary of State. Another woman, she was attending the European Alliance meeting in Switzerland. But trying to reach her was even more imposible. All satellite circuits were suddenly busy and there was no other way to get through. Then the group tried to reach the heads of the CIA, FBI, NSI, NSA, Homeland Security and the Pentagon, all to no avail. No other calls were possible because, by now, both cell phone and land-line systems were totally clogged.

At this time the first lady, now downright hysterical, was dispatched back to the White House in a tactical helicopter while the rest of the group moved to the base Com Center. Here they used the military RF communications systems to more fully assess what seemed to be a most dire situation. Once there, it didn't take long to arrive at a conclusion. At approximately four hours and three minutes after midnight, Eastern Standard Time on the seventeenth day of May in 2038, when the President of the United States went into the lavatory of Air Force One, nearly every other political, governmental, military, religious, business and social leader in the entire country had also simultaneously disappeared. In addition, a multitude of radio stations from such countries as Libya, Pakistan, Syria, North Korea and even China had just come on the air demanding the immediate release of their own leaders whom the United States was accused of having somehow abducted. Clearly, the problem was of even vaster dimensions than originally suspected and by evening there was no doubt, whatsoever. The entire planet earth was leaderless. Somewhat later it was also determined that the phenomenon had even extended itself downward into the underworld of illicit and clandestine activity. Anywhere and everywhere. Everywhere there was a structured organization of power of any significant magnitude.

THE ISLAND

In spite of the way all the old line anti-feminists like President Drukus felt about it, it was a time of increasingly more women in key governmental positions. In that regard Katherine Beaumont was the first woman to be elected Governor in her state. Rightly proud, it had been a long and difficult struggle. Even with her, lately come, second husband's money. Admittedly, he was a wealthy man but he had still contributed little to the actual campaign. But it was only later, however, after the honeymoon, that his true chauvinism really begin to show itself. Undoubtedly, the signs had been there. They had to have been. But she was far too involved in promoting her career to have allowed herself to openly acknowledge all the red flags.

He had pursued her more ardently than she had ever been in her life and had somehow convinced her that having him as a husband would provide additional fullfilment to her life. How was she to know? She had been happily married to the same man for sixteen years previously but he had been killed in an auto accident, leaving her distraught, lonely and vulnerable. Then along came Max. A bit older, but rich and handsome enough. A decent enough prospect at the time, she thought, even though he had been down the divorce-court aisle three times. Something else he had lied about, saying it was only once. As for why he had specifically chosen her, she was never completely sure. But whatever the reason, he had played a many-sided, deceitful game to get both their names on the same marriage certificate. And then the real truth

10

of things began to show.

Just like the country's President, he did not approve of women in politics. Or in business and a few other places. His bedroom behavior was equally crude and archaic. But it had not mattered. She had used what money he had given her wisely, had manipulated his connections to her advantage and been elected anyway. She had also quickly learned to sidetrack his rough sexual advances with minimal aggravation. That was the easy part. There were other deeper, hidden costs for having married the man that also showed themselves. They lingered there, haunting at times, the what she had traded for what, and the what she had given up to get what she had. It was not always a pleasant thing to live with, especially the part about having allowed herself to be misled so badly.

She was a good governor, however, and no one could ever deny that. Politically astute, tough minded and willing to deal with issues, some of which taxed her to the extreme. But, difficult as her career demands were, they had a positive side. Not only was there little time left over to dwell on the insufficiencies of her marriage, those demands provided her with a multitude of excuses for getting home late, not performing what he called her wifely duties and for avoiding his company in general. They also gave her considerable opportunity to attend social functions, meet new people and even to get out of town once in a while. But she had still made preliminary contact with an attorney. Even with possible damaging political implications, divorce was high on her list of priorities. Not only had her husband grossly misled her prior to marriage, he also continued the deceit with an old mistress. Without moral component, the marriage contract was thus rendered null and void and she acted accordingly.

But, even with their own sense of adventure, her resultant cautious and discreet encounters were extremely rare. And that was exactly what she had been thinking about the previous evening just before drifting off to sleep. The right man. Wistfully, she felt the need. Wistfully, the thoughts became the dream. Slowly, but smoothly, she slipped into the dream as she fell asleep, feeling herself caught up in someone's arms. A long, dancing, slowly advancing dream. Delightful, delicious, delirious perfidy, moving forward to the moment of ecstatic passion with great lucidity.

But then, suddenly, what was this? What weird, jarring, distressing change was this, right in the middle of her beautiful dream. How could it be? What was she doing lying down in the middle of an expansive, grassy meadow somewhere in broad daylight surrounded by what had to be thousands of people? Quickly, she got to her feet and looked around. The people were mostly male, but people of all races and nationalities and forms of dress. Some were even in the nude. And, by the looks of it, most of the nude ones seemed to be Americans. My god. What was going on? This new dream was even more limpid than the earlier one, she thought, somehow being in the dream and being very aware of it at the same time. These people, who were all these people and what were they doing here? What was she doing here, standing amongst them in her pajamas, looking at the confusion and bewilderment in their faces that matched her own.

Subconsciously, she fumbled at her pajama top and buttoned two more buttons to help hide the proportions of her bust line. Next, she looked down at her bare feet. God, such realism, the cool grass touching her toes. Then a small butterfly landed on her arm, folded its wings and sat there as though studying her. She was surprised to be able to see the fine lined, detailed structure of the black-marked, golden wings so clearly and the tiny antennae on the insect's head. She shook herself once, then again. What in hell was going on? She took a small step forward and banged her toe on a small rock, of which there seemed to be many around.

"Ouch," she cried out. It hurt. Damnit. It really hurt.

"My God," she said to herself. "This isn't a dream at all. It isn't a dream."

But that was utterly ridiculous. No, it was impossible. It couldn't be. But still.... Damn! She was really there. Here. Wherever. She had to be. It was not a dream. My God, it was real. There was no other way to account for it.

Desperately, she tried to calm herself, forcing herself to breath deeply, settle down and think it through. How could she have gone to sleep in her own bed and woken up to find herself outside in some completely unrecognizable, completely foreign place? And it was day, not night. It made no sense at all. But where was she? What was this place? At first glance it appeared to be a tropical island because she could see the blue of ocean waters through the palm trees in front of her. Yet, when she turned around, rising up in the distance behind was a pristine-looking, snow-capped mountain which, oddly enough, seemed to have its lower reaches partially blanked in a thin brown layer of smog. Very, very peculiar, she thought, still trying to control the panic, forcing her mind to work it through more completely. One minute she was lying in her luxurious warm bed, dreaming her lascivious dream.... But from there to here, instantaneously, without transport or memory of the journey. It was incomprehensible. How could that be? Yet here she was, now fully convinced of the reality of it, standing in full sunlight in her pajamas amongst a huge crowd of strangers who all had the same shocked look on their faces.

Then a funny thought passed through her mind. She was thankful it had been an unseasonably cool evening so she had worn her pajamas to bed instead of a that old tee shirt she loved so well. Worse, she might have been wearing nothing at all if she had let her husband have his way. What a horrible thought. Then, she too, would be standing there in the nude like so many of these less-fortunate souls. And then, in the midst of all that, another complete disruption. Laughter, growing louder, almost hysterical, and very close at hand behind her, coming from a swelling circle of people. Instinctively she moved nearer and pushed through the tightening pack.

"Oh, my god," she said out loud, temporarily shocked at the incongruity of it, for there, in the center on the ground, looking exactly as if he slid off a chair, sat the red faced, stammering President of the United States with his trousers and shorts down around his ankles. It was way, way too much. Like the rest of the onlookers, she could only laugh. At last. That unspeakable individual caught with his pants down. What could be more just? Nothing that she could think of. The laughter helped tremendously, breaking up the state of panic she had been sliding into but at the same time helping to reinforce the reality of what had happened.

But then, in the midst of it, another disruption as a male voice boomed, telling others to get the hell out of the way. It was the Secretary of Defence without his rimless glasses, wearing what appeared to be a silky looking, off-pink pair of shorts that did little to hide his skinny, hairless legs. Immediately he went to face the President.

"For Christ's sake, Stanley. Get up," he commanded, and extended his hand.

Taking the offered hand, the President pulled himself up, then reached for his pants. Without taking the time to tuck in his shirt tail, he quickly zipped them up. By then the laughter had began to subside and the Secretary spoke into the President's ear. President

Drukus slipped out of his suit coat and handed it over. The Secretary quickly put it on, the crowd parted and off they went, deep in conversation.

"Oh, my," Katherine said. "What next?" Then, helplessly she sat down in the grass, put her head down and began to cry. Tears and tears. Almost convulsively, every unrealized tear of an entire lifetime seemed to come pouring out. Impossibly, she tried to quit, to gain control, but she could not. Finally she was shaken by a hand on her shoulder and a man's voice in her ear. A vaguely familiar voice.

"Katherine? Is that you?"

It was more than enough to get her to stop. She did, and now she was quite mortified at having been so weak. It was so out of character for her, especially in front of this individual. She quickly dried her eyes on the sleeve of her pajamas, rose and turned.

"Oh. Jess," she said and bit her lip, determined to present a strong front no matter what. Then she looked him over with disappointment, wondering why it had to be him instead of someone else. Most anyone else but the fellow governor of her neighboring state.

"How come you're fully dressed when most of the rest of us Americans seem to be in our sleepware?" was the only thing she could think of to say at the moment.

Unable to help himself, Jess stared at the bustline he had once uninvitedly groped but could never get a second chance at. Instinctively, Katherine put her hand up, only to find the top button of her pajama top missing. But it served its purpose. The gesture brought Jess's attention back to the question asked and the answer finally occurred to him.

"Lucky, I guess. I was in Europe when it, this, happened. And I was just on the way back to my hotel after a meeting. That was in the evening. And what with the time differences, well…"

"Well, yeah. So be a gentleman and give me your suit coat."

"But, uh, gee....What if it gets cold or something? Can I have it back if I need it?"

"Still the same smuck as always, aren't you?" she told the man she had a very disatisfying encounter with at at regional Governor's Conference a couple of years ago.

"What's that supposed to mean? I thought we had something going between us?"

"Why? Because you once pawed your way under my blouse?"

"I couldn't help it. Your, umm, uh…. are so, uh…. Besides, I thought you liked it?"

Katherine's reply was to stare strongly back. Then she told him maybe he'd better keep his blessed coat.

"No, no. Here. I guess I don't really need it," he said as he slipped it off and handed it to her, then watched her closely as she turned away and put it on.

Big as it was, she pulled the garment close around her and said, "I can see I wasted a lot of time crying so stop being such a pervert and tell me what else you've found out so far."

"That's not fair, Katherine. I'm not a pervert."

"Okay, whatever. Just tell me what you've found out."

"Uh, not much, actually," he stammered, suddenly making an attempt at being manly. "Except it was universal, all happening at once, obviouly world wide as I said, which accounts for the fact that so many people don't have clothes on."

"I already gathered that. What else?" she asked, knowing that the inadvertant nudity probably excited him.

"Well, there seems to be no one here except leaders and power people. No working class for sure," he said, looking around again.

"Yes. I think you're right. That is very strange. It has to be significant. Whatever that's all about."

"Maybe we can find out. The President is going to have a meeting over by that tall rock there in about ten minutes. I was out trying to round up as many Americans as I could when I found you."

Katherine visualized the President with his pants down. The sight bouyed her slightly and she let out a little laugh. The thought of him trying to rally everyone around himself also added to it.

"What's so funny?" Jess wanted to know.

"Nothing," she said, because if Jess wasn't aware of the earlier scene she didn't want to try and describe it to him. Then it occurred to her.

"Ex-President might be more appropriate, don't you think? Doesn't look like there's much here to be President of."

"He's still our leader and I think we owe him our support. Maybe more so in the present situation."

"Damn, Jess," she said. " You're a smuck and an idiot both."

"How can you be so harsh, Katherine. How could you say such a thing?"

"If that man couldn't keep things together back in the real… My god. I was going to say, real world. But this one is just as real. Isn't it? I don't want it to be but I think it is. And if it is, I sure as hell don't want to wake up every day and know I'm stranded somewhere with such a bunch of deficient individuals as the president. What a horrible thought."

"Well, I have a different opinion of him and I think we should go to the meeting. Someone else may have also learned something, too."

Word had spread quickly. There were at least a thousand people, maybe more, mostly men, all gathered around a large, flat topped rock. It was a bizzare sight. President Drukus in his shirt sleeves, the Secreary of Defence with his skinny, bare legs showing and General Wells, Chairman of the Joint Chiefs of Staff in his silk pajamas, all on top of the rock. They were so totally engrossed in the importance of what they were doing that not one trace of embarassment was apparent. The Vice President, meanwhile, was seen to be peeking out from behind a tree along the edge of the clearing, afraid to show herself in the granny flannels she had worn to bed the night before as the General began shouting for order. Not something easy to come by with nearly everyone so occupied with their own concerns.

"It looks like Colorado to me," Katherine overheard someone say. "See that snow on those mountains in the distance, and all those Junipers?"

"Colorado is a hell of a lot farther than a few hundred yards from palm trees and the ocean," someone else pointed out.

"What about that brown layer hanging around the base of the hills? Christ. It looks like smog. We must be near a large city. Maybe Los Angeles."

"But the sun is in the wrong part of the sky for this time of year. I think we're south of the equator, myself," another person said, as the speculation continued.

"It's not Australia. Australia doesn't have any mountains that high sitting right on the coast line."

"Africa , then."

"Africa doesn't have smog like that."

"South America. Maybe Rio. That's a pretty foul place."

"But why?" Katherine wanted to know. That was the important question.

"Maybe some grand, survial of the fittest game," one of the group suggested with the same worried look on his face as everyone else. "There doesn't seem to be much here except what nature left behind, and what we had in our hands, or pockets or on our backs."

"Sure. But how do we know we are even still on planet earth? Those who happened to have cell phones with them say they don't fuction and some guy with a laptop computer and a wireless up link has the same problem. With hundreds of satelites in synchronous orbit, something should work.

"Pretty damned peculiar, I'd say."

It was at that moment that Katherine stopped in her tracks. Oh, oh, she said to herself and began cautiously scanning the crowd. Oh my. What if her husband Max was here too? Damn. What would that be like? The thought made the already frightening ordeal even more frightening.

"What's wrong?" Jess asked, noticing her suddenly nervous behavior.

"Nothing, Jess. Nothing," she silenced him and tried to ease behind him to hide herself. Thank god she was only five five and didn't have red hair.

By now the general was shouting as loud as he was able. Finally, he succeeded and silence prevailed. Then the President came to the front and faced the larger part of the crowd.

"Ladies and gentlemen. Your attention, please," he shouted in a raspy voice, standing as straight and tall as he possibly could as he surveyed his audience before continuing.

"First," he said, but stopped just as quickly, turned to the Secretary of Defense, asked a question and nodded at the answer.

"First" he began again. "We will say the Pledge of Allegiance. And since we don't have a flag with us, we will use this as a substitute."

With that he held up a crudely done flag drawn in red pencil on a used piece of legal pad the General had found in his pocket. Before he could start the pledge, however, someone a few rows back cried out.

"Would this be more appropriate, sir?" the man asked as he held up the briefcase he was still carrying. It had a full color decal of the flag pasted on it. It was the Attorney General, a true patriot in the President's eyes.

"Good man, Henry," the President stated as the briefcase was passed forward. The president bent and reached, slipped and almost fell off the rock, dropping the briefcase in the process. A second try was more successful. The President tried to hold the briefcase up high but it was quite heavy so he sat it end up on the rock beside him, put his right hand over his chest and began.

"I pledge.." But he got no further. This time he was soundly interrupted by a very loud voice from the center of the crowd.

"Sit down, you fucking idiot," a bulky, burly man dressed in black and wearing a swatstika arm band shouted. He was the head of the American Nazi Party. Reacting quickly, Bill Trunik, Chief of the FBI, pushed his way through, ripped off the armband and grabbed the man by the throat. Then, with his free hand he drew his revolver from his shoulder holster and pointed it dead blank into the Nazi's right eye.

"What's the matter, asshole?" he said. "Did you forget where you're at?"

"I don't have a clue where we're at," was the reply. "That's the whole point."

"And a pointless point because wherever we might be it sure as hell doesn't look like I have to read you your rights or get you an attorney, does it? Maybe I'll just shoot your ass and throw you in the bushes. Is that clear?"

"Yes Sir," said the newly turned coward as he tried to free himself. "I surely do. Yes Sir."

"Good. Now pay attention and show some respect," Trunik said as he shoved him aside and made his way closer to the rock. What he didn't realize, however, was that once it was back in it's holster, his prized revolver was undergoing a change of its own. It was slowly turning into a wax-like substance, as was most everything else made of metal brought onto the island by the new inhabitants. There would be no modern weapons here. Or anything else they had brought with them that could be used to hurt each other with.

"Thank you, Bill," The President smiled down at him.

Trunik nodded and the President began again- this time without interruption. After the pledge of allegiance was over he next informed the crowd that TV Evangalist, Reverend Billy Boxer was also amongst them and would lead them in prayer.

"Good grief," Katherine said as she listened to the words.

"What's the matter?" asked Jess, still unable to stop himself from trying to put his arm around her.

"Maybe the Nazi was right," she said, brushing him away.

"What do you mean?"

"The man really is a fucking idiot."

Jess was too surprised at her words to reply but found her explicit language to be a turn on. His hand slid down to her left buttock. Before she could react, however, a male voice behind them said, "Don't be too critical of the President."

Sliding away from Jess, Katherine turned to see who had spoken. A short, stocky man in a three-piece suit gave back a serious stare.

"Why not?" she asked.

"The President is still a little shook up about what happened."

"No kidding," Katherine said bruskly, looking at the person like he was a complete idiot. "Is he here all by himself?" Now she was irritated and angry. She began to move away.

"Were are you going?" Jess asked.

"Don't know."

"Can I come with you?"

"No. Please stay here."

"Hmm. Well, here then. Take my shoes so you don't hurt your feet," Jess said, looking at her bare toes. At this point he was willing to do most anything to maintain a connection with her.

"They're much too big," she replied. "I wouldn't be able to keep them on."

"Put my socks on, too," he suggested.

"God, no," she said, grimacing at the thought of it.

"Well, take the shoes at least and pull the laces up really tight," he insisted as he pulled off his expensive wingtips.

Reluctantly she obliged. The tight laces helped but they were still much too large. Better that than another damaged toe, however, she decided as she shrugged and moved off by herself.

By now Reverend Billy was up on the rock and beginning to speak.

"Thank you, Mr. President," he said patronizingly, then sanctimoniously closed his eyes and began to pray in a overly loud voice. "Dear Lord Jesus. Help us to understand why we have been removed from our homes and businesses and loved ones and placed here in this strange place without apparent food or shelter or guidance. We know that as human brethren we have all sinned and profaned and we ask thee to forgive us for we knew not what we were doing and we ask help in transforming ourselves into being better able to serve you."

"We ask also that you give us patience and strength that we may perservere until such time as you see fit to once again guide us all back into the temple of love and righteousness. And above all bestow mercy on all those who have been left behind for, without us, they are truly lost. Poor lost sheep who will flounder forever without the wise and loving help that only we, their leaders, are capable of providing. Blessed be the Lord. Amen."

But then he coughed slightly and continued. "PS, Lord. If this really is the Rapture come true then where are the streets of gold, the bountiful tables of food and drink and something comfortable to lounge on while harps play? Even worse, why are there so many deviant Muslims and other infidels here with us when the good book says that the Rapture was to be reserved for worthy Christians only. Help us to understand, Oh Lord, and endow us with strength that we can organize the situation according to conservative, God fearing principles. In the name of Jesus, Amen again."

With that he opened his eyes and looked at the President who gave him an approving nod, dismissing him from his position on the rock. Then, as Reverend Boxer climbed down the President informed the crowd that, as president, he was also Commander in Chief and as such he was declaring a state of emergency and placing the island under martial law. While the crowd was doing its best to assimilate that news the Vice President suddenly appeared at the base of the rock in her flannel nightwear without makeup, her hair all in disarray, and began shouting up at him.

"You can't do that," she stated as she questioned his ability to make such a declaration since it seemed quite obvious that they were no longer within the territorial United States. Not to be one upped, the President waved her away, stood up straight and again spoke loudly, declaring the rock he was standing on and all the surrounding territory for as far as he could see to be a legal possession of the United States of America. With that, he pulled the flag decal off the Attorney General's briefcase and placed it face up on the rock. He then ordered someone to toss him up a stone to put over it to keep it from blowing away.

"So be it," he stated with satisfaction.

"My God. Does the lunacy never end?" Katherine said out loud to herself. Damnit. What was she going to do? A part of her felt like giving up and crying again but she had made her decision. There would be no more of that, no matter how awful it became. But what? What could she do? Above all, she needed a plan. Whatever they had all become involved in, it seemed clear that it was not going to be easy. And for a woman alone amongst all these men, well.... that could soon become very dangerous. There were far too many hungry Jesses here and probably many more who were even worse. There were far too few women, too. No laws or law enforcement and far too few ways to protect oneself. And if nothing changed, if the situation continued for any length of time, if there was no prospect of rescue or return home, people would become desperate and wanton. Slowly she worked her way around the rock and through the crowd, evaluating her options. After careful reconsideration, maybe it wouldn't be so bad if her husband were there. Him she could handle and she hoped he would at least try and protect her.

She traveresed the crowd twice to no avail. Well, she decided at last. If not Max, maybe someone else. Except for running off into the trees and trying to stay hidden, there seemed little other choice. Several times she saw men whom she knew, or knew about, but systematically rejected them, one by one, without talking to them. Then, when she had nearly given up, a familiar voice called to her.

"Governor Beaumont," the tall, muscular looking individual said. "It's good to see you, even under such unusual circumstances"

"Mr. Briggs. It's good to see you, too," she responded with some hope, looking him over as she returned the handshake he offered. He was also from her home state. But he was fully clothed in jeans, sweater, boots and a small day pack on his back. Why was that?

"I was up in the mountains hiking. The moon was full, the night was warm so I just kept going. It was really beautiful out," he explained, to answer her unasked question. "And call me Howard."

"Fair enough, Howard. And Katherine, if you please," she said, evaluating the situation. Maybe she could make it work for her. Howard was the CEO of a very successful high tech firm whom she had met at a State held business conference a year ago. He was several years older than her, intelligent, resourceful and obviously physically fit for his age, the kind of man who demanded and recieved respect from those around him. Also important, he had a wife and was known to be faithfully married. A lucky find. But would he mind her tagging along? Would he look out for her if things became difficult? Those were the tough questions.

"What about your wife?" Katherine asked, looking for an excuse to further clarify things. "Was she with you?"

"Fortunately, no. Her mother was ill so she went back east. Thank god for that. Otherwise she'd probably be up in the mountains all alone right now. Then I'd really go crazy. What about you? You're married, as I remember."

"I was asleep in my own bed. My husband of sorts was down the hall in his own room. I'm sure he must be aware that I'm gone at this point, however. Doubt if I'll be missed much, though," she stated, somewhat surprised at her sudden willingness to share such a personal information with a stranger, realizing that it probably reflected on her fears about the stituation she found herself in.

"Well, I'd miss you if you were my wife," Howard said, however, trying to be comforting.

Katherine looked at him carefully, not wanting to misinterprete the comment. The look on his face quickly told her that it was of purely compassionate intent, however, and she felt relieved. At the same time she still evaluated him as a man. It was just one of those automatic things. And what affect did she have on him in that regard? Would she be able to control things later on, if it came to that? As for herself, well, even though it might be comforting, a sexual relationship at a time like this would probably be most unwise. In the meantime, there were far too many other things to be concerned with. Almost immediately, Howard addressed one of them.

"Is this ridiculous, or what?" he asked her.

"It's insane."

"Yes, but it's obviously real. We really seem to be here. In this strange place for whatever weird reason. And if so, maybe we'd better start taking it seriously."

"How so?"

"Go do something important. Want to come with me?"

She looked him over more carefully. Was he really inviting her to join him?

"Where are you going?"

"Well, it's quite warm here so shelter is not an immediate problem. But food and fresh water soon will be. A secure place away from all these people to get some sleep and to go to if things ever get out of hand would seem to be a good idea also."

"Not, if they get out of hand, but when they do, because we are trapped here with the world's biggest power brokers and ego maniacs. Sooner or later there has to be trouble," Katherine replied, her decision made.

"No question about that," Howard said, "and I don't think we want to be in the middle of it."

"For sure," she agreed, and with that they made their way through the crowd, leaving behind a disconnected scene that was rapidly deteriorating into a major dispute. Having heard of the land grab that the American President was attempting to make, President Pierre Pompou of France had also climbed up on the rock and pounded him precisely on the nose. Blood was spilled and the turmoil escalated. Then, as they made their way further into the

22

trees where it was quieter, they came across an attractive, blond woman sitting alone beside some bushes, sobbing deeply. The only clothing she had on was a skimpy pair of pajama bottoms.

"Hello," Katherine said and waited.

The woman stopped crying and looked up. Wiping the tears away with her hands she simply stared at them. Then she got to her feet, keeping her arms crossed over her chest. Most men would have been reduced to staring. Howard certainly noticed, but he had seen his share of good looking women before, one of the most exceptional of whom was his own wife. Suddenly, he missed her dearly. This one was several years younger but after a summary glance, he kept his eyes on her face, studying her. Katherine's mind was elsewhere. Poor thing, she was thinking, as her sympathies went out. She certainly understood what the woman must be feeling.

"Anything we can do to help?" she asked.

"I.... I don't know. What happened, why are we here?" she said, almost ready to start crying again. But then she pulled herself together enough to say, "I'm sorry. Why am I asking you? You don't know either, do you? Oh god. I want to go home."

Oh, god, is right, Katherine said to herself. Don't we all. And, unable to think of anything else that might be consoling, that is what she said.

"I'm just so horribly embarrassed and humiliated," the poor woman said. "And the very first people I ran into were all men from back, from... who I worked with. Several of them actually worked for me and here I am, topless. What a shock. Of course most of them couldn't say much. I was never aware how many men must sleep in their underwear. Only one had on pajamas and I always thought of him as the most masculine of the bunch. Isn't that a silly thing? Especially at a time like this?" she went on for some time, driven by anxiety and fear as they let her wear herself down. Then she apologized again and offered an explanation for her behavior.

"Maybe I'm still in shock. Just like everyone else, I would imagine."

"I would think something was wrong if you weren't," Howard offered.

At this point the woman took the time to look at them more carefully and Katherine offered her hand.

"I'm Katherine Beaumont and this is Howard Briggs."

"Deanna Holt. I am...   It was then that the two women recognized each other. Even though they had never met face to face before, they had both made the prime-time news at one point or another. Deanna had been the Head of the Department of Health, Education and Welfare with a solid reputation for good judgement in matters of public policy and Katherine was a strong advocate of women's rights and governmental reform. Deanna, however, was single. Childless like Katherine, but divorced since twenty-seven, she had devoted most of her career life to public service. At first they talked about their common plight but after some unfruitful speculation about what might have happened and what they might be doing there, Katherine again asked Deanna if she wouldn't like to come along with them.

"Where are you going?"

"To see if we can find food and water and a safe place to sleep. It might be better than staying here," she pointed out. "We thought it might be wise to get a head start."

"You're going alone? Just the two of you?"

"That's the plan so far."

"I don't know," Deanna replied, balking at the idea as something else occured to her. "Will we have to sleep on the ground? I guess we will, won't we, if we're still here. What about wild animals?"

"Well, I've spent a lot of time in the wilderness," Howard stated, "but it's always been the two-legged ones I feared the most."

It didn't register. All Howard got for his comment was an odd gaze.

"What about snakes? I hate snakes. And insects."

"Seriously, I haven't seen any traces of any animal life at all. Nothing but trees, grass and people."

'Nor I," Katherine added, "except for one small butterfly when I first got here."

"Okay. Thanks for the offer but I'd just feel safer with lots of people around. Especially men in a strange place like this. Even with my lack of proper clothing. As I said, there are several acquaintances from the Department here. They're all attending that meeting."

"How many are there?"

"About twenty."

"You're grossly outnumbered."

"I've worked with them, some for several years, and I have no reason to believe they would treat me with anything but respect."

"All of them?"

"There's only one or two I ever had any problems with.

24

Nothing serious. And they're both older."

Katherine's gut told her that it had all the ramifications of a bad scene but her ramped up scepticism went unheard so she quit.

But Howard kept on. "Seriously. No one knows for sure what's going to happen. Under the circumstances things may get a little rough."

Deanna was adamant, however, failed to see the point they were trying to make and stood by her choice.

"Okay," Katherine and Howard finally agreed, giving up. Deanna was extremely naive. But she was also becoming offended.

"Well, maybe we'll see you again. But please be careful." Then she took off the jacket Jess had given her and offered it. "Looks like you need this more than I do."

After they had walked away Katherine said, "I think she's in serious trouble."

"Twenty men and one woman. Very likely. Twenty men and a woman who looks like her...." The shake of his head couldn't have made it clearer.

BACK HOME

There were no appropriate words to express the effect the disappearance had on those left behind. Shock, disbelief, horror. They were all inadequate. The occurance was beyond the normal comprehension of even the most gifted of people, the immediate result of which was a paralysis that spread like an invisible wave across the country and around the world, knocking down old complacencies, destroying beliefs, pushing long held conceptions of reality over the cliff of rude awakenings to bring everything to an immediate and complete halt. Then slowly, as the wave ebbed and waned, the paralysis turned first to fear and then to panic. Suddenly, no one wished to be alone. Ever. Even for a few moments. Especially in the cities of America. It was there that humanity had it's most appalling difficulty in coping.

People refused to stay in their apartments, condos and homes, quite afraid that perhaps the end of the world was near. Instead, most of them collected in the streets and in the parks, milling around, worrying, speculating, drinking, ranting, coming apart psychologically. It was heyday for religious zealots. Twenty-four hours a day televisions and radios blared dismal disaster news and ranting religion. Ranting religion and the most vivid details of disaster caused by the disappeared who had been driving vehicles, flying planes, operating appliances, holding babies, turning the gas on but failing to strike the match. An hour of news, three hours of religion, round the clock. Denial, confusion, delusion, rationalization, mental disconnectedness, complete insanity. It was the end of the world, it was Christ refusing to appear in his promised second coming because homosexuals were getting married to each other, it was an out of control, massive governmental experiment, it was a lot of things. But whatever it was, mostly it refected on man's sinful nature. What else could it be? There was no other way to explain it.

Not too surprizingly, it was the fundamentalists who had the most difficult time of all. Being unable to reconcile their theories of God punishing the wicked with the fact that all their own religious leaders had also dissappeared, they slipped over the edge into lunacy and became murderous and vengful toward all who disagreed. It was nearly a week, however, of nothing more happening of any serious proportions before people finally began filtering back into their dwellings and some semblence of order reappeared. But they were all still immensely afraid.

In the suburbs the reaction was less severe. But not by much. There were still four suicides and one double murder-suicide in the somewhat isolated, small tract where Jack Briggs and his wife had their home. Other members of the group lived on in denial while several more seemed to grow increasingly unstable as the days passed. The situation was dire. And because Jack had been associated with the President, many of the rest chose the Briggs' home as a gathering place. Uninvited, they floundered in, seeking answers and reassurance. *It was ridiculous*, Jack thought. There weren't any answers that he knew of and he couldn't make any of it go away, either. No matter what. But there were other things he could do, and had to do, all of major importance.

His wife was three weeks away from giving birth. Truly enough, she was a strong woman but it had been an extremely difficult pregancy. As he had told the Secretary of the Navy on the plane when the president had disappeared, they had lost the first baby more than a year ago and there had already been two close calls with this one. She didn't need a house full of distraught people coming and going to worry about. Because she would worry about them. It was just part of her nature.

Then there was the issue of long term survival. In that regard, if the neighborhood couldn't get better organized, they would all be in serious trouble. And soon. Food and protection were major priorities. Beyond that his older brother, Howard, was also missing.

Probably as the result of the disappearance because he was the CEO of a fairly large corporation. But there was no way to tell for sure since he had been out on an overnight hiking trip alone in a remote area of the Colorado mountains. Needless to say, Howard's wife was extremely upset when he didn't come home. At times she was very nearly hysterical when Jack talked with her on the phone. This was one of those times and it was no better. Finally he was able to hang up.

"I'm sorry, Jack," his wife, Gail, told him as she sat on the large bar stool pulled up to the island counter in the kitchen area of the house, her pregnancy extremely obvious through the over sized robe she wore most of the time when she was out of bed. "I wish I could be of more help."

"There's nothing to be done. Denver is just too far away."

"Could she come here?"

"There is no safe way she could make the trip."

"But if I wasn't so incapacatated, we could go there."

"Don't even think about it. You've already been doing far more than the doctor wants," he said matter of factly, without criticism.

"I suppose I have," she reluctantly admitted. "But it's impossible to spend all day in bed."

"Especially for you. But you still have to take it a little slower. No more digging in the garden, and that's an order," he said, gently but firmly, as he came around behind, put his hands on her shoulders and bent and kissed her on the cheek, as he had lately gotten into the habit of doing. Ordinarily, he would have kissed her on the neck but felt that might be too suggestive and unfair at this point.

She turned her head a little so he could do it again and sighed as he stroked her hair. "Well, I'm sure glad you insisted on planting one again this year, that's all. And to have had the foresight to have made it even bigger. How did you know to do that, anyway?"

"There's some redemption in pulling weeds. I guess I didn't get enough of it last year. And the way you went after those vine rippened tomatoes, what else could I do."

"Too bad more of the neighbors haven't done the same thing. All of their lots have over two acres of good land. Just like ours."

"There's still time. Joe Drury down the street actually went out looking for seeds today. Hopefully he'll find some. Gardening is almost a lost art."

"Guess you had an unusual childhood."

"Yeah. My parents were always planting."

"Did they teach you to stockpile food, too?"

"Just part of the routine. Got us through a couple of emergencies. But nothing like this is going to turn out to be."

"You don't think this is just some wierd hallucination and that one day soon we'll wake up and everything will be back to normal? Of course not. So what's going to happen? There's no way a few small gardens are going to feed the whole neighborhood."

"No, they're not. And if we can't get all the neighbors fully engaged, we'll be faced with some tough moral questions. And soon."

"But what else can they do?"

"A lot. And again I thank my father. By the time we were teenagers Howard and I both were able to go into the woods and completely live off the land for as long as necessary."

"But most people never had that kind of childhood."

"No, they were too busy playing computer games and hanging out in the mall."

"They can't just be left to starve."

"They don't have to. It's a choice they have to make for themselves."

"Is that what tonight's meeting is about?"

"Basically. But I'm not too hopeful about the outcome."

"Why not?"

"I don't know all of the people here but so far I haven't met a single person in the whole neighborhood who's even capable of putting a door knob back on when it falls off."

"Except me. I can do that. Will it be okay if I come?"

"Only if you get back in bed and stay there for the rest of the day."

Immediately after the meeting Gail and Jack were back home where she was propped up in bed against a stack of pillows, sipping the tea he had made for her.

"I'm not sure they believed you," she told him as he sat there beside her, "about making nourishing soup out of cattail roots and that one cup of pine needle tea contains more vitamin C than an orange."

"That's okay. I'd just be happy if some of them would go and hunt deer, while there are still so many left. We could fill everyone's freezer up with venison. Wouldn't hurt to make some jerky, either, just in case." He didn't say just in case the power went out which he was sure it would some one of these days soon enough. She didn't need to hear things like that.

"Well, I wish there was some way I could help, Jack. I hate being such a burden."

"You are not a burden. You're about to become the mother of our child and that's more important than all of it," he said and took her hand. Then he brushed the hair back from her forehead and gently kissed her on the mouth.

"Well, you know what I mean," she replied with an appreciative smile as her deep blue eyes brightened. "I just don't like being so damned helpless. I've never had to spend a full day in bed in my whole life. And it couldn't have happened at a worse time. I'm so sorry, Jack."

"For what? Another two weeks and it will be over," he assured her. "And in a month you'll be out digging up carrots."

"And if all the neighbors start planting, too, we should be able to stockpile some food. I'm sure we can find a way to preserve part of it," she stated in a positive tone.

What a trouper, Jack thought. No wonder he loved her. Eight and a half months pregnant and she seemed to be handling the situation far better than most. Sometimes even himself. Not only was he worried about food, he was concerned about collecting wood for fireplaces when propane and fuel oil became unavailable. There were also concerns about safety from potential marauders if, or when, it really got tough, along with dozens of other equally important things. But then Gail's concern shifted.

"What happens to those who refuse to participate?" she wondered. "Do we just let them starve? Are those the tough moral questions you were referring to before?"

"Yes. Even with all the suicides and those getting ready to move away, we'll still have forty-one left to feed once stores and warehouses are completely empty."

"How long before that happens?"

"Technically, there may still be a couple of months of food supplies left in the pipeline but with all the panic and hoarding and hijacking, we'd be foolish to count on anything. Sorry to sound so damned dismal.

"Forty-one is a lot. Is that even possible?"

"If we can get everyone to pitch in."

"What about the ones who won't help or claim they can't?"

"Finish you tea. I'll get you another cup. Is there anything else you need?" Jack said, and got up.

"Not right now. Just answer the question."

"Harsh as it may sound, they're not getting any of our tomatoes."

"But Jack......"

"When they get hungry enough, they'll start learning to help themselves. If it comes to that, there is no other way."

"What about ousiders who aren't able to care for themselves. What about the ones with little children? What about looters? What do we do about them?"

"Tough questions. If we can unite the neighborhood and stand together, I'm sure we can get through this," he said, trying to be as positive again.

"I'm sure we can," she said, reaching for his hand. "I trust you implicitly," she continued and he knew she meant every word of it.

He would do his best. That was for damned sure. He'd die for her if he had to. It was that simple. And she would do the same for him. The confidence of that was but one of the many things he loved about her. But right now she was pretty helpless. The last thing he wanted was to have her feeling like she was a burden. He should have known better. As usual, her concerns were still about other people. Now it was the Taylors, their closest neighbor.

"They both seem to be extremely depressed," she said to him. "I hope you aren't, Jack. You don't seem to be."

"No matter what happens I'll never be depressed as long as you are with me," he said as he sat back down on the bed beside her and looked deep into her eyes. "And having a child to look forward to is a great blessing. I also know that if worse comes to worse the three of us can go off and live in the woods if we have to, just like I told you before."

"Just like pioneers. That sounds kind of exciting. I think. Or does it? Oh god, Jack. I don't know. I'm sorry. I guess I'm just a little scared," she finally admitted, trying to hold back the tears.

He took her in his arms and held her for a long time. Quietly. He knew better than to lie to her or to make false promises. He was scared, too. But that didn't obviate the fact of his own ability and determination. One way or another they would survive. She had to believe that. That is what he told her. Whatever it took. With or without the cooperation of the neighborhood.

"I know that, Jack. Regardless of the rest I know we'll be okay. But I think most of them trust you too."

"Hard to tell. But thank god everything hasn't collapsed. Small businesses are still operating. Some of the other people here are finally willing to go back to their old jobs and try to make things work without supervision. What else do we say to them? Obey the law and try to maintain order until better answers show themselves? But in the meantime prepare for the worst. Sounds a little trite, don't you think?

"Maybe. But sometimes it helps to confirm the obvious."

Okay, Jack thought. Good advice for most but easier said than done for himself. With all Administration officials gone, both in government and at the University where he taught, he didn't have a job to go to. Nor could he consider returning to the academic world he had left behind. Most of the educational system was shut down, from grammer schools to colleges. Where did he go from here, he wondered, as the questions kept coming. If thousands of human beings could suddenly disappear off the face of the earth, what next? Strange as that was, was that the end of it? What else might happen? Could he also somehow be seperated from his wife at this critical time? Would she be able to survive without him? And what about the baby? He certainly could get depressed over all that if he allowed himself. But he was determined not to. Gail had enough problems without having to try and cheer him up. Besides, he really enjoyed being around her all day. It had been a long time since they had that luxury and he was actually disappointed when Jenson Wilson, the oldest active legislator on Capital Hill and long time old friend, made a call, insisting that he sit in on a joint session of both houses of Congress the following day. He made some excuses but Gail insisted he go, promising she would behave and spend the day in bed.

"I'm sure Dana Williams will be by to check up on me as usual," she also assured him.

Doctor Milton Wisecough, M I T Professor Emeritus in Physics, was addressing the emergency session where Jack had a front row seat.

"Unfortunately," the Doctor was saying, "as of this moment we do not have one single shred of verifiable scientific evidence on which to base any sound conclusions that might account for what has transpired. Neither do we know if the victims were somehow captured and abducted or whether some grand, space time discontinuity swallowed them up. We do know, however, that the black hole recently discovered near the constellation Vega seems to be moving laterally with respect to normal universe expansion and is not only distorting the Higgs field but has a non distinct event horizon which is causing severe perturbations in the Plankian, deep space microwave background distribution curves as far away as earth. The zero point field is also behaving in a peculiar, non local way that seems to be violating parity laws for electron-positron particle pair creation."

Then he stopped, coughed, drank some water, looked around to see if he had everyone's attention, and continued.

"On the other hand," he stated. "Perhaps we are just the victims of some universal mass hallucination that has somehow pervaded the entire globe. If so, how does one verify such a phenomenon? It is a tautology. It may be true even if it is not true. There is no way to tell. Thus far the situation is beyond explanation. Rest assured, however, that we are in process of assembling a blue ribbon committee of top world scientists to formulate a self optimizing, artifically intelligent computer corellation program so we can begin to study the problem."

Jack had also been watching the audience as the professor was speaking. No one had a clue as to what the man had said. Not that it was meaningless, meandering bull. From the physicists point of view it was all factual information. It just didn't have a damned thing to do with the problem at hand and the professor knew it. Jack almost chuckled out loud. The man was purposely playing games with them, the old shit. And probably secretly laughing his head off, maintaining composure the whole time. Ha!

Having totally missed the point the Junior Senator from Wisconsin got to his feet. "Excellent idea," he said. "That's exactly what Congress should be doing too."

"What?" said the man next to him.

"Studying the problem. Form a sub committee of our own so we can have control over the proceedings and impeach anyone who is not completely forthcoming in response to questions."

"I second the motion," said Congressman Jones from Georgia. "But instead of scientists we need to pull together all the experts in the fields of religion and philosophy."

"Jesus, Bill," the other Georgia congressman queried, "Haven't you noticed? There aren't many of those kind left. Especially in the field of religion."

"Well, what about those East Indian fakirs or gurus or whatever they're called? And we need to include psychics and astrologers. We never would have seen such great strides during the Reagan years if it hadn't been for that kind of expertise. I'll bet some of them can already tell us what happened."

"For God's sake, what nonsense, you flag waving hypocrite. Don't you remember the Iran-Contra scandal? Ronald was one of America's most treasonist presidents."

"Well…Some patriot you are. Especially at a time of crisis like this."

"All right, all right," intervened Senator Billingsly of Arkansas. "We don't have time for that now. But I think it's still a good idea. So why don't we get started."

With that, an immediate wave of controversy swept around the chambers which, just as quickly and loudly, was interupted by the pounding gavel of the man who had invited Jack Briggs to the session, Jenson Wilson, now Acting Chairman in the absense of other duly appointed leaders. Jack watched him perform his duties with vigor. In many respects Jenson had been like a second father to Jack and it was he who given the recommendation for Jack's advisory post appointments. Unfortunately, as Jenson himself later admitted and apologized for, he too, had far over-estimated the President's capabilities and wisdom. But, with the disappearance, none of that mattered anymore and it was now their mutual desire to be of some service in solving the fallout of problems left behind.

"Order, order please. Order, damnit," Jenson yelled into the microphone and pounded the podium some more. Finally the noise subsided. Jenson might be physically old, Jack acknowledged, but he was still a match for many men half his age.

"All right," Jenson said in his still vibrant voice as the room stilled further. "Let's let Doctor Wisecough complete his statements to this distinguished body before we throw the meeting open to discussion." With that he nodded at the professor and asked him to continue.

Doctor Wisecough cleared his throat and stated that there was really nothing of consequence that he was capable of adding to what little he had already said.

"I'm sorry," he said, pretending to apologize, and sat down in a nearby vacant seat and promply fell fast asleep. Jenson peered at him for a moment over the reading glasses perched on his nose. Like Jack had done, he too, secretly chuckled to himself. He had discussed the worthiness of bringing the professor there earlier with Jack, who agreed that the only value might be to wake congress up to the fact that there probably wasn't any simple explanation for what had happened to begin with, otherwise everyone would already have known it by now. And since they did not, the real reasons behind the disappearance could only come from how the human race dealt with the dilema. And so much for that, Jenson said to himself and turned back to the delegation.

"For the remainder of the meeting can we all try and behave like adults," he admonished in a stern voice. "If you wish to be heard, raise your hand and stand up. Otherwise we will adjurn."

Almost immediately the conservative congressman from California jumped to his feet. "I have a question," he said, asking to be recognized.

Jenson nodded.

"I want to know why the entire staff of the CIA isn't brought in here right now. A dollar will get you a donut, they engineered the whole thing to begin with. "

"That's ridiculous," Cummings from Arizona shouted back. "Their upper echeon has disappeared along with all the rest."

"Exactly the point. Those devious bastards are capable of anything," said the Californian as Jenson again began pounding his gavel. Then Senator Trippy from Maine rose. As soon as it was quiet, Jenson gave him the floor.

"Gentlemen and ladies," he said in a powerful voice. "We are a rudderless ship and a rudderles ship is a ship adrift. Surely we cannot proceed along any significant direction without leadership or we will soon be awash on the rocks of the future. It is a time of great personal and public dilema that will command all our available resources, but, it is also a time of great opportunity for those of us who remain behind because we are consequently charged with the noble duty of gathering up the reins and steering a course out of this overwhelming predicament. Not only will it take immense courage and wisdom to do so but it will also take determined and consistant leaership. *Someone must steer the boat.* It is the only way. We must take it upon ourselves to select a new and competent leadership who will get us out of this terrible mess. *We need a new President.* And a Vice President, a Secretary of State and Speakers for both the Congress and the Senate. That, gentlemen, and ladies, is the real business at hand for this joint session and I say, let's get to it. The sooner the better."

Without hesitation a roar of approval rang through the auditorium and a motion to enact was seconded at least five times, forcing Jenson Wilson to nearly break his gavel, pounding so hard for order. Finally, after quiet was again restored, he leaned over the microphone and spoke in a clear voice.

"It won't work. And it won't work because..." he said , letting the statement hang out there for a long moment. "Because, there is no provision in the Constitution for simply appointing someone to fill such vacancies. The originators of this prestigious document somehow overlooked a prescription for handling such an adverse matter as we are trying to deal with. The President, Vice President, Secretary of State and The Speaker of the House are not known to be legally dead. For the moment they only seem to be unavailabe to do their jobs. Until such time as we can either verify their deaths or their incompetence, we are prevented from replacing them with appointed substitutes."

It was not what the group wanted to hear, however, and a subcommittee was quickly created to determine how the normal elective proccess could still be circumvented, legally or otherwise. That was followed by a series of antagonistic discussions that resulted in further motions. Both political parties gave action items to themselves to nominate candidates for the vacant offices so they could be promptly filled once they had sucessfully sidestepped the constitutional glitch. Then the entire block of New England congressmen got to their feet and demanded that all banks be closed immediately and remain so until further notice. Next, the Senator from Georgia insisted that what was left of the Pentagon start reprograming the nuclear arsenal for combat in outer space because the dissapearance of all the leaders had to be the precursor to invasion by some alien enemy. Someone else came up with a long list of reasons as to why it was no longer safe for Congress to have further sessions in the Capital Building. They should move across the Potomac into the subterranean emergency bomb proof complex.

It got even worse. Unable to maintain any semblance of order, Jenson Wilson laid down his gavel and walked off the floor. Jack got up and followed him outside. By now the sun had gone down. Regardless of the hour the Channel Five news team was still interviewing people at random in the street. At the moment they had a large proportioned older woman on camera.

"And why do you think all the leaders have disappeared, Alice?" asked the newsman conducting the interviews.

"Well, if you ask me," the stringy haired woman said. "They've been planning this for a long, long time. They probably stole the national treasury blind and now they're all in South America somewhere living the life of Riley."

"Why would they want to do that?"

"For two reasons. First, they're basically greedy or they wouldn't have gone after all the big jobs to begin with and second..."

"Yes. And what's the second reason?"

"I forgot... Oh dear, what was it?... Oh yes. Second, they probably just got tired of leading. Not that I blame them. Having to tell people what to do all the time. That would get awful stressful after while, wouldn't you think?"

"Quite possibly, madam," the newsman said and turned to a long haired individual in a shabby raincoat.. "And you, sir. What do you think happened?"

"You oughta know by now," said the man, running his fingers through his greasy hair.

"Really? And why is that?"

"God is clearing the decks for the Coming."

"The Coming?"

"The second coming of Christ, you idiot. What else do you think this is all about?"

"Well, maybe you're right."

"And maybe I'm not. Forget that! Christ wouldn't come back to such a lunatic world. It has to be the End Times. It's the beginning of the end of the world, that's what it is," he said, as he began to cry loudly. Then, in a complete turnabout, he jumped up and down a couple of times and let out a loud, "Yippee. The sinners all get to go to hell. And maybe I'll go with them."

Earlier that day in a different part of the country, but at the same time that Congress was embroiled in it's problems, a weathered looking young man sat in his pickup truck. Not wanting to get too close, he had parked across the street and half a block down from the, Toyoto of America, assembly plant. Here he watched the disorderly crowd of workers milling around outside the gates, carrying poorly constructed signs and banners and shouting slogans.

"We want our jobs, we want leadership.We want leadership," many of them were yelling in one form or another, although the voices were as disorganized and scrambled as some of the signs they carried. Several men also sat on the curb smoking cigarettes and drinking. One threw a beer can into the street, another, the half pint whiskey bottle he had just finished. Many other people were sitting on the sidewalk, leaning against the fence. Some of them were asleep, one small group had a penny ante poker game going.

"Looks like they could use a leader, all right. Doesn't it Dad," said the man's twelve year son who sat beside him in the battered old truck. "What's wrong with them, anyway?"

"Don't know. Maybe too many years of being told what to do all the time."

"But you don't have anyone telling you what to do."

"True," said the father. "But I work for myself. I know what has to be done and I just do it. Running a factory is more complicated."

"Why? Don't they know what they're supposed to be doing?"

"Well, you'd think so. But maybe it's not quite that easy," the man said, trying to explain the logic of it to his boy. "Building automobiles is a complex process. Someone has to be there to make decisions."

"Decisions about what?"

"Well, when something breaks down or they run out of parts or things don't go right.. Who's supposed to do what, when to start work, how much everybody gets paid, all kinds of things like that."

"Oh," said his son after a moment, acting as if he understood, even though he didn't. Then he asked, "Why do they run out of parts? Don't they know how many they need?"

"Of course they do, son. There's just a lot of parts. Sometimes somebody makes a mistake."

"Do they let them drink beer when they're working? Is that why they make mistakes?"

The father smiled at the thought of it as his son continued.

"And if they are out here doing this, um, what do you call it?"

"Demonstration."

"Demonstration. And there aren't any bosses or anyone around anymore to see it and tell them what to do, why are they doing all this to begin with?"

"Does seem pretty silly, doesn't it?"

"It's really dumb. You wouldn't let any of these people work for you, would you?"

"Not if I could help it," the man laughed.

The boy seemed somewhat relieved at the answer and sat there thinking. "Where will the new leaders come from?" he finally asked.

"They haven't decided how they can do that yet because it's not legal to take something that belongs to someone else."

"You mean the people who work there don't own the auto plant?"

"Very little, if any. It's owned by a lot of people. Most of them in Japan."

"Why do Japanese want to own something so far away?"

"It's good business, I guess."

"Well, why do people want to work for someone who doesn't even live here?"

"Because they need the money, too,"said the father.

"I wish money wasn't so important all the time."

"Me, too, son. But I guess we're stuck with it."

"But why do some people want so much of it?"

"Makes them feel good, I guess."

"Don't they have anything else to make them feel good?"

"I guess not or they would quit when they had enough."

With that answer the boy stared out the window at the demonstrators for a moment, then he said, "You own our farm, don't you Dad? It doesn't belong to someone else, does it?"

"No son. It's ours and it's all paid for."

"Do you think we'll be all right, Dad," the boy asked in return. "Without any government and all?

"Well, some folks think we're better off without them, but...."

No more had he said that than a confrontation began at the closed entrance gate along side the building which gave access to the loading dock, also clearly visible from the pickup truck. One of the low level, line supervisors who hadn't disappeared, had taken it upon himself to interfere with the demonstration from his protected place behind the high chain link fence. A bit of a bully back when the plant had been running, he was yelling loudly at the others.

"Get off the company property. Go home, damnit. Get the hell away from here."

Instead of complying, however, one man threw a beer bottle over the fence at him while others mocked and jeered. In turn the supervisor picked up the largest pieces of the broken bottle and threw them back across the fence. At that point five new bottles were hurled at him, one of which hit him on the head. He cursed and looked around, found a long two by four and picked it up. By now two men outside had climbed the fence and were about to go over the top. The supervisor prodded them with his weapon, trying to force them back but they laughed at him and called him nasty names. More angry words filled the air. The supervisor made a threatening thrust at one of the men's faces but the momentum of the board was too great and it slammed the man directly in the nose, smashing it badly. The man screamed in pain, let go of his hold on the fence and fell backwards onto the sidewalk, crushing the back of his skull. By then one rough looking demonstrator had already been to his own pickup truck parked nearby and had returned with a large pair of bolt cutters. The paddlock on the gate was cut off. Several other shouting men rushed inside, took the board away from the supervisor and began beating him with it. Two others, more than half drunk, climbed up on the loading dock.

"Damn, take a look at this," one said to the other as he hunched over one of several fifty gallon barrels, all with large warning signs on their sides, barrels that should have been inside, in the paint department.

"Acetone, man. It's acetone," and with that he managed to unscrew the plug in the top.

"Help me tip it over," he said as he got behind it and pushed.

With a great heave the barrel was over on it's side and a liquid far more volitile than gasoline was running across the loading dock and down the side. Gleefully, the instigator danced around, oblivious to the fact that he was stepping in the liquid and soaking his shoes.

"Give me your cigarette lighter, you bum," he hollered to his partner, who in turn reached in his pocket and tossed it over.

"Better back up a bit," he said, as he held it up, too drunk to realize that a vaporous invisible cloud of the evaporating liquid had surrounded them both and a large amount of the liquid had also run a considerable ways down the dock towards the breached gate and the surly group still beating on the supervisor.

At this point the man in the pickup finished responding to the question his son had asked. "I think we will be just fine, son," he said. "But if we're going to stay that way though, I think we'd best be getting home.

The truck started easily enough and he made a quick u-turn in the middle of the street. No sooner had he come around, however, than a tremendous explosion rocked the vehicle badly from behind and blew out the rear window. The first exploding barrel of liquid then ruptured the two next to it, and they in turn three more, causing another immediate and far worse explosion that tore the entire side out of the large building. The two men who had started the process had been totally incinerated in their tracks, while the flames, the heat and the shock wave reached out, killing another fifty five demonstrators who were either too drunk, too immersed in their own wanton behavior or just couldn't run fast enough to get out of the way. Needless to say, with no effectively working fire department, by the end of the day there was no longer any automobile manufacturing plant left for anyone to go back to work at, even if their leaders had all suddenly returned.

OFFICIAL BUSINESS

It was three weeks since the Disappearance, D-Day, as everyone now referred to it. Congress was still immersed in deep controversy. Thus far, neither political party had been able to compile a simple list of candidates for either the Presidential or Vice Presidential roles because more than half from both parties all wanted the top office. None of them would settle for second position. This also left the country without a multitude of other key officials that could only be appointed by the President. In the interim, however, some ambitious members of Congress had still written and passed several pieces of legislation. One of the first was to declare all disappeared individuals legally dead without the mandatory seven year waiting period. Not only would this allow the legislators to select new top executives, it would also permit individual estates to be legally passed on to others who could take control and begin running things in the private sector. Such things as oil companies, department store chains, banks, airlines and more. Unfortunately, all this legislation faced the same impasse. There was no chief executive to sign it into law. As one Senator put it, there was neither a legal chicken to lay an egg or a legal egg to hatch a chicken from. As a result, regardless of how much new legislation was hustled through Congress, it would all sit in limbo on the Oval Office desk until a way was found to seat someone in the chair behind it. Who, precisely did not matter as long as that person was a legally sworn US citizen over forty five. Even the janitor would do.

Fortunately, as history has repeatedly pointed out, Presidential decisions do not always have to be correct. The country, in fact, had been routinely victimized by severly incompetent chief executives right from the beginning and still survived. And, as Jenson Wilson had gone on record to state, Congressional performance had hardly proven itself to be any better. According to him, most legislators were grossly inept individuals who seemed to have a profuse knack for generating convoluted, overly complicated legislation that rarely solved the real problems at hand. This was because most legislation was created by somewhat bent minds to begin with, minds heavily slanted in favor of money and power and a warped sense of values. It was a view that put him heavily at odds with many of his colleagues. One of them was good old Senator

Billingsley who was from "The South," as he often made clear. Billingsley felt that money and power must always be restricted to a priviledged few. Dilute that and there would be real trouble.

"Look at all those damned movie stars and entertainers," he always said. "We let them live in this country and make tremendous amounts of money and what do those un American yahoos do with it? They join causes and start supporting crusades. Then they start screaming about the environment and the homeless and the diseased and who knows what all. Let it go on long enough and pretty soon the public begins to think that those things really are important. Then there's trouble. Big trouble. That's where us politicians totally screwed up. We should have put a lid on the amount of income one could make from such unorthodox things as singing and acting to begin with. Then those people couldn't afford to be so damned unpatriotic."

"But what about all the sports figures?" he was asked. "Some of them make even more money than movie stars."

"What about them? They're our perfect citizens. If all you know how to do is fight over a ball and your vocabulary is limited to twenty five words plus grunts and, yeah-man, you're not going to be out there saying rebelious things about the government. Not only that but they all die broke. And a lot of them are broke long before they die. That means they don't hoard their money or donate it to causes. They turn it over rapidly, buying Humvies and mansions and hookers and booze and all that other self indulgent stuff and that's always good for the economy.

"But what about Reagan? He was an actor."

"Yes. And a damned good one. But not in the Hollywood sense. He was such a good actor, he had everybody fooled. All those low budget, third rate movies were just a smoke screen. While he was hamming it up on film he was out sneaking in the back door of politics."

"Yeah. How so?"

"First and foremost, he was a right wing John Bircher from the very beginning. Everything else he did supported that purpose. And once he got moving he was so good at acting that half the time most people couldn't tell if he knew what he was doing or not. I happen to believe he did, however."

"Really?"

"Really. Take eating jelly beans all the time. That was a great one. People can relate to eating jelly beans, especially ordinary people. Then there was tax reform. Instead of tax instruction

41

booklets being four pages long when he took office, he upped them to one hundred and five pages. That alone made people respect the tax codes a lot more. And look how effective he was at building weapons. Think of all the jobs he created with the billions spent on nuclear arms, giving us the safety of ten times over kill instead of just one wipe out of the human race. There's a lot of security in being able to do that," Billingsley stated with vehemence.

"Good point," his adversary agreed.

"And just because his underlings got caught selling missiles to one of our worst enemies doesn't mean he committed a treasonist act. He was just moving with the times and there is nothing wrong with his being paranoid as long as everyone else was. Besides, the illegal funds were used to buy rifles for South American guerillas. Without them eighty six communists might have made their way through the jungle and clear across Mexico to the United States. The last thing we needed was bloodshed on own soil. So, there you go. An actor's actor. Especially the part about selling out to the Japanese in such a sneaky way."

"You mean that million bucks under the table for one speaking engagement?"

"What else. Christ, himself, never said anything in his whole life that was even a tenth of one percent as important when gauged by those standards."

"How could you even say such a thing?"

"Look at the facts. Christ died young and penniless. Not even a house or a donkey of his own. Just the clothes on his back. No designer labels, either. Just shapeless old, hand stiched clothes and scruffy sandels. Probably hand-offs from one of his disciples, poor man. Maybe he should have married someone who knew a good astrologer. Who knows? History is a capricious thing, subject to so many, seemingly inconsequential vagaries."

"And, as a matter of fact," Billingsley also stated as a case in point to his closer friends. "Perhaps the Holy Man deserved to die the way he did. After all, he was an activist. Served him right for all the fuss he created, saying all those terrible things about knowing yourself and trusting yourself. That's just not possible. It wasn't possible then and it's even more impossible today. Life is just too complicated to try and figure it all out by relying on one's own judgement. People need to stop trying. No wonder the world is such a mess and getting worse."

"And now," Billingsley was saying to Jenson Wilson as they pushed their way through the demonstrating crowd gathered on the

Capital Building steps. "Look where we are with all these damned, misguided fools shouting slogans and carrying placards and making grand statements about taking advantage of the situation and cleaning up the government. What the hell's the matter with them, anyway?" he said loudly in his Southern drawl, waving his arms. "The government doesn't need cleaning up. It needs to be left alone."

Unfortunately, Jenson didn't agree with him, but, instead of arguing he meerly nodded, made his way into the auditorium and onto the speakers platform. Thinking about the upcoming meeting, he gritted his teeth. Thus far he was deeply disillusioned with his colleagues inabilities to put aside personal interests and come up with viable proposals before the country fell completely apart. There was already heavy rioting in most major cities and in seven midwestern states the National Guard had voluntarily organized and gone into the streets to do battle with a leaderless militia. While congress floundered, the majority of the country was fast becoming an anarchy.

"Damnit," he said outloud, as he thought about it. They had to get a hold on the situation, and quickly, or they'd be out in the streets themselves, fighting for their own lives. With that he raised his arm and pounded on the podium with his new gavel, having already broken the old one. First, he addressed the Democrats.

"Gentlemen. Do you have a final list of Presidential candidates?"

"Just about," one of the members told him.

"Just about? What does that mean?" he asked with a groan.

"We've narrowed the field to ten for president."

"Good God. Is that the best you can do?" asked Jenson.

"We voted on it fourteen different times. It always comes out the same."

"What about you Republicans?" asked Jenson, looking to his left.

"The same problem. We are also deadlocked."

"Wonderful. That's just wonderful," he said in a sour voice.

"Goddamnit," he said into the microphone. "Doesn't anyone understand the mess we're in?"

"Excuse me, Sir," said one of the Republican candidates in a self rightious voice.

"What?" Jenson growled before he even looked at him.

"Well," came the snide reply. "I certainly don't think it's proper decorum to blaspheme before the joint houses of Congress."

"Really?" Jenson said as if considering the comment.

"Yes, really. And furthermore, it's far too important an issue to compromise on. What we do here will affect the entire future of our nation."

"No kidding. And how about what we don't do here? Did you ever think of that? Did you ever consider that what we don't do here will affect our future one hell of a lot more if we don't get moving," said Jenson. "Now sit down and let's get on with it," he stated and banged his gavel.

"*Idiots*," he said to himself. Maybe it was time to retire. He still had a little place in upstate New York away from the mobs where he might be able to live out his remaining years in relative peace. He fumed and thumbed through his papers, so busy with his thoughts that he didn't see the Congressman from Idaho stand up.

"With your permission, sir," the Congressman finally said in worried voice.

"Yes, what is it?" Jenson replied after looking up.

"I'd like to make a suggestion if I might."

"Yes. That might be nice," Jenson said. "We need all the help we can get so please remain standing while I first ask the Study Committee if they have been able to see their way around the Constitutional limitations we are faced with.?"

"No, we haven't," said the acting head of the committee. "Our forefathers didn't leave us any that we have been able to discover. But, we're still researching it. We've also hired Professor Popitt from Harvard as a consultant. He will be here tomorrow afternoon and has some opinions he'd like to share."

"I'm sure he would," replied Jenson as he looked at the congressman with dismay, then slowly turned back to the still standing man from Idaho.

"What did you have to say?" he asked.

"In the interest of expediency, I'd like to make a proposal."

"What the hell. In the interest of expediency, please go ahead. What is it?"

"Let's start with the office for President. Have every member present submit one name for the candidate of choice regardless of party affiliation. It's not likely everyone will vote for themselves. At least I won't, so that will start it off. Have five minutes to make a choice, then select the top dozen of those and vote on them. Cut the number in half and do it again till we're down to three. At that point let the majority vote receiver carry."

"Not too bad," Jenson said. "And to further narrow the field

I'm not a candidate either."

"Sounds like second grade to me," one of the senior Senators was heard to say.

"It's not right," said another. "It doesn't give recognition to the two party system of government."

"It will never work," someone else said. "We'll just have another deadlock.

"Seconded," a loud voice shouted from the rear of the auditorium.

With that the Pages were summoned and paper and pencils handed out. The first ballots were then promptly collected. By the time the entire proceedure had been completed only an hour had passed. It was a preposerous and unequaled record of efficiency for so vast a body of diverse individuals. Surprizingly, as the record showed, none of the candidates on the earlier lists of the Democrats or the Republicans were on the final three tallies and the winner for President turned out to be one Talamious T. Jackson, a pot bellied Senator from Florida who was renowned for his hilarious sense of humor and the obscene jokes he insisted on telling members of the opposite sex.

The Vice Presidential selection was equally smooth. With that completed Jenson suggested that the newly nominated President immediately select his Secretary of State while someone sent out for the proper dialogue for the oath of office.

"The Head of the Supreme Court is missing, too. Who's going to give the oath?" someone asked.

"I am," said Jenson.

"You can't. It's not legal."

"Well, we'll make it legal and we'll back up and make the foregoing elections legal, too, while we're at it. All in favor, raise your hands."

The vote was two hundred sixty three for, and three against.

"Have you got that written down?" Jenson asked the scribe.

"Yes, sir," he was told by the young woman who had been recording the minutes of all the joint meetings.

"Good," said Jenson. "Copy that last bit about it being legal over onto a separate piece of paper and hand it to me."

"In pencil, sir. All I have is a pencil."

"Good grief," Jenson replied and threw his ball point pen at her.

The scribe blushed, quickly copied over the last few lines and handed the paper to Jenson. At the same time someone else handed him a copy of the inaugural oath. With that, he summoned the new President to be.

"Now, Mr. Jackson. If you will please come forward, I will proceed to swear you in."

Jackson came up and stood in front of the podium with his back towards Jenson and smiled broadly at the faces in the auditorium.

"Turn around and raise your right hand, please," Jenson said, but the Senator was too busy basking in his new light. My God, Jenson said to himself. This was really cruel. The universe had blessed the world by getting rid of Stanley Drukus only to turn around and have him replaced by another misfit of equally stupefied hubris. "Damnit, Talamious. Turn around so we can get this over with," he said in a loud voice.

Finally Jackson faced Jenson and raised his right hand.

"Now, Senator. I'm going to read you the oath of office. At the same time I'm doing that, sign this piece of legislation that makes it legal and say, I do. Maybe if we swear you in and make it legal simultaneously we can somehow avoid any further complications."

"Gotcha," Jackson replied with a knowing smile as Jenson began reading the oath.

With that formality concluded, the Vice Presidential favorite was also sworn in. Jackson then took Jenson's hand and shook it heartily.

"Thank you," he said in a loud voice. "Thank you, thank you. Now we'll show these mothers what a good President can do."

"Well, before you do, I suggest you appoint a press secretary and make some announcements to get the public quieted down. Then get over to the White House and start taking care of business."

"Great. But what should I do with Mrs. Drukus, the old First Lady? I hear she's still there."

"Good grief," Jenson said. "Get out of here so I can go home and retreive my sanity."

The precedent setting, historical event made the five o'clock news. By seven o'clock a contingent of minor Wall Street partners made a further announcement. The market would reopen the following day and they fully expected a substantial recovery from the nine thousand point loss that had occurred with the disappearance.

"Thank God," everyone said. "Now we can get on with business as usual," and a sigh of relief swept the nation.

Except for Japan, there was favorable reaction throughout

most of the industrialized world. For the first time in over a month, most Americans and Europeans and Tiawanese got a peaceful nights sleep and looked forward to the morrow with renewed hope. Unfortunately, that hope was short lived. Neither the newly elected President, the Vice President or the Secretary of State appeared in their offices the following morning. Somehow, they too, had disappeared somewhere in the middle of the night. And, as the days passed, similar reports filtered in from around the world. Newly elected or appointed officials everywhere, as well as those who had assumed power through other means, had also kept disappearing under equally mysterious circumstances.

SECOND ISLAND

While the Westerners had been busy bickering over terrritorial rights, jurisdictional jurisprudence, pecking orders, preferential treatment and preservation of the previous heirarchy, Katherine Beaumont and Howard Briggs had gone exploring. In a matter of hours they had learned several significant things. First of all was the fact that they were indeed on an island and not part of some larger land mass. Secondly, although not immediately obvious, there was an abundant supply of food available. But it was not along the coast line or on the lower parts of the island. Higher up, in the middle reaches of the terrain, there were scattered groves of fruit trees everywhere and the varieties ranged from bananas and pears to pomegranits and avacodos. There was also wild asparagras and onions and artichokes and rubarb. There were even tomato vines, grape vines, watermelon and potatoes. Whatever it was all about, they were obviously not put here to die of starvation. Nor of thirst.

Although the snow covered peak that earlier seemed so far away was neither that distant nor that high, the snow melt still generated a number of fresh water streams that flowed down the sides and were readily available to drink from. Having learned this and having satisfied both their thirst and hunger, they followed one of streamlets upward towards the snow line. When they reached it, there were other surprises.

"This is really weird," Howard stated. "Not too many hours ago I was hiking in the mountains in Colorado and now, here I am on a tropical island with a snow covered peak. But not a very high one, however. Maybe four thousand feet. And even though the snow is melting, it certainly doesn't feel very cold. Neither does the air. It must still be about seventy degrees. And…"

"Howard," Katherine said, interupting him. "Look over there."

"A second island," he stated when he turned around. "But look at it. It's awfully barren in comparisson to this one. Flat. A few scattered trees, some ponds of water."

"Doesn't look very inviting. At least not from here. And not very big, either," Katherine pointed out.

"Actually, neither is this one now that we have had a better look at it."\

"How big would you say they are?"

"Maybe seven miles across and fifteen long for this one. More than enough for the amount of people here, however. Especially with all the food that is available. Second island there is about an eigth of that and doesn't look like it would support any life at all."

"I haven't seen any animals here, though. Or any birds. How about you?"

"No. Nothing yet," Howard stated as they sat down to rest.

Far below they could still make out the huge clusters of disappearees, most of them still closely packed together. Howard slipped out of the day pack he still carried, unzipped one of the compartments, removed the pair of binoculars he had taken with him on his mountain trip and began to scan the scene.

"Would you believe it?" he said, as he handed them to Katherine. "Looks like old Stanley is still up on that same rock waving his arms."

"But his audience has gotten a lot smaller," Katherine noted.

"All the ones with turbins are clustered over by the trees on the left. And that must be the Chinese way over there close to the water."\

"Interesting," Howard said, as she handed back the binoculars. "Wonder if anyone else left the mob and went exploring?" With that, he scanned the area below.

"There," he pointed. "A group of fifteen or twenty men headed up the slope."

"Do you think we'd be safe if they caught up to us?"

"Probably for now. Once they find the tree belt with all the food, it's unlikely they'll come any farther," he stated. But then he took another look at Katherine standing there in her pajamas. She was one sensuous woman. Like Deanna, who had chosen to stay behind, she was far too damned good looking for a place like this. Eventually, if they weren't careful, it could lead to trouble.

"But," he continued. "If we're going to be stuck here a while, who knows? And since there are only two of us.."

"And I'm a woman…"

48

"You never know," Howard said. "Best not to take any chances."

"What do you think we should do?" Katherine asked, pleased that Howard seemed to show a genuine concern for her safety.

"Let's keep going. We'll head on around to the back side of this so called mountain and check things out there."

Once around on what might be called the north slope of the singular peak, the terrain changed dramatically. Instead of grass and tree covered smooth slopes, it was a land of ancient upheaval and cataclysmic events, instead. Yet hardly barren. There was still an abundance of brush and small trees and other varieties of plant life growing amongst the boulders, the granite like inclines and along the rock shelves. Tinges and taints of green, shaded from light to dark, hints of red and orange, flower like creations of violet and blue.

"Awesome," Katherine said, as they sat down on a bench like stone to snack on some of the fruit they had gathered earlier.

"Yes," Howard agreed, then they ate in silence. When done, he rose and said, "And if you're up to it, I think we need to go a little further."

"I think you're right," she said, and also got to her feet. "The sun is moving across the sky. And if we're not on earth, we're at least on an earth like planet so it will be dark in a few hours."

"You're very observant. What else have you picked up on?"

"There's an abundance of vegetation but, as I said, I have yet to see any traces of animal life. No birds, either. And except for a butterfly that landed on me when I first arrived, I haven't seen another insect. And, by the look of the water, I wonder if the sea has any life in it. How's that for a woman from the city?"

"I'm really impressed," he said genuinely, as they started working their way into the rugged, trail-less region. After perhaps another hour of hard work they had only gone about three fourths of a mile but had gained some altitude in the process. Then they dead ended.

"What now?" Katherine asked.

"Back track and climb up around behind this boulder."

"You seem to be looking for something in particular."

"I am."

"Okay," Katherine said, and turned back. Not too much later, after some serious upward scrambling, they were behind the upper reach of the huge rock.

49

"And there it is," he said, pointing to a small bush growing out from the rocks.

At first Katherine was confused, but she went closer and then she smiled.

"I'll be damned. How did you know it was there?"

"Just a guess."

"But a good one. Should we look?"

Then a few minutes later, inside the cave, she said, "Wow."

"Perfect," Howard said. "Not too big, not too small. A place of safety when we need it."

"A long way from food and water, however. That's the only drawback."

"Maybe not. Let's get up top on the rock and take a look," he said, and began climbing with Katherine directly behind. Once there it was obvious that the rock behind which the cave was hidden was strategically placed and gave a good view of most of the backside of the mountain in all directions.

"Good enough," Howard said. "We also probably have the only pair of binoculars on the island so we should be able to see anyone coming long before they see us. And secondly, over there, less than two hundred yards away is another small stream so we do have easy access to water. But, unfortunately, we will still need to go back to the other side for food."

"But we can lay in a supply of apples and nuts and things that will keep longer, just in case."

"Exactly. So, with your permission, I think we should spend the night here. Maybe even several, until things settle a little. Once the shock of being here wears off for some of those people, who knows what they are likely to do."

"I fully agree. What a lucky find. The floor of the cave looks sandy enough to sleep on comfortably, the temperature is perfect and there is no wind."

"What could be better."

"Not much, I guess. It would be nice to have a stove, however. I always had a problem with raw vegetables."

Down below the new day was clear and cloudless. Additionally, the layer of smog that had hung over the land when they had arrived had completely disappeared, not to return for a long time. Then, at the point when the sun was highest in the sky, a single white cloud appeared directly over the island and briefly showered everything with large, warm drops of water, while on the peak snow fell quietly in an amount exactly equal to the amount that had thawed the day before and ran down the slopes. Likewise, for all the following days on First Island, it was always the same. It was always the same on Second island, too, except there it only rained every eighth day or so, and there was no peak for it to snow on. And, when the sun came up that second day, there was the President, most of his administration and a large number of those who habitually clung to that group, all asleep on the grass surrounding the same rock he had spent most of the first day standing on.

When they woke, they were also very hungry. They had been far too busy planning and power brokering to notice that the day had slipped by and too consumed with the President's new agenda to think of something so basic as food and water. That had always been left up to someone else. Unfortunately, such unimportant individuals as chefs, waiters and other service people had all been left behind and none of the administrative leaders present had ever had to take care of such menial tasks. Once the President learned that there was food on the island, however, he gave a direct order as their Commander in Chief.

"Scout it out," he directed, letting them know they had better return with his morning meal. They were also to try and find something to carry water in and bring that back to the site at the rock.

"What's this?" he questioned an hour later. "Grapes and bananas for breakfast? I need my sausage and eggs. How do you expect me to carry out my duties?"

"Sorry, Sir," he was told. "There doesn't seem to be any chickens in this place and no animals. Even if there were we'd have no way to slice up a pig, and nothing to cook things on. There's also nothing we could find to carry water in, either."

The President grumbled, turned sullen and pushed the food aside. Another hour later, however, when he thought no one was watching, he popped a handful of grapes in his mouth and peeled a banana. Then his thirst got the better of him and he was finally forced to walk the equivalent of about two city blocks to the closest stream, lay down on his belly and get a drink as best he could and to thereafter repeat the process every time he became thirsty. It was not a pretty picture. One would have to wonder what the voters back home might think if they could see him lying there, sucking and lapping at the water like some rejected dog. Especially since his crumpled, slept in clothes were now covered with grass stains and mud and his stubble of a beard started coming out blotchy and irregular. Back home he would have been mistaken for some drunk coming off a four day binge. But here it didn't seem to matter. The more surprizing thing was that, almost to a man, as well as the Secretary of State and the Vice President, both of whom were women, they maintained their ranks and never once questioned his authority or his agenda in this starkly new environment. It most certainly never occured to any of them to make an independent assessment of the situation to see if some other course of action might be more appropriate. They were Americans. President Barkus never doubted their loyalty for a second. There would be times, however, when he would wonder why the head of the CIA had become overly sarcastic and the Secretary of the Navy no longer appeared at staff meetings.

Regardless, most everyone else on the island had been more practical when it came to basic needs and had at least gone to sleep with a full stomach. They had also rapidly segregated themselves into groups peculiar to their nationality, or race, or profession, or lack of profession, and scouted out areas to call their own. Clothing was divided up so that most everyone soon had at least some minimal covering. Beyond that, though, there was no other concern for cooperation between seperate groups and, tragically, they all made the same mistake as the Americans. They quickly established an agenda characteristic of the political or social structure they had left behind. With such an attitude, this most diverse and divergent conglomeration of human beings forced together on such a small piece of real estate was hardly conducive to future peace and harmony.

"What's going on?" President Stanley demanded of his staff a few days after their arrival. "Except for the Brits and the Isralies, we now seem to be all alone here."

"No damned respect at all," said the lady VP. "Just because we don't have our high tech weaponry they think they can just ignore us."

"I think it's more complicated than that, Sir," said the female Secretary of State, who looked a lot more like a small truck than a woman.

"We have always been the *have* nation and the rest of them the *have-nots* but what with that abundance of food growing all over the place and no control over it, we don't have any leverage anymore. It's a very confusing situation and it's difficult to establish any kind of foreign policy. Especially when all the foreigners are right here with us, squatting on the land you already declared to be a possesion of the United States."

"I know, Madam Secretary, but that's your area of expertise. I'm sure you'll figure something out. In the meantime we have a great opportunity at our fingertips. Since all the world's leaders are right here with us, make up a contingent of envoys and send them out to promote global democracy. If we can convert them here, the rest of it will be a snap, once we get back home."

"What if we never get back?"

"We will. I found out that the head of that super smart organization, Mesmer, is here, too. He's convinced that he can establish our location on the planet by looking at the star field. Once we have that, someone can build us a boat and we'll know what direction to sail off in to get back home."

"It's called Mensa, Stanley," said the head of the CIA. "But I wouldn't count on it. They're supposed to be super smart but most of them can't even tie their own shoes."

Instantly, the President's eyes narrowed. Clearly angered by this sudden display of this first name lack of repect, he was about to respond when interrupted.

"I beg your pardon," said the Secretary of State, puffing herself up, "but I happen to be a member of that very elite group myself."

"No kidding? Tell me when to be impressed?" the CIA man said, mocking her. There was no doubt about it. He clearly did not like the woman. Never had. Not from the first moment he had first met her. And it had nothing to do with her being a woman. Basically, he loved women. He even wished that a woman was still in the country's top job. No, it was the personality. For a highly educated individual, the Secretary was the most superficial, shallow minded, self righteous, self centered, air head person he had ever met. And so distasteful and unappealing he couldn't bare to look at her most of the time. It almost made his skin crawl. But he looked now. He was totally fed up with the President's choice in appointing her to her post.

"Well," she said with great indignity, "maybe you should be..."

"Cut the crap," he interrupted. "Who cares? You're so far out of touch with the real world you don't even know it exists, or did exist at least, and it makes me sick to watch you walking around moon faced over Stanley here just because he's probably the first and only man ever to pat you on the fanny while you keep telling all those lies about what a great man he is just to keep him happy, hoping maybe he'll do it again."

"Wait a minute," said the President. "I have never touched that woman. Ever."

"Really? What about that CBS news clip last year where the two of you were walking across the White House lawn together and you had your hand on her posterior?"

"Well, that was an extenuating circumstance. She had just returned home from being thrown out of Iran and was so depressed that I took the risk and gave her a pat. I believe that has to be within governmental guidelines for good employee relations and besides that, that kind of talk will get you fired."

"It's a little late. I told the VP I quit three days ago."

"Maybe you did, maybe you didn't. But nobody in my administration resigns without my personal approval and that's final. But since you have treated both her and I with great disrespect I'm afraid I have no choice but to dimiss you from your office. Effective immediately."

"But technically you can't fire him, Sir," said the Secretary, responding from her own closed world of over-logic, devoid of common sense.

"What do you mean," the President bristled. "I'm the boss. I could even fire you if I wanted. Of course I would never do that. Not to you, anyway," he mellowed.

"Thank you, Sir. You are so kind. But you see he already resigned. And even if he spoke to you with disrespect he still stopped working for you before you terminated him so that becomes an invalid and illogical response that is unquestionably going to disrupt and confuse the fact that your patting me on the butt was as kind and noble an act as has ever transpired amongst us members of the political aristocracy."

"My God," said the ex head of the CIA, shaking his head astoundedly as he walked off.

Three days later the Secretary of State came back to the President's rock to report. By that time his staff had gathered rocks and branches in sufficient quantity to create some semblance of an office for the Chief Executive. He now sat on a medium sized rock behind a large pile of smaller stones which served as a mock desk and give him some sense of separation and importance. Tree branches were also laid out on the ground to define a perimeter of spaces like a floor plan in an attempted replica of the Oval Office.

At what might be considered the door to that office, a full Marine Corps Colonel stood guard, being the lowest ranking member of the military that had been transported to the island in the disappearance.

"Good morning, Madam Secretary," he said as she approached. "How can I help you?"

"I need to speak with the President."

"I'll see if he's available," said the Colonel and turned to look at the President who had been in full sight the whole time but sat there with his eyes half closed as though in a daze.

"Maybe we should wait a little. I think he's doing his morning meditation."

"Poor man. He doesn't even know what the word means. I'm sure he's just stressed. Maybe if I give him a neck rub."

"Good idea, Madam Secretary. Go right in," the Colonel said, and gave her a snappy salute.

With that, she entered the area, walked around behind and put her hand on his shoulder. He jerked his head up, opened his eyes and gazed up at her. "Just, a, resting my, ah, eyes," he said. "Yes, uh, oh yes. How was your, uh, how did your mission go?"

"I fear that I've failed you, Sir," she said, looking as though she were on the verge of tears. What was going on, she wondered. She would never have behaved this way back home. But then she had never slept on the ground before, either. And without a pillow or her teddy bear pajamas. And having to be around all these men all the time, especially when so many of them snored. That was the especially trying part. Nor had she ever gone without a shower and clean clothes and a toothbrush for more than a day in her whole life. And without any way of shaving, fur was growing on her legs and under her arms. How horrible. The situation was taking it's toll. She wasn't sure how much longer she could hold herself together. Thank God for the president, however. He had given her a special assignment to accomplish and even though she seemed unable to succeed at it under present conditions, it had kept her occupied.

"You could never fail me," he stated, consolingly, although she was as large physically as he.

"But I have, Sir. You gave me a job to do and I was unable to complete the assigned mission."

"Well now. Why don't you sit down here on the edge of my desk and tell me all about it. Since it's made of stones I don't think you'll hurt it."

"Yes, Sir. But could you just give me a, ah, something to cheer me up first?" she said and turned her right hip towards him.

That done, she sat on the stack of rocks and blurted out her story.

"No one will talk to the envoys I sent out and no one will even talk to me. All they do is laugh about our plans for global democracy and make very disparaging remarks about you. The President of France even said that if any more Americans show up in his area he will personally come back here and pound you on the nose again. If only we had something real to work with, Sir. Some carrots to dangle in front of them. Or something sinister to threaten them with. But we have nothing. And except for the Frenchman, none of the leaders will even consider walking over here to meet with you. I'm completely out of ideas."

"Well, don't you fret now my dear," said the President as he touched his lopsided nose which was still somewhat sore and would probably never look the same again.

"The Colonel at the door has been thoroughly briefed and is fully prepared to take Pompou into custody if he shows up. As for the rest of it, we'll just get the other members of my Cabinet in here and have another roundable meeting. Someone will have an idea."

"Where are they at, Sir? I haven't seen any of them for days."

"Over there in the trees playing checkers."

"How can they play without a board and checkers?"

"My people are clever. They scratched the pattern of a board in the dirt and found enough small white stones and black stones to do the job and they've been at it now for two days. Claim it helps improve their stategizing skills. Who knows. We might need that one of these days."

"What about our escape plan? How is that coming?"

"That Menstral guy bombed out. Says none of the star patterns make any sense and now that the moon is coming out, it is going around the planet from pole to pole instead of coming up in the, geez, what direction is the Atlantic from Washington DC?"

"East, Sir. The moon comes up in the east and goes down in the west. And it's called Mensa. Not menstral."

"Right. Except this moon doesn't do that so now we're really trapped. I'll never get to see my pineapple ranch again."

"Well…" the Secretary started to say, but was interrupted by a large, noisy group of people headed in their direction.

Once the collection of people had arrived outside the mock Oval Office, one man separated himself from the group and stepped forward. It was a fat, loud, demanding man, none other than

Talamious T. Jackson himself, the newly elected President of the United States, there to lay claim to the title, even if it was on some unknown island somewhere other than Washington DC.

"Jackson. What the hell are you doing here?" Stanley asked, thinking it rather odd that he was addressing the Senator from the south because thus far no members of Congress had appeared on the island. None that he was aware of, anyway. Clean shaven, too. And all decked out in a new three piece pin stripped suite. Suddenly the president felt like the homeless bum he must have looked like. That alone was enough to make him extremely angry.

"Well, it's surely not much to speak of but since I am, was, the last duly elected and sworn in Chief Executive, I must ask you to step aside and let me take my rightful place as President of the United States. Or what seems to be left of it, at least. I mean, is this it? Hmmm. Maybe I don't want the job after all."

"Want it or not, you're not getting it. No matter what," Stanley informed him., enviously eyeing the man's clothes. The pants were obviously too big around the waist but the jacket just might fit. And the shiny shoes.

"Oh, yeah. Well now I want it for sure."

"You can't have it. Besides, not enough time has passed to have had an election back home."

"Congress elected me, and the Vice President and then I appointed a new Secretary of State so your hunky lady here is also out of a job."

They argued steadily for ten minutes. Ten minutes soon became twenty, then it was an hour and then it was dark. Nothing had been resolved. By that time all that was left of the federal government had gathered around the mock White House and the last words of conversation were between Stanley Drukus and the Head of the Joint Chiefs of Staff, General Wells.

"Let him get some sleep," Stanley told the General, "but as your Commander in Chief, first thing in the morning I want you to take Jackson down to the beach and throw him in the ocean. And that is a direct order. But only after you remove his jacket and his shoes. Is that clear?"

"Yes, Sir. I hear you, Sir, but at this point I'm afraid I'll have to sleep on that one. I mean, I will sleep on it, won't I. But I'll have to review my thoughts on the situation in the morning, Sir. With your permission, of course."

"Well, I don't agree. But right now I have other important matters to attend to."

"Do you want me to round up the Cabinet so you can have your roundtable discussion you wanted before all the interruption?" the Secretary asked.

"No, cancel that. It will soon be so damned dark we won't even be able to see each other. Besides, I thought of a better way of doing things. Guaranteed to get far more positive results. Where is he? I just saw him a minute ago."

"Who, Sir?"

"That Trunik guy who runs the FBI. Oh, there he is. Bill, Bill! Get over here," the President shouted, waving his arms.

"Yes, Sir," Trunik said, coming to attention in front of his commander. "What can I do for you?"

"In the interest of national security, I'm sending you on a vital mission."

"Yes, Sir. Good, Sir. Very good. Checkers was getting to be rather boring. What is it?"

"Tonight I want you to take some of your best men and sneak over into the Arab territory and bring me back a couple of captives. I also want a couple of Chinks and Africans."

"Yes, Sir. Then what?"

"Find a secluded place in the woods where you can tie them up and keep them isolated."

"Great idea, Sir. But then what?"

"Then what? We are going to gather intelligence. We are going to find out what is wrong with those people and why they refused to talk to the Secretary of State here and what their plans are and all that stuff. And keep it quiet, will you. Top Secret.

PENNIES AND PAIN

Dr. Walter Heavypenny picked up a copy of his newly published book and handed it across his polished formica desk to a Miss Bernice Steinbla. It was a thick, heavy book of over four hundred pages entitled, "How To Deal With Leaderless Stress In Today's World."

Bernice looked glowingly at the bright colored jacket, then turned the book over to look at Heavypenny's picture on the back. There he was, sitting behind that same old desk, smiling through his bush of a beard and pointing his smelly old pipe off somewhere into the room. She squirmed a bit in her chair. As far as she was concerned, he was still the handsomest man alive.

"You may keep it," the good doctor said. "I've even autographed it for you."

Bernice opened the front cover, read the inscription and blushed slightly.

"Thank you, Doctor," she said and flashed him her best smile. Bernice was on the speakers committee for the Complete Life Exposition which had lost some of its key spiritual leaders and gurus in the disappearance and it was her job to locate new talent for the upcoming Los Angeles convention. The convention was big business by most any definition. Over seventeen thousand searching souls had showed up for last years event, and it was part of her duties to keep the lost spirits of the modern world on the profitable path to salvation.

The Doctor was a psychiatrist by trade and had been in the profession some twenty five years. In actuality, however, he was not overly intelligent, was rather poor at diagnosis, unduly insecure and always a little envious of many of his patients. That was partly due to a fatherless childhood and an aimless, alcoholic mother who had been the youngest bag lady Philadelphia had ever seen. This was further compounded by the fact that if Bernice's bedroom fantasy with him ever came true, she would most certainly be severely disappointed. And if he ever shaved off his beard and side burns he would have been completely nondescrip, plainer than beige wallpaper.

Ultimately, his signature became his saving grace, however, once he had found out how to use it effectively. This he had done in ever increasing amounts through the prescription of psychotropic drugs and sedatives to his patients, being professionally responsible for have hooked some thirty five hundred people on Valium and Prozac alone, over the years. He loved it. It saved so much time and trouble. And once the dosage was correct, they always came back for their follow up sessions and a renewal prescription. And if they kept taking the medication as prescribed they were too placated to dispute either his findings or his fees. In and out like a revolving door, there was a large amount of money in his bank account.

Not only that but it was a very effective way of dealing with people whom God had been more generous to than himself. Especially the women. In truth, he was actually quite intimidated by most of them. But rather than hold back or withdraw, his fear had manifested as a strong and active, but well disguised, dislike. And now, thanks to his professional training, he was allowed to persecute them in the most subtle of ways. That was most expeditiously done by simply telling them they were depressed.

Understandably so, of course. Wasn't everyone to some extent? Certainly. Nothing to be alarmed about. It was easy to treat, he had the exact remedy. Then, with their full confidence, he medicated them heavily. Once they were hooked they loved it, and they loved him, for he had helped them cope with the yappings of the modern world, to tolerate their boring husbands, their tedious, equal opportunity jobs, their time fading beauty, the trials and tribulations of menopause and more. He was the kind and saintly man who helped them get through the day so they could get up the next and do it all over again. No need to ever get into the messy business of trying to solve humanity's real problems. That was a good way to lose clients, not keep them, for if you freed them of their neurosis and budding psychosis there was never a need for them to return to the office. And even if he knew how to do that, how would he be able to go on living on the west side of L.A. in Santa Monica and have a new Mercedes every year if he did?

Of course, as a medical professional who had promised "to do no harm," he was strongly opposed to the use of street drugs and righteously lent his full support to the ongoing drug war because he sometimes lost patients to cocaine and heroin or some of the other recreational, mind bending substances in circulation. Things that led to dysfunction and overdose. What a waste, poor things. They needed intelligent regulation and supervision. That was what he and his colleagues were there for, that was his directed purpose in life.

And now he had published. It was an immediate best seller. His face was recognized widely and even though he had a number of sharp critics in the medical and psychological community, he was still in great demand as a lecturer. He loved it. Finally his life had an even greater meaning, or so he told himself anyway, even though deep inside he knew the book was nothing but a collection of trite efflufia. He didn't really have much of importance to say when he lectured, either, but he said it well and that was the important thing. Besides, if all these people were buying his book and coming to hear him speak, maybe it wasn't such extraneous animal matter after all.

At this point he looked back at Bernice spilling out of a dress that was much too tight for her ample figure and wondered how she had ever been able to stuff it all in there initially. He momentarily visualized seams splitting and smiled benevolently. He wouldn't mind getting his hands on those big jugs, he thought, as long as he didn't have to look at her face while he was doing it and as long as it could be done under circumstances where he wouldn't have to follow through. What the heck, his mind said, as he scanned possible scenarios while she prattled on about having him at the Expo this year. He had already decided he would like to go, but let her continue, sunning himself in her words until at last she asked the question directly.

"Well, yes," he said in response. "I think I can work it out. I was going to take some vacation time in there anyway, but I can set it aside if you really need me."

"Oh, Doctor. That would be wonderful. How can I ever thank you," she said, and bent over the desk to take his hand, once more displaying two straining piles of soft flesh that almost drooped to the desk top. From there they discussed the schedule, what picture of his to use in the publication, the split of proceeds from his lecture and all the rest until there was nothing left to talk about. By then his hands were itching terribly and there was a trite hint of a bulge in his trousers. He was about to get up, go around the desk and make a move on her when his receptionist interrupted. His next patient had arrived.

He acknowledged the message, shook hands with Bernice one last time over the desk and watched her sway out of the room. Then he buzzed his receptionist and told her to wait a few minutes before sending in the patient. Something had just struck home. The Disappearance. He thought of all the renowned personages who had disappeared. That's why Bernice had come to begin with. It wasn't just the politicians and the business tycoons, either. It had also happened to a large number of sincere humanitarians like himself. What was that all about?

"Damnit," he said outloud. Now he was worried. It just wasn't fair. Here he was finally reaching the pinnacle of success, the great American dream come true and someone or some thing might snatch it all away. Rather, snatch him away from it all, time warp him out or disintegrate him or zip him off into outer space, or whatever it was that had happened to all those other people.

"God," he said. It was an awful thought. Maybe he should cancel the agreement. He wanted to cry but was again interrupted, this time by a sudden pressure from within and he realized how long he had been sitting there with his legs tightly crossed. He got up suddenly, wishing he hadn't shared so many cups of coffee with Bernice, trying to check out her over ripe form. "Fat bitch," he said half outloud, and hurried for the men's room.

TRANSITIONS

It was the saddest ceremony Jenson had ever been to in his long life. It even exceeded the Kennedy funeral, which he could still vividly remember, even though he had only been twelve years old at the time. Such a dear young lady. Words were inappropriate. They would never be enough. And to have lost the baby, too. A double tragedy, the circumstances would probably haunt Jack forever.

The neighbor, Tom Piper, a block down the street had been home that day. He had borrowed an axe from someone and, looking to the future, had been wisely chopping wood. Unfortunately, it was a new experience for him, one he had little talent for. The only thing that saved his foot was the heavy boots he had been wearing. The newly sharpened tool still went through the thick leather, severed an artery and slashed deep into the bone. Jack had been out watering the garden when he heard the shouts for help.

"Damnit, Tom. Forget your pants and hold still. You'll bleed to death if we don't get a tourniquet on this," Jack said as slit open the leg of Tom's jeans with his knife and sliced off a piece of cloth long enough to circle the leg, tie a knot in and insert a stick.

"Hold this," he instructed, once it was twisted up tight. "And hang in there. I have to get your boot off so we can see if it's working and monitor it. Where's your wife? I see the car is gone."

"Out looking for supplies like everyone else. I'm glad as hell you were home."

"Jeez, Tom." Jack said once the boot was off. It would take more than a king sized bandaid to fix this. "We need a doctor." And damned quick. Not only was the wound deep and gruesome, Tom was growing pale. He would soon be in shock. Which left Jack without any other choice. Gail's pregnant condition was far too delicate for her to ride along. He'd have to leave her home alone if he was going to get Tom to the clinic. That worried him. There had been a break in on the other side of the tract two days ago and there had been cars cruising the neighborhood recently with some not-to-nice looking people in them.

Once the medical staff had Tom stabilized, Jack left. The necessary surgery wouldn't be till later and Tom would be spending the night. His wife could bring him home in the morning. Driving even faster than he had going to the clinic, the entire trip still took almost two hours. There was a brief wave of relief as he turned off the highway into their tract. But then, what the hell was that? he questioned as he came around the last corner. There was a battered old Ford parked in the street not far from the house. Damn.

"Oh my god" he said outloud as he rolled into the driveway, slammed on the brakes and jumped out. There was a body lying on the sidewalk near the curb. There was another face down on the grass. He ducked behind the car for safety and looked towards the house. There was another person crumpled on the front steps, the front door slighly ajar. The first two were deathly still, the third, apparently seriously wounded, was trying to move. Jack waited, listening. There were no sounds coming from the house that he could hear but there was a handgun lying beside the body on the grass. He went for it, picking it up on the run and darted around to the rear. The kitchen door was still locked as it should be. He fished in his pocket for the key, opened it and went in cautiously and quietly. Then he stopped. Nothing. Not a sound. He eased toward the doorway into the dining room and looked beyond into the living room.

A fourth body, a huge puddle of blood. He didn't recognize him either. He moved to the hallway and down towards the master bedroom. Another one, also dressed in camouflage fatigues like the two out front and the one in the living room. This one bearded and dirty looking, not so much blood on the floor but apparently dead too. Jack proded him with his foot, the gun pointed at the man's head, the safety off. He didn't move.

"Gail!" he said loudly. She had to be in there. She had to have shot this one. "Gail. It's Jack. I'm home. I'm coming in," he said, then peered around the corner and went in where his knees gave out and he collapsed onto the floor.

The barely alive man on the front steps was Mike from across the way, a thirty eight revolver in his hand, all six shots fired. He was in intensive care three days before he could speak. Hearing gunshots from his house, he had grabbed his pistol and come running. Fired upon himself, he had taken out the two in front. The man in the living room was already down. Gail must have shot him as he came through the door with Jack's deer rifle which was kept in the bedroom closet. The fourth one, the one Mike was not aware of, must have already been in the house by the time he got there, forcing Gail to retreat back to the bedroom where she had locked the door. But it was not a security door. Just a normal, paneled interior door, now badly splintered from being kicked open. There was one bullet hole through one panel about chest high. The man on the floor had two wounds. One had gone through the door, the other after the door was open. Either would have been fatal but not instantaneously so. The shotgun blast he had been able to get off before he died had tore into her abdomen.

What would he do now, Jenson wondered. Jack Briggs was a brilliant man in many respects, as his multi faceted career history would attest to. He had tremendous leadership capability, too. If only he had been interested in politics, he might even be in the Senate himself. But it was not to be. Jack was neither a team player or a man of compromises. Nor was his integrity for sale. In some respects he was a man out of step with the society he had been living in. But now with the disappearance, things were radically different. The country needed people like Jack if it was going to survive, Jenson felt. But with his loss and his sadness? And the bitterness he must feel under the circumstances? My god. How would he be able to handle it?

After the disappearance of Talamious Jackson and the others, Jenson Wilson still maintained some involvement with Congress but began spending more and more time at home with the woman he still loved after fifty years, helping her in the new garden she was planting. Jack, however, withdrew completely and retreated to his own empty home. Once the shock of his wife's and baby's deaths had begun to wear off, their absence had become real and devastating. They had died together, one wanting to give life, the other seeking it. But he had failed, society had failed, the world had failed and suddenly he was alone, more alone than he had ever felt in his life.

He refused to go back to the house, moved into a vacant one down the street instead, not really caring where he was at. And half of the time not really caring if he, himself, really lived or died. He could have turned to alcohol or to drugs. They might blunt or blurr. But in the end would solve nothing. What was, was, he tried to convince himself instead. Somehow he must learn to deal with it. If only he could get some sleep, however. If he could just sleep one whole night through. But he couldn't.

Then his brother Howard's still distraught wife called again. First, to extend more condolences to him and second, to seek his advice about the company she now seemed to own but knew nothing about. Without Howard there to manage, it was deteriorating rapidy. Perhaps he could be of help, Jack thought in his desperation. God help him, there was nothing left to keep him where he was. But the airlines were out of service and Denver was seventeen hundred miles away. He would have to drive if he was going. If he could find enough gasoline along the way.

Once he was in the car, driving demanded more of Jack's attention and gave him something exterior to focus on. As the miles piled up behind, the hum of the tires on the pavement became a lulling, background noise that ordinarily would have soothed and quieted his nerves. But not on this day, not yet, anyway. Try as he might, he couldn't get beyond the image of his poor dead wife on the bedroom floor. He forced himself to think about the disappearance and all its ramifications. What about the future, he wondered, not even sure he gave a damn. But he should. He had to. If he didn't, he might as well drive off a bridge somewhere. He reached for the radio and turned it on. The first thing that blared out at him was the latest top ten tune. "Baby, baby, baby. How I'd like to disappear with you," it went. "Disappear with you. Into the blue, into the blue. Baby, baby, me and you."

He punched the scan button and the radio jumped to the next station. More corrosive noises poured out. *Jesus*, he thought. Acid rock had returned with a vengeance, guaranteed to disolve your brain and eat away any sense of remaining reality. Perhaps it was written by and for people who had already lost theirs, a growing number, it would seem. He hit the scan button again, and again. If only he could find a single, normal voice in the tulmultuous onslaught. But what was normal anymore? What did that mean anyway? Whatever it might have meant at some point in the past, that earlier definition no longer, existed. The perverse was becoming the norm. At least if he gave any credence to what was on mainstream radio. And everything else he had become aware of since the Disappearance.

More and more people coped with their leaderless world by embracing weirdness. For the young it was even weirder clothing, behavior and music, all aimless, pointless and self destructive. Body peircing was but a faded memory of where it had all began. Now it was body carving and mutilation. The more tribaly oriented ones who had banded together in search of security had resorted to cutting off a particular toe or finger to display their affiliation with this gang or that gang, or an earlob, half an ear or possibly an entire ear if they wanted to make it flagrantly clear. Others completely scaped away an eyebrow or tore off a fingernail or two but the most prolific trend of all was body carving. Tatoo artists had thrown away their needles and used the surgeon's scalpel instead, to creatively disfigure human bodies on demand and for a price.

For some reason the most religious of clients seemed to demand carvings that caused the most excruciating of pain and purposely had their woumds packed with ink or dirt to prolong the healing process. They also loved to walk shirtless or topless to display their maimed and suffering condition. The most popular selection of all was none other than the Christian cross. It made its appearance on the back, the chest, the upper arms, maybe even the forhead, and, if the artist was skilled enough, some rendition of Jesus was hanging there, too, nailed to it with ink blobs in the destroyed tissue. Second to that came various depictions of the devil. People even had their eyes reworked to make themselves appear more sinister. Unable to grow horns, however, these followers gouged out deep holes in their scalps and did their best to pile up as much scar tissue as possible in those areas.

Finally, about to give up, Jack found a sane voice coming from a west coast talk show. The topic for the first program segment was the effect of the Disappearance on the quality of goods and services. The second half was to be on the psychological aspects of a leaderless world. At the moment of tuning in, one Carlton Hilary, former financial analyist and Dean of the Chicago Institute of Business Sciences was telling the host how happy he was to be there and how he hoped the host would keep up the good work because the country needed sensible programming like he presented.

"Thank you," the host replied. "And now, if you would, I'm sure the audience might like to have your views on the rehabilitation of the economy, if we can be so bold as to call it that."

"That's being bold, all right. Where do you want to start?"

"Well, how about food supply?"

"Know anyone living on a balanced diet these days?"

"Not here in Los Angeles."

"Nowhere else, either. Unless you happen to know someone who lives on a farm. For the rest, fresh produce is basically unavailable."

"Because of the failure of the agribusiness industry due to loss of leadership?"

"That's the immediate reason. But it's also because the large corporate owned farms forced all the small, privately owned farms out of business begininng over sixty years ago. That coupled with the hybridization of crops, monopolization of the seed supply, suceptability of engineered product strains to crop diseases and the complete failure to maintain adequate backup seed banks of native stocks, all tied together with the adverse effects of global warming."

"A complete disaster from beginning to end."

"Short term profit, power and politics."

"Seems like we've heard that before. What happens now?"

"Without leadership it's impossible to formulate any clear policy. And, without law enforcement, there is a lot of theft and piracy. Much of what could be available is ending up on the black market. There's nothing Congress is able to do about it either. As you know, no one in Congress is even willing to step forward for fear they will disappear with the rest. Off hand, I don't blame them but it doesn't help solve any of the problems, food supply included. Independently, however, some of the state legislatures seem to be doing a far better job of getting things done, even without Governors. Probably because there is a much smaller number of people who have to work together and come to agreement. And, in that regard, the thing that is keeping the situation together at all is that fact that small businesses are still functioning. While large corporations have, across the board, all lost their executives, small businesses have not lost their owners. But, if the situation persists, it will be a very long time before they can divide up the corporate pie into small, manageable amounts and run it in a small business manner. There will also be heavy reluctance to do that because know one knows for sure where the, *too big,* point is and most people don't want to risk disappearing also."

"I see your what you're saying. But getting back to the farmers, I understand that Congress has finally agreed to sell off all those burdensome hordes of surplus grains that have been accumulating for all these years."

"True, but they're getting a lot of objections from the farmers. For the first time in forty years the independents have a chance to become profitable again and they want the government to stay out of it."

"How do you feel about that?"

"In principal, I agree. But, I don't think today's farmers have to worry about competition from the governement's surplus grain supply."

"Why is that?"

"Because of problems in the food processing industry and the radical changes in peoples diets."

"Can you summarize those changes for our listeners?"

"Two things have happened and they are area dependent. The small town and rural segments of the population are turning more and more to fresh vegetables, fruits and meats which they buy direct from the farmer. Some people have even relearned how to bake their own bread again, after all these years. Processed meats, canned goods and prebaked, preservative laden pastries have almost disappeared from stores in those areas so people are also eating more fresh fish, venison, rabbits and other things that can be directly obtained from the environment."

"And the metropolitan crowd. What's new there?"

"You mean you haven't heard the latest?"

"What's that? Oh..., you mean..." the host said, as it dawned on him.

"Yes. The new line of hash and grass cheese dips."

"As if Bennie stew and Valium laced M&Ms wasn't bad enough. What's it coming to, anyway? Do you have any thoughts on that?"

"I believe your next guess is Dr. Heavypenny. Maybe he'll have something to say about it."

"Yes he is," the host replied, barely able to suppress a laugh at the thought of who he had invited.

By this time Jack was just getting onto the Ohio Turnpike, still headed west. "*Good God,*" he thought when he heard Heavypennie's name mentioned. "*He's actually going to have him on the program?*" One of Jack's neighbors had well intentionally given him a copy of Heavypennie's book right after his wife had died, thinking it might be of help. Needless to say, however, it was the first book Jack had ever burned in his life. He almost turned the radio off in disgust but decided he wanted to hear the rest of the interview with Carlton Hilary.

"Okay, said the host. "Let's turn to the industrial sector. And then, if we have time, perhaps you'd like to say a few words about the stock market."

"I probably should decline answering on both issues. Pessimistic as it may sound, things are really that bad. We have no idea what level of unemployment exists except that it's at least thirty percent with no indication of leveling off."

"What specifically seems to be the cause? I understand that demand for hard goods is still high."

"That's true, but the difficulty seems to reside within the work force, itself. For some reason the average production line employee seems unable to function without supervision. They claim it is unreasonable to expect them to work under conditions where there is no one to take charge and accept responsibility. Many are filing unresolvable workmen's compensation cases against the government because the government has been unable to step in and provide leadership. Somehow they just don't seem to understand what they are asking for under the circumstances and how impossible it is to give it to them. So, I only see things getting worse rather than better. At least for the time being."

Jack drove on, listening to the balance of the program, not surprised to hear that the stock market had once again been closed until further notice. With that the host opened up the show to telephone links with various parts of the world, inviting call-in comments. Surprizingly, it was the Chinese who seemed to be having the least difficulty with their leaderless state. In fact, the callers from that country seemed quite elated with the idea. In response, however, someone called in from Cincinnati and complained about talking with those Orientals in the first place because he didn't think they deserved that much freedom after so many years of oppression. With that, the host thanked Hilary for being on the air with him and took a station break.

Again, Jack was about to turn the radio off but there was something in the host's tone when he introduced Heavypenny that made him leave it on. Obviously, he had something else in mind besides helping the good doctor promote his new book.

Who were the real enemies the average person was faced with? Carlton Hillary asked, leading the discussion around in circles. Could it possible be themselves? Were they being helped along by the Heavypennies of the world they so blindly accepted? It was an interesting theme, one the ego bound, unsuspecting psychiatrist didn't even seem to realize he was playing into. But then Heavypenny took a surprizing sharp turn and began advocating a far more liberal use of drugs in society. Shortly thereafter, Jack turned off the radio in disgust. Somehow, it seemed that on many levels mankind rightly deserved the predicament it was in. Suddenly, he was very tired. It was finally time to find a motel.

Twelve hours of deep sleep helped. At least a little. Back in the car once more, still heading west, more miles disappeared behind. As they dropped away Jack forced himself to leave the past behind. Why the disappearance, he asked himself instead. That was challenging enough to keep his mind occupied. For a good long time. Not the 'how' of it. That was another matter. Even in the so-called, high tech world they lived in. Men on the moon, laser guided weapons and the internet were one thing. Physically bringing about the simultaneous disappearance of several thousand people was something else. No question about that.

The matter of "why," however, should somehow yield to rational thought. Shouldn't it? It had to, he told himself. If it had been a random happening, how could it have been so clearly split alone the lines that had occured. An odd conglomeration of people somewhere, maybe. An entire shopping mall full or a group of campers, or, whatever. But just leaders and a certain level of leaders at that... Bizzare and awesome as it was, that was far too precise. But it had happened. And since it was not a disorganized, scrambled, chaotic event, there must be reason behind it. There had to be. And if that were true then the implications were also clear. It must mean that the human race was somehow meant to try and understand it. What else could it be? There was nothing left. And, maybe, hopefully, after the initial shock and associated tragedy and hardship had worn off, it would not be beyond man's ability to see and understand. At least to some degree. It might even turn out to be quite obvious. Otherwise there would be no point to it. None at all, he decided. But then again, maybe he was wrong. Maybe it was nothing but incomprehensible madness from beginning to end. What then?

MIGHT MAKES RIGHT

Back on the island General Marcus finally persuaded the President not to have Talamious Jackson thrown in the ocean. He achieved this by pointing out a readily understandable fact. As many Americans as there were in this strange place, they were still in a minority and none of them should be wasted. After three hours the president saw the sense of it. Then, minus the new jacket and shoes which he kept for himself, and the nice new white shirt which the General extracted as payment for letting him live, the president put Jackson and the rest of the newcomers to work. Jackson was given the title of Operations Manager. His job was to find more tree branches and extend the outline of the White House on the grass so more of the President's staff members could have their own offices.

Jackson complained loudly, however. But grossly outnumbered and without any physical evidence to verify his claim to the high office, he finally relinquished and went to work, with the further understanding that he could outline an office for himself as long as it wasn't too big. Having to find and collect tree branches, however, with all the walking, bending and carrying was very difficult for him because of all his previously overindulged bulk. As a result, what he was able to accomplish was very minimal at best. Other than that he was openly welcomed because he brought with him a whole new chain of dirty jokes and a summary of everything that had happened back home from the time of the first disappearance until now. But, while the power play between himself and the President had been resolved peacfully enough, at least one other was in the making.

Ivan was a man of vision. He knew that preparation was everything. Do your homework and opportunity will come as surely as the sun in the morning. A product of the deep, dark forests of Russia, the dim streets of Moscow and several years in an American University, it was a lesson he had learned early, and he had the scars to prove it. And, because he knew what he knew, he took advantage of his time on the island, using it for prepartaion, knowing that if he was ready, sooner or later opportunity would present itself. And what he had done thus far was to secretly pull together an elite organization of specialized individuals that were there for the choosing. There were drug lords, gang leaders, smugglers, mercenaries and terrorists as well as other dealers in human misery and perversion to select from, all of whom presently had very little to occupy their minds and almost nothing to do with their time. He could have had them all on his team had he wanted and he would have had an army large enough and vicious enough to harass and intimidate everyone on the island. But it wasn't what he had in mind. There were precautions to take and standards to be adhered to. One was to stay away from those who might become envious of your power. Too much vigalence and wasted time.

"Good thing about our own Russian president," said Boris, who was of Ivan's closest allies from out of the past.

"One less power hungry mad man we have to worry about."

"But only three weeks and they beat him to death."

"I'm surprised he lasted that long."

"But the American president is still alive."

"Because American businessmen are too cowardly to kill anyone themselves."

"Yes. And there is no one here they could hire to do their dirty work."

"So, we are all stuck with him. But that is all right. We can have some fun trying to provoke him later on."

"Ha," Boris said, liking the idea.

Another rule was equally important to Ivan. Women were the greatest creations of God, most of them, anyway. And he respected and loved them dearly. As a result all the men were screened carefully. Anyone who had had anything to do with prostituion, hard core pornography, slave trading or other serious forms of human abuse were forbidden to join him.

"The other individuals to be excluded from our organization are the perpetrators of white collar crime," Ivan told Boris. "The junk bond dealers and inside traders, take over artists, corporate pirates of industry and banking, the comitters of fraud and larceny. Scum bags. They are all too weasiley, too small minded and self seeking, too egomaniacal and too greedy to be trustworthy. And far too hollow and transparent to be of any value. They have no code of conduct to live by and if the going gets rough they will all run like the rats that they are."

"I agree," said his friend. "I'll take a man of the street, anyday.

When they were done, the number of those picked to be part of the group was about four hundred, all sworn to secrecy about their united affiliation and convinced to wait until the proper time to come together en masse. That included forty seven women from different parts of the world, all self sufficient as any man in the bunch and equally capable of taking care of themselves.

"But what do we do with them all, now that we have made our selections?" Boris asked. "There are no business owners on the island to extort money from, there isn't even any money. And even if there were, it would be valueless."

"You are absolutely right," Ivan agreed.

"There are are no cigarettes, either. Or alcohol, or drugs. Nothing. There aren't even any music CDs to pirate. There are no commodities of any kind. What are we going to do?"

"In other words there is nothing at all to take charge of and control. Is that the way you see it?"

"The only possibility is women. They are in short supply. Unfortunately, they all seem to be well protected by the national groups they are part of. Besides, we agreed we will not take advantage of them."

"Again you are right," said Ivan. "And so far things are under control. Thus far there has not been a single rape or even one report of anyone even caught having sex. Certainly we would have heard of it. And none of our own people seem to have much interest. The men do not even joke about it. But I have serious doubts about how long that will last once they become more adjusted to being here."

"Well, at least I know you are normal."

"What does that mean?"

"I've seen you looking at that Israli woman with the hot green eyes and the big breasts."

"And what about you?"

"Well, yes. I have seen one I could get it up for, too."

"That is a good sign. But we still need to keep an eye on the situation. No woman should be forced into an unwillingly compromise, no matter what the circumstances. That is the coward's way. And we are not cowards. However, the members of our organization do need purposeful things to occupy their time. So, the first thing we need to do is to gather data. How many people are on the island? Where are they from? How big are they physically and what kind of condition do they appear to be in? Would any of them make suitable recruits if things ever came to hand to hand combat? We will begin first thing in the morning. Our people must be observant. Information is everything."

Within a week all the statistics were compiled in a protected flat area where it was easy to scratch numbers in the soft dirt. In total, there were seventeen thousand six hundred and twelve people on the island. Not surprizingly, the industrialized countries had by far the greastest numbers since their society was far more structured and over run with large corporations and big government. Five thousand Americans, only four thousand Chinese. Western Europe was also well represented. They were all criminals in Ivan's eyes in one way or another, however, but the total number of formally labeled criminal leaders like himself was only about eight hundred. Once the data was complete, every scrap of this information was recorded in a readily accessible part of Ivan's brain while the numbers written in the dirt were oblitereated.

In spite of some of their disreputable backgrounds, for the most part everyone was behaving themselves, although there was that old, continuing hatred amongst the Arabs for the Americans and the British. Two American businessmen and one State Department official had already died of a bashed in heads and now the Amercian president, the most despised man on the island, was clamoring for an international police force, to be under his control, of course. If something didn't change one day soon, there would be big trouble ahead. But it was not Ivan's fight.

"If they want to quarrel over petty nationalistic values, personal prejudices, bigotry, the passions of Allah or the piety of Jesus, let them do it," he told his own men. "We will wait for something better."

Other than that, life on the island had settled into a melancholy routine. Get up, find food, get a drink from the streams, mill around, talk, invent a new game to play or continue with an old one, argue, eat and drink and go to sleep. Or, wade out into the ocean and commit suicide. At first the despondent tried hanging themselves with grape vines but the vines always broke and they were left with sore necks. One person managed to slash his wrists with a sharp stone and slowly bleed to death but the preferred method was the readily available and beckoning ocean. The surprizing thing was, however, that no matter how far out they waded or swam, or from what part of the island, the bodies always washed back up on the beach into the same small cove. Every morning of late, there were always ten or fifteen new ones waiting on the sand. Since they had no shovels to dig with and no one seemed to care about the victims, they were left right there to rot.

It was a place the living avoided at all costs. To most, it was not something to even talk about. To Ivan it became a challege. If it kept up, within five years there would be no one left on the island but himself. But what could he do about it? He had no idea. Then one evening he quietly sauntered through the area where the majority of the Americans always camped out. It was enough. Now he had a plan. The first thing he did was to find interpretors and have a series of discussions with the Chinese, the Japanese and the Africans. Then he and his compatriots waited for the full moon and worked from dark to dawn.

For the Americans, the easiest way up the mountain to the food belt was through a wide, dry arroyo that led into the banana palms and then on to the rest of trees and plants that provided sustenance. There was another access about a mile further on and two more at even greater distances beyond that. The rest of the terrain was much too difficult for individuals who had spent most of their lives sitting behind a desk. General Simms, however, was an exception. He was always the first to climb the hill each morning, take off his shirt, lay it on the ground and fill it up with food. Then he would tie it up and use it as a carrier back to camp. On the morning after the last full moon he had slept much later than usual. When he awoke he was quite famished and began thinking about how good some bananas would taste if topped off with a few large handfuls of red grapes.

With that thought in mind he jumped to his feet with vigor and set off stridefully, his empty stomach rumbling louder and louder as he went. But then, coming to the last turn in the long path near the top, what the hell was this? His way was completely blocked. On each side of the well worn route was a formidable looking, well stacked pile of stones more than seven feet tall, just like the walls of a fortress. Both went up and beyond the crests of the side slopes for a good distance, making it practiclly impossible to go around, while the opening between the two piles was such that no more than two men might be able to pass between at once. But not right now.

The General found Ivan waiting there with over a dozen of his biggest and burliest men, all of whom carried clubs. Perhaps a hundred or two more stood along the wall, leaning against it, while dozens more looked down from on top.

"How dare you," General Simms bellowed when he found himself blocked.

"We dare," said Ivan with a smile.

"Wait until the President hears of this," said the General in a threatening voice.

"We will wait," said Ivan and turned his back on the General to talk to his friend Boris.

After the General finally stomped off, Ivan said, "Well, what do you think?"

"Looks like this is going to be very interesting."

"Yes," Ivan laughed. "They are going to hate us worse than sin. But I think we are going to have a good time with it while it lasts."

Two hours later the President arrived, angry and out of breath, having fallen twice, tearing both knees out of the trousers which were no longer recognizable as having once belonged to his best three piece suit. Standing firm in his role of Chief Executive, however, and thus being much too important to do such a menial thing as gather food, he had never been there before. His job was providing leadership, other people's jobs were to wait on him. Finally, however, when he stopped panting and with three more Generals to back him up, he said, "What exactly is the meaning of this? How dare you deprive everyone of food."

"We have no intention of depriving anyone of anything," Ivan answered quietly and civilly.

"What do you call this?" the President questioned, waving his arms at the piles of stone and the guards blocking the entrance.

"We will not deprive you of food. All we ask is that you begin to pay for it."

"Are you out of your mind? Food here is free, damnit. Who do you think you are, you and this bunch of, of, hoodlums?"

"You're right. Everything was free when we got here but as of today we happen to have control over a valuable commodity and we now desire a certain amount of remuneration for our goods," Ivan answered, maintaining his calm, matter of fact voice.

"What are you talking about? You're nuttier than a Texas fruit cake. There is nothing to give. All the money disintegrated long ago, as well as everthing made of metal," said the President and looked down at his clothes. "Even our clothes are of little value and would be good for only a few transactions. What would we do after that?"

"Go naked," said Ivan, kidding him.

The president was livid. "What?" he bellowed.

Ivan laughed. "Forget it," he said in return. "We don't want your scroungy clothes."

"Damn you. How dare you make fun of me."

"What else. You make it so easy. Now, do you want to eat, or not?"

The president glared at Ivan. Then he turned and looked at the three generals behind him. They shrugged and nodded in the afirmative.

"What then?" the president finally asked with a scowl. "There's nothing left."

"Not true," said Ivan evenly.

"What, damnit? What do you want?" the president asked, his voice rising rapidly in pitch.

Ivan waited for several seconds, watching the president's face closely. When he felt the man was calmer, he answered.

"I'll tell you, if you're ready to listen. And if you summon the rest of your so-called leaders."

"They are already here," the president said and waved his arm.

"I only see some generals. Where's the rest of your crew?"

All the president seemed able to do was stand and stare. Ivan returned the look, backed up by his large band of co conspirators. Seconds went by, then minutes. In the end the President was the first to yield. Perhaps it was his dismay at Ivan's effrontery. Perhaps it was his own hunger. Perhaps it was the growing sounds of discontent, anger and the grumbling of stomachs behind him. He turned and spoke to his three generals. The generals went back down the trail till they found some colonels. The colonels took off on a run back to their area and summoned the heads of the FBI and all the other governmental agencies and, half an hour later, brought them to the head of the line directly behind the president.

"This better be good," the president said, giving Ivan a mean look.

"Stones," said Ivan.

"Stones?" questioned the president, looking at him in disbelief. "Stones? What do you mean, stones?"

"Stones. Like those round, hard things there on the ground."

"What? Are you mad? You must have rocks in your head. Stones are worthless."

"Not any more. And you must have stones in your hands instead of your head if you expect to eat. Ten stones each as big as your fist for each piece of fruit from our garden. Consider it a tax. Maybe it's time you and your friends paid some."

"You expect us to pay for food with stones. I'll have you in irons when we get back to civilization."

"We'll hang you by the balls," said General Marcus, backing him up.

"Maybe," stated Ivan in a far more serious manner. "If we get back, and if I don't cut yours off first."

With that remark the General made a quick move towards Ivan but before he had completed a full step he found himself looking up at the sky, blood coming from his nose and excruciating pain from his groin.

The president gasped as he sucked in his breath and took a big step backwards from where he stood and once again stared at Ivan, reconsidering his position. Ivan again stared back. Eventually the President blinked and looked away.

"What if we run out of stones?" he muttered.

"There are thousands of them around," Ivan replied, knowing he had just won the first round.

"But some are bigger than others. Is a big one worth more?"

"They are all the same value."

"That's not fair," said the President.

"So...," said Ivan. "What is?

"Well, what about the disadvantaged who are too old or weak?"

"Be charitable and carry theirs for them."

The president again muttered something under his breath and shuffled back and forth. Finally he turned to General Simms and ordered him to start picking up rocks.

"But, Sir," said the general. "Need I remind you that I am one of the Chiefs of Staff?"

"And I happen to be Commander in Chief."

"Okay. Let me get some of my subordinates to help out."

"Hurry it up. I'm hungry."

"Yes, sir. I'll do my best."

"I'm hungry now," said the President.

Simms glared at him briefly but acquiesced and began searching the nearby area by himself.

"There, damnit," he said, placing them on the ground in front of Ivan, in two piles of ten each.

"Not there in the middle of the path, you fool. Over there out of the way," Ivan commanded.

The General first looked at Ivan, then he looked at the President, then he groaned and moved the rocks. At that point the President said, "I want two bananas."

Before he was allowed to collect, however, a group of Africans came to the head of the line and were immediately left to pass freely.

"What the hell is this?" the President demanded.

"Call it a lesson in social consciousness," said Ivan.

"Well, I know God put me on this island for a reason and I don't think he wants me standing around in line waiting on a bunch of third world no accounts just to get food."

"Who's to say. Maybe he wants you to learn some lessons, instead."

"I'm the President of the United States, for God's sake. I already know everything I need to know."

"That's your story, not mine."

"And what gives you the right to say that?"\

"I walked through your American area the other day and the ground was litered with uneaten food, lying there in piles, rotting away. Americans are the most wasteful creatures on the face of the earth."

"So what do you care. What business is it of yours? We have the right to use what's here any way we see fit."

"Very good. But for you, Mr. President, the price of your morning meal just doubled."

"What? You let those Africans get in free and now you want to double my price?"

"Maybe it's time someone showed them some consideration. However, you, and the rest of the Americans, will wait here at the gate. Once we have been paid, your order will be brought out. And... one more arrogant word out of any of you and the price will go up again."

The president's face turned crimson, but with an immense effort, he remained silent. Then he turned to the General and motioned for him to get more rocks.

"Just a minute, Mr. President," Ivan interrupted. "You get them and bring them here yourself. No one else. And while you're thinking about it, step out of the way so others may be waited on."

With great reluctance, the President stepped aside and angerly stared at Ivan who completely ignored him. Even his own men pretended they no longer knew him. Finally, after at least two dozen others had come forward with their newly gathered stones, he moved away and went in search of his own. By the time he returned, many more had already received their handout. As a result, the president, who could have had the honor of being Ivan's first paying customer, was about ninenty third. After that, news of the episode moved quickly down the waiting line of Americans and the pace picked up considerably as most individuals began collecting stones long before they got to the entrance. By noon two huge piles had been stacked up. In the afternoon, however, no one had to bring stones to buy food. Instead, they each had to carry the same number of stones from the two accumulated piles up the slope and add them to the two ends of the wall that had been built the night before in the moonlight. All in all, by dark another fifty yards had been added to each end of the wall, maintaining a full height of seven or eight feet the entire way.

The very first thing the following morning the President held a staff meeting, refusing to let anyone go for food until it was over.

"No matter what happens we are not going to put up with this kind of abuse. Especially from such low lifes as those Russian hoodlums. No way. So, first thing I want you military types to get out there and reconoiter the situation. There must be other ways to get up there to where all those fruit trees are."

"There is," said General Marcus. "I already checked it out."

"When did you do that? You didn't tell me about it."

"Yesterday afternoon. You spent the time in private

conference, remember?"

"I did not."

"Well, it sure looked like it to me. That bulky Secretary of whatever she's in charge of was sitting on your mock desk all afternoon and that Marine Colonel guarding your door wouldn't let me in."

"Oh, yes. I forgot. We were discussing foreign policy."

"It was pretty foreign, all right. All she did was gooney bird you the whole time."

"Well, gee..., " said the president as he brushed some dirt off the sleeve of his ragged shirt and ran his fingers through his hair to straighten it. "Well. Don't look at me like that. Tell me what you found out."

Before he began the General pulled a banana from his pocket, peeled it and took a large bite.

"There are..," he began before he was cut off.

"Wait a minute," said the president. "Where's my banana?"

"You have to get your own, remember? I distinctly heard that Russian gangster say so yesterday. We all did."

"Damnit," the president said. "You just got done saying there were other ways up there. Why didn't you use one of them."

"Exactly. Why didn't I? Well, first of all there are only three more ways to get up there, unless you're a mountain climber. The nearest is a good mile beyond the one that's blocked, but the Chinese beat us to it. They already have their own wall up and it's longer and higher than the first one. Not only that but they're not letting anyone through except for Asians, no exceptions. Period. The next one is another half mile further yet but the South Americans, the East Indians, the Indonesians, the Phillipinos and a bunch of others have that all locked up. No wall, just one hell of a lot of nasty looking people. And the last place to get up there is, quite frankly, just too damned far to walk everyday. Besides that, the Japanese and the Arabs have some strange alliance going and they are guarding it. And the way they hate us, I'd rather pick up stones anyday."

"Hmm," said the president, and stared off into space. "This might be a good mission for the Secretary of State. She seems to have a lot of extra time on her hands," he finally said, and scanned the group. "Ahh, there you are, my dear," he continued and gave her a funny litle wave. "What do you think? A woman with your personality can get things done a man wouldn't believe are even possible."

"Good idea," said the General. "I'll head on over and tell them she's coming."

"What's this?" said the President. "You mean you agree with me for a change?"

"No. I was just happy that I might not have to look at her much longer."

"And what does that mean?"

"That she probably won't be coming back. If you send that arrogant bitch over there, those people will throw her in the ocean for sure. Then maybe we can get something done around here because she won't be sitting on your stupid desk all day long with her lumpy legs hanging out and all that cellulite showing."

"I beg your pardon. How dare you talk to your Commander in Chief that way. Damn you." The president was livid and began ranting. But he knew he had best not antagonize the General too much. So, he finally turned and walked away, off into the woods to where the six prisoners were being held and tortured. When he arrived there was only one man left, hanging from the vines that bound him, his naked, bloodied and emaciated body nearly lifeless.

"What happened to the other ones?" he asked of the Head of the FBI, Bill Trunik, who had been spending a lot of time in the area, right from the beginning.

"The first four pounded their heads against the trees they were tied to until they killed themselves, stating that they were better dead than helpful to Americans. The other wasn't suidical, just kinda weak. Died two days ago. Wouldn't talk to us or eat his daily ration of plums. This last one here eats but he won't talk either unless you do something drastic and make him scream."

"I've never heard a grown man scream before. I wonder what that's like," the president said as he came closer, grabbed the captive by the hair, held his head up and slapped him hard across the face without result. Then he did it again.

"Don't do that," Trunik told with a smile. "That's sissy stuff. Here, he has one good finger left. Twist it backwards till it breaks. That will get you some response."

"What happened to the rest of them?"

"I got tired of rapping him in the face and gut with my fists so I started breaking his toes. Then I moved on to his fingers. I was just about to finish the job when you showed up. Go ahead. If that doesn't work I'll show you some other tricks."

Somewhat timorously the president found the hand with the one good finger and gripped it.

"Go ahead," he was urged. "It's actually kind of fun once you get used to it."

With that the president bent the finger back farther and farther until it made a sharp cracking sound. The poor Arab jerked in painful response but was unable to cry out as expected. He had died in that last moment, too weak to bear any more.

"Well, damn," the president said. "What a coward." Then he dropped the lifeless hand and gave the Trunik an order. "Go find General Marcus. Tell him to take some men and find some more. Only just Arabs this time. Have him bring back at least half a dozen."

While all this perversity was underway a new dignitary showed up at the wall where Ivan again stood with his friend Boris. He had just finished his own breakfast when he was informed that someone wished to speak with him. "Who is it?" he asked.

"Some old guy in a red robe," he was told.

"Right on time," said Ivan as he nodded to Boris with a knowing smile. "Send him up here."

A minute later the Archbishop of Burcanton appeared before him.

"His Holiness, the Pope, requests your presence for a meeting in one hour," said the Archbishop.

"I'm here now," said Ivan. "An hour from now I might be somewhere else."

"You don't understand," replied the Archbishop. "Not only is his eminence much too old to be climbing such a hill, he is also much too distinguished. He wishes you to come to him."

"Then give him my regards and my regrets."

"You mean you refuse?"

"I only give audiences to those who come to me."

At first the Archbishop was too outraged to speak. After a bit he finally managed to say, "God will never forgive you for this and neither will the church."

"And maybe God will never forgive you for being so stupid as to think he has nothing better to do than interfere in such petty affairs as ours. Now cross yourself if you must, and get the hell out of here."

MORAL PURITY

"Damnit," Jenson Wilson said to his wife. "I've been a member of Congress longer than half my colleagues have been alive.

Democrats, Republicans, war, peace, assassinations, resignations, good times and bad, but in all my years in office I have never felt myself to be under as much pressure as I have the last few weeks. I must be a complete lunatic."

"You're hardly that, dear. But maybe you should have quit entirely, back when you first wanted to."

"You're right. I should have. But they keep dragging me back into things."

"What is it this time?"

"I'm off to a briefing. Always urgent but probably the same old ongoing insanity."

"It's more than that, though. You're worried about something bigger, aren't you?"

"Yes. I suppose. In a lot of respects things are better because all the top administration officials are gone, along with all the extremest, right wing religious leaders and their special interest, slanted agenda. But the environmental movement has been set back fifty years, pharmacuetical companies still own the politicians and the FDA, and have three fourths of the population hooked on prescription drugs that they'd all be better off without. People have given up their basic freedoms in the name of freedom and security and still send their sons and daughters off to fight illegal wars thinking they are promoting peace. The stupidity goes on and on. Congress keeps going round and round in circles, lying to the public, and to each other, while almost every damned one of them would love to step into the President's job, or the Speakers job or any other job that's bigger than the one they have if they weren't afraid of disappearing and none of them gives a hoot about solving the real problems. So. With unemployment off the chart, Social Security bankrupt, small business failures twenty times normal, people starving and look what they did. They not only voted themselves a raise, they doubled their salaries. It's unbelievable."

"But that was last week. What's really troubling you, Jenson?"

"Maybe it's the hypocrisy. The conservatives sqaundered billions on an illegal war, gave corporations the biggest tax breaks in history and ram rodded themselves this huge pay raise in the midst of a severe economic depression. The family values nuts supported spending those billions on weapons while people back here can't feed their children, had no health care and go without basic human needs. Then the pro lifers wave their flags and cheer while thousands of innocent bystanders are killed by the bombs they insisted on paying for. And if anyone disagrees, they call them unpatriotic and want them locked up."

"You're right, dear. That's the deepest kind of hypocrisy."

"The bottom line is, they're neo-fascist loonies without an ounce of perspective. You can't have democracy without freedom and you can't demand that everyone love Jesus. And if that isn't twisted, idiotic dogma, I don't know what is. Demanding love obviates love. And if anything engenders an all loving God's wrath, that ought to do it."

"Pretty bizarre, all right. The only thing I never could figure out is if any one religion is the chosen religion, how come there are so many people with completely dissenting views?"

"Damned good point, dear. In the meantime there is so much animosity, hatred, and craziness out there and no damned room at all for a healthy difference of opinion. I still say they're all nuts, and frankly, they scare the hell out of me."

"What's going on?"

"Threatening letters, phone calls, sick e-mail, demonstrations on the Capitol Building steps. I'm surprized they aren't out in the front yard throwing stones at the house."

"Why? Just because you voice your opinion? That's what Democracy used to be all about."

"I know dear. And that's enough. Today I'm going to end it by resigning once and for all. To hell with it. I'm too old. I don't even care anymore."

"You are not too old. But, you are one of the few voices of wisdom left. They still need you."

"Not anymore. What they need is to learn to think for themselves."

Technically, there were still two separate houses to Congress but since the Disappearance they always met in joint session, always with the media present and always with the session broadcast live to the nation. It was as if they felt safer that way, as if the larger the group clustered together and the more public the display, the less chance of them disappearing individually. It also made for very strange politics and almost completely silenced any voices of dissention from amongst the ranks. What with the Congress almost unanimously voting to double their salaries, Jenson thought he had heard it all. But a coalition had been formed from the Southern States that had already spent another three million dollars of unapproved taxpayers money to design a mostrous memorial to the disappeared president, Stanley Drukus.

This pillar of stone was not only to be placed on the same federal land as the Washington monument, it was also going to be forty feet taller, considerably wider and far more extravagant. It would even have a blinking neon sign on the very top that could be seen from fifty miles away. As described, it was far more ostentatious than the Clinton Library, far more ornate than a gothic cathedral and far more obscene than a Las Vegas casino. Somehow, the worst President in the history of the nation was to get the largest, most garish memorial ever conceived. And, as if that were not mockery enough, there was to be a second memorial of similar design also pointing skyward just a hundred feet away. Almost as large, but not quite, it was to be dedicated to the president's sometimes friend, Reverend Billy Boxer, TV evangelist and scam artist extraordinare, no longer living in his mansion or riding around in his super jet, but off somewhere on the same mission as the president.

My God, thought Jenson. How could they? But, they had. Worse yet, much of the rest of Congress voiced agreement with the plan. What was another four hundred million dollars of the taxpayers money at a time like this. Construction should begin before the end of the month. Then they could all take a much needed, extended vacation so those coming up for re election could go home and campaign.

At his first opportunity, Jenson was on his feet. He yanked the microphone out of a colleague's hand and began telling the world it was time for a taxpayer's revolt. Congress was out of control, the nonesense had to end, the nation could no longer tolerate such insane madness. But no sooner had he spoken than the booing began.

"Well, to hell with it then," Jenson shouted into the microphone. "And to hell with all of you. I"m ashamed to be a member of Congress and I hereby resign, effective immediately."

With that, he dropped the microphone on the floor and slowly walked out of the auditorium, but it was silent now, as if they might have at last heard some truth in what he had said and were confused by it. Taking his time, he went to his old office where he collected as many of his personal effects as he could stuff in his jacket pockets and strolled the halls one last time. At last outside, he walked sowly down the long flight of stone steps, then stopped half way and looked around. He could only shake his head in dismay. He began to decend further. The usual crowd was there as always. No particular reason except maybe a lack of better things to do. The media were there also. Forever in need of a story, they had quickly gotten the word from inside and were already set to waylay him. He hesitated, considered going back inside but decided to stay. One last chance to express his opinion. With that in mind he again started down the steps.

Then a young man separated from the group and moved towards him. A rather wild looking man in a long black coat with a clerical collar showing through the unbuttoned top. Jenson turned to avoid him but to no avail. The man began to harangue. Jenson was an obstructionist. Billy Boxer was a savior. He deserved his memorial, even more so than the President. Not only was Jenson an obstructionist and guilty of religious bias, he was the devil himself. Maybe he was the anti-christ. Maybe it was his fault that the disappearance had occured.

Jenson raised his hand to protest and again tried to move away. But it was too late. The semiautomatic weapon was already out, pointed at his chest. Six shoots were fired in all. The first one killed him instantaneously, the rest simply emphasized the madness that had consumed the world.

Just hours away from his destination at his missing brother's house, Jack Briggs stopped at a small roadside cafe for lunch. It was then that he heard the news. The meal that he ordered went untouched as he sat through the broadcast. It ended with a report about the assassin's reasons for shooting Wilson. The man was the recent founder of an organization called CAMP. CAMP stood for Christain Americans for Moral Purity. As its leader, he had spent the last several months researching the backgrounds of Congressional members. Jenson Wilson had been especially tainted. He had been one of the originators of the bill that made abortion legal. He also supported family planning and promoted freely handing out contraceptives to the population and, worst of all, he had been heard to say that the twenty year old Mel Gibson movie that had been revived and reissued about the Lord was a gruesome, sadistic, sick production with twisted, sadomasochistic sexual overtones. Obviously he was unpure and grossly so. The unpure must be expurgated without mercy. As holy leader of the organization it was his God appointed duty to set an example for his disciples to follow.

"Don't you believe in the Ten Commandments?" he was asked by the newsman.

"Of course I do. You already know I'm a good Christian."

"What about, Thou shalt not kill? Didn't you just shoot someone?"

"That wasn't killing. I was doing God's work. That's why Jesus didn't come back right at the beginning of the new century. The way has to be prepared. Cleansing has to be done. Sinners must be punished."

"But I thought that was God's job and that's why Jesus came the first time. To help the sinners."

"You're just trying to confuse the issue because you're not a believer. Only believers know the truth."

My god, Jack thought when the broadcast was over. Religious righteousness had robbed the world of another valuable, venerable individual in a time of desperate need. Where would it end? All he could do was get back in his car and keep going.

Driving again, he reached his brother's house before dark. The first thing he did was to call Jenson's wife, now a widow.. He would come back to Washington, he told her. He could probably leave first thing in the morning. No, she said. Stay where you are. That's all the family you have left and that's what Jenson would want you to do. I will be all right. Maybe when a few months have passed and they get the airlines running again, we can get together. Please, Jack. Jenson and I were together for nearly fifty years. That's lot to be thankful for. I assure you I will be okay."

ALONE

For more than a month Katherine Beaumont and Howard Briggs had avoided all contact with the rest of the disappearees. To obtain food they always came around the island at mid afternoon and always approached the food belt from above so as not to be seen, gathered enough to last for three or four days and returned to their safe abode. During the rest of the time they had explored the entire north side of the island, from the mountain peak clear down and along the shoreline in great detail. They also added to the camoflague hiding the cave entrance, gathered several piles of small stones that could be thrown easily and collected branches that would serve as clubs and spears and hid them at various places around the area.

"Talk about returning to the stone age," Howard said as they sat up top on the boulder after a day of scrambling over the rough terrain, adding to their, just in case, defense system. It was a good humored remark for the most part.

"I think I've missed a lot."

"What? Sleeping in a cave?"

"Maybe. Until now the closest I've ever been to a wilderness was my back yard at home," she said before she realized he might have a different opinion of things. "Of course, without wild animals..."

"It's a sterile wilderness," he finished. "But still as primitive as it gets. And you've adjusted marvelously," he added.

"Yeah," she replied as she displayed her hands. "Look at all these callouses. And these dirty, broken finger nails. And..." She felt her stringy hair and glanced at her dirty bare feet. Then she turned her foot so she could tap the thick build up on the bottom. "And these are so thick I could probably walk over broken glass without getting cut. But..." and she smiled pensively. "There are a lot of things I'm not missing that makes it kind of nice also."

"Really? What would that be?"

She held up her hand for him to see. "Actually, keeping my nails manicured was a pain. Then there was the damned alarm clock. Social and political obligations. Everyone else owning my life. My offensive husband. Jeeez, " she sighed. "This is like the real vacation I never had. My heart rate and blood pressure are probably half what they were a month ago."

"It's good for that all right. Which is why I always spent a few weeks every year tramping around in the mountains alone. But it was also good to be back."

"Do you miss it?"

"I'm beginning to. My business, that is. I missed my wife right from the beginning but I built the company from the ground up. It was always a challenge. I lived for that, too. Probably never would have retired. Now I'm on permanent vacation," he stated, looking off into the distance. "I wonder if I can handle it?"

Katherine left it hanging there, didn't try to answer. What about herself, she wondered also. After they had adjusted and the newness had worn off. After the weeks turned into months and, god help them. What if the months turned into years?

"Well," Howard said after a bit. "I know one thing that would help. I'd give a lot to see a big old bear coming through the brush. About now I'd run over and give it a big hug."

"Just as long as it's not a bunch of crazy humans carrying clubs. That's what frightens me."

"I hear you on that one. But in that regard it's probably time we went back and checked up on things, just in case something major has happened."

"I suppose you're right. But would you mind if I stayed here? Somehow I don't feel all that safe around most of those people."

Howard looked at her for a moment. "Are you sure? You would be here alone all day."

"I think I would be just fine. Really. There's plenty of extra food. Probably enough for three or four days if it's just me."

"So it might be okay if I stayed overnight? Maybe not this time but if something came up and I needed to investigate further?"

"I think that if we are going to survive here and keep our sanity we both need to be as flexible and independent as possible. Beyond having this alliance we seem to have formed where we still look out for each other, of course. How about you?"

"Is that how you see it? An alliance?"

"For lack of a better word, yes. You've made it quite clear how you feel about your wife, even though she's not here. And I made some decisions about what lines I don't want to cross right at the beginning."

"An alliance then," he nodded approvingly. It was nice to have it clarified and in the open. "A good way to put it. Might solve a lot of problems in the future. I was wondering how we would handle that issue if it ever came up."

"You mean sex?"

"Bluntly put, yes."

"One of the reasons I trusted myself to go off alone with you was because I thought you were a man of honor."

"Dare I ask what some of the others were?"

"You're not a bully or a chauvanist."

"Hmmm. Well. I guess that's good. Makes me feel kind of stuffy, though."

"God, no, Howard. Anything but. You're also very intelligent, creative, physically fit, interesting."

"Good grief," Howard said with a smile.

"Well. Most importantly," she said, still trying to be serious. "After spending how many days together? We were going to keep track. But, just as well. Probably a month. And I'd trust you with my life. I hardly think that makes you stuffy."

"I hope not. And thank you. I'm quite impressed with your character also."

"You're welcome. As for character, looks like this is going to be some kind of test, all right. And not just for me and you but for everyone here on the island. Especially for the women. Getting involved could make things dangerously complicated."

"Good point. Not be a good place to have a baby, either."

"Fortunately, most of the women here are older. But if they get a bunch of guys fighting over them, there will still be a lot of trouble."

"No doubt about that," he nodded. "So I'm glad we're friends and partners."

"More than that. Family."

"Sounds good to me."

"Me, too. But for the record. If it ever came to the point where I might want to get involved, you would still be my first choice.."

Howard blushed heavily and turned away. "Well, then. First thing in the morning I'll head on over to the other side and take a look around. See if there's anything we need to be aware of."

"Sure you won't change your mind and come along?" Howard asked, early the next morning.

"No," she said after some consideration. "Until we know how things are going, you're probably better off without me."

"Hard to tell. Well, it's a long walk over and back. If I should stay the night, will you be okay?"

"Of course. I'll count the days. If you're not back in four, I'll call missing persons."

"Fair enough. And I'll check up on Deanna Holt, the woman you gave that coat to. I know you've been worried about her."

As she watched him go she wasn't so sure she had made the right decision. It was probably the first time in her entire adult life where she had been left entirely alone, without other people nearby, without the sounds of civilization somewhere in the background, without at least a phone at hand. She'd never even been on an overnight camping trip. And certainly not all alone. At first there was a mild touch of panic, a compulsion to shout out and run after him. But she suppressed it, forcing herself to sit there long after Howard had disappeared, dreading the idea that he might be gone more than a day or two. Gotta stay busy, she told herself. Do some more exploring, or something.

Finally shaking herself free of the anxiety and fear, she rose and began working her way barefoot down the mountain, her goal the cliff like shoreline. The first few times they hiked the slopes she tried wearing the clumsy, oversized shoes Jess had given her. But with the fit so loose, they were actually dangerous and soon abandoned. Calluses were better. And while her feet had rapidly built up protective layers, it was still a difficult task over the rough terrain.

There was but one small section of accessible white sand. Somewhat difficult to get to, especially alone, it was also the one place where the bottom sloped gently enough to walk on. She slipped out of her clothing. Some clothing, all right, she thought. A pair of deteriorating pajamas. Then she waded out and swam several laps back and forth. Coming in, she walked the sand, letting the warm sun dry her body. She hadn't had a tan since she was a teenager and decided she liked it. She wasn't so sure about all the hair that was beginning to grow on her legs, however. But, what the heck. There were no media helicopters overhead. She obviously wasn't going to be on camera for a while.

Forgetting personal hygiene, she began examining her surroundings more carefully. If only there had been one small tide pool with some sea life to poke around in. If only there had been one small sand grab scurrying around. If only there had been one small strand of kelp in the water. But there was nothing. She dropped to the sand and sat there motionless for a long time, suddenly feeling very sad and lonely. Not even a hint of breeze, the ocean was mirror smooth and endless. So was the silence. It frightened her immensely.

It was mid afternoon by the time she made it back. She was exhausted. And in considerable pain. Without Howard there to help her up over that first series of smooth rock faces that backed up the sand of the beach, she had lost her grip and fallen, harshly twisting her right wrist. She didn't think it was broken, just badly sprained. She hoped. Serious enough by itself but she had damaged it further getting out of the trap. That was the problem.

She considered staying there for the night, sleeping on the sand in the hope that it might be better by morning. But if it wasn't just sprained, if she had broken it instead, it would also be worse. Much worse. And she wasn't sure about the tide, or how far in it might come. What then? And if her wrist was broken and she couldn't make it out, how would Howard ever find her? She didn't know when he would be back. The cave was far up the mountain. She could wear herself out screaming and he might never hear her. So, through tears and agonizing pain, she fought her way over the obstacles and up the hazardous slope. Dumb and damnit, she chastised herself.

Finally. Tired and in agony, Katherine made it back to the cave. Even though well concealed from below up on their private boulder, she still crawled in under the branches of a small overhanging tree that shielded her from above and tried to rest. But the pain was too intense. She couldn't sleep. At dusk she stopped trying, managed to eat some fruit, moved farther out on the boulder to where she could see the oceans horizon and remained there. Her wrist had turned an ugly black and blue and was swollen badly. There was no way to describe the pain except to say that it was excruciating. Where was Howard? Her determination to remain brave and manage being alone was beginning to slip. Would he make it back home tonight. Home? Wasn't that interesting? Thinking of it in those terms. Had she been on the island that long? Or maybe she was giving up hope. Was this all there would ever be?

It was mid morning on the fourth day when she thought she heard voices. Had Howard brought someone back with him? Her first inclination was to jump to her feet and start waving but something held her back. Instead she peeked out from her vantage point up on the boulder. And froze. It was a group of five. Howard did not appear to be one of them. They were not that far off, either. A couple hundred yards at the most. Where were the binoculars? Back in the cave. She retrieved them quickly and crawled back out to where she could again peer over the edge. Confirmed. Howard was not with them. Had something happened? Why else would they be here? Oh my.

They were still coming in her direction. Cutting the distance in half, they stopped. They were looking around, pointing at different things, talking profusely. She could hear it clearer now. The dialect was totally unfamiliar. Then they were moving again. This time they stopped almost directly below. She didn't dare try to look. Slowly she eased herself backward towards the entrance to the cave, staying flat as possible. For some reason she didn't go into the cave but crawled far back into the brush further on and waited. Not an easy feat with her damaged wrist as she bumped it once and almost cried out. It was still grossly looking and very tender. But she managed to hide herself as best as possible. The voices were dimmer now but she could still hear them. Sometimes they almost seemed to be arguing. What was that about? Then it occured to her. What if they found something that signaled her and Howard's presence in the area. Howard had always been very insistent about picking things up. Orange rinds, banana peals, eveything. They also made a consistent effort not to disturb what plant life was there so as not to leave evidence of any trail.

But,she had been here alone for days now. Had she been as careful as she should have been? She tried to think her way backward. Damn. The slightest trace and she could be in trouble. Suddenly she didn't feel very safe. Where was Howard, anyway, she fretted and thought about the closest stash of primitive weapons. If they began climbing the boulder, a spear might be best. She could probably get a few of them if she caught them by surprise just as they came over the top edge. But with her injured wrist? Hell, she wouldn't even be able to hold a weapon properly, let alone use it.

Damnit. What was going on? Ten minutes must have passed. Then more. Almost on the point of hyperventilation, perspiring profusely, it seemed like forever to her before the voices started moving away. She relaxed a little and crawled out of her hiding place. At last she was able to look. They were leaving, headed in a direction on around the island. She crawled farther out on the boulder on her belly and watched through the binoculars. Then one of he men stopped and turned around. Geez, she swore. He seemed to be looking right at her. Had she given herself away? What now? But then he turned back around and caught up to the rest of the group. She let out her breath and relaxed a little as she continued the surveilance. Not the best looking bunch by any means. Long hair, scraggly beards, weathered faces, dark eyes. All fairly tall, dirty but obviously physically fit and fully clothed. That meant they weren't from her side of the planet.

Count myself lucky, she said, almost outloud. Then another voice softly calling her name. The most welcome thing she had heard in days. She looked around and there stood Howard with a mean looking club in his hand. He was smiling at her. At first it was almost impossible for her not to jump up and give him a tremendous hug. But she resisted, still getting up quickly, not about to smile back. Suddenly she was angry. Where the hell had he been? Damnit. Injured as she was, she might have been raped, or killed, or who knew what. So she just stood there, saying nothing, hiding her right hand behind her.

"Are you okay?" He was concerned now.

"I hope so. Are they gone?" she asked, nervously turning around to check.

"Yes. Well out of sight," he assured her.

She took some deep breaths, relaxed a little more, then let loose with a flood of questions, not all of them in a very pleasant tone.

Howard laid down the heavy club, then slipped off his back pack. Opening it, he handed her a shiny red apple. She took it with her left hand. Then he emptied out the rest. Enough food for several days. She rolled the apple around in her hand, finally took a big bite and sighed. They sat down together.

"How was your trip?" she asked after a few moments, glancing at him as she asked. It wasn't quite a glare.

He looked back at her, holding her gaze. "First I need to know if you are really okay? I mean with everything. You still seem a little shook."

"I.. Yeah... Well, I guess I am. They scared the hell out of me. Especially when they were right down below. Must have been there twenty minutes. I wonder what that was all about?"

"They were having lunch. Left a pile of garbage."

"What? How do you know that?" She stared at him.

"Came up behind them about two miles back. Could hear them from a long ways off so I just stayed out of sight and followed. I went higher up once and tried to get ahead but it was too open. Thought they saw me the first time they stopped back there. Then, when they stopped below, I was able to skirt the area and climb up above," he said, and pointed.

"Jeez, Howard. I was here dying of fright and you were there the whole time? Why didn't you come down?"

"Too many small rocks. I was afraid I might make knock something loose. But I had my eyes on you. Every move. And I was ready."

She turned her head and looked at the club he had carried. It was big enough to knock a man's head off with a single blow. She was beginning to feel bad about being angry at him. Just one thing. Did he really have to be gone so long? This was the fourth day. But, hurt or not, she had better get over it.

"Okay," she said, trying to lighten up a bit. "How was it over there? Tell me what you found out."

"Hmm," he replied." I wasn't able to find Deanna. But a couple of people claimed to have seen her recently and said they thought she was all right. As for the rest of it, I'm appalled."

"Bad, huh?"

"You thought having the president standing up on that rock declaring the island to be a possesion of the US and the French president beating him on the nose was ridiculous. Christ," he said, and went on for some length, giving her more details.

"Well. I guess I'm glad I stayed here," Katherine said after letting it settle for a bit, not sure she really meant it. Too bad she wasn't a man. Or at least had some decent clothes to hide herself in. She would have liked to witness some of it for herself. Maybe next time.

"So. How did things go for you?" Howard then asked, scrutinizing her face.

"Actually, it was, ahh, interesting."

"Interesting? Come on, Katherine. You can do better than that."

She held out her damaged hand. There were tears in her eyes. She bit her lip and fought the emotion.

"My god, Katherine. What happened?"

"I," she sniffed, determined to be brave about it even though a big hug would have helped. Better not to risk that, however.

"I was climbing down to the beach and..." she went on to explain.

"Let me see it," he said and supported her arm very tenderly as he examined it. "Looks like hell."

"Hurts like hell," she answered. "But not as bad as it was."

Empathetically, he looked at her with concern. "Jeez, Katherine. I'm really sorry. I shouldn't have stayed so long."

"Nonsense. It was my own damned fault."

"Yeah, but.... Damn. What if it had been more serious? I never even..."

Howard looked so upset Katherine almost wanted to reach out and console him. It was a good lesson for both of them. Instead she moved on, continuing the previous part of the discussion.

"You're right. Forget the wrist. It will heal. It's already beter. As for the rest of it, well, in all truth it was still difficult. Very difficult at first. Especially that first night alone. I didn't even feel safe in the cave. It got claustrophobic so I tried to sleep out here. For some reason being able to look at at the stars helped but I still didn't sleep much. The second night wasn't much better. But, by the third day the pain was better and once I stopped feeling sorry for myself, something else started happening," she said and waited.

Howard remained silent, giving her a chance to search for the words she needed.

"Strange. I... it was like I was moving away from myself. Slipping sideways back and forth into some odd psychological time zone or some other mental space somewhere. Then I'd have to jump up and do something for a while. Except there wasn't anything to do that I was able to do. So, I'd sit back down and let it happen some more. The hardest part was in trying to shut down the mind, to keep it from rattling on and on."

"The internal dialog," Howard said and tapped his forehead with his finger.

"Yes. That's it," she replied in quick agreement. "The internal dialog. Once I finally got some control over that, everything gradually became easier. I had heard of things like native American vision quests and I though about hermits and pioneers living way out somewhere all by themselves, the hunters and trappers living alone, all those kinds of things. So I just decided to try and really shut down and see what happened. Last night I slept reasonable well and today... Today I found myself slipping into a kind of timeless place where I think I could have sat here forever if I had too. And then I realized that you have obviously already been there since you said you used to go up in the mountains alone for days and days. So you knew what it was like. Didn't you?" she asked, watching him closely.

"Well, yeah. I guess I did," he nodded.

"That wouldn't be one of the reasons you stayed away so long, would it? You wanted to see if I could handle it."

"Are you angry?" he asked apologetically, still feeling guilty.

"Instead of just being stupid and getting hurt, what if I'd done something really looney, said to hell with it and jumped off the cliff into the ocean?" she wanted to know.

"I had a lot more faith in you than that or I wouldn't have left you alone at all. I hope you believe that."

"I do. I can see that now. And it was important for me to go through that."

"Except for the visitors. That was dumb of me. I didn't think anyone would be coming over here. And I'm sorry I let them scare you so bad but it seemed the wisest thing to do. Let them pass on through believing there's no one here. And now that they've satisfied their curiosity and know there's no food on this side, it's doubtful they'll be back. Maybe they'll pass the word and keep a few others from it, too. Let's hope so," he said and started apologizing all over again.

"Enough," she said and admonished him. "You have no idea how much stronger I feel about myself now."

They were quiet again. The silence between them much warmer. Then Katherine continued.

"How to be completely alone with oneself," she said. "I never realized how important that might be. I'm glad you trusted me to handle it. I mean it," she continued, giving him a sincere look as she spoke.

"Me, too. I guess. Well..." he shrugged and raised his eyebrows.

"Seriously, once I got past the panic stage I really enjoyed being able to just sit here and think."

"Well," he acknowledged. "There is a lot to think about, that's for sure. Especially if we can learn to be honest with ourselves."

"That's the hard part. How badly one can delude themselves. Back in that other world I always thought I was in complete control of my own life. But it wasn't true. I may have choosen a path and set things in motion but after that I just became a victim of the clock and the calendar, outside pressures, other peoples demands and on and on. And I get so caught up in it I didn't even realize what was happening. Even when able to enjoy a certain level of power, as I was. And I can see I wasn't alone. It seems to happen a lot. Before we realize it we become defined by our position and our interactions with other people almost to the point where, in the end, we don't even know who we are. At least for me. Once I took office I was totally surrounded by the job. Day and night. The governor. An image which was beginning to take over my identity. I don't think that was very healthy."

"Really? Why not?"

"Don't you see? Because it's so one dimensional. I used to wonder about people who were always summing themselves up with one word. I'm a lawyer or a doctor. A police officer or a mechanic. But maybe that's all there was for them. Or maybe thinking that way made it easier for them. Or that's all they allowed themselves to be. Or maybe that's all the people around them allowed them to be. I don't know. Then I became, the governor. Jesus. And I started doing the same thing. Wow."

"Well, you've certainly have been wrestling with it. Any conclusions?"

"I'm not sure. Did getting elected really prove anything? Did anyone else actually care unless they personally had something to gain or lose?"

"Why should that matter? It was about you, not them."

"I suppose you're right."

"Forget the rest. What was important to you at the time?"

"I guess it was the challenge. I was damned if I was going to let anyone tell me what I could or couldn't do with my own life. But once I took the oath of office the real excitement was over. The glory was gone. I still did it, though. And I did it well. But it was so totally damned consuming. And it wasn't me. I wasn't meant to be a public servant. Or any other kind of servant. Too bad I didn't realize that earlier."

"What if you had been a man and had been drafted into the military?"

"Hmm, well, I believe I would have refused to serve. I guess I never felt I ever owed anyone anything, country included. What about you? Were you in the military?"

"God no. And never under that son-of-a-bitch."

Wow, Katherine thought, looking closely at Howard. She had never heard him swear before. This should be interesting.

"That was Bush, right? I was a teenager when he left office. But he went down as the worst president in history. I remember that part very clearly."

"Sick and stupid both. A complete moron. But, I have to admit, it wasn't entirely his fault. No one can create that kind of disaster by themselves. He was aided and abetted by the most dimwitted, corrupt congress ever. And flag waving fools coming out of the woodwork. And eager young idiots who couldn't wait to pick up a gun to prove their manhood, and...." He stopped for a second, catching himself before going off into a harangue. "Jesus. Still makes me mad as hell just thinking about it. Sorry."

"I know. Even I got embarassed about it when the subject came up."

"There was a lot to be ashamed of."

"Not a good time in history."

"Still isn't," Howard said, shaking his head in confirmation. "We almost worked through it and then, along came Drukus. God."

"Maybe the disappearance was a good thing. He seems pretty harmless here on the island."

"Don't count on it," Howard spoke with a scowl. "All his key players are here too. He'll think of something."

SOME VERY BAD MEN

They still hadn't made a calander and didn't try to keep track of the days. Dumb if they had. Counting would become depressing, only serve to remind them how much time they had been imprisoned there. It was already too long. Why bother. But, without keeping track of the actual days in between, Howard still went back around the island to where all the people were at somewhat regular intervals. Maybe every two or three weeks. But after Katherine's previous exerience, never more than a day at a time even though she kept assuring him that she would always be discreet. Then it was time to go again. Katherine's wrist had completely healed without any permanent disability and she felt good. She made the decision to accompany him.

Beginning early to provide extra time, they started out. Bathing in the stream every day, she was as clean as could be but her hair was long and matted, her armpits were bushy and her legs atrociously hairy. What was left of her pajamas was tattered and stained. She had to look like the bag lady from hell so who would ever want to bother her? She would take the risk. They reached the fruit trees by mid morning. Once there, however, Katherine changed her mind, not too sure as to why. Was it vanity, or fear? Something else?

Didn't matter, she decided. As a man, Howard would attract much less attention alone than he would with her in a place where women were in such a minority. Wasn't the whole idea to maintain a low profile and stay out of trouble if at all possible. Of course, and she would feel better remaining behind. She would gather supplies while he was gone instead. If all went well, he would be back by the time the sun had moved approximately forty five degrees across the sky, the equivalent of three hours. It was their only way of telling time and Katherine had become quite good at judging it.

"I'll meet you here by the pear trees," he said, after everything was settled, and started out. There was a trail of sorts, headed downward. Katherine followed him with her eyes until he disappeared amongst the trees, then she set to her own work.

They were the strangest trees, she thought, as she began gathering. No matter how heavily they were picked, they were never barren. As soon as a pear or an apple or an orange was removed a new bud would appear and a new piece of fruit would replace it within a matter of two or three days. Wouldn't that be something to have in the yard back home? It was very odd indeed. But it was not unusual in it's present setting. Everything here was very strange in one way or another. In spite of the warm climate, the abundance of food and a more than adequate supply of fresh water, the island was completely devoid of all animal and bird life. There were no insects of any kind and no fish in the sea. In spite of all that the main island still had a certain stark beauty to it, however. For some reason, even though entirely flowerless in the normal sense, the plant life was still quite varied and sometimes striking. Trees and bushes and plants all had tremendous differences in size and shape and texture and coloring. Until then Katherine had never before realized that there could be so many delicate shades of green and brown.

Then there was the sky, immensely blue, sliding from pastel at the horizon to deep indigo at the vertical. And the sea, dead as it might be, was a different blue in the distance, always shimmering, becoming lighter as the water depths decreased, finally turning a heart wrenching tourquoise in close, crystal clear to the bottom, looking always like the perfect jeweled Pacific atol she had once flown over in times past. Daily it had beckond to her from high on the mountain where they had their cave home. But once down at the shore it was too lifeless and dead up close and the distant horizon far too flat and empty and disturbingly far away. Thus, all in all, the island offered an agonizing beauty that left her yearning for what she might not always have appreciated back home but now desperately hungered for. For hours and hours she had sat alone on top of the protective boulder that hide the cave and wondered at it, loving it in her private way, trying to embace it, to understand. She did it in the daytime and often at night when the moon was up. Was it also the same moon that humans had ventured to and landed on almost seventy years ago? she wondered. The size was right, the features were very similar, perhaps tilted a bit, maybe from a slightly different angle in space. She was never quite sure. Howard agreed. He didn't know either. Did it matter? Obviuously not, but for some reason she had begun thinking about it again, once Howard was gone and she was alone.

The day was warm and comfortable as always, just as every other day had been thus far and she worked slowly but steadily, gathering together a variety of fruit and fresh vegetables, all that they would be able to carry comfortably. Then she loaded much of into Howard's back pack and more into his long sleeved shirt so that it could be tied into a bundle and wrapped it up. Next, she took off her still intact pajama top, as she was in the habit of doing lately, and loaded it, too. It had taken a while, but they had finally become somewhat accustomed to the semi nudity between them. Howard was still very married in his own mind and she was still as determined as ever to keep things on their present footing.

But exactly how much longer would that be possible, she wondered, as she continued with her work. For the rest of their lives? And how much longer could they go on living like this, anyway, where the only challenge seemed to be nothing more than to just go on living, one day almost exactly like the next, day after day after day. Did living like this even have any meaning beyond just that? If so, what? And if not, what then? No wonder people were commiting suicide down below as Howard had previously reported.

Finally the task was done. It had taken her little more than an hour, she estimated. There was still time for a decent nap. She scouted the area, found a small clump of bushes, placed the pack and the two bundles of food inside and layed down in the middle, seemingly out of sight to any would be passers by. Or so she thought.

She must have been more tired than she realized for she slept deeply for nearly forty five minutes. Then, in a matter of seconds, she was wide awake. Someone was laughing, men were laughing. It was gluttonous, rough, male laughter mixed with crude language. Suddenly she was very frightened. Quickly she got to her feet and backed away as far as possible, crossing her arms over her breasts in the process.

There were three of them, bearded, scraggly, course looking, all aroused by her partial nudity. At first her mind went blank with fear as panic nearly over came her judgement. Her first impulse was to run but in her mind she knew that would be futile. With three of them, they would catch her easily, and if she showed fear, they would feed on it. Not only would she be brutily raped, she would probably be killed in her resistance, or worse, taken captive. What to do, what to do, she questioned, as she studied them carfully.

There was but one chance, she decided. It was small but maybe she could make it work. Summoning all her reserves she forced herself to stop shaking, forced herself to stare back at them, forced herself to look them over carefully. The big one, he must be the leader. She took a long, deep breath, exhaled slowly and looked him straight in the eye. Her gaze was steady, the fear no longer obvious. He hadn't expected that and the three men stopped their advance. Then slowly she smiled at him, confounding him further.

"You," she said in her most confident voice. "You and me. Not them. No. Make them go away."

Surprized and astounded, he looked at her. His English was limited but he understood. "You and me?" he repeated, quite confused. How could he suddenly have become so lucky?

"You and me. Not them," Katherine said again. "Make them go away, " she said strongly and pointed.

The man looked more carefully. She was half his size and she was alone. But she didn't seem to be afraid. Could it be? How lucky could he get? She wanted what he wanted! He turned to the other two and motioned them to go. At first they did not respond but he barked at them loudly. Slowly they retreated. Twenty feet away they stopped. "More," Katherine demanded. "More. In the trees, over there. More."

"More," said the man, thinking of his own good fortune, helping her. "You can have her when I'm done."

Finally, when they were completely out of sight, she stepped out of the bushes into the clear and motioned him to follow her around behind the additional cover. "Ah, ha," she said and lowered her arms so he could see her bare breasts. Then she looked down at his pants. It was her only chance.

"Take them off," she told him, and motioned as she did so.

He grinned with a lewd pleasure and looked down, then began fumbling with his belt. She took a slow step forward so as not to disturb him, her arms at her sides, waiting till his pants were down around his ankles so he would be most vulnerable. A little closer, one last small step.

The distance was now exact and she took a deep breath. Then, with both thumbs rigidly extended, pointing upwards, she raised both arms with a fear driven strength, jamming her long, ragged nails directly into his eyes. Perhaps the surprise was too much or the pain too great, but he did not shout out. Instead his head came up as the blood poured from the deep injuries and she took a last step, really in close now, and rammed her knee into his crotch with her all her might. He groaned, crumpled and went down. But it was not over. Blinded, fighting the pain, he flailed about with his arms, reaching for her. She saw a rock, picked it up, came in behind and bashed him on the skull. Now he was quiet. But for how long would she be safe? How long before his friends became impatient and wanted a taste of her too. Clearly, it was time to run. Run she must. But quietly, she must do it quietly. She turned and took off, circling the area in the trees where they had gone, heading downward in the direction Howard would be coming from, running, running, running. Down the hill, through the trees, round a thick clump of bushes when, almost out of control, she slammed into another human being, almost knocking him down.

"Katherine! What is going on?"

It was Howard. He had caught her and held her, keeping her from falling down, looking her over to see what might have happened.

At first she was stunned and breathing so hard she couldn't speak. Then slowly she gained control and looked up at him still holding her. It was the first physical contact they had ever had. He let her go. Still shaking from the frightful experience, she backed away and told him what had happened.

"My god," he said. "Are they still up there?"

"The one may be dead. I don't know. But the other two will be waiting. Maybe they found him by now."

"One way or the other, we have to finish it," Howard said. "We can't risk having them follow us back to the cave." He looked around, walked to a nearby tree, broke off a large dead branch and hefted it. It made a substantial club. "Ready?" he asked, and she nodded, not so sure she wanted to return to the horrid scene.

With Howard taking the lead, they made their way slowly and quietly upwards. As they approached the area of Katherine's confrontation they heard talking in the trees.

"They're still in the same place," she told him in a whisper. "Maybe we can skirt around and get away before they know what happened."

"We can try," he replied, but no sooner had he said it than the voices became louder. Now they were yelling at their other friend.

"Hurry up, you dog. We want a turn too," they shouted, laughing. And when there was no response, they did it again. Then it was quiet for a moment. But not for long. Howard and Katherine could hear them walking towards the bushes she had been caught in. Now they were talking again but they were not making jokes as a string of loud curses filled the air.

"Too late," Howard stated. "Let's go," he said and circled around to get behind them, darting from tree to tree.

One of the men swore again loudly, then the other.

"Stay here out of sight," Howard told Katherine when they were but fifteen or twenty feet away. Then he stepped out from behind the tree, the club in his right hand, hidden behind him. At first they did not see him. He used the time to get several steps closer and stopped. "Hey," he said in a loud voice and stood his ground.

At first they were surprized. Where was the woman? Surely she could not have beaten their friend so badly. It must be this one. He had to be the one. They came closer, eyeing him carefully, staying apart, wanting to get him between them. Howard waited. The first man was now a meer five feet away. Another step, just another step, Howard said to himself. Another step it was and the club came up, swung with full strength, bashing itself across the man's knees as a scream of pain left his mouth. The other one stopped momentarily but then rushed in with a yell. It was pause enough. The club was up and swinging again, colliding with the man's rib cage, producing a loud crack as bones shattered. Then more painful screaming as he too, went down. But it was hardly over.

Fighting the pain and angry as an injured bull, the first man down quickly rolled to within reaching distance of Howard standing over the second man on the ground and threw his burly arms around Howard's legs, throwing him off balance, making him lose his grip on the club. Beating on him with his fists, Howard was unable to free himself. Vengfully, the man clamped down on Howards bare leg with his teeth, sinking them deeply into his calf, drawing massive spurts of blood.

Katherine, who had by now come out from behind the tree and was watching the battle from a safe distance, came forward. Avoiding the desperate thrashing around, she circled in and picked up the club Howard had dropped and began beating the man across the back and the legs. Finally he let go, lying there with hate in his eyes, looking up at her. Then he swung his arms at her, missing her legs by inches and she wielded the club again, hitting him on the head. Now he was silent.

She turned her attention back to Howard. He was on his feet once more, had found a large rock and was ready to use it. Then, looking closely at the condition of the two attackers, he dropped it.

"Are you all right?" he questioned Katherine.

"Yes," she said, catching her breath and coming towards him. "But we had better do something about your leg. It's bleeding badly."

"I think the bastard bit through an artery," he said and sat back down, trying to apply pressure with his thumb.

Katherine went to find the bundles of food still wrapped in their clothing, tore the sleeves off of Howard's shirt and returned. By then Howard had the bleeding stopped but it was a serious wound, deep and ugly. "God, I hope it doesn't get infected," he said, as they did their best to bandage it.

"Do you think you can make it," Katherine asked.

"We certainly can't stay here. No telling if this bunch has other friends. "

It was nearly dark by the time they were safely back at the cave. With great difficulty, Howard had climbed to the top of their private boulder where they sat looking towards the setting sun, eating their last meal of the day in silence. A hint of red expanded across the horizon, separating the blue of the ocean from the darkening blue of the sky. Another hour and it would be completely dark. By now Howard's leg was swollen and miscolored. He was also clearly in pain. Eating quickly, Katherine climbed down and went to the nearby stream, collecting large plant leaves along the way. These she wrapped in her pajama top and soaked them in the water. Returning, they were placed over the wound and wrapped securely. Back in the cave for the night, Howard propped his wounded leg up on a small pile of brush Katherine had also gathered and tried to sleep.

In the morning he could hardly walk, his lower leg badly swollen and painful. He hobbled outside, found a place in the sun and spent the entire day there exposing the open wound to as much sunlight as possible, hoping it would help sterilize the injury and let Katherine wait on him and bring him food. Water was the difficult part, however. They had brought back half a dozen coconuts several days earlier but they were as yet unopened. At first Katherine tried beating them against the boulder. Then she laid them on top of one rock and beat on them with another. Howard struggled up and tried also, but to no avail. Finally she found a fairly heavy rock, flat on one side but pointed on the other. Dragging it closer to Howard, she placed it on the ground, point up. Then, with her holding the coconut on top of the point and Howard slamming it with the largest rock he could yield under the circumstances, they drove the sharp end into the shell, piercing it. After first drinking the milk, Katherine managed to beat on the coconut some more and finally divided it neatly in two. Once the meat was scraped out with a stick and placed in the sun to dry, Katherine had two bowls to carry water in, saving Howard many painful trips to the stream. Later in the day she rested along side of him and encouraged him to talk.

"Tell me what you learned from your excursion down below," was the first thing Katherine wanted to know.

"Frankly, I was pretty shocked. Most of the people still haven't stopped to take a serious look at where they're all at or what they might even be doing here. They just picked up where they left off at home and are still trying to force the same old rules and regulations on everone else around them but no one seems to see just how ludicrous that is and how stupidly they are behaving. Leaders impose, followers, follow. And then there is the White House laid out on the ground with sticks," Howard went on, describing it to her.

It was almost impossible to stop laughing, even for Howard, although it made his leg hurt even worse than before. When they did, she asked him what else had happened. He told her about more suicides and all the bodies in dead man's cove. Also, the Arabs still hated the Americans with a vengence and there was serious trouble brewing between them. Christian and Muslim religious leaders were both sending misionaries to the other side trying to convert each other and that created another kind of conflict. A Russian Mafia figure had built a stone wall and gained control of the food supply, blocking off access from below. The Americans were planning a retaliation. The Southern Baptists were blaming the whole affair on American liberals and the President was still behaving as outrageously as always and every time he left his mock White House the same old corporate power brokers would lead him off into the trees and tell him what they thought he should do, so he blusters around all day, still convinced of his godly importance.

"They're all crazy," Howard stated. "Misdirected as the President is, most of them still just keep falling in line behind. Never learned to think for themselves back home and don't seem able to do it here. Even under these extreme circumstances. That's rather discouraging."

"You're much too polite, Howard. It's depressing as hell. Weird and difficult as this place is, it is still an opportunity to learn something, and, if that turns out to be the criteria for getting off of here, most of them will be long dead before it happens."

"Maybe their God can fix it for them if they pray enough."

"They'd better hope so or this place is in for a lot of trouble."

"Well, I haven't done any praying but hopefully I've learned something. Hard to tell, though, under the circumstances. However, if I knew I was going to be back home tomorrow, or even in a month or two, I'd still say it has been one of the most important things that has ever happened to me and I'd never trade it away."

"Really? Why is that?" Howard asked. It was an interesting point of view.

"It's been a shocking but significant change of perspective.

Just being here. Learning acceptance. Not trying to prove anything, knowing that is not necessary. Sitting in the sun, feeling the breeze, becoming a part of the nature that's here, not separate from it. And most of all, thinking, wondering, experiencing the awe of it all. The great gifts of consciousness and awareness, emotion and sensation. Being alive to be alive. Today for today. I am beginning to believe that this is not just some flukey thing that happened. You don't just separate all the leaders from the rest of the population by accident and land them on some remote island. It could only have been done with great intelligence and planning. The real reasons for it have to be in finding out why. What we can learn? What should we be learning ?"

"I guess I'd have to agree with you," Howard said after some consideration. "When you put it that way. And suppose you do get a chance to go back. What would you do differently?"

"The truth? I would probably resign the governorship if it still exists. Isn't that something? I never would have believed I'd see the day when I'd say that. And to think I even had aspirations for the Presidency. Another woman in the White House. I think I had a good chance, too, the way it was beginning to come together. But no more, thank god. As we have talked about before, too many compromises just to promote a career. Then I'd like to work on my personal integrity. Kick my husband out of the house regardless of the consequences, learn to live simply and think clearer, learn to be scrupulously honest with myself about myself because I'm finally beginning to see what my behavior was really costing me."

"What do you mean?"

"My own home was not a joyous place. The minute I stepped in the door I had to shut down all my feelings. Now, looking back I can see that once you start shutting down in one area, it soon spills over into others. After while you're not sure what you really feel about anything, or if you're feelin at all. Maybe just going through the motions while other things take over as priorities. And that's about where I was at, tough and hardened, taking care of me and to hell with the rest of it. Perfect, of course, if I was going to stay in politics."

"Your point is well taken. I admire you for your courage."

"Well, perhaps. But what about you, Howard?"

"I'm not completely sure yet. I haven't quite come to grips with this leadership thing. I can't believe that taking the lead position is wrong, in and off itself. There has to be more to it than that. But I do know one thing I would like to do for sure."

"What is that?"

"Take my wife off to some tropical island like this, but one that has animals and birds and flowers on it. Talk to her, listen to her, try to find out what she is really all about, listen to her priorities. I love her dearly but there are so many little things I have missed, or don't know, or was always too busy to try and find out about. She seemed happy being married, but was she really, or was I working too hard, away from home too much, taking her for granted. Then, too, has she had enough life experiences, has she really had a chance to explore all the things she ever wanted? Have I been totally fair and given her the chance and the freedom to grow and expand as fully as she might want? Or, have I imposed my standards and my morality on her? And shame on me if I have because, if I did, I am now beginning to see that I may have also cheated myself by never getting to know the person she might have been if things were different."

"What if she wanted other men?" Katherine asked, quite astounded by what she was hearing. Suddenly she felt a twinge of envy. How come she had never met a man like this? Maybe there weren't any except Howard here and then maybe he was only what he was after having had to endure the experience of separation and loss. How did she know? And then she realized she had asked a very tough question. Perhaps one she had no right to.

"That's the toughest one, isn't it?" Howard replied anyway, looking serious. "The real test."

"Definitely," she responded in a subdued voice.

"No one owns another," Howard continued. "Technically, I wouldn't have the right to intervene. Emotionally, it would be very difficult. But legally and religiously imposed faithfulness is not morality, no matter what the church or the state may claim. In the same light, marriage vows are a farce. No one should be forced to honor a promise made at twenty at a time of passion, or ignorance and immaturity, for the rest of their lives. That's just another form of tyranny, subtle as it may be."

"People should only stay together by choice, not by mandate."

"Yes. And no outside group or agency should have the right to interfere. Except maybe where children are involved. That's a whole other issue. Fortunately, or unfortunately, we never had any."

Katherine watched him intently in the light of the setting sun. "Well," she said. "I am very happy to have met you, Mr Briggs. .....I've had so many men in my life, both before and after I got married, but I never met a one who ever saw me as much more than

108

a sex object or a business or political opportunity."

"So, as you said, your marriage wasn't very good?"

"It was horrible. A bargain made in hell. I wanted his money, he wanted my looks and my connections as Governor. But I never loved him. I didn't even like him and I cheated on him from time to time. But I don't think there was any hypocrisy. We didn't do the classical, love, honor, obey part. We had a simple one page legal contract. It didn't say anything about sexual faithfulness or privilage. There was no morality attached to it, either. And none intended, at least on my part. We haven't even been in the same bed for over two years."

"He didn't care?"

"I think a man always cares, especially the ones who see women as possessions. But he really never knew what I was doing because I was always very discreet."

"What about him?"

"I think his feelings were hurt because I wouldn't sleep with him so he always had some frumpy looking female somewhere on the side, trying to flaunt it. He even brought one home once but I just laughed her out of the house. It was the one time when he almost hit me."

"Well, after what you did today, he's be a damned fool if he ever did," Howard said, looking at Katherine's face, studying it. There was concern in his eyes.

"Yes, but I almost killed two other human beings. Maybe I did."

"But you didn't. I checked. They were both alive and groaning when we left."

"But maybe the first one will be blind. Maybe I blinded him."

"Maybe. Maybe not. But you could have been killed, yourself."

"That would have been better than the other alternative. And they would have had to kill me before I let that happen."

"I don't doubt that one bit and I'm overwhelmed by the way you handled it. I'm not so sure I could have done so well under the circumstances."

"But you finished it in the end. Otherwise I might not even be here now."

"Well, neither of us had much choice, did we?"

"I'm not so sure I could do it again, however, if it came to that."

"Let's hope you never have to. I should never have left you

there alone."

I't's not your fault."

"Perhaps not. But I'll never leave you alone again over there."

"I'm flattered, Howard. Thank you for your concern."

"God, Katherine. We have been together for many long months now. I have watched you, studied you, listened to you. We have shared our food, our cave, our concerns and our hopes. I have come to see you as a most remarkable woman and I would hate to have anything happen to you."

Katherine stammered and tried to speak. There was a tear in her eye. She wiped it away. "Oh my," she said. They were sitting very close together. Howard put his arm around her shoulder. Automatically, she leaned into him as the last small slice of the sun disappeared over the edge of the world. She sighed and relaxed. "God, it feels good to be held," she said.

"It feels good to hold you."

"It's been a long time."

"Yes."

"I hope .... I don't want to.... I......."

"Don't worry. You're still safe. Long as it's been, my own wife is still very much in the picture, and with this bum leg hurting the way it does, well..."

"Well, I wish there were more men like you around. Didn't you say you had a brother?"

"I did. About your age. But he's also married. They were about to have a baby back when I disappeared. I hope it went well. There were some serious complications. Anyway, I'm sure you'd like him, even if he isn't available."

ANOTHER DISAPPEARANCE

At the same moment Howard was telling Katherine about his brother Jack, his own wife back home was talking to that same brother.

"They found Howard's Jeep about a month later," she was saying. "But as for him, nothing. Not a trace. As bad as it may be, I can only pray he disappeared with the rest of the leaders. At least there is some hope that way. Someday they may all reappear, wherever they are."

"It's never easy, Margaret," Jack Briggs said to his sister in law. "And not knowing doesn't help."

"But you have had such a deep loss, Jack. And Howard is your brother, too."

110

"I know. It's been difficult. That's the problem, I guess. Trying to keep going. And what about the corporation? What's happening there?"

"I'm sorry, Jack. I just don't know. It was always his thing. I never got involved. All I know is that it has essentially come to a standstill."

"Well, tomorrow we can go down and take a look. It would be different if they were just making toys or pencils. But special purpose electric motors, motor control units, computer peripherals, tooling, all those things are important if the country is to keep going. There must be something that can be done."

"I hope so, but Howard was always a hands on type of manager. He never had a cardre of vice presidents and managers running around like so many firms of that size do."

"I don't think it would have helped. If he had, they probably would have disappeared too. The big question is, how do you run a business without some form of leadership? Where's the line? Size has something to do with it, obviously, since small, independently owned businesses weren't affected."

Even though the company had well over eight hundred employees and there were no Vice Presidents or titled Department Managers, it had run quite well when Howard had been in control, with nothing but supervisors over the various functional areas. As a result, there was no one who had any broad, interdepartmental experience capable of coordinating between them. After two solid weeks of both individual and group meetings and evaluations, however, Jack discovered several persons who had the potential. Not a one wanted the job, however, for fear of disappearing also. In an attempt to solve that problem Jack instituted a policy of early morning meetings between all the supervisory personnel, with himself acting as coordinator. What had gone wrong yesterday? What did they need today to make things run better? And, looking ahead, what needed to be done to keep it going forward in the future?

As a new challenge, the plan worked quite well, as new challenges often do. Each supervisor organized his own area to suit himself, hiring and firing, establishing wages, determining responsibility. But then, it too, began to fail. And while the supervisors were very good at getting their own subordinates to work together, they were very limited in their ability to work together amongst themselves. Some had more employees than others and felt they deserved more pay. Some felt others were not doing their jobs as well as they should and they were working harder than necessary to take up the slack. The list became longer and longer. Some of them, of course, just plain didn't like each other. Daily meetings deteriorated into fault finding, back stabbing and generalized complaining. From the beginning, however, Jack had decided that he was not there to manage. His sole function was to chair the meetings and demand that they be constructive, but it became more and more difficult. Then one day it was too much.

"All right," he said, pounding the conference room table, interupting the ongoing argument. "How do you expect to accomplish anything this way? Don't you get it? You have to work things out amongst yourselves and if you can't do that we might as well quit. I don't care if you have to stay here all day and all night and all day tomorrow. When you think you have a plan you can live with, I'll be back."

Maybe it was just too large of a group or maybe it was just too much to expect to begin with. It was hard to tell, but they did try. They didn't stay all night but they were all there until past ten and they began again the next morning. By evening, however, it all seemed clear. The group of supervisors were just not capable of working things out on their own.

"I don't know what to do, Margaret," Jack told her at last. "Other than taking over entirely. At first they were full of sincerity and cooperation. But once the crisis of the moment is over they all fall back into the same old ruts, expecting someone else to keep them focused and make the tough decisions. I have taken a lot of notes over the past few weeks and have personally evaluated each and every one of them. If I had the freedom and if I dared, I know exactly who I would fire and who I would promote, who would get more money and responsibility and the whole bit. But I don't want to do that."

"What if you just advised me and I did it instead? Do you think that would work?"

"I'm sure it would for a while, just like before. But in the long run, no. Things are always in flux. If you weren't completely involved on a day to day basis and able to make ready decisions, it wouldn't work over the long haul. And if I'm there full time, advising you from behind the scenes, they would resent me and wouldn't respect you, so we'd still be in trouble."

"Maybe we should just lock the place up until Howard comes back. And if he doesn't, well, none of it will matter anyway. He did put enough money away for us to live on for a long time, however. And with him gone....."

"Let's not give up just yet. Let me try one last thing. Five of the group have to go. They are definite trouble makers. A few more need some serious job counceling but I think they will be all right, and the rest should be able to cooperate if we can set it up right."

"But Jack. That may be overstepping. I don't want you gone, too."

"Well, maybe I won't. On the other hand I don't believe everyone who disappeared is just dead. They have to be somewhere. So, if worse comes to worse, what the heck. Somehow I'm not afraid of the possibilities. It might even be interesting to find out. Wouldn't it be something if I could even locate Howard and we could figure out what went wrong. Maybe, just maybe, once we understood that things could be turned around and a person might somehow be able to get back. Wouldn't that be something? There has to be a way. I just can't believe it's a forever kind of thing," Jack told her earnestly.

"But what if you're wrong?"

"Then I'm wrong. But without my wife and baby, half the time I don't feel like going on anyway. Besides, I don't think it will happen. I won't really be running the business in the strict sense of the word. I'll just be making a few management decisions."

That was it. A few management decisions. Secretly, however, Jack was intrigued with the whole idea of the disappearance and it was a fundamental part of his nature to want to know the bigger truth. As a result he spent a lot of time thinking about it in his idle moments.

All the changes he had talked about with Margaret had been accomplished within a week but Jack was still making the major decisions and fine tuning the group as it went along. At this point he was very hopeful. Another relatively trouble free week passed. Now if they get through a few more like it, maybe everyone would settle in and the place would go on functioning in a proper way. And if he could bring the business to a point where it could operate without someone on top of the pile making all the big decisions, well, then maybe he could take some time off, go his own way and Margaret wouldn't have to worry. And if Howard did by chance return, things would be all in order, waiting for him.

On the particular morning in question Jack had come down to the facility early to get things started. He had his coffee, did a quick tour of the engineering area and came back to Howard's old office.

Sitting down behind the desk, he started going over progress reports. He stopped for a moment, wished he had brought another cup of coffee from the machine, leaned back in his chair to rest and began looking out the window. Howard had done a superb job of landscaping when he had the building put up. It was a park like setting full of trees and shrubs, very pleasant and relaxing. What was he doing in here? Why wasn't he outside, Jack began to wonder. Enjoying the fresh air. He leaned back in the chair a little further, put his feet up on the desk and shut his eyes momentarily. He could have drifted off into a short nap but was soon subjected to a rude jarring instead. At first he thought the chair had tipped over. When he opened his eyes, however, he found himself sitting on the ground in the grass, completely unharmed.

"What the hell?" he said out loud, as he looked around carefully. Doing his best to subdue the burst of anxiety he felt, it took a while to register, even though in the back of his mind he already knew what happened.

"Well, that answered that," he said to himself as he layed there for a bit longer. Then he got to his feet. Everything about himself seemed intact and he felt just fine. "Ha," he said "How about that? I did it and I'm still alive."

No sooner had he made that statement, however, when he was approached by two grubby bearded, dirty looking, half dressed men. "Well, well," one of them said with a British accent.

"Another new arrival. Haven't had any in a while."

"And look at those fancy clothes," said the other, checking Jack out. "How about sharing some of them with us? Be a friend and we'll give you a guided tour of the island."

Jack sized them up, their appearance immediately telling him that things here were obviously much more primitive than back home. But even though they looked very shabby, they were alive and seemed to be in good health. So that was something. Survival here was possible. But what had the experience done to them, that was the question? Were they safe to be around? They weren't as big as he was but there were two of them and he was alone and without any knowledge of what it took to stay alive in this place. Still, after a hard look at them he was sure he could handle them both if he had to.

"Sorry," he said, cordial enough. "I came to see some friends who may need them worse than you." Then he patted his jacket pocket, remembering. "But I do have a couple of cigars you can have if you give me some information."

"Cigars?" the smaller one questioned. "Jesus, I used to smoke a good cigar now and then. But they're worthless here. There's no way to light them," he said with anger and Jack took a step back.

"Wait a minute," the other one said. "What the hell. We're not going to hurt you, mate. And even if there's no way to light a cigar here, I still wouldn't mind chewing on one just for the taste of it," he continued and reached out.

"Well, let's see, Jack said as he felt through his pockets and also came up with a book of paper matches. He struck one and held it out while the first man lit his cigar. The second match would not light, nor would any of the rest of them. "Same problem we had when we first got here," the man said and offered his cigar to the other one who was able to get a light for his own off of it."

"Well, now. That is downright wonderful," the second man said. "There aren't any keys to the kingdom but what can we help you with?"

"I'd like to know where all the Americans might be, if I'm correct in assuming they're here also."

"They are, they are," he was told. And not only did they tell him that, they told him about the food and water situation, the strange politics amongst the various factions on the island, the serious trouble that was brewing for the Americans if they didn't stop listening to their demented President sitting on a rock in a White House made of sticks, and many other things.

"Yeah. It's too bad," said the bigger one, letting out another puff of smoke. "Even us Brits won't have much to do with them anymore. And that says a lot, if you know what I mean."

"Doesn't sound good," Jack acknowledged but he had heard enough so he thanked them sincerely and headed off. As soon as he was out of their sight, however, he took off his jacket and shirt and dropped them on the ground, grinding dirt into them. Then he scuffed up his shiny shoes, rubbed dirt on his pants and face and mussed up his hair. It would have to do for now. Hopefully he looked like he had been there for a few days anyway.

Once in the American area he was very cautious. The last thing he wanted was to be recognized by the President or any other administration official who might be there, especially after what the two British individuals had told him about the fomenting trouble. He wasn't about to be pulled into that mess, no matter what. But at the same time, neither did he wish to start out by antagonizing anyone. Later, perhaps. When he had nothing better to do. In spite of all his other difficulties back home, there had still been time left to do some serious thinking about what had gone before. In particular, about the reign of President Drukus and his corrupt administration. And where that had been leading. Nationalism could be a dangerous thing, as world history had indisputably proven, particularly when a nation was in the grasp of individuals corrupt enough to tamper with the fundamentals of its own democratic process and constitutional integrity. And obviously, it was still going on here on the island. That was appalling.

For the time being, however, he was in a difficult position. Dirty, ragged, wearing odd remnants of clothing, hair down to their shoulders and equally long beards, it was almost impossible to tell who was who. But somehow, in spite of that, he still had to find Howard. That was his single priority. His older brother had to be there somewhere. Even if he couldn't recognize him immediately, surely Howard would still be able to recognize Jack when they came across each other. All he could do was to keep moving and try to stay out of trouble.

After spending several nights sleeping on the grass under the trees and questioning scores of people, he had learned little. Howard had to be here somewhere with the rest of the Americans. Didn't he? Or had something else happened to him? Was he all right?

Jack's concern for Howard's welfare was beginning to grow. Then one day he happened to over hear a small group of men talking about all the good looking women they had left behind and how they wished they were still back home, or at least had some of the women here with them.

"One of the best looking ones I ever met probably still is, " a very scraggly looking man named Jess stated. "At least she was here, anyway. She was here the first day. Man, what a body."

"What do you mean, was? " someone else asked.

"Damned fool me," Jess said. "I gave her my jacket and my shoes. And what does she do? Disappeared with some big tall dude. Older guy. Never saw him before or since. Wonder why not. I've sure been looking for them, all right."

"Sounds like the couple that beat up those three guys up on the mountain. Blinded one guy, damned near killed the other two. They're still looking for her, last I heard. And the guy she was with."

"Does anyone know who the man was?" Jack asked, but they all just shook their heads.

"Well, what about the woman?" Jack continued, addressing himself to Jess. "Since you seem to know her, does she have a name? And where is she from?"

"Katherine Beaumont. Governor, ah, ex governor of Colorado."

Colorado, Jack thought. Howard's home state. Now that was something. Jack was silent but pleased with the information. Not wanting to give anything away, however, he shrugged as if he had lost interest and withdrew.

"Someone's coming," Katherine shouted down to Howard lying in the sun, just loud enough so he could hear, his still unhealed leg propped up.

"How many? And how far away?"

"Less than a mile. Just one. White male. Must be a newcomer. Not much hair on his face and wearing a full set of clothes. Do you think we should try and hide?"

"Not yet. Just stay down and keep an eye on him. Tell me what you think when he gets closer. Keep your head down."

Katherine flattened herself out on the top of the boulder and watched the approaching figure through the binoculars. "Shirt, pants, shoes and a sport jacket. A little dirty but in pretty good shape. And the way he's making it across that rough terrain I'd say he been hiking before. There, he stopped. He's looking at the ground like he's tracking us. Do you think we left any signs?"

"Only to an experienced outdoor person. I'm going to try and make it up there. How far away now?"

"Maybe half a mile. Better come up the back side."

"Right on. And we'd better be quiet, too."

By the time Howard made it to the top of the boulder with his injury, the man was less than a quarter mile away. When he was settled, Katherine handed him the binoculars. Howard refocused them for his eyes and held them steadily on the lone individual until the man was less than three hundred yards away. He lowered then for a moment, rubbed his eyes and looked again.

"My god," he said. "It's not possible. It can't be. My god," he repeated again and again and slowly worked his way to his feet, trying not to put too much pressure on his bad leg.

"Who is it, Howard? What's going on? Do you know him?"

"God, yes," Howard said with a huge smile and started to shout and wave. "Jack! Jack! Up here. Damn, it's Jack. It's my younger brother. The one I've been telling you about. My god,

Katherine, I don't believe it."

Katherine was completely shocked by Jack's presense. Howard's own brother? The one he talked about from time to time? What a strange coincidence. It seemed impossible. What was he doing here? How had he found them? They had been hiding out on this side of the mountain for all these many months and not a single person had ever come this far around the island, deliberately looking for them. But here he was with short hair, about a weeks growth of beard on his face and a suit of clothes still in relatively good condition. Suddenly she felt subdued and self conscious, wondering how she looked in her ragged clothing. Fortunately she had rinsed off in the creek that morning and combed through her hair as best she could with her fingers but she was still convinced that she must look absolutely terrible. Especially to one who just come from a place where they had soap and shampoo and razors and lipstick and, and... But then, argue as she might, so what. Jack wasn't there to see her, he had come to find Howard.

No two men had ever greeted each other so warmly and it was still a happy time, even under the disparaging circumstances. Jack kidded Howard about how badly he looked, said he didn't recognize him at all with the long hair and the beard and was at first inclined to turn around and run.

Finally, Howard settled down somewhat. Then he apologized and introduced Jack and Katherine. They both put out their hands and shook. Initially, all Jack could do was stare at her. Her face was growing red. She felt her suspicions coming true and she wanted to run away. How embarassing. But why was he hanging onto her hand so long?

"My pleasure, Governor," he said at last, and looked questioningly back at Howard.

Howard shook his head, no. "We haven't, a, we aren't, we, ...," he struggled to answer with the truth, obviously quite embarassed by the whole thing.

"Seriously, Jack. Oh, I know. But you see, I, uh, she... we... And I still consider myself married," he went on and on as Katherine also blushed even more profusely and looked away, suddenly realizing that for some as yet unknown reason, it was important to her that Jack believed what Howard was saying. "So, with no disrespect for Katherine, I'll continue to hold out for Margaret, just in case I get lucky and go back. And, since you're here, it tells me she still exists back there somewhere."

"She does. And she is quite well in spite of also missing you pretty badly. We had breakfast together five days ago before I went off to work at *your* corporation, trying to put the finishing touches on a plan I started to initiate. But, looks like I stepped over the line a little."

"No kidding," Howard responded light heartedly "You always were a little impulsive."

"Can't say I'm totally disappointed, though. Now I get to look at both sides of things," Jack said. But then his eyes found their way back to Katherine for a brief moment and he looked very troubled.

After a moment Katherine said, "Well, guess I'll go for a walk so you two can catch up on everything."

"That's not necessary," Jack said. "Why don't you stay."

"Absolutely," Howard agreed. "After all this time together you're part of the family."

"Are you sure?" she questioned again.

"Of course," both men said, and with that they all set down in a triangle. The first thing Jack questioned was Howard's bandaged leg. Katherine and Howard both took turns telling the story.

"It looks swollen. Is it infected?" Jack asked.

"You should have seen it a week ago. Thanks to Katherine here, it's finally getting better. She's been gathering different kinds of plant leaves to see if they have any healing qualities. There's a dark colored, broad leaf variety that seems to working."

Katherine smiled and explained how she had put the leaves in the coconut shell and ground them into a mush with a stone, then applied them to the wound like a poultice.

"Pretty clever woman," Howard complimented her.

It was the least she could do for the person who had saved her life, she said in return. For a moment Jack felt a twinge of envy. While he believed Howard's claim that he was being faithful to his wife, they certainly had developed a deep and caring relationship between them. He had almost forgotten how lonely he had been since his wife had died but now, suddenly, he missed her very badly. Then, almost immediately, having no way of knowing what had really happened, Howard began asking him about her and the baby.

With great difficulty, Jack talked about it as best he could. Howard was obviously badly shaken by the news. Katherine, too, sat silently, also touched by the pain. Finally, after a long silence, Jack changed the subject to other things. The discussion continued until nearly sunset. Then they made their way back to the cave where they dined on the stash of food Katherine had brought back the day before.

"Now we had better go collect some leaves so we can make up your bed," Katherine told Jack.

"Wait till tomorrow," he said. "I'm happy as hell just the way things are. And that sand looks pretty comfortable compaired to where I had to sleep the last few nights."

"Okay," she agreed. "But then you have to tell me what it's like to sleep in a bed. And what a steak or a pork chop tastes like. It's been so long I can't even remember."

In the morning they began again, catching up on the rest of each other's lives, comparing notes and sharing opinions. Eventually they got around to Howard's business.

"What do you think you did wrong, Jack?

"I'm not totally sure," he said. "I hadn't made any major decisions in several days and everything seemed to be working just fine. Then, the one minute I take to lean back and relax, boom, here I am," he continued, and recounted the story about sitting in Howard's chair looking out the window and winding up on the grass of the island. "Can't say I was totally surprised, however. On one level I was quite aware it could happen so I guess I was somewhat mentally prepared."

Continuing, Jack explained what he had tried to do to keep Howard's business operating in more detail. When done, Howard was silent for several minutes. Then he said, "That's it Jack. That's the answer. I'm sure of it."

"What?" Jack asked. "How could it be? Obviously what I did didn't work or I wouldn't be here."

"No, not that. I think you were on the right track but maybe you didn't carry it far enough. Of course, since you didn't own the business, there was no way you could."

"And maybe I wasn't on the right track at all. There doesn't seem to be much room for experimentation, does there? But I still agree with you. There has to be an answer. A lot of leaders of smaller groups didn't disappear. Along with a very few who had organizations of reasonable size. And if I had owned the place or had full authority to do anything I wanted, what do you think should have been done? What would you do now, if you had the chance?"

"Sell it."

"What are you talking about?"

"The solution. That's what needed to be done. Sell the business to the employees. Help them make it into an employee run business. A co-op of sorts. Joint management and participation, shared responsibility, complete sharing of all profits. Damnit, Jack. That's the kind of thing that ought to work."

"Well, you may be right. It would cerrtainly have solved your problem because then you'd have been out of it."

"That's not what I meant."

"I know. Just kidding. Seriously, though. You had half your life invested in that company. Do you really think you could have just given it up? What would you do? You don't have that golf cart mentality."

"I know. But my priorities have certainly changed. And there are other, far more importants things than operating a business."

"For an old workaholic like you who was always running out of challenges? What, for example?"

"For example, like I told Katherine, I would carry Margaret off to some desert island."

"After being here for more than half a year? I would think that would be the last thing you'd want."

"Not so. Maybe Katherine can explain it to you some time. We've had a chance to discuss things like that to some extent. What with all the spare time we've had on our hands. But now, what say we get some sleep? You've had a busy day."

Happy as he was to have disappeared and still be alive, and to have also found Howard alive and reasonably well, it was still a restless night for Jack. He kept waking up, thinking about everything that had happened. And Katherine. He couldn't stop thinking about Katherine. What a surprise. And the more he thought about her, the more restless he became. My god. He had never been caught so unaware in his life. And to have her here, sleeping in the same cave not all that far away. He listened for the sound of her breathing. Was she awake like he was or had she simply dozed off, giving him little thought. Stringy hair and all, she was the most beautiful, sensuous being he had ever met in his life. Between her and the excitment of having found Howard and all the rest, his mind raced onward and onward. Try as he mighht, he couldn't get everything that had happened into a manageable perspective. Eventually the moon came up and there was light enough to find the cave opening. He rose and went outside. Hours went by before he crawled back inside to try again. He dozed off and on. Finally he went into a deeper level of sleep. When he woke at last, the sun was at least two hours high in the sky and he was alone in the depths of the cave. Slowly he got up and went outside. There was no one around. "Howard," he called out.

"Up here," Katherine called back as Jack began climbing up the boulder. When he reached the top Katherine was sitting there alone. As she rose to her feet, Jack stopped dead in his tracks and could only stare. She was completely topless and solidly tanned.

"Oh dear," Katherine said as her face reddened and she crossed her arms over her chest. "I forgot. It's so warm and pleasant here all the time that we just got in the habit of not wearing many clothes. Especially since we only have one set and there isn't much left of them. My uh... apologies," she stammered and looked around, blushing even more heavily. "Oh dear," she said again. "I guess I left my top down below. Maybe I better go get it."

Jack still couldn't speak, he could only stammer and stare. Finally she gave a little laugh and dropped her arms. "Oh, what the heck," she said at last, trying to be casual about it. "It's really no big deal. Once you get used to it. Especially here under these conditions, living like early indiginous cave people."

"I, well...it's just that, that you ....are...., very, very attractive," he said and blushed heavily himself.

She laughed lightly in an attempt to deal with what seemed to be happening but not really trusting it. He seemed to be as intrigued by her as she was by him. Under the circumstances, how was that possible?

"Me? Stringy hair, no makeup, unshaven legs, haven't seen a bar of soap since I left home. You'd better take another look," she stated but raised her arms to cover herself again and looked away. Then she returned his gaze, trapped by his eyes. There was something else she was very glad about. Much as she might have wanted to, she was happy that she and Howard had never crossed the line in all those long months and she hoped beyond reason that Jack would believe that. Would he? Did he, she wondered, unable to look away.

For a while that was exactly all Jack could do, too. Take another look and continue looking. He took a step closer, feeling helpless, knowing that his own face was red and had to be betraying him, wanting to take her in his arms. But then, with one last great effort he stopped and forced himself to turn away. Finally he was able to speak again. "Where's Howard?" he asked in a serious attempt to change the focus.

"He's not here," she said after a long hesitation, both disappointed and relieved at the same time. They did need to talk about Howard. That was for sure. And certainly more important at the moment .

"Where did he go? Not far, I hope. With that leg of his."

"I mean, he's not here. He's gone", she stated, watching his face, not knowing quite how to proceed.

"Gone?" Jack repeated.

"He was here. I woke when he did and I heard him leave the cave. He started to climb up here to the top and I wasn't more than thirty seconds behind but when I got up here...he..."

At first Jack was puzzled. "What do you mean? Did he fall off and.... Then he smiled broadly.

"Wow," he said. "Could it be? Do you think that's what happened? Did you look everywhere?"

"Very carefully. There's no other way to explain it."

"Damn. Maybe it really is possible. Not only to come here but to also be able to go back. Do you think so?"

"A two way street. Wouldn't that be great?"

"What else could it be?" he asked, both of himself and of her and waited, thinking about it. Then he smiled again, "Isn't that something. Just think of it. I'd sure like to have seen Margaret's face if he showed up looking like a wooly mammoth. But maybe he went back to the mountains where he disappeared from. Then it will still be a while before he gets home. I hope she doesn't have a heart attack when he gets there."

Katherine pondered the immensity of it. Could Howard really have returned home? It was a while before she could respond. When she did, it was with caution. "That means there's reason for hope, isn't there," she said, more in question than in statement. "I mean for us, for all the people here?"

"It certainly looks that way." he said, looking into her uncertain eyes. She had been here on the island for such a long time. So long maybe she had given up, he thought. Or at least partially given up. Poor woman. But without hope of return, what else was there? No wonder some people walked out into the ocean. But if Howard was really gone, which he certainly seemed to be, then there was little left but to believe that he had returned back to that other world they had come from.

But she still wasn't quite ready for the idea of it. "Maybe that's just a fanciful dream. Maybe it's not what we think at all. Then what?"

"I know," he replied, trying to be encouraging. "But I still believe it's a two way street. Just the same way I always thought that the disappearance was a real happening. That Howard and all the other people, you, had to be somewhere, had to still be alive. I never could have imagined this place but I knew in my own mind that none of you were just extinguished like blowing out a bunch of candles. I guess that's why I eventually took the risks I did with Howard's business."

"Are you saying you deliberately wanted to test it? That you wanted it to happen?"

"Indirectly, yes. I guess I did. It was just too big of an enigma."

"Well, here you are. Now you know part of the truth anyway. And by now Howard should be in a position to know another part of it."

"God, I hope so," he said, showing his concern.

"What else, Jack?" she asked, studying his face. "You've obviously spent a lot of time thinking about it."

"I have. But probably not enough. Still, I don't believe I stepped over some invisible line somewhere. And I don't believe that's what caused the original disappearance you were caught up in, either. Not completely. There must be more complex reasons behind it than that. But I also like to think that my own desire and curiosity played a part in getting me here. And, if that's true, then it's not a simple black and white thing at all, is it. So....Maybe if ..." he stopped, his train of thought lost in the moment of being with Katherine. What he was saying was important, he was sure of it. But his mind shut down and he became silent, not knowing how to continue.

She was also silent for a period of time. But she hadn't given up on the subject. Not yet, anyway, as her next question pointed out.

"Obviously it has something to do with power, or giving up power and control, don't you think?" she finally asked as she sat back down on the rock and looked off into the distance.

"That's seems to be part of it," he agreed, coming back to it. "But, like I said, I don't really think it's all that simple." he continued, knowing that nothing was simple anymore, as long as he was in her presence. "Do you?" he asked as he approached the place where she sat, and lowered himself, being careful where he faced so that he wouldn't have to look directly at her nudity. That would never work. If they needed to talk about abstractions some more, that was the only way he would be able to manage it.

"Apparently not," she replied. "Because I made the decision to resign my office and completely change my lifestyle if I ever got back at least a couple of weeks ago. Maybe even a month, and I'm still here."

"I'm glad you are," Jack blurted out. "Or, at least I, well, you know what I mean. You shouldn't be here at all as far as I'm concerned but then, how else would I have met you?"

"Thank you," she said quietly.

"Sorry," he responded after some thought. "That's being selfish. I didn't mean it quite that way. I think if anyone deserves to go home, it's probably you. At least as much as Howard. You took care of him and everything."

"It's okay, Jack. I understand," she said, so full of conflicting emotion. Both happy and sad.

More silence. Then, "I never would have thought it possible," Jack said at last.

"What?" she asked.

"To, ... damn," he said.

"What's wrong?" she asked.

"I... Nothing, I guess. Just so many things happening at once," he said, lying about it, trying to push aside the power of her presence and the overwhelming attraction he felt for her.

Then, hoping she hadn't seen how weak he was feeling, he brought the conversation back to where they had begun. He knew it was dumb but for lack of something better he asked her why she thought she was still there, since she was just as serious about her intentions to give up her position and power as Howard had been. But just as quickly, he regretted it, hoping she wouldn't take it the wrong way.

"I wish I knew," she said without offense. "And I agree with you. It seems much too complex for there to be some singular criteria involved. And who is doing the deciding? Is there some kind of grand, super committee sitting up there in the sky taking notes and making ongoing updates about people's behavior? That's pretty spooky, isn't it, like God back in biblical days. Misbehave, turn into a pillar of salt. Or wind up on an island with the world's biggest loonies. And that reminds me. Did you hear about the President landing in the grass with his pants down when he disappeared?"

"God no. Tell me."

Jack had never heard anything so funny in his life and he

laughed accordingly. Then he told her the other half of the story. How he had actually been on the airplane when the President had disappeared.

"But on the grass with his pants down in front of all those people. Geez. If only it could have made the six oclock news back home."

"That and him sitting on a rock patting the Secretary of State on the butt in a White House made of sticks."

"Do you think the good citizens would still vote for him?"

"Unfortunately, yes."

"Which says that so far most everyone has missed the point. Of course when it comes to human affairs the pendulum always seems to have to swing pretty far in the wrong direction before enough people get the message. So, who knows how it will end."

"Well, if it is a wake up, by who's decision? Doesn't mankind have free will? Don't we have the freedom to foul things up if we want? Maybe even to destroy ourselves as a race? Who has the right to interfere with that? God?"

"Perhaps. If there were a God in that sense. But if there were and he or she was a caring God, things never would have gotten this far out of hand to begin with. And if God were all powerful and wise, why mess around this way. Why not just show up one day and issue a mandate? If anyone disobeyed, start throwing lightening bolts around. Or do the pillar of salt thing. Then there wouldn't be any doubt as to who was in charge of what."

"Or inject them full of universal love or some other such obscene thing. When you try to put religion in the equation, the whole scenario becomes as completely ridiculous as President Drukus with his pants down," Katherine said, but this time she didn't laugh at the thought of it.

"And that's the beauty of religion," Jack agreed. "Nothing has to make sense. If it did, the world would have something much better to turn to for guidance at times like this."

Katherine nodded and they went back to being silent again. "Hungry? she asked somewhat later.

"I am," Jack said. "And why didn't I think of bringing something with me when I came. I went right through the fruit trees on the way."

"No problem. There's more than enough in the cave. I'll get it," Katherine said and got to her feet.

Jack rose also. "Let me help," he said.

"Why don't you fluff up that pile of leaves. We can sit there. It might be more comfortable. And give me your jacket. It will be easier to carry that way."

Within minutes she was back. This time she was wearing her tattered pajama top. Every bit still as beautiful in Jack's eyes, he was glad she had put it on. He hoped that he could now at least look at her when then talked without feeling like he was being leacherous.

"The cook is off duty," she kidded. "So it's bananas, pears and apples for the main course and grapes for desert."

"If I had known for sure I was coming I would have brought wine and candles," Jack said, realizing he was still in trouble. She might no longer be completely topless but every time she moved, her breasts bounced beautifully inside her worn garment. Howard must have had a will of iron, he decided. How in the hell did he ever stand it? But, knowing Howard for what he was, he had probably kept his resolve intact. Even if he, they had, damn, what difference did it make under the circumstances, anyway? None, he hoped.

"Yes," she said, and put the food down. "That would have been nice."

They sat down face to face. He took a banana, partly peeled it and handed it to her, then took one for himself and they ate in silence. When they were done, she said, "It really bothers you, doesn't?"

"What does?"

"Me, without a top on."

"You have no idea. You'd bother me if you had on a down filled parka."

"Really," she teased and gave a little laugh. Then she said, "Well, in case you haven't noticed, Jack Briggs, you bother me too."

Speechless, Jack could do nothing but stare into her eyes. She rose, got on her knees facing him, took both his hands, placed them on her breasts and leaned into him, kissing him on the mouth.

ALONE AGAIN

It was by far the longest any man had ever made love to her in her life. And on top of a large boulder at that. Love and tenderness and lust and stored up passion, over and over. The afternoon disappeared into rythms of ecstacy and brought the full moon at dusk which rose higher and higher and moved a good distance across the sky before they fell asleep where they were, too exhausted to climb down to the cave. Katherine slept deeply, waking but once to put her pajamas back on because the night had cooled. Then she snuggled up tightly to Jack and began to dream about being back in her own room in Colorado. An evening breeze was coming through the open bedroom window. Early morning sunlight streamed in and warmed the wall next to her bed. Her soft, delicious, comfortable bed. She was in a bed, her own bed, sleeping. Her bed, with clean silk sheets and soft, fluffy pillows. What a beautiful dream. She could lie there forever.

Then she heard bird songs. Birds. Beautiful creatures. How she had missed them. One of them in particular was very stricking. It sounded just like that funny little canyon wren who used to sit on the window sill and belt out his repertoire, his voice sliding down the musical scale as he sang. There, he did it again. It sounded so close. Suddenly she sat bolt upright and stared. Chest thrown out, head cocked to one side, right there in front of her, the little bird stared back. Then he opened his beak and began singing his heart out all over again.

Shocked and overwhelmed, it was impossible to move, but she knew it to be true. She had returned. No need to pinch herself or to scream and shout. Her heart might burst instead, from the extreme emotion of it, and it took a long time to assimilate the change. But where was Jack? she agonized, and ran her hands down over her body where he had touched her and held her and re lived the night in her mind. Oh my god, she sighed. Why wasn't he there with her? Where was he? Nothing was more important and nothing was more devasting than to be there without him.

At last she was able to get out of bed and go to the large mirror over the dresser. What she saw was almost as shocking as being back. Except for the fact that she was still wearing the same old tattered pajamas she had put on in the middle of the night, she almost didn't recognized herself. Slowly, she removed the top and let it drop to the floor. Her hair was matted and dirty and sunbleached and nearly a foot longer than she had ever worn it, but it was otherwise healthy enough looking. Her skin, although deeply tanned, was also soft and smooth and blemish free. She was slimmer, too, and in spite of the dirt and the hair on her legs, she thought she looked younger than before. Certainly she was in far better physical condition than she had ever been. Happily, then, she stretched and turned and viewed herself from as many angles as possible. She must get in the shower and clean up, but so far she liked what she saw.

There was soap and shampoo and a razor and brushes and soft, thick towels. It was all such sheer ecstacy. She had almost forgotten about them. Such simple things, but they would have been treasures back on the island. She would never take anything for granted again.

Much later, toweled and dried and combed and brushed, she looked in the mirror again, even more pleased with herself. Then she went to the closet. At least the bastard hadn't thrown her clothes out yet. It took a long time rummaging through the luxury of so many different things to wear but in the end the only thing that seemed comfortable was a simple pair of jeans and the loosest fitting sweat shirt she could find. Then, at last, it occured to her that she was hungry. What time was it, she wondered. She almost went to the window to look at the suns position in the sky but then remembered about clocks.

It was still early, not even seven oclock and the house was quiet. Maybe he's not even home, she thought. She hoped he wasn't. Not yet, anyway. She needed time to adjust. Quietly she walked down the long, carpeted hall of their large two story house to the other end. The door stood open and she peered in. There were two nude bodies on the bed. A dark haired woman lay with her arm draped across her husband's over sized chest. Slowly and very cauitously, Katherine pulled the door nearly shut and quietly backed away. Downstairs, she made her way to the kitchen and to the refrigerator. Well, he must not have fired the maid either because it was fully stocked. My god. Eggs and sausage and hash browns and toast and, wow, coffee. It had been at least seven months since she had a cup of coffee. Maybe longer. And that was something else she had to do. Look at a calender.

Anxiously, she piled a huge mound of things on the counter by the stove and began to cook. Fifteen minutes later she was outside on the patio ready to make a glutton of herself but the colors of the flowers growing in the yard distracted her. Carrying her over loaded plate, she stuffed her face as she went, making the rounds of all the potted plants and flower beds, stopping at each new variety that was in bloom. Of course she remembered them because she had planted them in the first place. But she had never seen them like this before in all their vividness. Eating, stopping, bending over to look closely and to smell the different fragrances, setting down her dish to gently touch some of the petals, verbally saying hello to them, telling them how beautiful they were, then back to the table to sit and stare, impossibly trying to absorb it all. Finally, a second cup of coffee, and a third. She was almost done with the third cup when she heard a noise and looked up.

"My god. Katherine. For Christ's sake. Is that you? What the hell is going on?" her husband exclaimed as he stood there in his overweight nudeness, his lady friend hiding behind him. Then, realizing the implications of the other woman's presence, he motioned her away.

"It's okay, Max," Katherine said. "She can stay. Just go put some clothes on first."

"But Katherine. Where have you been, where did you come from, how did you get here? Jesus. I thought you were dead, or gone forever, along with all the others. Does this mean they are back, too? My god, is it true? Think of the implications."

"I don't have the answer to any of your questions, Max. And, even if I did, I'm certainly not ready to discuss it yet. Besides, how can I talk to you this way. You look so ridiculous with your big belly sticking out and that bare assed woman hiding behind you."

Badly embarrassed and confused by Katherine's appearance and attitude, Max and the woman retreated back into the house. Five minutes later they were dressed and back, Max stammering his head off, trying overly hard to be friendly and accomodating.

"Cut the crap, Max," Katherine said with bold authority. "Go make yourselves some breakast, then pack your bags. I want you out of here in an hour."

"But," he started to say, and stopped. Then he said, "God, Katherine. I can't. It's Tuesday and I have a whole series of business appointments. And if all the top execs are back along with you I'd better be first in line with my stock broker. Damn. I can make a killing if I hurry."

The use of the word Tuesday shook her badly. There had been no days of the week back on the island. They were all the same and after the first few weeks no one even bothered to try and keep track. There were no months, either. Or schedules and meetings and outside obligations. There was only a timeless time and a simple flowing of days and nights all ironed out together, flowing by. Suddenly she felt off balance and insecure and unresponsive. Readjusting was going to take a while. A long while. No doubt about that. But it didn't change her resolve. "Sorry, Max," she finally replied. "That will all have to wait. An hour is all you get."

It was early morning, the sun was almost up. Jack was lying

there next to Katherine, halfway between sleep and awake, his arm draped over her, his hand under her pajama top feeling the warmth of her body when suddenly and without warning, she was gone. It was instantaneous. She was gone just as Howard was gone. Shocked, he sat up quickly, knowing there was no place to go and look for her. She was irretrievably gone. He got to his feet and swore loudly. Damnit, damnit, damnit. This most intriguing, beautiful woman, gone. Damnit. Why so soon? Why couldn't they have had more time together? A few more days. Something. Better yet, why couldn't he have gone with her? He swore again and was silent. But then he told himself that really was being selfish. At least she had made it back and she had been on the island for a lot longer than he had. Good for her, he thought at last, and there was some blessing in the idea. With that he climbed down from the boulder and went to the creek where he got a drink and washed himself as best he could. Now what, he wondered. With both Howard and Katherine no longer around, the situation reminded him of the vacant house he had left behind back home. It was all too intense. He would never be able to stay here by himself, either.

Back at the cave he ate the rest of the fruit that was stored there and left. Might as well do some more exploring, he decided, setting out in the opposite direction from which he had originally come. Circling the island in that way the first group of people he should encounter were the Japanese. Since one of the languages he spoke was Japanese, why not give it a try. That's where it had all began, anyway, hadn't it. He had been on the plane with the President, headed towards Japan. And then the President had gone into the lavatory. And now, here they all were. Americans and Japanese and everyone else. Undoubtedly, the Japanese leaders they had set out to see had to be here too. Maybe he would at last get to meet them.

BLOODY GROUND

With all the walls and the conflict over the food belt, Jack stayed high on the mountain and descended into their territory from above. Prepared for the worst, he was not met with the hostility he might have been, however, but with open curiosity instead. Although the Japanese had been at extreme odds with the American administration back home and their underhanded politics, they didn't blindly hate all Americans and hadn't been gunning them down in their city streets like some parts of the world were doing. Feeling relatively safe, Jack wandered around, reacquainting himself with the language and the mannerisms, then began looking for a single receptive individual in ernest. At last he came across an older man who looked in need of clothing, and offered him the jacket he had carried with him in exchange for his indulgence. The man listened and bowed, seemingly impressed with Jack's facility for his language, offered him a a gift in return, as was customary, even though it was only an apple and they sat down together under a large tree to talk.

Jack had chosen wisely. The man seemed to have accurate information on nearly everything that was happening on the island. Probably the most important thing that he learned was what was going on within the Arab community. When he did hear it, however, he was not all that surprised. Actually, what else would one have expected?

For the last few weeks large segments of the Arab world had been busy grinding sharp points on sticks with the use of rocks, gathering up tree branches that could be used as clubs and accumulating palm sized stones that could be thrown easily. It was totally in keeping with foregone history. More than two hundred years of European interference and pillaging of treasures and resources and more than half a century of American oil piracy, Christian contempt for Middle Eastern values, political meddling and disruption, covert assasinations, cover ups and conniving had left an indelible mark on the middle east psyche. The Arabs may have all too often seemed to have turned their backs, but they had not forgotten. Resentment had accumulated and pressures had built and no one had had the good sense to stop stirring the explosive mixture, especially the arrogant Americans. Not even here on the island. It wasn't a time bomb, it was a human bomb waiting for a spark to set it off.

True to form, Stanley Drukus, President of the United States, international trouble maker, bar none, was that spark. And his delusions of granduer. And a maliscious, semi fascist Secretary of Defence with a snarly face, and an overly agressive group of war hawks from the Pentagon and a disenfranchised group of followers who took pride in beating up anyone who appeared to be weaker, all of whom were still egging him on, right here on this small atoll, pushing him into ongoing confrontations he was only too happy to become involved in. Little had changed.

It had been the same back at home. The only difference was that, back there, the President had also been vehemently supported by voiciferous American conservatives and an equally disinfranchised American public who seemed to have obtained sadistic pleasure from seeing their nation bomb, straff and murder innocent men, women and children of other defenceless nations whose only fault was that they had been so bold as to tell the Americans to mind their own business. So, righteously, the President had been the front man, always able to convince the taxpayers that it was sound foreign policy to continue spending billions of dollars on war. So what if they were short on health care and social services and their standard of living had taken a beating. At least they didn't have to spend their hard earned money on those trite video games anymore. What for. Turn on the TV. The news was full of blood and guts from the front lines of ongoing aggression. There were real cities being blown to hell and real bodies lying in the streets and real guns going off and real body parts flying around and it was addictive as hell and almost as good as a chemical high anyday.

And then, after all that, Drukus had the affrontery to declare that he was once again going to try and democratize the entire Middle East. No. It was not a new idea. It was a resurrected something that had been tried once before by a equally surreptitious President and even greater dotterel in the too quickly forgotten past with disasterous results. But where that man had failed, he, Drukus was the one person who could now make it happen. He knew it for a fact. Just ask him. Of course all of that was back in that other world where the administration had nuclear weapons, stealth bombers, high tech weaponry and a wealth of misguided adherents who were willing to march off and commit further human atrocities in the continuing name of protecting America's freedom. But, so what? In spite of the fact that none of that armed might existed here on the island, the President still kept on pushing. Unfortunately, threats were the only real weapons he had but he used them lavishly. The major one was, "If you don't cooperate, when we all get off of here and back home to the real world I will have your foreign aid cut off and we'll barracade and boycott and bomb you if necessary."

The Chinese laughed until they hurt, the Europeans scoffed and the rest just shook their heads but still he persisted, and coerced and intimidated.

"Just wait," he would say and harangued some more.

But they were empty threats and most groups knew it. To the best of their knowledge no one had ever gotten off the island as yet except by getting themselves killed or by committing suicide. So who was he kidding. They were all here to the inglorious end. Whatever that might turn out to be. So let him yell and threaten. He'll die here with the rest of us, they said and turned away.

Still, in spite of all the opposition, he somehow managed to build up a haphazard coalition of allies, even though most of them would be totally valueless in a tough situation. Didn't matter. It sounded good. Then he came back to the Arabs and went to work on them, carefully at first because he soon became extremely afraid of the very tall, bearded one with the turbin who always stood out at the perimeter looking at him, looking through him with fathomless eyes, studying, waiting, waiting. But then he surrounded himself with fifty of the biggest and strongest Amercians who happened to be there with him and he became bolder, almost passionate in his quest.

The Arabs, meanwhile, had listened but said nothing, then had withdrawn into the shelter of thick forest farther around the island and isolated themselves, now seriously engaged in making the weapons the President knew nothing about as yet. At first he was relieved by the quiet. In fact he misguidedly viewed the lack of ongoing response as some kind of victory. Surely they had been intimidated and given up, he told his staff. But then, after a few weeks of absolutely nothing, he began to worry. He also missed the ongoing conflict. The six additional Arabs he had his men capture some weeks back had also been tortured to death and he had no one else whose fingers he could break, so he was uptight and frustrated. Quiet was distressing. Confrontation, however, was a chance to flex some muscle, a chance to intimidate and control and give him identity. The head of the FBI had been ordered to capture some more but had been unsuccessful thus far. Without that, there was nothing, and it made him feel unimportant and impotent. And that was where Jack erred. Leaving the Japanesse behind and wandering the island, he had become too open in his visits to the American area. One day someone from the administration finally recognized him.

"Jack who?" the President said when he was first informed.

"Briggs. Jack Briggs. He was on the plane with you when you disappeared. The nuclear weapons expert and the guy who speaks Japaness and about five other languages."

"Okay. And so what?"

"So what?" one of his personal advisors said to him. "The Arabs live over there close to the Japanese. Not only does he speak Japanese, I believe he also understands some of the middle eastern dialects."

"Yeah but he was never a power player or anything, so what's your point?"

"My point is maybe we could get him to go in there and gather some intelligence for us."

"And then what?"

"Then we might have a better idea how to play those damn Arabs. We haven't gotten a bit of information out of any of the ones we've tortured to death so far. And, if that doesn't work, maybe he could help smooth things over with the Japs and they could be our allies, too. If we're really going to take charge of things here on the island we need all the help we can get. What do you think?"

"I think it's the best idea I've had in a long time. Now get him in here so we can talk to him."

"Sorry," Jack said, once they had confronted him. "I'm not interested."

"But you're part of my advisory staff," the President said, "and that is your new assignment."

"And I'm afraid I must refuse."

"You can't refuse. You're on my staff."

"Was on your staff. A lot of things have changed since then."

"I don't remember terminating your employment. Did I terminate him?" the President asked of the same personal advisor who had recognized Jack to begin with, and then answered his own question. "No I didn't and I ought to know if I did or not."

"Maybe not," Jack said. "But your disappearance did. And if that' not good enough, I still refuse."

"Well. You're still an American and it's your patriotic duty to follow my orders."

"An American by birth but even that is getting to be rather embarrassing. Especially here. So that's as far as it goes. And in my opinion, the kind of patriotism and blind loyalty to nationalism you are talking about is what got us in so much trouble to begin with. And if that makes me a traitor, so be it. I will not help you in your misguided mission while there is still some chance for peace."

"Well, just be careful that I don't charge you with treason. You wouldn't stand a chance defending yourself because I'm about to appoint a whole new Supreme Court and I don't need the approval of Congress on this one either, because they aren't even here."

"I'll keep that in mind," Jack said. "And you this. You don't have an ocean and a high tech military between you and your enemies on this small parcel of real estate and if you keep perpetuating your odious actions, you are headed for serious trouble."

"Ha," the President said, rising from behind his pile of stones desk, angry now. " Don't think you're fooling me with high toned words like odious. I know what that means so just you remember that if you're not for me, you're against me, so I hereby prohibit you from ever entering the American area again under threat of incarceration," he declared with hostility, his voice rising, while unconsciously his right hand grasped one of the many fist sized stones that his desk was made of.

"Thank you," Jack said, eyeing the stone in the President's hand, knowing full well that if the man actually picked it up to throw at him, the situation would become far more personal than he had hoped for. But, what would be the point in bloodying the man's nose another time? The French President had already done it twice and the President obviously hadn't learned a thing. He certainly wasn't worth that kind of an encounter. Still, Jack stood his ground and stared firmly back into the squinty eyed face until the President dropped his rock and finally looked away. Then Jack left.

"Man, I'd sure like to break some of his fingers," the President said when Jack was out of range. Now get the head of the FBI in here. We need some fresh prisoners to interogate."

Well, he didn't have to worry about being recognized any longer, Jack thought as he walked away. But he was not about to stay out of the area, either. He still had a few friends there and if he wanted to see them, he would. As for his one man effort to make people more aware, he didn't know. Up until then he had always pointed out to almost every American he came in contact with just how much the rest of the world despised them and where that might lead. Unfortunately, most of them negated his claims and brushed them aside. "We have the most powerful nation on earth. Even here on this island," they assured him, parroting the President. "They'd have to be crazy to go up against us."

"Right," Jack would reply and move on. And, when he was away from the American area and there were Arabs around, he would wrap what was left of his shirt around his head, making a turbin of sorts. He didn't really speak Arabic as some people claimed but as long as no one looked too closely or tried to engage him in real conversation, it seemed to work well enough. And, having the easy way with languages that he did, he also listened closely, and learned key greetings and expressions that quickly became of value. For the most part, however, he spent his time away from all the turmoil. He had found another vantage point part way up the mountain on the populated side of the island and spent most of his nights there, just in case, but he still came down in the early morning to walk through the various areas and see what was going on. It was on one of these ventures that he learned the distressing news.

The Americans were capturing Arabs and torturing them. The President had recently bragged about it to the English PM, the PM had told the Australians and the Australians told the French and within days the infamy was common knowledge. Even the Arabs knew it by now, although the President kept dismissing that possibility. After all, they had never mentioned it and had removed themselves from all contact with the Americans. Certainly they never would have behaved that way if they knew the truth. As for the rest of the world, it was no big surprise. Americans do what Americans do. There were no human rights organizations on the island. Why get involved? Jack, however, was appalled.

The moon had come up sometime after midnight and by then Jack was inside the American area searching. Having to be cautious and quiet, it took him nearly an hour to find the captives. They were all there, all six of them, all stripped naked and each tied to a separate tree, their own clothes used to gag and bind them. Surprizingly, however, there seemed to be only one guard on duty and he was sitting on the ground with his back up against his own tree some distance away. Equally odd, and clear enough in the moonlight, the guard had long grey hair and a long gray beard. Hardly a threat to most anyone, Jack thought. Were the Americans that callous? Was the old guy even awake? It was hard to tell since he was so quiet.

Carefully, Jack moved in closer, stopped and threw a small stone in the direction of the prisoners to check. Although he had appeared that way the guard had not been asleep. He looked around briefly but did not get to his feet, shifting his position instead, trying to get more comfortable. Under the circumstances Jack could have walked in and easily overpowered the old fellow but he didn't want him to see his face and be recognized later. Since his hair and beard weren't very long, that would be much too easy. Of course he could find a rock and bash the guy's head in. But, he didn't want to kill him. He only wanted to rescue the prisoners. With that he got down on his hands and knees. Carefully, like a cat stalking its prey, he moved in. But then he stopped and backed on out, moving a ways into the woods. How silly. If he was going to behave like a bandit, why not look like one. With that he removed his shirt and gently tore off one sleeve, put the shirt back on and tied the sleeve across his face like a bandana.

When he came up behind the guard this time, he was walking upright and still made it all the way in without being noticed. A short pause, two quick steps and he was around the tree, one hand over the guard's mouth, the other grabbing him by the neck and lifting him.

"Not a word and I won't have to hurt you," Jack said quietly. "Do you understand?"

The old man nodded, surprise and fear in his eyes as Jack removed his hand from his throat.

"Good. Off with your own clothes now," Jack told him, "and quickly."

The man took off his shirt and then his trousers and Jack had him back up against the tree. That done, Jack tied his hands together with the pants legs and used the shirt to make a gag. Then he made his way to the prisoners, motioned then to silence, and began untying them one by one, indicating that they should dress and wait. He was nearly done with the last one when a loud voice boomed out. "Who the hell are you? What do you think you're doing?"

Damnit! There had been a second guard all along, off somewhere and now returned. Too bad for Jack. This one was much younger and stronger and quickly had him by the arm. He had also torn the mask off Jack's face before he could react. Then Jack's first blow caught the man in the stomach. The second was a hard uppercut to the jaw and down he went. That over, the last prisoner was soon freed and Jack was leading them through the trees, determined to escort them back to their own area. Fortunately, they hadn't been held very long and were all strong enough to make the journey. The only problem that remained was the second guard who had gotten a look at Jack's face in the moonlight.

A few hundred yards away from their home territory, Jack bid them goodbye in broken Arabic. They, in turn, still seemed to be puzzled by having been rescued by an American but three of them thanked him before walking away. By then it was getting light out. The sun would be up in half an hour and Jack headed back into the cover of the trees. It was then that he heard the sounds. They came from a very large group of men coming his way. Staying well out of sight he watched as spear and club carrying Arabs moving quickly through the night towards the south end of the island, the place he just rescued the prisoners from. There were at least a hundred of them, probably more. It had finally happened. But there was nothing he could do about it now. Even if he ran all the way back he would never be able to get there in time to warn anyone.

The actual battle was not a major event, however, by most standards. Once it began, it had lasted less than twenty minutes. When it was finally over the ground was soaked in blood. Looking at it, though, no one would ever have been able to tell if it was American blood or Arab blood, Christain blood or Muslim blood. Shocking and inconceivable as it might be to some, all humans bleed and all human blood is the same. But in spite of all that, the truth was that not a drop of the blood was Arabic and all the President's fifty strong bodyguards lay dead in a pile, along with another twenty or thirty British and Americans who had been too foolhardy to flee. As for the President, he was purposely captured alive, along with the Vice President, the Secretary of Defense and the British Prime Minister. Their clothes were stripped from them and used as bindings. Then they were dragged off to the Arab territory and lashed to the trunks of trees as runners went out to summon the rest of the world leaders. The trial would begin when the sun reached its zenith.

The list of charges was long, the deliberation short. Thousands of innocent men, women and children were dead because of these four. Unanimously, they were all guilty of war crimes. But, wait a minute, said the Norwegians, the Swedes, the Danes, the French and, with the exception of the British, almost the entire European community. They are also guilty of crimes against the rest of humanity. They had refused to abide by the Kyoto initiative, to reduce pollution and green house gasses in particular and had placed the future of the entire world in extreme jeopardy.

"Good enough," was the answer. The penalty was still death. Hang them, that was the way most of the leaders wanted it done.

"No. Not good enough," said the Arabs. "That is much too easy, we have a better way."

"What is that?" they were asked.

"We first need to see if they can bleed. They will be given food and water and kept alive for as long as possible. Everyday, however, everyone with a grievance will be given a rough piece of stone and allowed to rub away a small patch of skin and draw some blood. When enough skin has been worn away and enough blood has been drawn, the criminals will die. Hopefully, it will not be quick."

"Yes, but that Vice President person is a woman. That seems a little cruel and unusual."

"Yes, but who was out there helping promote all the atrocities in a loud voice? And who said all the killing was vindicated because the rest of us were infidels? And who does not dress properly and cover herself but flaunts herself like a harlot instead. And, well.... that's enough. Isn't it? How else should she be dealt with? Do you want her to have a quick death instead?"

"Well, maybe you're right," agreed the European leaders. "But we will not hurry the process by scraping away at them, too. Instead, we will come every day and jeer and point out how badly they have abused the rest of mankind with their arrogance and stupidity and help you keep them alive to suffer as long as possible."

"That is very thoughtful," some of the Arabs stated. "And we thank you."

"But wait," a handful of other men stated as they came forward. "How can you do this? They saved us from the hell of our dictators."

"Yes. And what do you Sunnites know with all your self proclaimed tolerance. They killed your aunts, uncles, brothers, sisters and children. Do they not matter?"

"Perhaps, but they are dead and we are still alive."

"Yes. And now you have explained how it was that these bastards were able to get away with it."

"Perhaps, but you Shi'ites are such trouble makers. And who appointed you Caliph anyway?"

"I am not caliph. I am the Grand Ayatollah of my people. And since we are the ones who captured these criminals, we are the ones who will decide what is proper punishment for them. So if you want to do something for Allah, go capture your own prisoners and deal with them the way you think is proper."

Shouting and name calling between the Arabs quickly broke out and it looked like another battle would be waged amongst themselves. Before any blows could be landed, however, the Secretary of State came running in, sobbing madly, throwing her huge body down in agony at the feet of the President. "You can't do this," she wailed. "God will punish you."

"More than likely God will punish us if we don't," they said, suddenly unified again, whereupon the President had the audacity to join in.

"Ha," he said with an immense smirk. "You infidels forget one thing. God is on our side, not yours."

"Well, ha to you, Mr President," they replied in turn. "If God were on your side how did he ever let you get yourself into such a mess as this?"

With that the President's face turned blank and he became too confused to respond. But the Secretary was undeterred. "I'm not leaving him," she said. "You will have to torture him over my dead body."

"No," they said. "We will punish him over your live body and soon you will get tired of his blood dripping in your face and leave. If not, we will string you up too. With all your bulk there will be a lot more skin to scrap off and there will be more fun for everyone because it will take a much longer time for you to die."

Back in their own area the rest of the Americans were shocked and apalled. What affrontery. How dare anyone attack the United States of America's elite citizonry like that. Who in the hell did they think they were? They would pay dearly for it, one way or another. That was for sure. But first they must rescue the President and the three others and bring the Secretary of State home before the few clothes she had left got all blood soaked.

Unfortunately, General Wells, Head of the Joint Chiefs of Staff, had been killed in the original melee so General Marcus, also with five stars to his credit, took charge. He assembled everyone who was in the military, the FBI, the NSI, the NSA, the BMC and civilian law enforcement. The Heads of Homeland Security and the CIA were excluded, however, since they had obviously underestimated the Arab threat by an unforgivable amount and were now being considerd for trial by military tribunal for deriliction of duty. In the meantime it was their assigned duty to drag all the dead bodies down to Dead Man's Cove where they could rot in peace, since there was no other way to get ride of them. Not a pleasant job for sure because, among other things, the island was lacking such critical items as body bags.

"Listen up," General Marcus said in a gruff voice to the nearly one hundred dedicated individuals assembled in the clearing before him. "This is to be a covert insertion into enemy territory. They will never expect us to regroup so quickly," he said confidently, "so we will go tonight, just as the moon breaks over the water. There will be a diversionary force of all the non military people and a main rescue party comprised of the rest of us. I will personally spearhead that group into the heart of the enemy occupied sector, secure our position around the President, release the captives and extract everyone safely back to our own area. The diversionary force will..." he went on, outlining all the minute details of the mission.

"But what will we use for weapons, General?" someone in the group asked. "They have all those sharp sticks and clubs."

"Surprise, gentlemen. Surprise. That will be our greatest ally. Most of those people will be lying around bragging about their foray into our midst and sucking on those red grapes like they're always doing so they won't have time to pick up their sticks or clubs. From that point on we use our intellects. We are all educated men. Certainly we ought to be able to outsmart a bunch of camel jockeys whose brains have atrophied in the desert heat. What do you say to that?"

"Hip, hip, horah," came a shout from the rear.

"Good," said the General. "Give me another one."

"Hip, hip, horah," went a dozen voices.

"Better," said the General. "Now, all together." And together it was, as the multitude joined in for the final round that was heard half way round the island.

The Head of the FBI, leader of the diversionary force was confused. So was everyone else who was with him. They should have been well within enemy lines by now but there had not been a single Arab in sight. They waited briefly, then went several hundred yards farther. Still no one. How could they create a diversion if there was no one there to have an encounter with, they questioned. Finally someone thought they heard voices still farther ahead. Arab voices. Good, said their brave leader and hand signaled to keep going. Cautiously, they moved onward, alert and poised to whatever might appear before them. What they hadn't noticed, however, was that their group was steadily growing smaller and smaller from behind, like a lizard losing small pieces of it's tail. Maybe if they hadn't done so much whispering and feet dragging they would have noticed more of the muffled noises at the back of the line where, one by one, their members were being thumped on the head with stones and quietly dragged into the bushes. Eventually, the tail of the lizard had all but disappeared and, at last, when their number had been selectively reduced to ten or eleven, one of them turned around and said, "What the hell...?" but it was too late. Simultaneously, an equal number of Arabs stepped out from behind the trees that concealed them and dropped them in their tracks with a single blow each.

Thus far General Marcus thought he was doing considerably better. Skirting quickly from tree to tree, they had not encountered any resistence either, and considered themselves to be within striking distance of the target site. Another fifty yards and the General signaled a stop. They would wait here in silence until they heard the diversionary force let out the war cry they had agreed on earlier. But they waited in vain and they waited a long time. Regardless of what undeterminable thing might have happened, however, the General had made a commitment and was determined to press forward. They would free the President at all costs. He gave the signal to advance and they moved another hundred yards closer to their goal, then stopped again.

"What's that?" he whispered to the Colonel, who was right on his heels.

The Colonel put his hand to his ear. "Sounds like a woman whimpering, sir," he said. "Maybe it's the Secretary of State."

"Big as she is, she'd be a whimperer, all right," said the General. "That means she's at the President's feet. So pass the word and prepare to move in. General Max is to take the left flank, General Barnes on the right, and we'll go right down the middle."

Within a swift ten minutes the left flank had circled around and bumped into the right flank without incident of any kind. No one had seen or heard a single Arab. The same held true for the General. All he found was the Secretary of State, entirely alone, tied to a tree in the middle of a small clearing.

"What the hell..?" he said, also abiding by the rules of proper exclamation under the circumstances.

"They took him off in that direction about an hour ago," she sobbed loudly. "And I've been here all alone the whole time. It was awful. I've never been alone in my life."

"What do we do now?" the two four star generals asked the five star general.

"We came to rescue him and by god, we will rescue him," General Marcus stated. "Colonel, you untie the Secretary here and provide her overly ample bottom safe escort back home where you will stay by her side and protect her with your life if need be. The rest of us will proceed in the direction indicated until we either find the President and free him or until we engage the enemy and eliminate them. Now move out."

"Yes, Sir," they all said and saluted him in the moonlight.

Again, they advanced slowly into the night, every eye and ear focused forward, but again without regard to what was happening in the rear. Then, a silent hand over the mouth of the last dedicated soldier in the line to keep him from crying out, a quick thump on the head with a rock and a quiet lowering of the body to the ground to be carried away. Since the General's troops were all getting rather tired by then and the line gradually strung itself out further and further, the attritional process became rapidly more efficient. At last General Marcus stopped and turned around. All he saw was but three men behind them.

Once again in the tradition of the military, he said, "What the hell?" but once again it was far too little and far too late. A dozen men armed with sharp sticks stepped out from behind the trees and surrounded them. "What the hell," he repeated again in complete shock.

Then the tall man with the turbin and the cold, hard eyes that the President had come to fear, stepped forward and confronted him. "All Americans are evil and should be put to death," he said, "but we will spare you this one time if you will learn to leave the rest of the world alone."

"But you're just a damned terrorist," the General said. "You don't speak for the rest of the Arabs."

"And how do you know who I may or may not speak for?" he said. "One way or another they are my people and they have your President in custody. I'm just making sure they keep him until he has paid for his crimes. As for yourselves, be thankful you are still alive. Now go and tell the rest of your people to leave the rest of the world alone before we hang you up and peal your unwashed hides off."

Of course, Jack realized. What else was to be expected? The Americans were just too bullish and brazen not to have tried to get their leader back. Nor did they have a choice. They needed him as much as he needed them. Perhaps more. And whether or not the White House was but an outline on the ground made of sticks, or a bad dream, they still needed someone to report to and bring order to their lives. Never once did they see it as some utterly ridiculous,

144

silly game. Without structure, all would be lost. Sitting around in the sun philosophizing, enjoying the scenery and the climate would never do. Challenge, turmoil and problem resolution were what they lived for. Especially turmoil. That, and the taste of blood. The cause might be completely bogus, the morality of it shameful, the end result counter productive and debasing, but it didn't matter. As long as they kept themselves busy enough there wasn't time to think about the deeper aspects of their behavior or to question what they might be doing on the island to begin with. Obviously, there would be more trouble ahead.

After what had happened Jack spent most of his nights up on the mountain. Because of the wall Ivan and his companions had put up, however, it was always a rather long hike. To get back and forth he was forced to circumvent the wall's southern end. That meant he had to be at the beach during low tide to get around. If he misjudged or something happened, he was trapped, either up top or down below. Obviously, it was time to meet the one called Ivan, he decided after the second mishap and hoped nothing rash would happen in the process. Ivan had at least five hundred nasty looking men on his side and every damned one of them seemed to have a built in grudge against the rest of the world. But then, on the way over to seek him out Jack began to wonder. What a fool. Negotiate so he could freely use Ivan's gate? Good grief. With what? Maybe it would be best to find some unguarded portion of the wall to climb over and take his chances.

But still, he had never heard of Ivan or any of his men actually having killed anyone as yet. They had beat up a few, everyone knew that. But only after that someone, or someones, had tried to bully their way through the gate and gotten physical about it. That didn't seem too unreasonable under the circumstances. If the President had the right to try and declare the entire island to be a possession of the United States, Ivan and his men had the same right to build a wall and claim control over the food belt. Or did they? Didn't matter. Ivan's claim was backed with muscle, the President's with bluster. And that brought up another point. Ivan was one of the few people on the island who had earned some respect. So, what the hell. Even if Ivan told Jack to kiss his butt, he would still like to meet the man first hand.

NEW ALLIANCES

The guard at the gate seemed surprised to find him coming down from above. Who was he and who had let him through, the guard wanted to know. And how did he get up there in the first place?

"I came to see Ivan," Jack said, speaking in his best college acquired Russian, which evoked a brief look of surprise.

"You haven't answered any of my questions," the man still responded in turn.

"Nobody let me thru. I live up above most of the time. And I thought I might just stop by and meet Ivan. No offense to you, my good man, but he is the one in charge here so I thought it best to say hello directly. My name is Jack."

"Really now?" the man said, looking him over more carefully. And what makes you think he would like to see you?"

"I don't. Just thought I would ask."

"He is a very busy man," the guard stated. "Why do want to see him?"

"It's a personal matter. But there is no hurry. I'll just sit here and wait."

"I can not leave my post until my relief comes. It may be quite a while. Are you sure you don't want to tell me what this is all about?"

"It's not a problem. My belly is full from all the food I ate, so I'll just take a little nap over there by that tree while I wait"

The guard looked at him suspiciously, trying to understand his motives. After a moment he turned his head and whistled loudly. Nine rough looking individuals quickly appeared.

"He wants to see Ivan," the guard said as the men promptly surrounded Jack.

"You look like you are lost," one of them said, gruffly enough. "Are you sure you don't need an escort back to the gate?"

"Happily, if you like. You can show me after I have had a chance to talk to Ivan."

"You are a bold one," the man said, pulling himself taller. "Do you have an appointment. Ivan only sees people who have made an appointment."

"No. But maybe one of you would be so kind as to go and ask," Jack said as they looked him over even closer. "Well. Either way," Jack continued. "Since there are so many of you I guess you can all just beat the hell out of me. Or you can leave me alone and let me sit down while someone goes and talks to Ivan. I promise not to run away."

The biggest one of the bunch said, "Okay, whoever you are. Come with us. We'll go ask him and then maybe we will still beat the hell out of you. What do you think of that?" he said with a big grin that was joined in by all.

Surrounded by the pack, Jack was taken about a quarter mile along the upper side of the wall until they came to an almost fort like, rocky outcropping. They turned there and made their way up the slope another hundred yards into a small, flat meadow where about a dozen men were gathered, some watching, but most of them on their hands and knees playing a game like marbles with small, round stones. The big man, apparent leader of group, went over to the marble players, bent down beside one of them and spoke for a brief moment.

The one spoken to nodded, then put up his hand as a signal to wait. It was his turn at the game. He bent lower, eyeballed his target and thumbed his small stone off with a vengence.

"Ha," he said with delight, then got up, turned around and looked over at Jack. After a short pause he moved nearer. It had to be Ivan. Jack watched him closely, trying to determine what kind of trouble he might have gotten himself into. It was hard to tell. Ivan was just as bearded and long haired and bedraggled as all of the rest of the men on the island. Still, there was still a certain demeanor to him as he stood and carried himself. He would have stood out in a crowd wherever he was.

Stopping directly in front of Jack, Ivan gazed at him intently. "And what can I do for you?" he questioned in a firm voice, while motioning to the men that he wanted some privacy.

Jack waited till they were alone before speaking. "You must be Ivan, so I will get right to the point," he said, again in his Russian.

"Good," Ivan responded, continuing to look him over carefully. "It is the only way to do things."

"My name is Jack Briggs and I would like to have free access to your gate in the wall back there, to come and go as I please."

"Well. That is to the point, all right. But really now. Are you someone special that I should give you such a priviledge?"

"Probably not," Jack replied. "But I thought we might be able to talk about it."

"Well, I don't know," Ivan said, now switching to English that was every bit as good as Jack's Russian. "I have found few Americans I like doing business with."

It was Jack's turn to look surprised.

"Yes," Ivan continued. "I can honestly say that. I did actually live in your country for a few years. So, let's continue in English. I could use the practice just like you and your Russian. And tell me why you want to discuss this priviledge you ask for. Don't you think you need to do a little work for your food like everyone else?"

"I don't need it for the food. I can get all I want here or elsewhere. I would just like to have a shorter way up and down the mountain."

"What for? What's up there? All the people are down below."

"Sometimes I like to be away from all the craziness so I can get a good nights sleep."

"You have a place up there?"

Jack shrugged in reply.

"Makes a little sense, I suppose. But you're still an American, aren't you? That doesn't say much in my book."

"There's little I can do about that. But that doesn't mean I agree with what they are doing."

"That is good to hear. With that attitude maybe we can negotiate. What do you have to bargain with?"

"Not much. Maybe nothing. I'm sure you have a lot more than I do. And now that you mention it I can't possibly imagine what I might offer you that you don't already have?"

Ivan laughed heartily. "Are you joking? Here, in this place? How about a bathtub with hot water and soap? How about a stove with an oven and some freshly baked bread? How about some vodka? Yes, Vodka would be very nice. Can you do that?"

Jack laughed also. "No. I was thinking about making some wine, however. But if that were available it would probably only add to the craziness."

"Wine, huh? Maybe we can talk about that some more, sometime. But for now you are saying that you really have nothing to bargain with. So why should I grant you your wish?"

"I don't know. Maybe you shouldn't. I just thought I'd ask. And besides, I've heard so many bad things about you I thought I'd like to meet you and see for myself."

"So you think I am bad, is that it?"

"Not too bad. You do have a sense of humor."

"I hope so. It would be impossible to survive here without it. But having a reputation for being a bad ass, as you Americans say, certainly serves a purpose, wouldn't you agree?"

"It does have its advantages. Bad is all some of them understand."

"And what is it that you think about me, now that we have met?"

"Too early to tell but you sound reasonable enough and you didn't just arbitrarily have my head bashed in before we had a chance to talk."

"Yes. That would have been a presumptuous act. I try not to be so arbitrary about things. And since you didn't come to try and impress me or to bully me, I'll tell you what. I will pass the word and you may come and go as you choose. Maybe you can even stop and say hello once in a while."

"Well, thank you," Jack said, somewhat surprised. "I appreciate it. Good. Thanks again. I'll let you get back to the game you were involved in." And with that he headed back towards the gate in the wall.

"Wait," Ivan said before he had gone very far and Jack returned. "Even though you don't claim them, are you still able to mingle with the Americans?"

Jack shrugged. "Depends. I had a little disagreement with the President but now that the Arabs have him I feel fairly safe down there," he said, leaving out the part about having been seen by the prisoners' guard who had torn his mask off. "Which is not very often any more. Frankly, I prefer the Japanese. I have made some new friends there."

"Very good. But it is the Americans that do have something I want. Unfortunately, as you already know, they would love to also bash my head in if I were to go there. And those of my men, too."

"They would do worse than that, I'm afraid. So would half the other people on the island. But I can't help you with that."

"I know. It's quite hopeless at this point and I wouldn't even want you to try. It is something else that I have been concerned about."

"Okay. As long as I don't have to harm anyone, tell me, and I will see what I can do."

"Yes. Well, it's what I would call personal and frankly I am a bit embarrassed. But, who is to say," Ivan replied and looked at Jack carefully to see his reaction. Jack, however, remained neutral and waited patiently.

"Well, can you believe it. It seems so silly, I suppose, but, well, I would never speak of it to any of my own men. They would think I was being a fool. And maybe I am. So, Mr. Jack. Since maybe we can be friends I have to ask if you are familiar with this tall woman with the blue eyes. She is slim but built, as you might say. Dark hair, about my age, perhaps?"

Anyone else might have reacted differently but looking at Ivan's face and quickly remembering his own agony at having first lost his wife, Gail, and then Katherine, he had some idea of what might be on Ivan's mind.

"I don't think so," he was forced to reply, however. "Maybe if you could describe her a little more."

Ivan continued, providing Jack with everthing he could remember about her.

"Yes," he nodded at last. "I may know who you mean. She might be the one. She was an administration official in the Department of Education, if I'm right. Her name is Deanna Holt."

"Ahh, yes. Deanna. That is the name I heard. You know her then. That is good."

"I only know who she is. I've never come across her here."

"Well, it doesn't matter. Maybe she can teach me how to write in English," Ivan replied, trying to downplay his interest.

"Is that it? You want to learn to write English? Why? You certainly speak it quite well. Very well, actually."

"For a Russian, you mean? Would you believe I have a degree in political science from an American university? Maybe not. Doesn't matter," he stated and waited. "Well, okay, why not. The truth is that many weeks ago she would come up here when I was at the gate. But always in the company of a group of men who seemed jealous of her. Still, we could not help but keep looking at each other. Sometimes we got to say a few words before we were interrupted. It was clear to me that there was a lot of that chemistry stuff. I think she felt it, too. Then once we talked for several minutes while the men were gathering stones for the wall but when they caught us they seemed very angry. She has never returned since that day. I don't know. Maybe it sounds dumb to you but I have become concerned."

"Well, I can understand that. I just hope you don't want me to kidnap her for you, however."

"No, no. Nothing like that. That would prove nothing. I don't want to own her. I would just like to be able to talk with her some more. Maybe even spend some time together. With her permission, of course. That is what I want you to do if you could. Make the arrangements."

Now that was interesting, Jack thought. Must have been some strong chemistry. But, then maybe the woman didn't feel the same way. What then? What was he getting himself into? He didn't want to be pressured into compromising some poor woman just to have free access in and out of Ivan's area.

"I don't know," he replied. "I have never been a match maker before. Maybe she'll think I'm totally crazy. What then?"

"I assure you. It would be entirely up to her. All I ask is that you present the idea of a meeting."

Jack was still sceptical and his face reflected it. "If I could do such a thing, can you guarantee she would be safe?" he asked.

"I have a suspicion that she would be safer talking with me than being where she is," Ivan replied.

"How would you know that?"

"Because I saw how they treated her. And after she did not come up anymore I overheard some of them talking about her. It was not with good intentions, I assure you."

"You may well be right," Jack agreed at last. "I'll try and contact her."

"Good. I will pass the word. As I said, you may come and go freely in our territory regardless of the outcome. But I also ask that you hurry. After you learn what happened to the Americans last night, she may be in even more danger."

"I have a pretty good idea but I didn't stick around to see the outcome."

"Such fools," Ivan replied and went on to tell Jack about all the details.

"Not good," Jack agreed. But it was out of his hands. There was nothing he could have done. Whatever was underway would have been all over by the time he could have managed. But it was still was a huge escallation in the trouble between the island factions and he was sorry to hear about it. There were serious ramifications for everyone living there. Himself included. And what about the woman? He might be stupid to become involved but now that he had met Ivan... Well, the man was not an ogre or a criminal. And, in spite of all his power, Ivan was but a man out of character in his role, hooked on a woman who might bring him considerable trouble in the future. But then, what if Katherine was still here?. What if she was the one in the prediciment Ivan had postulated? Didn't leave him much choice, did it? Irregardless, the final decision must be hers, he vowed. Then he repeated that condition to Ivan.

"Agreed," Ivan confirmed. "But be careful. They will string you up if they suspect you are aiding me."

No kidding, Jack thought. And if they catch him for freeing

the prisoners they would also break all his fingers before they did.

But how to find the woman, that was the question. After the defeat of the Americans who had gone to rescue the President, everyone was being very cautious, what with all the men being bearded, long haired and scraggly, with deeply tanned and often dirty skin. Europeans, Americans and middle easterners all looked quite similar at first glance. Some middle easterners also had blue or green eyes and spoke English reasonbly well. So did some of the Russians. And, from what Ivan had related, Deanna might be being held captive. Maybe even worse. It was urgent that he find her as quickly as possible. But even with those killed in the battle and other conflicts and all the suicides, there were still about forty four hundred Americans left on the island. They were broken up into smaller protective clusters and groups scattered over a large, irregular area.

Since she had been a part of the governmental beaurocray, he began his search among those who had settled in the areas closest to the so called White House. No one seemed to remember her. He was about to move on when there was loud shouting behind him.

"That's him. Stop that man. He's a traitor," came the high pitched voice of an older man. "Stop him."

Jack turned just in time to see that it was himself that was being pointed at and before he could move he was piled on and dragged to the ground. While he was being held down his accuser came over and kicked him soundly in the ribs. That did it.

"You son-of-a-bitch," he said and angrily fought his way to his feet. After some sharp, hard blows they backed away. Too many bananas and too much time lying around under the trees, most of them were not only older than Jack but in poor condition. But there were just too many. He was still completely surrounded and, capable or not, they all looked like they still wanted to fight. The little older man came as close as he physically dared and glaring madly at Jack.

"We got you now, you damned traitor," he screeched venomonously.

"And who the hell are you and what is your problem?" Jack spit back. "And what the hell gives you the right to kick me, you little weasel?"

"Because I know who you are. You're Briggs and you're the guy who refused to go spy on the Arabs for the President and now they have him and it's your fault. That makes you a traitor in my book."

"Well, stuff your little book and just remember that if you kick someone when they're down there's going to be repercussions."

"Oh, really. Such as what, big guy? I'm one of the president's best friends," he sneared and stupidly stepped closer as Jack's fist landed squarely on his nose. It wasn't meant to hurt him seriously and it didn't, but it did cause the blood to run. Continuing the surprise, Jack tripped one of his captors, shook off two others and backed away. For the moment it was a standoff. Then, just when he began to think it was over there was another face in the crowd staring at him. It was the guard who had seen him in the moonlight two nights before.

"I see you caught the bastard," the man said as he came nearer with venom in his eyes.

"Yeah. He's a traitor, all right," said the little one, holding his bloody nose. "Any man who would refuse a direct order from the President needs to be punished."

"What's that got to do with it?" said the guard. "What are you talking about?"

"He refused to go spy on the Arabs for the President and now we've captured him."

"Spy, hell. That's the guy I was telling you about before. That's the guy who let all the prisoners go."

"What?" the little man said, having to breath through his mouth. "Somebody go find some strong grape vines. We need to string him up."

Jesus, Jack said to himself. Were they serious? That would be a lousy way to die. Here on this god forsaken island at the hands of a bunch of loonies. That didn't suit him at all. He looked around, seeking the weakest side of the ring that surrounded him. And that little wimp was moving back in, too. Probably to kick him again when he thought it was safe to do so. Okay. If that was all the dumb little shit understood, then he could be first. Then the two behind him, egging him on. And then, run like hell. Before Jack could make his move, however, there was another strong voice from the back of the crowd. One that sounded vaguely familiar from somewhere in the past but one he was unable to identify at the moment.

"Excuse me. Let me through. Get out of the way, damnit," said the man in a husky voice that demanded attention. A big man with strong shoulders and a few inches taller than most of them, but just as fully bearded and long haired as the rest.

God, I know this guy, Jack thought. But who is he? It's been a long time. Was it Sam Birnstead? The Secretary of the Navy? The man who had also disappeared off the plane with the president? He knew he had to have been on the island somewhere but, strangely enough, their paths had never crossed. Why was that, he had wondered at times, thinking maybe he been killed or something earlier on before Jack had arrived. Clearly not, it now seemed. But why had he suddenly shown up and what was the outcome of this likely to be? Either way, he was prepared as ever to land some blows and beat his way out of there.

Elbowing his way into the inner circle the big man looked closely at Jack. "By God, it is you, isn't it. Damn Jack, how are you anyway? It's been a long time," Sam said and held out his hand. Jack shook it gratefully, realizing he might still have one ally in this mess.

"What's going on?" Sam asked. "Looks like you've got yourself into a bit of a mess here."

"Guess you could say that," Jack responded with a touch of hope.

"He's a turncoat traitor. That's what he is. And we're about to hang him for what he did."

"Damnit Wilford. You always were such a hot headed, trouble making little wimp and I don't want to hear anymore from you so somebody else please tell me what's going on."

About three people all began speaking at the same time and it took several minutes before the whole story came out. Jack had refused to help the President and Jack had freed the Arab prisoners on the same night the President was taken hostage. The first part was one thing, freeing the enemy was something else. He deserved to be hung.

"Well, isn't that interesting," Sam said to the crowd, looking around. "But you're all jumping to conclusions."

"Doesn't look like it to us," the men closest in said. "And what do you know about it?"

"Maybe more than you do, so pay attention. As most of you know I was the Secretary of the Navy and while I may have maintained a low profile around here and stayed on the sidelines I do happen to know one thing. Mr. Briggs did indeed refuse to spy for the President but he would have been entirely within his rights to do so, if that was all there was to it. What none of you know, however, is that it was also part of a more complicated, classified scenario. But now that the president is in trouble and unable to straighten this out himself, I feel compelled to come forward. The

154

last thing we want to do is hang an innocent man. So, the truth is Jack was supposed to refuse to spy on the Arabs on purpose to make himself look like the bad guy in this mess. Once that was set up he was given an official assignment to come in late at night and free the prisoners. Which is exactly what he did. It was all part of the plan and he carried out his mission very well, I must say, risking his own life in the process. It became necessary because the President had realized he had been given bad advice by some of his key people and made a big mistake in taking prisoners. But just openly releasing them would not have been good policy under the circumstances. That wouldn't have looked good at all. So he set this thing up and Jack here was brave enough to risk getting caught in order to help out. You should all be giving him a medal instead of causing so much trouble. Still, I realize your intentions were good so I'm not going to ask you to apologize. But I do want you all go back to what you were doing and leave him alone. Otherwise I'll help him beat the hell out of the bunch of you."

At that point no one moved. They all stood and looked at the Nav-Sec. What a story. Sounded like a bunch of crap but who knew for sure. And since there was no way to check it out they were left to face the more immediate truth of who stood beside Jack. There was no doubt that he was probably the biggest man in the crowd and not a one of them wanted to be the first to come to blows with him. But they weren't quite ready to concede, either.

"I mean it, damnit," Sam said in a strong voice. "Especially you, Wilford. Take a hike before I thump you on the nose myself. And I won't just make it bleed. I knock the damned thing clear off."

Looking shocked, Wilford raised his hand as if to protect himself, turned around and walked away. It was enough to break the impass. So, after a respectful moment, the inner core began seperating themselves and left the area. The rest soon followed. Jack finally relaxed, shook his head and grinned. "That was one hell of a story," he said.

Sam grinned back. "Yeah, that was fun. I haven't had an interesting confrontation since I've been here. Thanks for the opportunity."

"Thanks, hell. You probably saved my life."

"Okay, so you owe me one. Jesus, Jack what are you doing here? I left you back on Air Force One. But then I heard some talk a few days ago about you telling old Stanley to kiss off. Still didn't seem possible that it could have been you. Let's take a walk and you can bring me up to date."

"It's a pretty long story."

"With my schedule, the longer the better. Did you really free some prisoners? I'd heard rumors about them but was it really true? Drukus really did that?"

"Him and Trunik, the head of the FBI. There were others before that, tortured to death."

"Jesus. I didn't know that."

"Me either, till just recently"

"Shameful bastards. I guess I should have stayed plugged into what was going on. But things were getting so ludicrous I did a drop out instead. Moved around the island so I could be away from it all. Just happened to be passing by when all the fuss started."

"Damned lucky for me. I loved your story."

"That little wimp Wilford is a trouble maker. An ex Wall Street broker. Biggest crook on the block, I'm told. Somebody is going to stomp him good one of these times. But anyway, what were you doing there?"

"Well, I got myself involved in trying to help a friend locate someone else before it's too late. Or maybe it already is. I don't know, but I promised I'd try. But I should have known better than to have come through here."

"Mind if I ask? Who is trying to find who?"

"Well, the first one is Ivan. The Russian who built the big walls up on the mountain. He doesn't dare show his face down here so I promised to help."

"Ivan, huh. I sure want to hear the rest of that story. Who's he looking for and why do I sense another problem? Couldn't by any chance happen to be a woman, could it?"

"Well, yes, actually. How did you know?"

"What else would be worth all the trouble in a place like this?"

"I see your point. Problem is, he thinks she's being held captive. It's Deanna Holt, the Secretary of Education. Do you know her?"

"No. I'm aware of who she is but I don't recall ever meeting her. What's it all about?"

Jack did his best to explain it in a reasonable way.

"Do you need some help?" he was asked after he completed the story.

"Okay, sure. That would be great. Might save some time if we could split up. Let me describe her for you," Jack said and continued to do so, hoping his information was accurate enough.

"All right. Let me see what I can do. We can meet later and

compare notes. We need to catch up on old times, too."

"Good. I have a lot of questions for you. How about down by the beach by that big domed rock to the west of here? Are you familiar with it?"

"I think so. I'll find it, anyway. Say about an hour before dark?"

Sam had taken the area south of the White House while Jack moved off to the north. It was a difficult process. By early evening, however, with about an hour to spare before he needed to meet with Sam, he had finally located her amongst the group Ivan had described. But it was only after passing by the third time. What he had remembered was an attractive, poised and confident woman very much in control. What he saw now was someone totally unwashed and unkempt, long stringy hair, dirty face, dirty finger nails and torn clothes, resigned looking from a distance but hostile and defiant when approached, staying away at the edge of things as much as possible, even though one or another of the men was always trying to bring her back into the circle. A dark, malicious undercurrent ran through the group which Jack pretended not to see on his final walk through the area, wondering how he would ever get to talk with her without arousing suspicion.

Eventually he thought he recognized one of the men. Maybe he could engage him in a conversation. It was easier than he thought as Jack him led him around a variety of subjects, purposely ignoring the woman while hoping for opportunity. It came as one of the other men in the group said something to her in a harsh voice.

"What's her problem?" Jack asked off handedly, being deliberately negative.

"That one?" the man said. "Would you believe she thinks she's really special. But look at her. Won't even wash herself in the creek."

"Why do you even let her hang around?"

"Are you kidding? There's only one woman for every hundred and fifty men so we kinda took charge of her, if you want to put it that way. But there are only twenty two of us. We figured that in time we could get her to take turns but she fought like hell and we didn't want to just rape her, so we waited. But what does she do? She completely stopped taking care of herself. Look at her. She's disgusting."

"So, why don't you let her go?"

"No way. We still have plans."

"Really?"

"Yes. She has put us off long enough."

"What are you going to do?"

"We're going to pick one of our members who will have the fun of being the first to take her down a notch. Once that has been clarified, then we all get our turns. A chance to sleep with a woman once ever three weeks is better than none at all, wouldn't you say?"

"And you don't care if she is willing or not?"

"Hell no. We're on an island, man. And we get to make our own rules."

"Hmm. Well... How are you going to decide who is first?"

"If we had money here, it would be easy. We would have a lottery. But we will think of something. We all agreed it has to be done within the next few days, however. So if you have any ideas, maybe we will give you a chance at her, too."

"I don't know," Jack said as he looked at her critically. "I don't think I'd be interested. But then," he continued, scrutinizing her as if he were making an evaluation. "Maybe if I could talk to her a little. The only way to be sure is to take a closer look."

"Go ahead," the man said. "Take your time but don't get any big ideas just yet."

Deanna had become aware of Jack's presence the moment he had set foot in their area. It was what she had become. Highly observant and extremely suspicious. Nearly paranoid in her attempt to survive, she noticed everything. It was the harried, fearful existence of a frightened animal and she loathed what she had been reduced to. There were times when she felt so hopeless she was almost willing to give in. What was the point of going on? Sometimes she thought she would just antagonize them all so badly that they would simply kill her and get it over with. At other times she was determined to survive. But it was becoming less and less of a priority.

The real tragedy was that these were all men she had known back home. She had worked with them on several levels and seemed to have had their respect. One of them, the man Jack had been talking to, was even one of her assistants, damn him. But he had turned into one of the worst. Obscene, conniving, denigrating, she hated him the most. And, for him she had made a special vow. If he personally ever touched her she would find a way to immobilize him before she died. She would kick him, bite him, scratch his eyes out. She had found a hard, dagger shaped stick of wood which she had cautiously ground a sharp point on by rubbing it against a stone and she carried it hidden in her ragged clothes. If it came to that, if he dared touch her, she would would kill him if she had the chance. And if not and they all joined in and took her by force, that was when she would find a way to kill herself.

Just look at her. God, she could hardly stand to live with herself as the filthy, disgusting individual she had purposely let herself turn into. So far, however, it had worked. It had kept them away but it would not last. She knew that. Eventually they would overcome that, too, because they were sinking further and further into their own degeneration. The bottom was not far off, either, and as Jack approached her the survival side of her nature was instantly highly alert, wondering if this was but another deviant she might be forced to deal with, even though on the surface she feined a convincing disinterest.

Quietly Jack introduced himself. He told her his name, what he done back home, how long he had been on the island and, no, he was not a friend of the man he had been talking to. He was only seeking information, his sole purpose for being there was to find her and talk to her, nothing more. At first she was extremely cautious and highly sceptical, then she seemed to become embarassed and looked down at her tattered, filty clothing.

"Then why are you here?" she demanded, raising her eyes to meet his and boring into him.

"Ivan would like to see you again," he said softly.

At first she seemed confused, then there was a small flicker of light which she quickly subdued.

"You mean...?" she questioned and nodded in the direction of the mountain.

Jack nodded back.

"Yes," she said, scornfully. "I suppose he wants a piece of me, too."

"He assures me it is much more complex than that."

"And what does that mean?"

"He remembers you from before. He was really very fascinated with you. And he is also concerned about your safety since he has not seen you in some time."

"Then why didn't he come looking for me?"

"He couldn't do that. The President has told everyone he wants him dead. It seems Ivan badly embarassed and insulted the man."

"I know. It was one of the most refreshing things that has happened here."

Jack chuckled at the idea and saw that Deanna's face softened slightly.

"Yes," she said, after a brief wait. "I remember Ivan very well. I thought he was quite charming. There was something gentlemanly about him, too. But that was a long time ago. As you can see, a lot has changed." Again she looked down at herself and then around at the men who were now her captors.

"But he has not forgotten you. He says he thinks of you all the time and he is worried that something bad may have happened. He wasn't sure but he thought you liked him too."

"Well," she said, reluctant to admit it at first. "Okay, yes. I guess I did. We used to flirt with our eyes and talk a little until these men became jealous. After that they made me wait down below when went for food. And now they never let me leave this immediate area."

"That explains why you never came back. And why he was right in being concerned."

"Really? It's hard to believe anybody here even gives a damn. Besides, since then all I have heard is that he is a terrible man. A criminal, I believe."

"Perhaps he was back home. But then again, perhaps he wasn't. It's hard to know the truth. Here he is an opportunist. And a very clever one. I also think he's probably very honorable in his own way."

"Interesting," she said, and then she was silent for a long time. "But I think it's impossible," she replied. "He cannot come here and I would never be allowed to leave."

"Nothing is impossible," Jack assured her, holding her with his eyes. "Not even here."

"Hmm," she said, considering his statement. She didn't believe in love at first sight. Attraction, yes. Longing, perhaps, maybe something bordering on lust. But love, no. Still, like it or not, there had been a magnetic quality between her and Ivan that had stirred something deep inside, and, understood or not, it was still there. "I'll give it some thought," she told him. "Maybe if you come back tomorrow we can find a way to talk some more."

Jack hadn't believed in love at first sight either. Not when he was younger and until he met his wife. And then Katherine. And now, looking at Deanna, he remembered them both very clearly. Somehow, it seemed that Deanna and Ivan at least deserved a chance. Of course there was another side to it. Having stepped into the picture he felt he had a certain responsibility for her safety. Sooner or later these men would be abusing her. But how long before the Arabs came storming in again, too? And if they did, her fate would be even worse. At the same time all he had was a sketchy opinion of Ivan. Maybe she wouldn't be safe there, either. But, everything considered, he still trusted Ivan the most. Even so he couldn't frighten her into making that choice. It had to come honestly. The only alternative was to take her to the cave and let her live there. But why would she go? She didn't know whether she could trust him any more than the others. Poor woman. What a horrible situation to be in.

"Okay. Tomorrow then," he said and started to turn away.

"Wait," she said. "How would I find him if I decide?"

"I would have to take you there."

She studied him very carefully. "How do I know I would be safe in doing such a thing?"

"You don't," he said honestly.

"I understand. But would you stay with me and bring me back afterwards."

"Of course."

"Early in the morning then. By the creek. Near the old tree. I'll try and sneak away by myself."

"Good enough," Jack said.

Jack was at the creek shortly after sunup but Deanna was nowhere in sight. He circled the old tree, went to the creek and scooped up a handful of water for a drink. It was then that he heard her behind him.

"Hello," she said, somewhat nervously.

"Well, look at you," Jack replied as he surveyed her.

"Do I look okay?" she wanted to know.

"Better than okay," he stated. "What a transformation."

"It's the best I can do under the circumstances," she explained. "I'll have to let my clothes and hair dry as we walk."

"Either way, you look great," he complimented her, wanting to put her at ease.

"You must have had a wretched opinion of me last night," she said. "But I purposely let myself become as unappealing as possible to keep those men away. Unfortunately, I never thought it would be enough and I was becoming very concerned."

"I assumed that's what you were doing. You had every reason to worry. You were also right in that I don't think they would have waited much longer."

"Well, your coming was a blessing. It forced me to reevaluate my entire situation."

"How is that?"

"Regardless of what happens today I have resolved never to return to that bunch and I have further resolved not to be defeated by what has happened by being here on this island. Somehow I will survive. If not with Ivan, then I will hide in the woods or I will climb the mountain and live alone but I will never be a slave to anyone, ever again, and live in fear."

Jack didn't have to look too closely to see that there was a fire in her eyes that matched the determination in her voice. "Good for you," he stated.

"Just how well do you know Ivan?" she asked after they had walked a good deal further. "And what do you think of him?"

"I hardly know him at all," Jack replied honestly. "But I have watched him from time to time and I've asked a lot of questions of those who were willing to talk. So, at this point I'm not completely sure what I think. I do know he's more than just a Russian hoodlum, however. He actually went to school in the States and has a degree from some University which at least accounts for his English proficiency. Other than that I feel he reflects what is given to him. Treat him with respect and you get respect. Treat him badly, don't turn your back. I hope that's not too damning."

"Not at all. It somewhat confirms my own opinion."

"Well, If you choose not to go with Ivan I can still show you a safe place," he told her. "Actually, there are two of them that I know about. There is one hidden cave on the far side of the island where my brother and another woman stayed for more than six months and I recently located another up here on this side just below the snow line. If necessary, I can bring you food and keep you informed of the things down here."

"No one ever goes up there?" she asked.

"I have never seen any evidence of it."

"That's odd, don't you think?"

"I don't know. Maybe not. Fear keeps them huddled together and pushes them to keep all the old ongoing craziness they brought with them alive. So, I guess if a person can conquer their fear then they can learn to be alone. Part of the time, at least."

Deanna didn't know what to say but she began to relax a bit, feeling she had finally met someone she might be willing to trust. Never completely, however, after the experience she had been through, but enough to continue the risk. At the same time Jack was seriously hoping that Ivan was every bit the man he claimed to be and that he would respect Deanna's rights as an individual the way he had avowed. He also realized that by taking her to him he was honor bound to follow up and make sure she was treated properly.

Ivan was true to his word. Before they arrived at the agreed upon place, Jack carefully scouted the surrounding area and found him to be entirely alone. Deanna had told Jack that she would stay an hour and see what she thought, so he took her in to meet him. At first the three of them talked together. Then Deanna gave Jack an approving nod so he left them alone, waiting some distance away where he could watch, but not hear, what was being said. The sun rose higher, an hour's worth of angle. Then two and then three, as Jack watched their movements and body language. They stood the entire time. It was almost like a dance. Her arms were crossed over her chest at first, Ivan's open, several steps between them. She brushed her hair out of her face and looked down at her clothes, then back at him. He looked at her, too. Always there was eye contact, but he never stared or tried to assess her body or her clothing. Without realizing it, they circled each other, round and round. Purposely, however, he never once took a step directly towards her, never hurried her in the conversation or pressed for answers. When she was silent, he waited. Eventually, he leaned against a tree. Strangely enough, she went to the opposite side of the same tree and leaned up against it also. There they were, back to back, the tree between them, but they no longer spoke. Deanna looked up at the sky. Ivan looked up at the sky. What now, Jack wondered as he got up and went over to where they were. At first surprised, they both turned to look at him. Ivan nodded at Jack, while Deanna gave him a reassuring smile. Then Ivan moved away from the tree and started walking back towards his camp.

"Thank you," Deanna told Jack quietly, then turned and walked to catch up to Ivan.

The next day Jack returned to the American area to continue his discussion with Sam Birnstead and to make sure nothing had gone wrong and Deanna had somehow returned. He decided to check on her first. Having invented the story about how he would not be interested in the woman, he looked for the man he had talked to the previous evening but he was soon accosted by one of the others whom he had seen bullying Deanna.

"Hey you," the man said.

Jack tried to ignore him but was grabbed by the arm.

"Take your hand off me," he said.

"Not until you talk to me, damnit," the man said, but before he knew it Jack had turned, grabbed his wrist and had his arm up behind his back. There was a cry of pain. He thought it might fracture.

"Okay," Jack said. "Calm down before I break it off. My name is not, hey you, so if you have something to say, be polite about it. Do we understand each other?"

"All right, okay. Now let me go?" the man conceded.

Jack slowly released his arm and the man stepped back.

"Now, what is your problem?" Jack asked.

"Never seen you around before last night, but you were there talking to our woman. And, guess what? This morning she's gone and never came back. Maybe you had something to do with that."

"Your woman?" Jack said with an angry look in his eye. "How did she get to be your woman? It didn't look like there was anything consentual about it to me."

"Doesn't matter," the man said. "Here we make our own rules."

"Well, if she's gone as you say, I guess you didn't do a very good job of owning her, did you?"

"What's that supposed to mean?"

"It means you are all a bunch of sick bastards."

"Well, if we ever get our hands on her, she'll be sorry she ever ran off."

"Really? Sounds pretty tough for someone cowardly enough to try and enslave a woman."

"Yeah. What the hell do you know about it?" the man said, backing up a bit.

Jack took three steps forward so he was almost nose to nose. Looking down at the man, he spoke with even more anger than he had when he was kicked by Wilford.

"I know that if it ever happens again, there are a bunch of guys here who will take you and every one of your friends and smash all your balls between a couple of rocks. One ball at a time. Is that clear enough?"

At first the man was too startled to move and could only stare back in fear. Then he dropped hs eyes and retreated to a safe distance where he stopped and turned.

"Better watch your back, sucker," he said visciouly as he spat on the ground and quickly slunk off.

"Good advice," Jack said to the man as he watched him retreat, tempted to go after him, but let it go. He wasn't there to try and straighten out every obnoxious little bastard who came along. Plus, there were getting to be too many of them to bother with. Let someone else have some of the fun.

"Damn right," he also said as a reminder to himself. From here on out, living on the island would indeed require one to watch their back. Something he had better start paying more attention to. Especially if he was going to run around freeing prisoners and helping women in distress.

Ivan took Deanna on a long walk through the region above the wall. He first introduced her to Boris and a few of his closer friends. Then he took her to another walled off area where most of the women from his group lived together. It contained both a public area and several smaller cubicle like enclosures for those who wanted more privacy. Outside a small stream ran downward almost adjacent to the eastern wall of the structure, tumbling over a small waterfall into a grotto like pool ringed with a dense growth of trees and brush.

"They take their drinking water from the falls and the pool below is for bathing. Men are not allowed in this area without permission so you will have whatever privacy you want. The women will all look out for you till you become more acquainted. You will be quite safe," he assured her. Then, one by one, he introduced them.

Looking back, Deanna wasn't at all sure what she had expected when she had so boldy walked off with Ivan. All she knew was that she didn't want to be figuratively dragged off to some wretched cave where she might be forced to do battle with him. But this! She could never have imagined.

Deanna had been married twice before. The first had been a flaming disaster. Lots of flames and fuel for passion, all turned to ashes within a year. A year before she was old enough to vote. The second had been based on more practical considerations. They were both professionals pursuing seperate careers. He in medicine, she in government. Their goal was children and a horse ranch out in the rolling hills of Virginia with his career being the dominant element. It didn't stand a chance. She was far too attractive, he was bellied and bald by thirty, his profession eating up the hours of the days, six or seven days a week, every week. Feeling neglected, she became angry and hurt, then just plain bored, joining this, joining that, absent nearly as much as he toward the end.

There never was a horse ranch, no chilren and no Virginia, only a townhouse in DC. Just as well. Jealousy and controlling behavior on his part drove it into the final wall where the seven year relationship died in a huff, never to be repeated. For her, at least. But Deanna was resilient and optimistic. She still liked men but had never found one that stirred her being and stimulated her brain both at the same time. And then there was her debasing, fear ridden experience here on the island. Would she ever be able to trust a man again? A few days ago she would have said, hell no, with a vengence. Today was more than just a surprise. The relief and the respect he was showing brought a tear to her eye. She turned and blinked it away.

As for Ivan, it was inbred thing. When it came to women, force was meaningless. If you had to use force, you ended up with less than nothing because, in the end, they would hate you. Someday, given half a chance, they would stab you in the back. Women were not about conquest. If it wasn't mutual, it wasn't worth the trouble. And as far as Deanna went, well, he would protect her with his life. That he already knew.

"If you need anything, tell Kira here. If you want to talk I am usually back that way with the men during the day but in the evenings we all gather together. Maybe tell stories, sing a few songs, whatever we feel like. And now that you are here I wonder if you might show me how to dance. I would love to dance with you. Not like we did this morning, around that tree. But together, the two of us."

She smiled with more surprise. Not only had Ivan turned out to be an honorable, considerate gentleman, he was also a bit of a romantic.

"I'd be more than happy to," she said warmly. Time would tell, of course, but for now, absolutely. Months of pain were already melting away. She would love to give him dance lessons and continue to hope.

Shortly after his encounter with the one who had helped keep Deanna captive, Jack came across another face he recognized from out of the past. But not at first. It was only after she caught him staring at her that he made the connection. It had been a long time ago and with her tangled hair and worn clothing, it was quite difficult. More manish now than before and more stern looking, she had been the Dean of the University where he had gotten one of his earlier degrees. My god, he laughed when he thought about it. That one was in psychology, of all things. He had other aspirations back then.

"Dean Whitcomb," he said as he came up to her, hoping he hadn't embarassed her.

She scrutinized him carefully but it was obvious she didn't know who he was.

"I'm sure you don't know me," he said in confirmation. "But I was a student at the University some years ago. Are you still, were you still the Dean when this happened?"

"Well, I'm pleased to meet you," she said, warming a little. "Yes I was. And with only a year and a half to retirement. Isn't that a ridiculous concept under the circumstances?"

"Well, yes. Along with a hundred other things we used to attach so much significance to. So. Can I buy you a drink or something?"

She laughed. "Maybe we could go down to the beach and talk a bit," she said after some consideration. "I haven't been there in quite a while."

"I'm always surprised that there is almost never anyone down here," Jack said when they arrived. An immense stretch of white sand greeted them. There were also palm trees and crystal clear water close in that went from turquoise to deep blue further out. At first glance it might have been Fiji, or Moorea, or Bora Bora, except for the lack of people. None but a single, older man who sat alone under a palm and gazed out to sea, seemingly unaware of their newly arrived presence. When they came closer, however, he rose slowly and turned to them.

"Hello," he said rather timorously when they near enough. "Nice to have some company," he continued weakly, after they returned his greeting.

"Are you all right?" Dean Whitcomb asked him, somewhat worried about his glum looking appearance.

"Nothing serious. I'm just a little depressed," he said. "It's all so very discouraging."

Judging from the length of his hair and beard and the condition of his clothing, the man had obviously been on the island from the beginning. Dean Whitcomb commented about it not being easy to be there for any great length of time.

"It's not the place," the man said. "Except for the absence of

167

life forms other than humans I'm quite pleased with being here. It's actually quite beautiful when you stop and take a look. And it certainly has been interesting."

"Then what is it?" Dean Whicomb asked. "Do you miss your family? That's certainly understandable."

"No. Families all gone. Just me, anymore. The problem is my computer. If I just had my computer. Or even that old typewriter I threw away twenty years ago. Hell, I'd give my left arm just to have a stack of paper and some pencils. But, no such luck, right? Here I am, helpless in the middle of the opportunity of a lifetime. Helpless, I tell you. And it hurts like hell."

"I'm not sure I understand. What do paper and pencils have to do with it? Maybe you could elaborate a bit."

"Yes, well, sure. I could do that. But it's a rather long story."

"Under the circumstances I don't see that as a problem," Jack said. "Do you, Dean Whitcomb?"

"Absolutely not. Why don't you tell us, Sir, Mr.... we didn't get your name."

"Well, I recognize your name, young lady," he said to the Dean. "You were head of that college back in upstate New york. I was a Harvard man, myself. Doctor Blumford Yates at your service. But I like to be called Professor. That's what I was for most of my life. Until my fourth wife passed away, anyhow. That's seems to be the reason I'm here. It's her fault, you know. If she hadn't died a few years back she'd be here now and I'd be home writing another book. Of course it wouldn't be half the book I'm unable to write here."

With that Professor Yates looked back and forth at their faces, studying them, trying to decide if they deserved to hear the rest of his story. Finally satisfied, he went on.

"Except for a year in the Amazon and six months in New Guinea, I taught companion courses in Anthropology and Sociology for twenty seven years. My third wife had just left me and my life was my own for a brief period of time. Then the mother of one of my students got her hooks in me and I'm married again. Turned out she was the owner of this retail conglomerate, richer than God but never let me touch a penny of her wealth. That didn't bother me and neither did being wedded again because I didn't meddle in her affairs and she didn't meddle in mine. All I had to do was to be home Friday evenings for a formal, sit down dinner with her friends. Other than that we had almost zero impact on each other's lives. Then, three years ago she passed away. Lord knows, I certainly could have handled that easy enough. But she threw me a real curve and a half, damn her, when she died. She made me her sole heir. One day I'm a happy, unharried professor, the next I'm the owner of an impossible tangle of large companies. That was a damned mean trick and she didn't even have any relatives who wanted to contest the will or I would have given it all to them. Not even her daughter objected. Strange, huh?" Remembering it, the man stared out to sea for a long time, then at last he smiled a little and continued.

"Well, after I finally got over being mad about it and since I didn't care about the position or the money I decided to have some fun. I hate lawyers so the first thing I did was to escort the entire legal staff out the door. Didn't even give them a chance to clean out their desks. Then I dumped seven company presidents and twenty six vice presidents, ten or twelve technical advisors and every other empire building, entrenched individual I could find. I tried every thing I knew to screw things up because I was making a case study of it, taking notes and all. It was going to be my next book. But the damned thing wouldn't leave me alone and it wouldn't go away and it kept making more money than ever so I made myself CEO, moved into the home office and really took over. And then this happened and here I am."

"That certainly could be disconcerting," the Dean said, appearing to agree with him.

"Yes, well, even winding up here didn't upset me too much. And in a way I was glad because I didn't have to deal with all those snarly business matters anymore. No, here I am, that's for sure. But without my computer or my old typewriter or even just paper and pencil. Think of it. This place is a sociologist's and anthropologist's dream. Look what's going on in the way of human behavior. If I just had something to take notes on I'd have a book that would get me a Nobel Prize and a Pulitzer Prize both. With all the bizzare behavior that's happening here it would go down in history as a classic. Assuming I could somehow get back to that other world to get it published, that is."

"You're saying that's the source of your depression?" Jack asked. "What about all the demented behavior that's going on all the time?"

"Oh that. It's beautiful. Perfect. What an opportunity. What a surprise. Who would have guessed it would turn out the way it has. I never would have predicted such a situation. Every sociological theory ever presented turned completely upside down and I'm right here in the midst of it all. But....... damnit..... No paper and pencil

169

and maybe no way home," he said. "Far worse than going from professor to billionaire. The most awful situation I have ever been in."

"Not as bad as getting yourself killed in the midst of all this conflict?"

"Well, yes. There is that, now that you mention it, I suppose. But when I go into someone else's area I always make sure they know I'm only there to observe and nothing more. So far it seems to have worked."\

"And up until the last few weeks it was mostly a war of words. Now it's clubs and spears and rocks and serious numbers of people are getting killed. And no matter what, you are an American, you look like an American and, just like back home, the rest of the world hates no one else as bad as Americans."

"Yes. You are certainly right on that score, thanks to our fearless leader. Too bad he didn't disappear through a crack in transit somehow. But then the situation here wouldn't have been half as interesting, either. Now would it? And I wouldn't have half as much to ponder over."

"What exactly do you find worth pondering over?" Jack asked. "At least from your sociological, anthropological view point."

"Except for a few punk gang leaders, almost everyone here is roughly between forty and late sixties. A few older, big time money men in their seventies. Average education level above the norm, but greatly lacking in the arts and humanities. Highly competitive, hard driven, type A personalities addicted to power and status. Insensitive, unreflective, self serving. Did I miss anything?"

"Not much."

"So here they are, suddenly dropped into what had to be a very traumtic experience for all of them. But look what happened? Professionally, I would have expected a completely different set of reactions."

"Really? How so?"

"In such an extreme situation I would have expected people to have sorted things out in a far more logical manner. First, analysis and evaluation. A shocking event has occured. New and strange environment. Only leaders are present, everyone else has been left behind. No structure, no rules, nothing. A completely new chance to start over and do what might be best for the common survival. A chance to ask, what is this all about? What happened? Why in heaven's name are we here? What are we supposed to be getting out of this? But instead.... Did any of that happen? Did anyone even sit down longer than five seconds and discuss it? Was any attempt ever made to find out who might be better qualified than who to organize and lead everyone towards a more compatible situation? Or, for that matter, since all us so called leaders are here for a reason, a reason as yet unknown it seems, does anyone in particular even have to be in charge? Maybe we were supposed to try and work it out some other way. Who knows? The only thing that's for sure at this point is that it's much too late for any of that now."

"Yes. It's certainly beginning to look that way," Dean Whitcomb agreed. "I have become very discouraged with the entire chain of events. Now we'll never know what great opportunities might have been lost. What do think happened to spoil it, anyway?"

"Professionally, I'm as baffled as you are. Maybe we all became so good at denial back home, never wanting to look at the real problems that everyone just retreated into the same old psychological void. All this sudden freedom and lack of structure was just too frightening for most of them, I guess. All imagination, creative, intuitive, humanistic skills and normal curiosity were immediately suppressed. As a result we wound up with almost nothing to work towards or compete over so the former political and religious leaders postured and haggled and bullied and wallowed around in religious nonsense and political pettiness, trying to keep the same old game going as back home. And, sadly enough, they succeeded. After that, the rest was quite predictable."

"Like flag waving and arguing about whose side god is on and killing each other with a vengance or getting depressed and wading out into the ocean to commit suicide at a rate that's at least ten times the norm for back home," Jack stated.

"Exactly," said the Professor. "Except here there is also something else involved which makes it even more distressing."

"What do you mean?"

"Here we have a repeat of the same scenario as back home except here it's easier to see the true dimensions of what's going on. There is no media to sensationalize or distort the truth. The ranting religionists also don't own television and radio stations and can't hammer away about righteousness and the Rapture and being the only ones who will go to heaven. What an absurd concept. Anyway, in like manner the government can't edit or propagandize or disort the truth quite so easily either, even though they are just as sinister in their attempts to do so. And yet, on it goes. Heading down the same old road as always."

"Well I think it's very tragic," Dean Whitcomb said. "But the old administration certainly doesn't speak for all of us. And if a poll were taken I don't believe their views represent even half of the people. Most of it is just hype from highly vocal supporters. So, without a doubt that means that the rest of us failed too, didn't we? And badly, because we didn't stand up and shout the crazy fools back down and demand something better. And now, if we are not careful, they are going to get us all killed."

"And not care one bit as long as they can save themselves."

"But they can't save themselves because they don't realize they are their own worse enemies. It's not the Arabs who will have done them in. They are just the instrument. But with equally crazy leaders who also allowed themselves to get sucked into the melee."

"Well, nothing makes a fundamentalist feel more like a cornered rat than a difference of opinion. And what could be more dangerous to them than that?"

"Yes, and now that the military men never came back from their rescue attempt, except for that one General, and the President is tied to a tree, slowly bleeding to death, where do we go from here?" Dean Whitcomb asked.

"It's a critical situation," Jack said. "But as for the President being tied to a tree, he has no one to blame but himself. If he had had one ounce of human decency in him, the first thing he would have done would be to make a sincere and humble apology to the Arabs for all the innocent people he had killed when he was back home and beg their forgiveness. Not that they would accept it, of course, because they seem to have an equally strong and warped mindset about things, but it would still be the decent thing to do. Without that we have what we have. Conflict and war. Sounds kind of trite even saying it, however. At least here. And in that regard I strongly believe that if your own group of dissenters is going to survive, you need to separate yourselves completely from the rest of the Americans. You also need to do it quickly and get the message out that you are not part of the ongoing insanity."

"Yes, you may just be right," Dean Whitcomb conceeded.

"Well, its your choice but I'm convinced that what has happened so far is just the beginning. So, if you feel you need a place to hide, I can show you one. Unfortunately it is very limited and only a few could come."

"Thank you, Jack. I'll give it some serious thought. For now, however, I think I would rather stay and work on the problem. How about you? Will you come and help?"

"No, because I don't want to become caught up in some antigovernment crusade. I would do better on the other end of it, trying to get as many people to withdraw as possible and remove themselves from the conflict. I hope that doesn't upset you too much but under the circumstances I think it's the best way to have peace."

"Well," said the Professor. "While some people might see that as being cowardly and want your head for refusing to take sides, I personally applaud you for your courage."

"Yes, Professor" Dean Whitcomb responded. "I may have to agree with you. I'll certainly have to give it some thought, anyway. I guess that also means you are out of it too. Or do you have other plans?"

"No. It's such a fascinating moment in our island history that I'm going to try remaining neutral for as long as possible and keep on observing. But I have also been doing some jogging lately so, if it becomes necessary, I'll just run like hell."

The following day Jack was back in the American section, again looking for Dean Whitcomb. The more he thought about it, the more he was convinced that the peace loving segments of the American community needed to seperate themselves from the rest if they wanted to avoid the brutality that could only escalate. He had already covered most of the territory except for the area around the White House. Not wanting to go there he had purposely left that to last. That was where the conservatives and the religionists spent most of their time and he didn't want to be dragged into another melodramatic encounter. At first he walked the periphery without success, then made his way in closer. Damn, he said to himself ruefully, when he was still about three hundred yards from the White House itself.

"Howdy, my good fellow," a slick sounding man dressed in the remains of what had once been a very expensive, hand made Italian suit said, stepping right in front of him "You're just in time. This is your lucky day. We only have seven more left."

Jack stopped, took a large step backwards, then tried to go around.

"Wait, wait," the man said. "Hear me out. Today I can make you a really special deal and even reduce your down payment by ten percent."

Good grief. Another guy who's been been on the island far too long, Jack decided. But he didn't look viscious and he didn't look like he was about to go away, either, so Jack simply stood his ground and waited.

"Well, obviously you don't know who I am but don't worry about that," the man began again.

"Just remember that I'm here to help you and I can certainly do that because back home I was head of one of the largest legal firms in the country. And see that gentleman over there, the portly dude with the bald head? That's Joe Dunbee and he was the CEO of the nations largest real estate firm and together we have collaborated to bring the island citizens one of the best deals imaginable."

"Well, I'm happy for you," Jack finally responded, "but I really need to be going."

"No, no. You don't understand," the man said and took Jack by the arm and pointed off to his left. "There. See all those stakes in the ground? Those are the boundaries of the islands choicest residental parcels. Can you believe it? The President himself gave us a land grant of about thirty acres right here not two hundred yards from the White House. Just before he was captured, poor man. How tragic. But his cabinet also had the good sense to zone it residential, site built homes only, if you can believe that. So... here on the island, just like back home, every individual has the God given priviledge of land ownership with all its irrevocable property warrants. As a result the fortunate individuals who purchase these lots gain the right to build on them, fence them off, sell them and so forth. What else could you want or ask for?"

Jack shrugged and started to walk away. This guy had lost it for sure.

"No, no. Don't leave," the man insisted. "You're probably just worried about the down payment so let me explain it to you before you make your decision. I can see that you certainly wouldn't have any trouble with it at all because you are young enough and healthy enough to handle it easily."

"Look. I'm really not interested. Now could you please get out of the way?"

Completely undaunted, however, the man rambled on. "You probably think I'm crazy, don't you, because there is no monetary system on the island. And you're right. So we borrowed an idea from that wild Russian up on the mountain. It's all about stones. Get it?"

"Stones?"

"Like I said. You're young and healthy. You can collect stones as well as anyone. Only three hundred as a down payment for the lots out on the edge next to the trees and only five hundred and twenty three for these really prime ones here just down the path from the White House. Now how is that for a deal?"

"And what exactly are you going to do with all the stones?" Jack asked, having decided he had to hear the rest of the man's story just to see how nutty it could really get.

"Well, me and my partner over there kept these two big lots here for ourselves and we feel that, rightfully enough as I'm sure you can understand, looking like the gentleman you are, that we should be as prosperous here as we were back home. So, with that in mind we would like to have appropriate residences on our own parcels and that they should at least have stone walls instead of just sticks laying on the ground which seems to have become the standard so far."

"Well, if you feel the need to claim ownership to something to feel prosperous, you're doing the right thing," Jack said. "And, if you can convince other people to build a house for you in the process, I guess I could at least listen."

"I hope you're not being condescending."

"I'm not being condescending."

"You certainly sound like it."

"Well, what did you expect?"

"I must admit you have a point."

"So tell me the rest of it."

"What?"

"The rest of your sales pitch. Sounds like you worked pretty hard on it. The down payment.... I think that's where you were at."

"Why waste my time. I'm sorry I bothered you."

"Not at all. And you're right. I'm not interested in being a part of your venture. But I am a little curious as to what some people are willing to do just to be a part of something. So, if you don't mind sharing just this once."

"Yeah, well, sure, I suppose. Why not. And, when you put it that way it does seem a little ridiculous, doesn't it. Damned ridiculous, actually. But that's how it all began. Deliberatley taking advantage of boringly obsessive people. Not only did we con the President and his cabinet members, we conned all his loyal supporters. And not only that but they are building us each a house and bringing us food every day of the week. Jesus, do you realize how hard we have laughed about it. Hell, it's this kind of insanity that helps keep us sane. If that makes any sense?"

"It does," Jack affirmed and smiled. "So how did you manage it?"

"Same old tried and true BS as back home. Make them want to belong to the club. Squatters versus ownership. Have small lots and big lots to invoke some status and make the ones closest to that mock White House the most prestigious. The bigger the down payment and the higher the monthlies, the bigger the debt. The more debt you have, the more important you must be. It never seems to fail. And here, of all places, people need to feel important. All we did was capitalize on it. Stones are the medium of exchange. Down payments paid in stones, monthly payments paid in stones, the number of which depends on the price of the property. The first seven buyers, however, had a second option. Once the down payments were made, they could bring a certain amount of food instead of rocks. But that has to delivered once every week. Alternate the days between the seven buyers and we, the sellers, never have to go up the hill again to get things for ourselves. What could be better?"

"Not much," Jack chuckled. "Thanks," he said.

"My pleasure," the man replied, seemingly quite refreshed with having found someone he could be totally honest with.

He offered his hand. Jack shook it and walked off. This time, however, as he continued on his way he took a closer look at what else was going on. Most of the buyers who had already made their down payments were gathering long sticks and doing what the President had done. They were making outlines of houses on the ground. As he walked around he saw outlines of two and three bedroom houses almost completed. Most of them were being constructed by single men or men whose wives had been left behind, but, for everyone of them, there was a woman waiting there to see if she could move in with him when it was done. There were also two married couples. One couple had co managed their own large company back home while both members of the other couple were from high governmental positions. The husband of the first couple had quickly put together a four bedroom floor plan and, when Jack happened to be passing by, the wife of the second couple was out at the side of their own outline, ranting at her husband.

"I don't care how far you have to walk to find more tree branches. They have four bedrooms," she said loudly, pointing to the neighboring lot. "And I want five. And the fifth has to be right here where I've put these scratch marks in the dirt, right next to the library."

Was it hilarious or was it pathetic? Jack wondered, because they all seemed so ostentatiously serious about what they were doing. And, if he should come by some moonlit night, would he find them all asleep there on the ground, confining themselves to the area they had designated as being the master bedroom? More than likely he would. With that he almost wanted to turn and run, but he controlled himself and walked away instead. He really wanted to find Dean Whitcomb again. And he also wanted to introduce her and her group to Sam Birnstead, since Sam had agreed with Jack about them moving and had offered to help. In order to do that, however, he still had to walk past the White House, itself. That turned out to be almost as distressing.

Coming up to it, there were two tall sticks driven in the ground. Tied to one were the remnants of an old, and once white, shirt flopping in the breeeze. It had red horizontal stripes wiped on it with pomegranite juice and blue stars dyed with blueberry juice. Unfortunately, the blueberry juice was not color fast and the stars had smeered badly from the rain. On the other pole hung four yellow ribbons. As Jack remembered it, the Secretary of State had on a yellow blouse the last time he had seen her. Now she would be walking around in her bra. A black one, no doubt. Not that she really needed it. Actually, she might be better off without it, because then everyone might think she was an overrfed man and leave her alone.

At last Jack found Dean Whitcomb. She was back at the beach, along with two other older, dignified looking men but the Professor was nowhere in sight. "I never realized how much I loved the sand and the water until you came here with me," she said after she had introduced her companions.

"Yes. It's actually very beautiful to look at but I wouldn't recommend swimming."

"Really? Why not? I know it's completely lifeless so there are no sharks to worry about."

"True. But wade out a ways sometime, into deeper water."

"You mean it's not safe?"

"Safe enough but very strange. It's salty like a sea should be but it also has another rather foul taste to it. Smells a bit too."

"That is strange. What do you think it means?"

"Take another look out there. Now tell me what you don't see."

"All I see is water."

"I know. But if it was a normal, what else would be there?"

"Of course. Besides no fish, there is no seaweed, either."

"Exactly. No sea weed, no algee, no plant life of any kind. No coral either. Nothing. The sea is totally dead."

"That's very bizarre what with so much vegetation here on the land. What do you think that's all about?"

"I don't know. But I have a feeling that if I figure it out, I'm not going to like it."

"That sounds very ominous."

"Possibly. But that's not why you came back here."

"No. But I'd like to talk about it some more sometime. Right now I brought Joe and Bob along so we could have a strategy meeting of sorts." With that she went on to tell Jack what the men's backgrounds were back home and how they had taken what he had said earlier quite seriously.

"Not only have we decided to disavow any connection with all the Americans who still look to what's left of the present administration for leadership and policy," the one named Joe stated, "we are in effect, going to announce a political seperation from them entirely and demand not to be dragged into their petty pursuits. What do you think?"

"It's a great first step. And, a necessary one. But solve the problem? Not at all," Jack said, disappointed that they hadn't seen the most important side of it.

"Really? Why not?"

"Because it's not an "island" problem. It's a decades long problem that has been constantly aggravated and worsened by American arrogance and injustice for longer than most everyone still alive can even remember."

"So, what are you trying to say?" Joe asked. "What would you do?"

Jack weighed the question. The two men seemed astute enough. But they also seemed somewhat naive. Would they listen?

Dean Whitcomb, however, had picked up on his concern. "It's okay, Jack. We understand the gravity of it. But you seem to have had more contact with other factions on the island, so tell us straight out what else you think we should do."

"All right. Like I said before, not only do you have to make your political separation loud and clear but you also have to move. It's mandatory. The separation must not only be ideological but also physical, and far enough away to be clearly significant. And.... probably the quicker the better."

"How do we do that? Where would we go?

"There's a good place further around the coastline another couple of miles where Sam Birnstead, the former Nav Sec stays."

"But that's still a long ways."

"Hopefully, far enough to save your lives, if it comes to that."

"What about food? It's a long ways back to the gate in the wall."

"The fruit tree belt ends right above that area. Ivan's wall is there, too, but I have a feeling we might be able to negotiate some kind of deal."

The three of them looked at each other. "Well," they said. "It's not like we have to take time off from work to make the trek. Or that we need to hire a truck to move all the furniture."

Reverend Billy Boxer had also been rather busy the last few months. Or at least his sheep had been. But he had provided the two most important ingredients, guidance and inspiration. Let them not forget that. Besides, a man of God of his caliber should never have to stoop so low as to do anything quite so physical himself. No. Copying the tactics of the real estate developers, he had been busy keeping his parisheners busy, making him a church and bringing him food so he didn't have to walk up the mountain so he could spend more time praying for their lost souls, poor things. But, that was as it should be, too. What with his closer connection to the Master, he had a much better chance of being heard than they did. So, everything was righteous and in order, as it was in heaven so be it on the island, he would shepherd his flock in good faith, poor souls. Halaluhua. Amen.

And there it was, all laid out on the ground, just like the White House. The one major exception was that he wasn't using sticks taken from trees. He was recycling. The outline of his church was made up of all the discarded banana peels and old apple cores. And with so many people here and with little else to eat, there were a lot of them. They were better than sticks, too, because, if you criss crossed the banana peels and put the apple cores in the middle, you could stack them fairly high. And what with all the eating folks had been doing, his church walls were now almost two feet tall.

He hadn't received any divine inspiration as yet, however, on how to make a stained glass window with religious icons in it but the church did have a stone alter and a cross made of drift wood tied together with the tie he had been wearing when he had disappeared. Unfortunately, the tie was sun faded and becoming weak. The cross arm was badly skewed and the little Jesus figure made from a lump of clay found near the stream was also half dissolved from the rains and distorted so badly it looked more like a beheaded puppet than a member of the holy trinity. But that was what the Lord's work was all about, he kept telling himself. Difficult at best. And since I am in his service, he said, I will walk in the shadow of death and keep plugging away. Too bad, however, that the Americans weren't on better terms with the rest of the people on the island. Think of that. With all their banana peels added to the pile, his walls would have been ten feet high by now.

The previous night Billy had slept quite well in spite of a full day's worth of prayer and agonization over the fate of his good buddy, the President. Before going to sleep he had taken a spiritual vow to spend the next day fasting and praying and making sure the Arabs knew he was starving himself to death over their atrocious behavior. But some where in the night it all went astray and first thing in the morning he found himself devouring bananas and grapes like he would never get enough. Pieces of grape vine worked well in the wall, too, he had found out. Sort of tied it together and gave it strength. He was just in the process of finishing his breakfast and putting the left-overs on the wall when he looked up to see a mass of people going past the church, headed west towards the sea shore and around the island. He stared. What was going on? Had someone found the face of Jesus etched in a tree somewhere, or on a stone. Wow. That would give the sinners something to think about. They could even build a new shrine on the island and charge admission. Five banana peels per visit. That ought to do it.

Looking closer, however, none of the group looked like they were in a religious fervor because surely someone would have come and told him first. So what was happening? Then he spotted Dean Whitcomb, whom he had debated once back in college and lost badly to. At first she tried to avoid him but he made his way into the crowd and confronted her.

"It's really quite simple," she said. "We're leaving."

"Leaving? Where can you go? It's only an island."

"Hopefully, far enough away so that the rest of the islanders won't associate us with you. We are, in effect, seceeding from the union."

"But why? Why would you do that?"

"For a very long list of reasons I don't really care to discuss with you at the moment."

"But, but, but, but you can't do that. What about, united we stand, divided we fall?"

"What about it, Billy?"

"Well, I'm not sure. But what you're doing is the most

180

unpatriotic thing I've ever heard of."

"Oh for god's sake, Billy. You haven't said anything intelligent in your whole life," Dean Whitcomb said and walked off to join the group.

DEBT PAID

General Marcus had gotten almost no sleep since he had been ruthlesly shamed and defeated by the Arabs, and the death of nearly a hundred of his troops hung heavily on his head. He felt embarassed and humiliated and stupid and maybe he was but the more he felt it, the angrier he got. Worse, although the President was still alive two nights ago when he had stealthily gone into the area and located him, he was being so well guarded there was no way he could rescue him without help. A lot of help. He was so well guarded in fact that the General could barely make out that he was still alive until near the end of his observation when he saw the President turn his head and begin swearing at one of his captors. Nothing came of it, of course, except that the captor shoved a banana in the President's mouth to keep him quiet. How mortifying. If only he had an AK-47 in his hands. By God, would he show them then. But he didn't and the General really had all he could do to keep himself from rushing out from behind his cover and tearing the man's head off with his bare hands.

"But what about the Vice President, the Secretary of Defense and the British PM," he was asked after he had returned.

"What about them? They are secondary individuals and that makes them expendable," was all he would say as he continued wracking his brain for ideas.

At last, to tired to even move, the General layed down under a tree to get some rest. As exhausted as the man was, one would have thought he would have slept for three straight days. But no, two hours later he was wide awake, having had an extremely vivid dream.

"That's it," he said when his eyes popped open and he got up and began his search. Appropriately enough, he found what he was looking for to be a part of the White House itself. It was a strong, straight stick about seven feet long and as big around as his arm. Immediately he went to work, carefully scraping and grinding away at one end until he had brought it to a sharp point. With that completed, he hefted it, getting its feel by making practice lunges at some invisible target. When he was satisfied, he set off with a vengence towards the Arab area in broad daylight.

There were just too many damned Arabs in the world, he decided, as he slowed his pace and dodged from behind one tree to another to stay hidden from view. Finally, after a long zig zag course through the woods he arrived at his goal. He was but twenty feet from where the President and the rest of them were tied up and slowly bleeding to death.

"Well," the General said to himself as he heard the President swearing incoherently at his captors once again, who at the moment only numbered five. "The man is tougher than I thought."

Then it was time. The General lifted his sharp stick, holding it out as a lance like a brave knight in shining armor and with a most frightening, blood curdling scream coming from deep inside, he charged with all his might. The scream was so loud and horrifying that the guards were temporarily immobilized and when the President first saw him, a happy smile came to his face. Then, as the General closed the gap between them, it quickly turned to fear and suddenly it was over. The General's spear had gone straight through the middle of the President's chest and became lodged in the tree he was tied to, whereupon the General fell to the ground and began crying like a little boy.

It was a strange and twisted kind of justice. And very lopsided. If it had been fairly proportioned, the president would not have been run through by one of his own people after only a few short days of being tied to a tree. He would have hung there for a year. And every day at least a hundred people would have come by and scrapped off some skin and made him bleed for all the tragedy he had heaped on the innocent during his time in office. Hopefully, by then, Stanley Barkus would have gotten a small glimpse of his own contribution to the long, sad chain of events he was resposible for before his life was punctuated with a spear. Not speared through just once, however, but at least a thousand times. Maybe more.

Completely dumbfounded, the duty guards could only stare. Finally, they called for their leader who had also heard the General's war cry and was already on his way. There was a long string of harsh words in Arabic punctuated with hand waving and gesturing and moving about. Then the leader went to the General, bent over and slapped him hard across the face, then twice more. Finally the General stopped crying as the guards dragged him to his feet.

"Your own President," the leader said in English. "You must have hated him pretty badly."

"No," said the General between sobs. "I loved him so much I couldn't let him suffer any longer. I owed him my life. If he hadn't started the war with you guys, my career would have been all over a long time ago and I would have ended up in one of those extended care facilities wearing diapers in my old age. Putting him out of his misery was the least I could do under the circumstances."

The leader stared in disbelief, scratched his head, then gave a command to his men. The men moved forward and with all the strength they could muster, finally freed the General's lance from the tree and removed it from the President.

"I'm ready," the General said, coming to attention and sticking out his chest. But he waited in vain. At last he said, "Well, get it over with. I have nothing to live for now."

"That's not what we had in mind," the leader said as he handed the general back his sharpened stick. "We thought you might want to do us a favor and finish off the rest of them."

"The rest of who?" he asked. "You mean the Vice President and those people?" he queried with a most incredulous look on his face.

"Who else?" said the Arab leader.

"No way. Let them hang there and suffer. I never liked those two sons-a-bitches and that other bitch anyway," the General said and handed the spear back to the Arabs. "Now will you hurry up and run me through so I can be laid to rest with the President."

"Sorry, old man," the leader said. "Now get out of here before we have to carry you."

"But I insist."

"And we refuse."

"I vehemently insist," the General said.

"Well, we don't know what vehemently means so will you just get the hell out of here."

"Then give me back my spear. I'll find a way to do it myself."

"Sorry, old man. Too late for that."

"Then hold it up so I can run into it," the General demanded, his voice at the point of breaking.

"You should be so lucky," the Arab leader told him.

"But, boss," one of the men said. "I thought you said a good American is a dead American?"

"I did. But after the act this one comitted I'd rather have his own people take care of him."

Stupified, the General was no longer able to speak. He stared morosely at the leader, took a long last look at the President's body, then turned and slowly shuffled off.

"Not that way, you fool. Your area is back there."

"I know," said the General. "But the closest way to suicide cliff is this way."

At this point the Vice President gathered together enough strength to speak in a loud voice.

"Wait a minute, General," she commanded. "I'm the President now, thanks to you, and as your new Commander in Chief I am ordering you back to the American sector to mount another rescue mission. Only this time I expect you to make a success of it. You have two days to get us out of here. Do I make myself clear?"

The General stopped just long enough to hear the new Chief Executive out. But then, without a word of acknowledgement he continued walking in the same direction he had started out in.

ONWARD

Two days was correct. It took two more days before the Vice President, the Secretary of Defense and the British PM all expired. By then the Secretary of State had moved into the White House and claimed it for her own. Since the rightful heir to the high office, the Speaker of the House of Representatives, had somehow remained behind with the rest of Congress, the Secretary of State was able to empower herself. Immediately thereafter she called together what was left of the government. They met out on the grass in front of the White House where she made new appointments to fill all the vacant posts resulting from the conflict with the Arabs. "You are the new Secretary of Defense," she said to the Colonel who had freed her and dragged her back to camp.

"And the Secretary of Commerce is the lucky individual who gets my old job and..."

Down the list she went, re forming the administration. When she came to the navy, she said, "Well, we still have the Nav Sec with us so we can skip that one."

"No you don't," said Sam, who had been hanging around in the background. "I haven't been on this team since I got here and I'm not about to start now."

"And just exactly what do you mean by that?"

"Just what I said. I'm not against you but I'm not for you either and I want no part of anything you intend to do from here on out."

"Well," she said indignently. "I guess that explains why we don't have any navy. You haven't even bothered to build one canoe in all this time, let alone something useful like a sailboat. Why is that, anyway?"

"Really? I do happen to have a canoe but you're not getting a ride in it. As for sailboats, if you don't know the why not of that one, I'm certainly not going to try and explain it to you."

With that she turned around and looked at some of her new appointees. "What's he talking about? What's wrong with sailboats? Which one of you knows?"

The new Secretary of the Interior raised his hand. "Madam President, perhaps I can help you," he said, waiting.

"Well, don't stand there. Speak up, man. Help me out here."

"Yes sir, mam, your honor, uh, Mrs. President. You see, someone climbed the mountain there way back when. Not me, of course. I'm too old to be stomping around in that white stuff. But I believe it was actually the Nav Sec there. Probalby the only one on the island who would have bothered but the story is that from up there you can see at least a hundred miles out in every direction."

"Okay. So what? What's the point of your story?"

"Yes. Well, the point is that there's nothing out there and no place to go."

"How can you say that? There has to be something further out."

"Well, sure. Perhaps, anyway. But how to get there. We have light breezes here but they're not strong enough to power a sailboat and there are no prevailing winds so if you did happen to get started you would never get anywhere. Or, if you happened to get a little ways from shore you'd probably end up being stranded out there and starve to death. And so, well, there you go."

When he stopped talking the new President looked at him sceptically but said, "Hmmm. Gerald, isn't it? Your name is Gerald, right. Good. Okay Gerald, since you seem to be so well informed I'm making your the new Secretary of the Navy instead. Consider it done. So, what's next? Who can I find to take your place as the late Interior Secretary. You there," she pointed and continued on with her original agenda, adding six more names to her cabinet posts.

With that completed, she outlined her new agenda. The first item was the Arabs. "For the sake of world peace we cannot let these mavericks get away with the great atrocities they have committed against humanity. Tthe loss of our President was not only our loss, but a loss to the entire planet, even if we may personally no longer be dwelling on it ourselves. Furthermore, there will never be peace here on this new island home of ours, or back home, unless we can democratize each and everyone and convert them all to our good family value way of thinking with conformity and uniformity. And should that become impossible then we must exterminate them completely. God's will is not to be questioned, but to be obeyed."

"Holy damn," someone was over heard to say. "She's as delusional as Stanley."

"Worse," their companion pointed out as the first female President on the island continued.

"We must not be deterred in our duty," she said. "But, before we pick up weapons we shall try diplomacy. In other words, we will do our best to intimidate them. After all, there are still more Americans on the island than any one other single group and, with that in mind, we will send forth a delegation. To lead that delegation I hereby appoint the former President's dear friend, Reverend Billy, to head it up. Where are you Billy? Raise your hand so I can see you. No need to be so shy now...... Ahhh, there you are. Good to see you. Take as many of your loyal parisheners with you as you see fit. Go to the Arabs and tell them we will forgive what they have done. But only if they turn over that bunch of hooligans who rose up from their midst and took away our high officials. We need to bring them to trail and hang them."

What, Billy thought to himself? Me? Go talk to the Arabs in person? Oh, no! Almost paralysed with fear, it took him a long time to respond. What could he say, what plausible sounding excuse could he make?

"But, but, Ms. President," he stammered at last. "Maybe it would be best to send someone else. I still have my flock to attend to and that is always a most difficult daily challenge that is making extreme demands on me. So much so that I was about to name a couple of assistants to help out in this time of great need."

"I understand, Billy. It is a time of great tribulation, no doubt about that. But your country is calling you. I am calling you and God is calling you."

"Well, gee," he said, his mind racing around in circles, feeling the pressure from all the eyes that were now on him. How had he ever let himself get backed into a corner such as this? Why hadn't someone gotten sick this morning so he would have had to attend to them? But, no. Here he was, caught short, never able to think quickly on his feet, without a plausable sounding, side stepping excuse in sight. So...What else could he do? There wasn't time for a pleading prayer to his maker.

"Well," he said again. "If it really is that important, how can I, a servant of the Lord and a servant of my country, refuse. So, I guess I have no other....I mean I, gee, well, I guess I accept. How soon do we have to, oh my, leave?"

"Just as soon as we attend to this second item on the national agenda. In my opinion we would also be more successful here if we had a White House more in keeping with the status of our great nation and with the high office I now hold. Don't forget, we are still the world's only remaining super power and we should never let the rest of the world forget it. The solution to that problem is, however, quite easy and it is with great pride that I present it to you now. Would you like to hear what it is?"

The response was over whelming and the air was full of responses such as, Yeah, good grief, sure, and, well, why not, and, go ahead, get it over with, so she proceeded.

"I will not call it a tax," she said, "for that is a frightful word. So, we will call it a priviledge instead. Twice a week I want every American to do their patriotic duty and bring the largest stone they can reasonably carry here and place it on the pile. Soon the pile will become a wall, and then another wall and another. Within six weeks we will have a White House made of stone. And while that is going on the Secretary of Defense will dismantle the old building, saving all the heavier, straighter sticks which will be summarily sharpened as spears and put in the national arsenal in case of emergency. The rest will be used to try and make a roof."

"But where will we get all the stones?" someone shouted out. "Ivan already has most of them and if we put the rest of them in the White House, how will we be able to get food?"

"I have but one answer," the President said. "And in the words of one of our greatest Presidents of all time I say to you now. Tear down that wall!!"

There was a murmur in the crowd. The murmur turned to a cheer and the cheer rose to become the second crescendo that could be heard almost clear around the island within a week. At least it was heard by the Arabs.

"Here we go again," they said. "Those damned fools never learn?"

Deanna's first six days on the side of the mountain passed quickly enough. But they were not entirely conflict free. Two of the twenty women she had been sharing space were clearly jealous. They had both wanted Ivan for themselves and soon told her so. Even if he had shared them both, they would not have objected, they said. They might even share him with Deanna, if that was what it came to. If only he hadn't been so stubborn about it, all the time claiming such a liason would become too complicated. What kind of excuse was that? And telling them that eventually they would find other men to spend their days with, instead. Most of the other women would too, he assured them, when they were ready. Didn't matter, they still wanted Ivan.

As for the rest, well, there were at least ten times more men than women in their group. But that was hardly a problem even though there were no rules because Ivan had made none. Do what you want, he had told them right at the beginning, and that included the women. But only as long as it doesn't go against the wishes of another. Everything must be completely and mutually consentual. And, as long as some poor lout doesn't fall too helplessly in love with one of the women and start causing trouble, everything should be okay. As for himself, however, how many of the women had shared his bed, Deanna seriously wondered, but was determined never to ask. None of the women there ever claimed he did, though. At least not in her presence. But they said other things. Mostly about her character.

"We're disappointed," one of them told her.

"And why is that?"

"We thought all American women were arrogant, self centered bitches and we would would have some fun messing with you. But you ruined it."

Deanna laughed. "That sounds like a compliment. I hope. Thank you."

"Especially those two, Nadya and Kirana. They're very jealous."

"I know. They already told me."

"Well, don't worry. If they ever did anything serious and Ivan learned of it ...."

"He wouldn't. I'd find a way to handle it myself."

"Hmm," said Tanya, the one she was talking with who nodded with approval in a sign of acceptance. Welcome to the club. They would be friends. Tanya was one of three women who also spoke English and had been assigned to serve as an interpretor.

Another woman approached and said something to Tanya in Russsian.

"A visitor comes to see you," she related to Deanna in turn. "He waits outside by the, what is the word? Banana. The banana tree."

"Do you know who it is?"

"Nyet," was the response as her eyebrows went up. Deanna was supposed to be Ivan's woman. That was the story. But now a stranger had shown up. She had to learn to understand some Russian. There was always chatter amongst the other women when she returned from her visits with Ivan and a few even rolled their eyes at her. None of it seemed maliscious, however, but she wanted to know. But another man showing up. That brought some skewed looks and a different kind of unknown commentary. Who could it be? Certainly not one of her former captors. They wouldn't dare. There was only one other.

It was Jack. As yet none of the women knew of the role he had played in getting her there.

"Look at you," he said with an approving smile.

"What?"

"You're ten years younger."

"More," she said with a happy smile. "I'll never be able to thank you enough."

"You already have. Just look at you."

"A safe place to sleep, a dip in the pool every morning, don't have to beg for food, I'm allowed to go anywhere I want and everyone treats me like a human being. I don't know what would have happened if you hadn't come along."

"I can't even imagine what it must have been like."

"No cops on the street. No way to call 911. Total humiliation and helplessness. Living without hope. I would rather have been in jail."

"Ivan is the guy who sent me. Is everything okay in that regard?"

"An absolute gentleman. And very intuitive. No pressure whatsoever. Hasn't even tried to hold my hand as yet. Helping me get my trust back, I guess."

"Seems to be working."

"Yeah," she said with a big sigh as she wiped away a tear. Then she gave him a serious look.

"Damnit, Jack. I never met a man like this before. Or one like you. I have a feeling the two of you are somewhat alike. Except, there always was that chemical thing with Ivan. And now..... what am I going to do? I think I'm half in love already."

"That scares you?"

"Immensely. Especially if it doesn't work out. What would I do

189

then?"

"Be friends. I think he will always be your friend."

"And you, Jack. You're my friend. I know that."

"Always. But speaking of that........"

"Ah, Jack. Good to see you again," Ivan said as he approached, holding out his hand.

They shook and smiled at each other then Ivan turned to Deanna, still with a smile but of a different kind, deeper, their eyes locked together. He asked her how her morning had been. Her response was positive and up beat. The three bantered back and forth for a few minutes, then it was time for Jack to leave. Or so he said, and did so graciously. Looking back at them as he moved away he noticed that their hands had found each other. He grinned and kept going.

Long walks allowed them to continue their discussions. But they were never long enough for Deanna. The nights helped, however. Additional time with each other as everyone gathered together in an open clearing when the moon was up.

Some members of the group had hollowed out pieces of log and used them for drums. There were also sticks and rocks to beat on and one clever individual had removed the pulp from the inside of a long plant stalk and made a didjeridu. There were also hollowed out coconut shells to tap out tunes on. And, yes, she was teaching Ivan how to dance.

"Well," Ivan said to her on the seventh evening. "I will never be able to thank Jack enough. I wonder what I could do to show my appreciation," he said to Deanna.

"You?" she replied. "I owe him my life. I will never be able to repay him for that. But there must be something we can do. Sometimes he seems so lonely. I wonder why?"

"I don't know. He has never said much about himself. Of course I actually only met him the day before he brought you here. And that was because he came to see if he could come freely through the gate when he wanted. That's what started it all. I think he spends his nights higher up on the mountain."

"And probably alone. That's how we can help."

"How?"

"Invite him to the evening gatherings. The company would do him good."

"Yes. I should have thought of it myself. I can introduce him to some of the women. I'm sure one of them would like him well enough."

"I'm sure they would but I think it goes deeper than that. I think there is already someone else back home. And, speaking of nights, you have never shown me where you spend your time sleeping, either. Is it a secret?"

"Of course not. But what's to see? It's not exactly the Hilton."

"Show me," she said, so he led her away to a place in the trees about a hundred yards distant where a leanto had been constructed. There were several more scattered around, all respectable distances away.

"Well, like I said. It's not much, but it's home."

Deanna looked it over, then put her head inside for a few seconds.

"Hmmm," she said, looking at him directly. "There is only one problem."

"Really? It has a problem? What is that?"

"It's more than big enough for two and you are sleeping alone."

"I, well..."

"Well, is right," she said as she took his hand and pulled him inside. "We have both been doing that long enough."

"I'm impressed," Jack said to Ivan a few days later, watching the intermingling crowd in the moonlight. "It's like a folk festival."

"Indeed, but it is entirely improv. Would you like to sing for us?"

"Maybe later," Jack said as an excuse while a woman and three men belted out a Russian drinking song.

"I wonder what it is?" he continued after they finished and the roar of approval died down.

"What do you mean?" Ivan asked.

"Thousands of people on the island from all over the world but your group is by far the most cohesive and conflict free of them all."

"I don't know about that but we have to be doing better than the Arabs or the Americans."

"Why do you think that is, Jack?" Deanna asked.

"Building the wall was a unifying force. So is having control over the food supply. But it goes beyond that."

"It didn't start out that way. That was never our conscious intent. The only thing I knew was that our people needed something constructive to do to keep it together in this place. Having all that

191

power also made them feel important and we had some good times telling the world's leaders to ... well, you know," he said, looking sideways at Deanna.

She laughed heartily, Jack followed and soon they were all doubled over. Then they were back to being serious again.

"I think it had some other positive benifits, too," Jack said. "The more time people have to spend looking for stones, the less time they have to squabble."

"What about the evenings? How did all this come about?" Jack asked.

"Just one of those things. One night after the wall was all up and everyone else had finally accepted all the silly rules we made up about getting the food, we got together to celebrate a little. Somehow it caught on and we just kept doing it."

"It's a good thing. Another part of why your people seem more at peace with being here."

"Do you think so? Sometimes it's hard to tell. You know that old story about walls. They keep others out but they also keep you in. So, occassionally we take the risk and sneak around down below. But it is not the same as with you, coming and going freely. So, I'm sure we miss a lot of things too. But for now I am very happy," Ivan said as he put his arm around Deanna and hugged her.

"Not nearly as happy as I am," she said and kissed his cheek.

"And I'm happy, too. For the both of you," Jack said, even though seeing them together sometimes accentuated his own solitary life. Would he and Katherine have been equally happy together if she were still here? He thought so. But before he could dwell on it, Deanna continued.

"And I think his idea for the wall was one of the best things that could have happened. Like you said, good or bad, it gives people some structure. Every day they have to deal with it if they want to eat."

"Yes, I'm sure you are both right. But sometimes I get a little tired of it. I know some of the men feel the same way but I think we all realize the importance of it for now. So, we will wait and see."

"You don't seem concerned about the new President's intent to tear it down," Jack said, giving Ivan a grin. "Didn't think so. Sending that revivalist preacher out might just do it."

"What is that?" Ivan asked. Neither he nor Deanna were aware of that aspect.

Jack explained Billy's presidential mission.

Ivan laughed, then became serious. "Maybe you should stay

up here with us for a few days until we know how it ends."

Try as he might, Reverand Billy could not think of a single reason as to why his mission should be canceled. But for three days in a row he had at least been able to come up with a succession of excuses to stall the actual moment of marching off, flimsy as they were. Then, as he ran out of inventions, he began blaming the new President, a woman. What an unnatural thing. A female for President. How absurd. His friend Stanley never would have done this to him. But then how did Stanley get himself into such a mess to begin with? How did he do that, anyway? And end up dead, leaving Billy in such a predicament. Damn him, it really was his fault, wasn't it? He never should have taken that sermon Billy had given about an eye for an eye so seriously. Heaven help him, poor soul. But, now what?

That question was answered directly enough on the fourth day when the lady President gave him an ultimatum. Proceed as instructed or the government would confiscate his new church building.

Reluctantly, Billy picked thirty of his most fervent parisheners and had them gather as many white T-shirts as they could find. Or T-shirts that used to be white, since without soap to wash things in everything had a dinghy taint to it. But they did their best and with the shirt remnants tied to sticks raised high in the air as signs of truce, they marched valiantly off. When they were almost to the Arab area, Billy stopped them and lined them up, side by side, in two columns. Then, with the biggest of the flags in his own hands he shouted out the command to move forward and to begin singing, "Onward Christian Soldiers." It was the one and only hymn they had practiced and that is what they sang at the top of their voices. Onward Christian Soldiers is what they were still singing clear into the heart of the Arab territory. All of them except for one. That poor distressed soul had started out with enthusiasm and conviction, directly behind Billy, but as the singing continued and Billy's high screetch of a voice kept drowning out his own he began dropping further back in the line. Worse, he also stopped singing.

He couldn't sing because other thoughts began to plague him. Things he had always known but had been sucessfully able to rationalize away. Until now. Back home, one in six children in the US went to bed hungry at night. Billy was a multi, multi millionare. His private plane alone, cost twenty five million dollars. How many children would that amount of money feed? The house he lived in cost over ten million. It had eleven bedrooms and fourteen bathrooms and only two people had lived there. There were maids and chauffeurs but they all had seperate cottages. And then there were the three limos and five Cadillacs, not to mention the ninety three foot yacht he kept in the Bahamas and only used to haul around other equally rich and over indulged personages. And what about the fact that the man had always spent enough on his clothes alone to keep five families in food. What was that all about, he began to ask himself over and over and the more he asked, the further back in line he fell. Then there was the thing about being born sinful. And God let people murder his only son to absolve the sinful? It was really difficult to understand the logic of that one. Wasn't that condoning murder? But two thousand years ago? What about all the sinners who came after that? And then there was the symbol of the holy son hanging on the cross with nails through his hands and feet. That was really dismal, disturbing and downright gruesome, with all kinds of negative connotations attached to it.

It was also extremely depressing to think that sex was so dirty that Mother Mary wasn't allowed to procreate in a normal way. And why did God temp poor Eve with that apple if he knew ahead of time she would't be able to resist it and, and, and, oh, my. It was migraine creating stuff, all right. And none of it made any sense except that Billy was a hypocrite who was also the President's buddy and sleep in the White House when he went to Washington and in turn hauled the President around on his yacht that ate up thirty gallons of fuel for every mile it went. Fuel paid for by guilt ridden, coerced parishioners who sometimes went without life's necessities to be able to mail Billy in a contribution. And what about the ex President, that self proclaimed man of God who seemed to think that the Ten Commandments only applied to other people and not to him.? And not only that but.... But here he was, marching along behind this, this... what? Why? Why was he doing that? That was the question. And maybe to his death. Did that make any sense at all? No, it did not. Blind allegiance had to be some form of insanity, he suddenly decided, and that was that. But why had he always been so amenable all these years? Try as he might, he coudn't find an answer to that one.

But of course he didn't have to ask anyone else. In his own heart he knew. He had always known. He had been afraid. He had been so afraid, he was afraid to admit it. He didn't want to go to hell. Hell was a really bad place reserved for sinners, full of fire and eternal damnation. He had believed in hell. The truth shall set you free, he remembered his boyhood pastor always shouting at the congregation. Jesus is the truth and if you don't embrace Jesus you will go straight to hell and burn and burn and burn. Oh God, he didn't want to do that. Who would? Jesus, what a mortifying, immobilizing thought. And now, like a lightening strike the bigger truth hit him. It was all a scam. He had been duped. He had been lied to and ripped off, mentally, morally and financially. They didn't give a damn about his soul. All they wanted was his mind and all those crisp dollar bills he had been conned into putting in the plate over the years. It was about control, power and money. He had been violated. He had been mentally and spiritually raped. Damn Billy. Damn them all. Damn himself. What a fool he had been. But no more, damnit. Enough was enough and with that he stopped and dropped his white flag on the ground.

"Dear God, strike me dead if I am wrong," he said and turned around, waiting to see what would happen, still half prepared to be zapped.

The rest of Billy's group, however, never misssed a step or a beat and heartily pushed onward, singing their hearts out. And, since not a single Arab came out to meet them or greet them or even to look at them or obstruct them, they kept on marching and singing and marching and singing until they had passed entirely through the Arab area. It was only when they ran into a group of Japanese sitting around chattering that they knew they had gone too far. Much too far.

"About face," Billy commanded, then scurried back around so he was again at the head of the line. "Onward," he cried, and back they went, still singing, even louder than before.

This time, however, they had only proceeded a few hundred yards when they ran into a solid wall of Arabs all armed with sharp sticks and clubs. Billy stopped singing. The men directly behind him also stopped singing but those in the rear seemed unaware and continued, verse after verse, still marching in place as they did so. Then Billy looked closely at all the spears. One particularly sharp and dangerous one was pointed right at him. He quickly lowered his white flag, removed the white shirt from the stick it was on and held it up between himself and his adversary and peaked over the top. The spear was still in place, the spear holder staring back at him.

"I need to speak with your leader," Billy was finally able to mutter, feeling like he was six years old again, facing an angry father who was about to belt him for slipping five dollars out of his wallet when he was napping. Then he trembled and remembered that he had also wet his pants on that occassion. With that he crossed his legs slightly and repeated his demand.

"There are no leaders here," he was advised in broken English.

"But we came to negotiate," he said, standing as tall as he could and leaning forward. It wasn't that he was short. The problem was that he was very narrow shouldered for a man and rather hollow chested. More accurately, very hollow chested. Taking big breaths and leaning forward helped but he still came across as a wimp. If only he had one of his custom tailered suit coats on with the big shoulder pads and that extra little bit of padding behind the lapels. Then maybe he would get some respect. But he didn't so he spoke loudly and as deeply as possible with his limited lung capacity.

"How can we negotiate if there is no one here in a decision making capacity. I find that to be completely ridiculous."

"Well, too bad. The decisions have already been made. This is our territory and you do not have permission to re enter. And, if you don't make those idiots stop that damned singing, we will beat you to death here and now.

Billy turned to his group, gave a loud shout and waved his arms. Finally it was quiet.

"We have come on a peaceful mission," he stated again, still doing his best to appear stalwart. "And we demand to speak with your leaders."

"You should have called ahead," said one of the men. "They are very busy today and cannot see you. They are very busy tomorrow, also. In fact, they will be very busy for at least a month."

"But that will never do," Billy said. "This is of vital importance to us all."

"To you, perhaps. But not to us."

Billy was getting frustrated and the put offs were making him angry. But he hadn't been poked with a sharp stick as yet, however, and that was encouraging. So, controlling his apprehensions, he stubbornly stood his ground and kept repeating his demand, talking so fast he hadn't realized he was no longer being answered. Neither did he see the slowly advancing spear point until it touched him on the chest and gave him a mild jab. At last. The real message penetrated his skull.

"All right, all right," he said, backing away and mellowing his tone of voice. "If that's the way you want it perhaps you could bend down with us here and I'll say a little prayer. Then maybe you could please step aside so we can go home."

"No prayer to your false God and no permission to pass. We cannot allow you back into our area."

"Well, we'll see about that," one of Billy's bolder disciples said as he pushed his way forward, only to be bashed with a club and knocked to his knees. Then another one tried it and received the same treatment.

"But how are we going to get home?" Billy demanded. "You're here and Ivan's wall is up there."

"Go that way," he was told.

"But that's the ocean. And there is no beach there to walk on along this part of the island," Billy said, and looked around.

By then a group of stick bearing Japanese had also gathered behind them. "Don't even think of it," their leader said. "You won't be spending the night here, either."

With that, Billy's people helped the two injured ones to their feet and they reluctantly headed towards the ocean with the Arabs quickly closing in behind, filling the gap, making it impossble for them to back track. As they walked Billy could think of no other appropriate hymn to sign under the circumstances so he kept repeating his version of the Lord's Prayer over and over until his voice gave out. Then they marched in silence. At last they reached the cliff overhanging the water. It was not a high cliff, actually, barely forty feet tall and the shore line below was without rocks and provided a clear drop into the ocean. Everyone stopped.

"Please. In the name of Jesus, you cannot do this," Billy pleaded. "We will go home and tell our new President to leave you alone if you will just give us one last passage through your area."

"In the name of Jesus it is much too late for that," he was told. "But look, you only have to swim about a mile. See the sand around there. If you can make it that far you can walk the rest of the way back."

"It's impossible," Billy responded.

"It's impossible," said the rest of Billy's group.

"How do you know? You haven't tried it yet," one of the Arabs said and jabbed one of Billy's men in the ribs with his spear, forcing him over the edge. By now Billy was on his knees, praying and pleading, but to no avail.

"Tell him about the Bible, Billy. And that commandment about not killing," one of the men said.

That brought Billy to his feet again. "I don't want them to laugh at me," Billy responded. "We're Americans and with our track record... what could I possibly say?"

"Well, they shouldn't kill us just because of that. Should they? We don't have anything they want."

"That's not the point," Billy said. "Sophisticated, First World people like us only kill for power and profit. Third World infidels like these kill for vengence or even just for the heck of it."

"Looks like we're screwed," Billy's man said.

"Probably true. But just because we're all about to die doesn't mean you couldn't choose your words a little better," Billy chastized him. He was about to make some further comment but, before he could, more spear jabs quickly followed and another dozen of Billy's delegation went over the side. The rest tried to turn and run but were quickly knocked down and forced over the edge, leaving Billy standing all alone. Fearfully, he looked at all the spear points that were now pointed at him and all the scowling faces of the bearers. He stammered, he pleaded, he begged, he called on every deity he could think of and then he cursed loudly. Jesus had let him down. The church had let him down. Civilization had let him down. It was not his fault, not a bit of it. So, now what? There was nothing left to do. He wiped his hand across his face to brush away the tears. Then the expression on his face began to change. Slowly at first, but soon enough he was smiling, then he became downright happy and slapped his knees.

"Halleluhja," he shouted. "I'm going to be a martyr." he said with exhilaration. "A martyr, a martyr, a martyr," he chanted, dancing around with a wild look in his eyes, then tripped and tumbled over backwards into the sea, letting out another long halleluhja. But then, just before he hit the water a young boy's face flashed before his eyes, the young boy he had so malisciously molested so many, many years before and he suddenly realized his whole life had been a sham, a cover up and a warped attempt to compensate and supress other desires. Dear Jesus, he screamed. But Jesus didn't hear him, nor did anyone else because he hit the water before the sound could leave his mouth.

Moving closer to the edge and looking down, the Arabs watched closely. Billy was the only one who had failed to come to the surface. The rest were swimming as hard and as fast as they could, but all very badly.

"Is that what must be done to become a martyr?" one Arab asked.

The man next to him only shook his head. "He was even dumber than that camel of mine who got lost in the desert. None of them will make it back and by tomorrow all the bodies will wash up in dead man's cove. The rest of the Americans will think they were all cowards and comitted suicide."

"Well, what's wrong with that? It's the truth, isn't it?"

RELOCATION

The distance between First and Second Island was less than the length of two football fields and at low tide the water was less than three feet deep in the middle, but, few people ever went there. There was one fresh water spring to drink from but the rest of the water on the island was in the form of small ponds. These ponds all had a greasy slick on their surfaces and smelled like old motor oil. There was also very little that was edible. A few heavily thorned berry bushes grew here and there along with a scattering of banana palms whose fruit never totally rippened. Most abundant of all was a wiry, vine like plant that produced a bitter tasting variety of squash. There were also tall, broadleaf trees growing in clutches but it was nearly impossible to take advantage of the shade. Thick, thorny underbrush grew tightly around them that was extremely difficult to penetrate. And, as if all that were not bad enough, a stagnant, brown hazy cloud hung low over the island. It smelled exactly like big city smog and filtered the sun, making everything take on the hue of an ancient, faded photograph from the past. Needless to say, no one had ever bothered to stay the night. At least not until the original group of arrivals on First Island had all been forced to stay there.

The Iranians and the North Koreans were in the lead, followed by the Syrians, the Iraquis, the Palastinians, the Saudis, the Turks, the Libyans, the Egyptians and even a dispersed group of Malasians. They came howling into the original American area at the crack of dawn, rounded up everyone in sight and herded them all to the south side of the island just across the water from Second Island. As planned, the tide was out so the attackers screamed and threatened and prodded and whacked away at the American's backs until they had forced the approximately seventeen hundred Americans of this group to wade across. Few resisted, but some turned on the attackers and for a while the shallow stretch of ocean between the islands was red with blood. Then, once all the Americans had been finally forced across, armed guards were posted all along the shore of First Island so no one could return.

The other American group led by Dean Whitcomb, newly relocated further on around the island, however, was far more fortunate. The majority of the members of the anti-American coalition involved in the attack had no interest in pursuing them. If anything, they were quite pleased. Not only had it shown them that there were still a few Americans who had some brains and did not blindly follow after their leaders, it also reduced the number of Americans left to be dealt with to a more managable size. Thus far everything had gone much smoother than had been expected and once it was clear as to who was in control of what, the Arab leaders shouted over and said it was necessary for the new American President and other top officials to wade back across so they could be informed of the new set of rules that were to be imposed upon them.

"We're not coming," the Americans shouted back.

"Your choice," said the enemy leaders and started to walk away. "There's very litle to eat and drink over there, so if you want to breath foul air and die of starvation, go ahead."

"Is that true?" the president asked her advisors.

"I don't know," was the most common reply. "I've never been here before."

"Well, find somebody who has and hurry up about it."

They did. And the enemy's assertions had been correct.

This revelation quickly promoted a short and very heated debate amongst the President, the new Secretary of State and the new Secretary of Defense. Then the Secretary of State called out, "Wait. We're coming," and the two Secretaries set out, leaving the President behind.

When they made it back across and stood before their rivals, they were told, "Since you are all so dumb as to let that big block of lard be your leader, she must come over here, too."

Finally, after considerable shouting back and forth, the President also waded back across, displacing a considerable amount of water in doing so. She was about to make some derogatory comment about the whole thing but decided against it, and, for the first time in several years, listened instead.

"Too bad you have wasted so much of our time," the Arab leader said. "We were going to tell you the new rules about how you could come back here to get food but you put up too big a fuss. Now you will have to wait until tomorrow."

"Tomorrow?" the president said in an outraged voice, staring back in a despicable way. "Tomorrow? Why?"

"Do you also have a hearing problem?" the Arab asked, staring back until her eyes finally dropped. Then he waited some more. "Well," he said. "Maybe I have one. I didn't hear your answer."

"I, I, a, a, I...."

"Good. Now turn around and go back across to your new home. Our guards will be here all night. Anyone attempting to cross before we get back will be dealt with severely," he said in a harsh voice and drew his finger across his neck for emphasis.

The following day the coalition leaders did not return until nearly noon. When they came, the President and her staff were waiting anxiously on the opposite shore. By now every skinny banana and berry on the small island had been picked and eaten and they were still hungry. But for those in command of the situation, that was not good enough. Now the Arabs wanted every American governmental official and every religious official who was there to come across so they could all line up in a row. In spite of the fact that the tide was part way in and the water was another foot or so deeper than it would have been in the morning. The Secretary of Defense was sent back to summon them. When that was finally done, Arab and Korean men with pots made of coconut shells filled with a bright purple dye came down the line of half drowned people. Dipping into the shells with sticks whose ends had been mashed and frayed into paint brushes, they placed a large dab on every forehead in the line and made the recipients lie down in the sun until the spot was completely dried. Then they were sent back. Last to be branded were the President and the members of the Cabinet but they each received two dye spots on their foreheads instead of just one. While they were lying on the ground letting the dye set, the rules they were to live by were reiterated to them.

"The dye penetrates deep into the skin. It will not wash away. If you try to rub it off it will make a deep wound. Everyone with the double mark will spend the rest of their nights here on Second Island. Once a day you will be allowed to come back across to get food but if you are caught over here at night, you will be killed. The rest of the people with you must spend at least one month on that island. Then, if certain conditions are meet, they may be allowed to relocate. They, too, can come for food once a day. All persons will be escorted from here to the orchard area and back. All food, however, must be eaten on this side of the channel. None can be taken across. That way, everyone must come and get their own. If

201

you think this is unfair, you may be right. Or maybe not. We don't care."

AND THEN THERE WAS FIRE

Just to prove that he could do it, Jack built a fire. It really wasn't that difficult. Using a long shoelace and a strong stick, he made a small bow and used it to spin another straight stick on top of a piece of dry, soft wood. But, of what use was it? The temperature was always moderate on the island and there was nothing that really needed cooking. Nor was the knowledge of how to start a fire something that needed to be shared. If anything, it could easily become a menace. So, having built his small fire, Jack, in turn, put it out and quickly forgot about it.

The idea of fire itself, was not to be forestalled, however, since Jack was not the only person on the island to have the knowledge of how to create one and not long afterward others began making their own. Within a short time one of the major users of fire was the Catholic Church. It was found that the branches of certain small trees burned slowly and uniformly and made good substitutes for candles. Historically, the Church had always burned lots of candles. The church on the island was no exception. It also had one thing the people back home did not have. That was the Pope.

Surprizingly, the old man was still alive. Bent, crochety, feeble, archaic, drooling in his sleep. But, far too stubborn to die, he still issued mandates and edicts and talked about papal infalibility. And, just as back home, he was still surrounded by the same subordinates who basked in the shadow of his power, subordinates who had blessed people with holy water with one hand and molested helpless nuns and little children with the other, all in the name of God. How deep can hypocrisy ingrain itself? How many levels are there in the church? How many layers are there to the human mind? None of it mattered, however, because always more people brought their freedom and the integrity of their minds to the sanctimonious and laid it at their feet. It had been true back home, it was still true on the island. The only positive thing about the island was that there were no children on it to molest and almost no women of the cloth to abuse because women did not have positions of power in the church. As a result there was no one for the righteous heirarchy to get their sick hands on except each other and the few twisted souls who still attended the holy masses. As an organization, the church was just as corrupt and destructive as ever, and just as broken and near death as the supreme being who ran it.

But without a doubt, it too would one day soon stumble and fall and never be able to get up again. In the meantime, however, it still bumbled dangerously along.

Shortly after their arrival the Pope had appointed one of the Archbishops keeper of the calendar and he kept the record of the days and weeks and months and had reconstructed all the holy days to the best of his memory so they could be honored. Mass was still held every Wednesday and every Sunday and confessionals were always available night or day. The church itself was also made of sticks, just like the White House, but the sticks of the church were stood on end and lashed together with grape vines to form an enclosure. Although the Pope had also talked about putting up stone walls to take their place, everyone was always too busy to put it into effect. Still, it would not be a real church until it had a roof over it, the Pope insisted, so longer poles were gathered and the structure covered over. The Africans, whose area was nearby, always laughed when they saw it, however, for it made no sense to them.

"Christians put up a structure and call it a temple and say you must go inside it to find God but we always thought God was every where so the best place to talk to God would be outside in the presence of nature under the sky where the beauty of all creation can be seen."

"What would you know," they were told in return. "You are nothing but wayward heathens who have never known the love of Jesus, and he is the son of God."

"But we don't need Jesus to love us to make us whole, or to act as our intermediary because we are all God's children. We just need him to leave us alone so we can go on loving each other."

It was an ongoing dispute. The Africans had a good time with it, the Catholics took it very seriously and were deeply bothered by such differences of opinion. As long as it persisted there would always be a few small shreds of doubt festering away in the dark, shuttered, hidden recess of their minds where it might grow and destroy all the many long years of dogma that had been planted there. To protect themselves they would have to make a concentrated effort to convert these uncivilized beings to the ways of Christ. Not only that but the church could always use a few more members. Members were needed for tithing and since the only thing of real value on the island was food, tithing was done by bringing food to the Wednesday and Sunday masses so that church officials did not have to run up and down the hill to get their own.

They were also seriously considering having an extra mass or two during the week because some of the fruit did not always stay fresh for the period in between, especially since some of the parishoners were getting lazy and always grabbed the first thing in sight.

As back home in Europe, the island Vatican was also surrounded by Italians. Unlike it's main counterpart, however, the island holy domain was very plain and boring. There were no priceless treasures of antiquity stolen from the middle east to fill it's halls. Or confiscated oil paintings to hang on its walls and no possibility of someone ever creating a painting on its ceiling. Regardless, the church was still visited by people from around the island who still considered themselves to be Catholic and who, for the first time in their lives, could come and get a close look at a bent old man who had long outlived his time of value.

Other interesting people also came. One of them was a woman named Carlotia. An extremely attractive, middle aged , generously proportioned female, she had an agenda all her own. Her father had been an Archbishop, her mother a nun, often raped by her father. But no one on the island knew that but her. No one ever knew exactly how he had died, either. Except her. It was another thing she had never talked about it, back then, or now. The rest of her background was also a complete mystery but she began sleeping in the trees adjacent to where all the church officials had made their home. Then, cunningly she began seducing ever male in the church heirarchy who still had some heterosexual drive, starting with the lower echelon and working her way up. But once she had them firmly hooked and they began begging for more of her favors, she spurned them and moved on up the chain. Eventually, she got to one of the Cardinals.

Crotchety, barely able to perform as he was, she hooked him worst of all. It was a special challenge for her since he always slept in the same area as the Pope and usually only a few feet away. After just two brief encounters in the woods he became so obsessed with her that she was able to sneak into his bed one moonlit night and get on top of him. Rather than the risk of getting caught being a deterent for the old man, it became a turn on instead, and he was having the time of his life when Carlotia purposely began to moan and groan very loudly. He barely seemed to notice, even when she succeeded in her intent of waking up the Pope.

Aghast at first, the Pope rose up on his elbow and shook his head in disbelief. Then, when he was able to sit up, he noticed a group of Cardinals on the perimeter all trying to sneak a peek and he knew it to be true. Surprizingly, when he finally recovered from the shock, the Pope said not a word to the Cardinal. The Cardinal wouldn't have heard him anyway. Totally drained, the Cardinal was off luxuriating in some place even greater than a Catholic heaven, transfixed, staring up at the stars while Carlotia stood there in her beautiful nakedness, smirking at the Pope. The Pope's chief personal attendent moved in and helped the decrepit old patriarch to his feet, hoping he wasn't about to have a coronary. But the Pope was able to stand erect, put his hands in front of his eyes so he wouldn't have to look at Carlotia and began summoning his voyeuristic underlings to his side.

"Get some vines and tie her up. Tightly. It's almost morning. We'll deal with her then. After I have personally heard each and everyone of you in the confessional."

By then there were another two dozen nobel volunteers all wanting a closer look at the woman and hoping for a chance to touch her. The Pope pointed to the Cardinal's tattered red robe lying on the ground.

"Cover her up first," he ordered. "Then get back in the trees and get on your knees. And stay there until I give permission to leave."

It was nearly noon before all the confessions had been heard. There were so many of them. This devil of a woman had tainted almost everyone in his island equivalent of the Vatican with her sinfulness. Overwhelmed, he was forced to lie in the shade for another two hours to get some of his strength back. Still not completely recovered, he sat on a rock while he made his pronouncement.

"Back home we were restricted by the laws of the state," the Pontiff said in a weak, ratchety voice. But while his voice might have been feeble, his eyes were full of fire. "Here we are not. As in times past the church is once again the law and the laws of the church and the laws of God will prevail. Mankind, having been born into sin, is weak and sinful by nature. You are men of the cloth and you must repent. Ask God for forgiveness and you can be forgiven because the Savior knows you would not have strayed but for this wicked temptress. It is her evil that has created the problem. She is a handmaiden of the devil and does his work and her punishment must be harsh and swift. It is my pronouncement therefore, that she be burned at the stake until her malicious soul has been liberated from her sinful flesh. We will do it now."

At first, most of the men were shocked at the Pope's decree but several quickly rushed forward to help lash her to the stake that had been driven into the ground so they could paw her body one last time. Once she was fully restrained they piled up leaves and dried sticks and every man who had touched her carried a candle to the pile and helped light it. Then, as it burned, they danced round and round the pyre and hurled obscenities at her under their breaths so the Pope could not hear. Disappointingly, however, never once did she do something so ordinary as to scream. At first she meerely smiled and shut her eyes and was silent. Then it began. Her voice was loud and strong and vibrant and clear and penetraing as she heaped curses upon them all.

"Damn the Catholic Church," she said. "Damn the Pope and damn everyone of you who put a candle to the fire and damn all of the rest of you who did nothing to stop it or put it out. You think you have the power of God behind you but I have a power behind me that is far older than your God has even been in existence and many more times more powerful for it comes from beyond the space and time of men and I have the power to speak it so I say to you now that the Catholic Church is damned and will never survive another decade, neither here on the island or back home where we came from. The Pope is damned and he will be dead and rotting before the fullness of the next moon, destroyed by one of you who has known my body and is espescially cursed. And all of the rest of you are damned and will never be able to leave this island and return home. And now, to show you the strength of my power, the fire will no longer burn at my feet. But my earthly body has been too badly injured for me to go on living, so I will give it up. But you must look at it for days to come because no fire will be strong enough to destroy the rest of it. And as you do so, my curse will surround you and sink deeper into your own flesh and penetrate even into your souls and I will return, time and time again, to haunt you down through the eons whenever you should reappear so that you are cursed both here on earth and in your own despicable after life."

Then, at the very moment she stopped speaking, the fire, which by now had almost totally engulfed her from foot to head, began to dwindle and soon went out. Every one gasped and stepped quickly back and looked at the one standing next to them in awe and fear.

"Light the fire, light the fire," the Pope ordered in his raspy voice, so the men piled on more dried leaves and sticks and tried again and again to rekindle it, but to no avail. They tried again in the afternoon and again the following day but it would not burn so they left the charred body hang there because everyone was far too afraid to touch it or even get too close. After a time of three full days, however, it was gone without a trace. None claimed to have moved it and no one knew where it had disappeared to. To the last holy man, they all swore it was the absolute truth. And no matter how many times the story was retold later on, it was always the same, biblical in proportion and importance. Clearly, the Devil was alive and well. Much worse, he was here with them, on the island and he had resurrected his own helper, the witch of a woman who would not burn completely. Hurridly, they began collecting small sticks which they tied together in the form of crosses that they carried about wherever they went and waved in the faces of sceptics and disbelievers. They even slept with them.

Whether or not that was the proper terminology for it, the witch burning incident was a major turning point in the history of the island. Originally there were one hundred and seventeen thousand, four hundred and twenty seven people trapped there. Within the nearly eight months that had ensued until the fire was started at the woman's feet, approximately twenty one thousand lost souls had waded too far out into the ocean or had jumped off the cliff. Another fifty five hundred or so had simply let themselves starve to death while thirty five thousand five hundred and ninteen had been mercilously beaten to death or run through with sharpened sticks. Only ninety seven had died of natural causes, leaving less than fifty thousand remaining. Not only had the Catholics set fire to a woman's feet, the extremely barbaric nature of the act triggered an outbreak of other violent behavior that swept around the island like its own wildfire, out of control. Old hatreds renewed themselves more brutally than ever before, issues that had once been resolved burst back into view and violence, and old prejudices reappeared and deepened into open conflict.

Chechenians bashed Russians and Russians bashed Chechenians, Turks killed Armenians and Iranians killed Turks, East Indians beat at the Pakistanians, Palistinians attacked the Isralis, Philippino Muslims killed Philippino Christians, Hindus hunted down Buddhists, Mexican seperatists killed Mexican nationalists, Argentinians attacked the British and Americans fought with nearly everyone. Shi'ites killed Sunnites and Sunnites killed Kurds. On and on it went. Most malicious of all was the night the white South Africans surrounded a large grassy area where several hundred black Africans made there camp and set it on fire, killing them all. Almost everywhere torches blazed in the darkness and few felt safe. For practical reasons, however, Ivan's area went untouched. Nor did his own men go to war, they only guarded the walls of their enclosed area and kept the peace for those who came for their daily rations.

More than two hundred Americans on Second Island fell prey to others on their daily excursions back to the main island for food, but as yet the relocated Americans of Dean Whitcomb's group were not pursued because it was generally too far away and everyone was too busy fighting their more immediate neighbors. But in spite of it all and even though they had old grudges of their own, the Chinese and the Japanese still managed to seperate themselves from the mayhem and did their best to go their own peaceful way, even showing some signs of cooperation now and then. The major thrust of the otherwise island wide holocaust lasted a little over a six weeks. When it finally ended, several thousand more people were dead. Even the Pope himself, was gone. True to Carlotia's prophecy, his most probable sucessor to the papal high office had forced him to walk round and round in a circle until he had over exerted and died of a heart attack.

There were corpses everywhere, to be stepped on and stumbled over, but now, with the advent of fire, bodies no longer had to be dragged all the way down to dead man's cove to be disposed of. They were simply stacked up in large piles and burned. For a time the stench of scorched flesh was almost unbearable. For the most part the smoke rose straight up but instead of disipating into the atmosphere it formed a thick, disgusting cloud over most of the island that hung there statically like a bank of smog, just like the one over Second Island. When it rained, it rained through the cloud but never washed it away. It was not completely opaque, however, and some sunlight still filtered through, but it was dirty brown and weak.

"Have you noticed," Jack asked of Ivan one day. "It is slowly becoming cooler here?"

"Yes. The diminished sunshine is having its affect. Look at the leaves on the trees. The fruit does not grow back so readily, either."

"And if it contiues we will need to have a fire for ourselves at night to keep warm."

"Then we will be in really big trouble."

"No doubt. To stay warm the people will burn all the dead wood first. The cloud will get thicker, the weather colder still. Then they will burn the live trees down below. Eventually, if enough more do not die in the meantime, they will begin to burn the fruit trees and when the food supply gets too short, they will begin killing each other over that."

"It is a dismal picture," Ivan stated.

"Yes, but not entirely hopeless," Jack said. "While everyone else was butchering each other the Chinese and the Japanese have been working together and have at least found a way to make clothing."

"Well, that is interesting. Maybe we can get some from them."

"It's not likely because it's a very tedious and time consuming process. But, I have watched them do it so we can make our own if we have to."

"Maybe we shouldn't wait too long," Ivan said and turned to Deanna who had never left his side since all the trouble began. "What do you think?" he asked her.

"As usual, you are probably right."

"Well," Jack said. "There certainly is no lack of raw material. They use this long leaved catcus like plant here which just happens to grow nearly everywhere on the island. Pull off a leaf, like this. Lay it on a flat stone and beat at it gently with a stick. If you do it right it separates into strong, thin, flexible fibers which are really quite soft. When you have enough of them they can be woven together in the same way a rug is made. But it becomes a piece of cloth instead and is really quite warm and durable."

"It does look like a tedious process, but I think the men could do it with some practice. Too many of them do not always have enough to do and that can become a problem."

"Good idea, husband," Deanna said to Ivan. And then to Jack she said, "You notice how I call him husband now? He pretends he doesn't like it but he always gives me extra affection when I do."

"Well, you are a wonderful woman. How could I not be affectionate?" Ivan said with a happy grin. "And which of the men should we teach first?"

"Men? Don't forget. We also have about fifty women in the group."

"Other people on the island will have to learn, too. Eventually, everyone on the island will need warm clothing if the temperature keeps dropping."

Even though the body count was preposterously large, the hostilities were still far from over as new hatreds took the place of old ones and the bloody mayhem continued. Surprizingly, the Americans who had relocated had experienced the fewest number of casualties, along with the Chinese and the Japanese. The Americans relegated to Second Island were only safe as long as they stayed there but were always in extreme danger when they went for food. There was nothing that could be done. Not yet. They weren't strong enough to free themselves and no other group was brave enough to want to help.

Now, the Syrians and Lebanese were fighting each other. The Kurds and the Turks battled, the Egyptians and the Palastinians hammered away, the Isralies beat on everyone, and so it went. Africans also fought Africans and South Americans fought other South Americans as the island sank further into its own kind of dark ages. Living in despair and constant fear, others comitted suicide in droves. Ivan, wisely enough, and with Jack's encouragement, had at last given up the idea of controlling the food belt. With the labor of his four hundred and twenty three loyal followers, all of whom were still alive, they relocated large portions of the wall to make themselves a high stone fort that could easily be defended while still enclosing more than enough fruit trees for them to live off of. At night torches were lit and burned along the ramparts so posted guards could see any potential attackers.

At first, free access to the food seemed to increase the fighting because it was one more thing to do battle over. But as soon as it became apparent that there was no shortage as yet, it eased a little. Still, the barbaric conflict raged. Middle aged men who should have otherwise been playing golf or reading a good book or hanging out at the club swapping stories, mercilessly pounding away on each other. Clubs and spears and stones. Einstein had said that if there was ever a nuclear war the next one would be fought with clubs but it hadn't taken bombs to bring this one about. All it had taken was man's inability to understand himself and to embrace his fellow humans. While politics and religion were both claimed to be major contributors to the destruction and downfall, in the end it was because most of them were a lot like the previous President of the United States. They were just mindless, insecure bullies at heart who needed someone else to abuse to make themselves feel good. Then at last, when the island population had been brutally reduced to a third of it's original size, two more bands of sworn enemies encountered each other. They stood all lined up, weapons in hand, face to face, and waited. Finally the leader of one band stepped forward and threw down his club.

"I have had enough. I will fight no more. Kill me if you must," he said and turned and walked away.

Stunned, the rest looked at him.

Then the other leader said, "Nor will I fight either," and threw down his own spear.

It was a small start, but suddenly, for the survivors who remained, everyone was tired of waging war and over night, peace drifted across the island and all was silent.

"What happened?" Deanna and Ivan asked Jack . "Is it really over? Has everyone actually stopped fighting?"

"All the major bullies are dead," Jack replied. "The ones who are left have to do their own fighting and they are usually too cowardly to do that. But, maybe they should have all killed each other, and the rest of us, too. It's not going to be easy."

"Paradise lost." Deanna lamented. " Even without birds and animals, it was still a beautiful place. Perfect weather, abundent food, plants and greenery, a great view and a real opportunity to do something besides slaughter each other. But now, my god..."

"Paradise lost," Ivan repeated.

"And now we are having our kind of nuclear winter."

"What's that?" Ivan asked. "You mean the cold?"

"Yes. After a nuclear war the atmosphere becomes so thick with smoke and ash that it keeps the sunlight out and the planet becomes colder."

"Our little world is doing that, all right. Even the snow cap has moved down the mountainside five hundred feet," Ivan replied.

"And they're still burning bodies," Deanna stated.

"Pretty crazy, huh?"

"Yes, but what about disease? If they stop cremating and drag them all down to the cove, can't handling dead bodies spread illness?"

"That's one of the other strange things about this place, remember? There are no communicable diseases. At least none that I'm aware of."

"But there is religion. Some sects still believe the dead have to be cremated."

"That's a communicable disease, all right."

"Wouldn't you think people would begin to understand just how destructive beliefs can be."

"They already do," Ivan said. "Just don't dare admit it. Otherwise all the killing would have been for nothing."

"Well, what's left of the population better begin cooperating for a change, or very few of them are going to be around much longer."

Ivan shrugged and raised an eyebrow. "Guess we'll find out."

"But.. the cold weather may be a good thing," Deanna said hopefully. "Every one will soon need clothing. That will go better if they all help each other. The same with shelters."

ANOTHER PILE OF STONES

No longer being forced to stay on Second Island after the fighting had ceased, the Americans held captive there quickly moved back to their old area on First Island.

"We lost half our group in the conflict," one of the survivers said to Jack one day. His name was Boyce, looking and sounding rather pathetic in a search for sympathy.

"Stupidly so," Jack said with little empathy. Who was this old guy? And why had he waylayed Jack, Ivan and Deanna? Odd fellow. Looked like he should be walking with a cane, all bent over like that and skinny as a stick. Couldn't even grow a decent beard, as though it had moth holes in it. Both eyes didn't seem to point in the same direction all the time, either.

Boyce scowled and did his best to give Jack a despicable look. And he also just stood there, not about to let them pass on the narrow pathway.

"Well. What else would you call it?" Jack said, caring less and less.

Boyce looked at Ivan to see if he might have any sympathy for him but none was noted. The same with Deanna. Jack realized he should have never said anything to the man in the first place. Now the guy seemed to feel that he needed to defend himself.

"Yeah, well...I guess we didn't see it that way," Boyce said in an aggressive tone with a squinty, sideways look.

"Guess you didn't," Jack said, shaking his head, trying to go around him.

"How can you say that. It's not fair to judge us. You weren't here."

"Thank god for that." Jack responded and moved off the path. Enough of this old fool. Ivan followed.

"Too good to hear me out, are you? That's the problem. They were just like you. Thought they were too good to pay attention to the President. That's what did it and before we knew it, it was too late. And there we were, trapped on that horrible little island."

Now it was Deanna's turn. "What should they have payed attention to?" she asked as she came up to him.

"She wanted to do a preemptive strike against those abominable middle easterners."

"She?"

"The president. Who else?

"Right. And she couldn't get enough support?"

"No, no. That wasn't the problem. We had a show of hands. It was a hundred percent. But when she asked for volunteers not a single person came forward. They all had the same excuse."

"That wasn't very creative. What did they say?"

"You're much too sarcastic. I'm not going to talk to you, either. Even if you are a woman."

"Jeeez," Ivan said. "What a dip. Is that a good word, dip? Let's get out of here."

"See, see. You're just like they were. All of you. Don't want to see it through."

"What? Listen to your drivel?"

"No. And I know who you are. You're a leader, not a fighter. That's someone else's job. That's what they all said. Every last one of them. Leaders don't get their hands dirty. Find someone else. What do you think of that?"

"That's the American way," Ivan said with sarcasm.

"How dare you. Who are you to talk that way?"

"I'm a Russian. We do things differently in Russia."

"Yeah, well," Boyce said, raising his eyebrows. "Jesus," he went on, staring off into the distance.

"So what would you know. We were the ones who were degraded and forced to spend all those horrible months on that tiny island. Made everyone mad as hell. But, I guess we don't have to worry about that anymore," he continued, looking like he might cry.

"Why not?" Deanna asked, not knowing why she felt a sudden tinge of sympathy. Maybe it was because the man seemed so pathetic.

"You mean you haven't heard the tragic news."

"Obviously not. What happened?"

"Well," he said with difficulty. "Well.... She survived all the challenges and the turmoil. Along with the new VP and the new

Secretary of State and all the rest of us. And then....Oh my," he said and began to cry.

"Good grief," Jack said none too quietly. But he caught himself, guessed he'd be polite and hear the rest of it because Deanna seemed interested. They waited but it didn't look as though old Boyce would ever regain his composure.

"Excuse me," Jack said as he stopped another man who was passing by. Another old guy. Bald but bearded, beady eyed and suspicious. Taller than Boyce and half way healthy. "Sorry to bother you but did something happen to your president?"

"Sure did," he said with a big smile that showed all his brown stained, crooked teeth. "Sure as hell did," he went on as he looked them all over, frowning heavily when he glanced at Boyce. "Want to hear about it?"

"Might as well," Jack said with resignation.

"Hmmm. Well... The president and her phony cronies had spent all those long months wearing those branding marks that had been painted on their foreheads. They were humiliated and laughed at by every Arab they came in contact with. They even spit on her. Once she spit back and they slapped her until she wet her pants. Ha. You should have seen that. Ha, ha, ha, ha," he laughed and kept on laughing until Boyce came out of his state of glum and walked up and punched the man in the stomach.

"How dare you," he shouted with a livid face. "Have you no respect for the dead?"

"Wait a minute," Jack said. "Are you saying the president is dead? When did this happen?"

Boyce started stammering. "She, she.."

"Not you," Jack said. "You," he pointed at the other one. "What's your name?"

"Bart. I'm Bart and good riddance," he said and ducked behind Ivan so Boyce couldn't reach him.

"All right," Jack said loudly. "Boyce! Go over there and sit down. And," he said to Bart. "Cut the commentary and get on with it."

"Yes, sir. Well, like I was saying. Good rid... Woops, Sorry. Okay. So once all the major fighting was over and we were all able to leave that desolate hell hole we were trapped on, she went over the edge. Night and day all she did was rant. Revenge, revenge, revenge. But, when she learned that all of the people personally resposible for her embarassment had gotten themselves killed in battles, she finally shut up. But she never gave up. No sir. Then she found out that there were still two Caliphs on the island who were still alive. Didn't matter that they had sat they whole thing out. She still tracked them down and tried to find some Americans to help her. She vowed to have them beaten to death. Of course she got a lot of sympathy from people like this yo yo here," he said, waving at Boyce.

"Can you imagine?" he went on, quieter now so Boyce couldn't hear. "And then, once that was accompished, she was going to rebuild the White House and Boycey boy there was going to move in with her. I kept saying, I hope she was a sound sleeper cause if she had ever rolled over on him in the middle of the night she woud have sqashed him like a bug. Ha," he laughed and had to force himself to stop.

"But, when it came time to pick up a weapon, well, guess what? Same old story. No troops, no support team. So there she was, big as a truck, all alone, standing there with a club in her hand yelling at these two poor guys. Then they started laughing at her, along with about a hundred other people who had followed behind to see what might happen...."

At this point Boyce jumped to his feet and started yelling about how did Bart dare to diminish the president's memory. "Just because the club she had was too big and she lost her balance and tripped and fell and hit here head on a rock and killed herself. I mean, gee whiz. How can you make fun of her for that?"

All Jack, Ivan and Deanna could do was to look at each other and shake their heads. They turned around and started to walk off but Bart caught up to Jack and grabbed his handmade jacket.

"Wow," he said before Jack could react. "I didn't notice those. Where did you get the fancy duds? Are they warm? I could sure us something like that the way it's getting so damned cold anymore."

Finally, Jack thought. Sharing their new skills was the main reason they had come to this part of the island. And since most of Ivan's enemies were no longer alive or in power, Ivan had also accompanied him into the American area. Deanna had insisted on coming along, too, assuring them that she would be safe in their company. The three of them were each dressed in their own hand made clothing. By this time a curious crowd had began to form around them and a barrage of questions began.

"Can I feel it?

"Does it scratch?"

"Is it warm?"

"Looks a little bulky to me."

"Must weigh a ton. How do you move around?"

"Where did you get it? How can we get our own?

And then people started asking questions about Jack's and Ivan's hair and beards. Crude and ragged looking, they were still considerably shorter than those of anyone else. With a little more attention to detail they would have looked almost as good as some of the homeless people back home. Everything is relative, however, and most everyone was curious as to how they had done it. Some brave souls on the island had previouly experimented with trying to burn their hair and beards shorter but it was dangerous, smelled like scorched chicken feathers for days and looked worse than if they had left it alone.

The crowd was pushing in and the noise level was rising. Jack stood up on a rock and shouted for attention.

"This is great," he said. "We appreciate your interest. So, if everyone will hold the questions for a while, we'll do our best. What do you want to talk about first? Clothes or hair?"

Surprizingly, even though many of them were dressed in complete rags full of holes, sleeves missing, half a pant leg or none, the men still wanted to have a haircut and shorten their beards. The women voted for clothing but since they were heavily outnumbered, Jack stayed on the rock and began. He had also brought a medium sized hand woven bag with carrying straps along. It was quite heavy. He reached into it and removed two pieces of rock. The first one he held up was shiny black and irregular shaped.

"This is flint, and since we seem to be living in the stone age, it is most appropriate for our primitive society. I actually found it several months ago but felt it wasn't safe to share at the time. Everyone was doing a good enough job of killing each other with clubs and spears the way it was. But now that the serious fighting seems to be over maybe we can put it to a more peaceful use."

He then held up the other stone. "I'm sure you've seen enough of this around. This is granite. If you lay the flint down on another, bigger rock, hold it firmly and strike it with the granite, you can chip off different sized slivers. It's called flint knapping. Takes a little practice but it can yield some very useful pieces. Some of them are very sharp. Sharp as a razor blade, if anyone remembers what one of those is."

At this point he reached back into his woven bag and took out a bundle of large leaves wrapped up in a protective ball. Unwinding the leaves, he removed a smaller piece of flint that he had previously prepared. Then he motioned to one of the men up front who had the most hair on his face. Taking his beard in hand, Jack deftly whacked away at it, shortening it by half.

"Wow," a man in the front said loudly. "How about me?"

Jack shrugged. "Okay. But that's it. I have six large pieces of flint and I'm willing to show you how to chip them into sharp pieces, but the rest is up to you," he stated, nodded to the man and quickly chopped off about six months worth of growth from his beard.

Then it was Deanna's turn. Deanna who has also used some of the flint to shave the hair off her own legs and drew a lot of extra attention because of it.

She held up a handful of long, thin but tough plant leaves that looked like fan palm fronds. Nothing new, they were very prolific on the island. All anyone had to do was turn around and look. She pointed out the presence of some of the plants nearby but no one could connect the plants with the clothes so she gave them a brief demonstration.

"With a little experimenting you can also make sleeves and pockets and learn to sew them all together. For those who are interested, gather up a bundle of raw material and come up the mountain to where the old gate in the wall still stands. First thing tomorrow."

Then she began answering questions. She was in the middle of the first one when Jack bent close to Ivan.

"Looks like there might be trouble," he said and nodded towards the side of the crowd.

A group of ten or eleven tough looking men stood grouped together. They were all that was left of the original twenty three members who had held Deanna hostage for nearly six months. The rest had run afoul of other scoundrals even more obnoxious and sadistic than they were. But those deaths hadn't mellowed the survivors one bit.

"Jesus. Will you look at that. It's that Holt bitch that got away from us. Damn. All cleaned up and everything," one of the bunch said in a loud voice.

"Damn, is right. Look at that body. Christ, I knew we should have started banging her right from the beginning. Might have taught her a lesson, snooty bitch. Probably would have liked the bunch of us climbing her once she got used to it. Then she wouldn't have run off."

"She might like it even better now that we're down to eleven. Think of it. We could all have a little every day."

"How long have you been here?" one of them asked another. "Is she alone? I don't see anyone with her."

"Got here just a few seconds before you. Don't see anyone around."

"Good. Once the crowd thins out we can make a grab for her."

"Do you think it's safe?"

"Most of the people here are too damned timid to interfere. And this time we'll drag her off somewhere farther away."

"Yeah. Then we'll show her what life's all about."

Too excited about what they had discovered, they hadn't noticed Jack or Ivan in the background. As for Ivan, he was livid with anger, but restrained himself and spoke quietly to Jack. Unbeknownst to Deanna, some of Ivan's strongest men had also followed along. They were out there, Jack had noticed when he was standing on the rock. He nodded to Ivan and Ivan moved off, with Jack on his heels. Once behind the interlopers, Ivan let out a soft, bird like whistle. Twelve men responded accordingly. Within an eye blink everyone of the roguish bunch had his arm twisted so far up behind his back that it almost broke and had a strong hand over his mouth so he could not speak. Quickly and quietly they were escorted back into the trees. By the time they were out of sight of the crowd there had been two sharp cracks and two broken arms from resisting too strongly. But, agony or no agony, they were not allowed to cry out. Then a third one made the mistake of kicking backward into his captor's shins and there was a third sharp noise.

Ivan faced them one at a time. When they realized who he was they became even angrier. The hand was removed from the first ones mouth. A mouth controlled by a brain too stupid to keep it shut.

"Look at this. It's that goddamned Russian who stole our woman. You filthy bastard," he spit out before Ivan slammed his jaw shut and glared at him. Then Ivan asked Jack for a piece of his flint.

With two quick slashes Ivan cut a groove down each of the man's cheeks. Then he ripped the man's shirt open, exposed his belly and carved another line down the middle. The man called him a bastard and called Deanna a whore. Ivan's knee came up and caught him in the groin. The man cried out in pain and doubled over.

"Get his pants off," Ivan said, and it was quickly done. "Here," he said to Koslov, one of his band of men, a bulky bruiser with spite in his eye. "You know what to do."

Koslov bent over, a sadistic grin on his face. Now they had a proper amount of the fool's attention.

"God, no. Anything but that. Jesus, God, please. Anything. Kill me first."

As if he hadn't heard, Koslov's hand kept moving downward, followed by more begging. Then he laughed. "Damn, boss. Not much there. Hardly worth the trouble."

"Your choice," Ivan said.

Koslov grinned and squinted. "Yeah," he said and continued with the sharp edge of the flint moving closer. "Why not." But in the end he passed the critical parts of the man's anatomy and made a long slash down the inside of each leg.

"That was for practice. Next time it will be the real thing," Ivan told the man who had curled up in a ball on the ground once they freed him. "Now get out of here while you are still alive," Ivan said in his most sinister voice, nudging him with a foot.

Almost in shock, it took the man several seconds to recover. Hurting badly from the knee to his crotch and totally shamed, he limped away, dripping blood as he went. The three men with the broken arms were released next. Then Ivan sized up the remaining eight. One had wet himself badly and was snivelling like a three year old. A good kick in the rear sent him on his way.

"Who else has anything to say?" Ivan asked, menacingly.

One man was dumb enough to make a semi coherent quip in a low voice about Deanna's decency to the one next to him. The recipient of the comment eyed Ivan fearfully and shuddered badly, began twitching and jerking and started to wretch. When he recovered he was separated from the rest and also sent on his way. By now the one with the mouth finally realized that his own life might be in jeopardy. He got down on his knees and began praying. One of Ivan's men put his foot against his side and pushed him over. He layed there for a while, eyes bulging out in fear and began to crawl away. Pummled with laughter, they let him go and that left five.

"Who's next?" Ivan queried. It was so silent they could hear the tree leaves rustle in the slight breeze. "Anyone care to tell me what they might have learned from all this?" Ivan continued.

No one dared look at him. Ivan sat down on a big rock. Jack

sat down on a big rock and Ivan's men sat down in the grass, leaving their prisoners standing where they were. Nobody moved, not a word was spoken. Finally, one of the captives started to cry, softly at first, then louder. So did another. Two minutes later they were all bawling their heads off and Ivan, Jack and Ivan's men got up without a word and walked away.

Moving back towards the original crowd they noticed Deanna still actively engaged with the people there. She didn't need to know what had just transpired but someone would always accompany her whenever she left the mountainside. No one else from their group would be allowed to come back into the American area alone, either. Women would always have multiple escorts no matter where they went, men would at least move in pairs. Except for Jack, of course. No one was about to impose rules on Jack. Not even Ivan.

As for Deanna, she personally would not have wanted to witness the violence. What she might have enjoyed instead was to flaunt herself in front of her old captors. To let them know she had survived their abuse and done well at it. But they knew it now. And they would never forget. The only difference was that she didn't know that they knew and she might never find out. But it was done.

With that issue resolved, Jack bid them goodbye.

"I want to see if I can find Dean Whitcomb and the Professor and some of their friends to invite them up for the big bonefire tomorrow evening. Then I'm going to look for Sam Birnstead. Haven't seen him in a couple of weeks. I hope nothing has happened."

He came across Dean Whicomb almost immediately but after more than two hours of looking for Sam, he gave up. The sun was going down and no one had had seen or talked to Birnstead in more than a week. No one knew where he might have gone, either.

Days later, as Jack made trips to the oriental side of the island he was further surprised. Some of the older, wiser members had also gone missing but no one seemed very concered.

"We don't know what happened," he was told. "One minute they were here, the next time we looked, they were gone. We thought they went into the woods to relieve themselves, or whatever. Maybe they went for a stroll around the island. Nothing to be worried about. People come and go all the time."

"Yes. But when they go they usually come back. The fighting has been over for weeks."

"Now that you brought it up, it is a little peculiar."

"How is that?"

"The ex communists, the criminals and all those kinds are still here. The ones who are gone were not invoved in those things. In fact, they refused to play follow the leader and spoke out for the rest of us so we wouldn't make that mistake ourselves. We have a lot to thank them for. I hope they are okay."

Had they gone the way of Howard and Katherine, Jack wondered. Is that what also happened to Sam. Sam was one of the most peaceful guys on the island. Often a mediator but never a participant in a fight. Of course, big as he was, he didn't have to worry about many people trying to pick on him anyway. But after all the mayhem you could never be sure. Still, Jack seriously doubted that anything bad had happened to Sam. So, where were these people? Were they back home? Gone like Howard and Katherine. It was the only thing that made any sense to him. And, if so, were they all safe?

Were Howard and Katherine safe? Or as safe as possible. The world back there was not such a great place to be, either. At least it wasn't when Jack had left it behind. Howard would be able to take care of himself. He would also be able to take care of his wife, Margaret. But what about Katherine? Was she okay? And then he thought of his wife and the child that was not to be. It was probably over two years now, as best he knew, that he had lost them. But it might have been a century. So many terrible things had happened in between.

Gripped by the emotion, Jack walked off. He kept going until he was half way up the mountainside. Then he sat down in the grass and watched the early moon rise. God, what he wouldn't have given for a shot of brandy. A whole water glass full. The whole damned bottle.... If only he had a picture of her. That was what bothered him the most, the one thing he wanted to hang onto above all else. He felt he should have still been able to visualize her clearly. But he could not, even after the nine years they had together. He could no longer see her face in detail and it hurt him badly. But he remembered her as being very striking and beautiful. He knew her eyes had been a clear deep blue, that her skin had been soft and smooth, that her voice had been husky and seductive and her smile gentle and captivating. But only as descriptive passages, not sharply defined details, leaves blown by the wind, all muted now, retreating into the fog of the past. Had it all been real? What if he was mistaken and she were still alive, along with their child, and back there alone. What then? Would they have been able to survive without him? Or was it all just a dream, a beautiful, sad and lonely dream. There was nothing here, no hard evidence to press against, not one small trinket, not one other person that had known her who could confirm any of it. What the hell!

Leave it alone, he told himself. Just because he couldn't see her that clearly anymore was not a reason to feel guilty. Except he did. And it hurt. And sometimes it was his own private kind of hell.

Damnit, he said to himself. Damnit, damnit, damnit. Suddenly he didn't want to be on the island anymore. He *did not* want to be there. He swore again and got to his feet.

Burning wood crackled and popped, sparks scattered outward and upward as twists of smoke rose into the evening air. There were at least two hundred people gathered around, faces and bodies illuminated by the roaring glow of the huge bonfire, the one sane use fire had been put to since it was first introduced on the island. Led by a lone woman with the flames as her backdrop, they were singing Russian folk songs. She was not a big woman but she had a big voice, strong and melodious with a range of several octaves. She could have been an opera singer. Maybe she had been one back home. If not, she had missed her calling.

It was a very primordial, tribal like affair. Unkempt people with long hair and scragly beards wearing bulky, crude looking, hand woven clothing, beating on hollowed out coconuts and pieces of wood and clacking sticks and stones together, dancing self invented steps and chanting away in the night. In one extreme it touched the dawn of human beginnings. On the other it might be serving as the lamentable end.

Jack stood alone, off to the side, watching and listening, his face also lit by the flames. Tonight was the weekly, cross cultural gathering up on the mountain at Ivan's location where hundreds of people usually came. There was singing and dancing, story telling, sometimes the work of an amateur playright, an occasional poem or whatever else came to mind. It was about time, an exchange long overdue, working well, helping to promote good will. But the island still contained it's vein of disgruntled trouble makers who would never be satisfied to leave things alone. And that was the way it was. Feeling melancholy, Jack began to sing along.

Much later, after the fire had died considerably and most everyone had wandered off, Jack and his five closest friends collected around the diminishing flames and growing pile of embers. Deanna and Ivan, Dean Whitcomb, the Professor, Jack and Ivan's friend Boris, along with several others from their group. Deanna had planned a fashion parade.

Bulky, baggy, all of the same drab color except for one creative woman who had tried to dye her inspired version red with strawberry juice, the participants walked around the fire to show off their latest creations of hand woven grass apparel. Strange, alien-like beings in the firelight. There was also more conversation and laughter and two more songs before the six of them were finally alone together. Ivan seemed preoccupied. Jack thought he knew what was bothering him.

"Well, if you think everyone still needs more to do, why don't we build a monument," Jack said offhandedly.

"A monument?"

"Just a thought. Like you said. Keep good minds occupied. Not just with games. Hard work is good therapy too. We can't build a rocket and go to the moon but maybe we can invent some task to take it's place."

"But there are still so many people here. How could building a monument keep them all busy?"

"Build a big monument. The bigger the better. As stupendous as it can get."

"Sure, Jack. Out of what? And where would we put it?"

"Maybe down by suicide cliff so if someday a big ship goes by they can see it and come and rescue us," the Professor said with a grin as the rest laughed at him.

"Actually that's not a bad idea," Deanna said. "Not the ship part because who's kidding who? But up on the edge of the cliff. It's still a very spectacular location in spite of its name."

"Well, great. But what kind of monument?" Boris asked.

"And what would we make it out off?" Dean Whitcomb wanted to know.

"How about stones?" Jack proposed.

"What else?" Ivan put in. Liking the idea, his mind was already reviewing possiblities.   "Since we're no longer trying to control the food belt we seem to have a large surplus of those."

"Thousands actually. Maybe even millions according to my last estimate," Jack stated.

"Yes. And most of them are one hell of a long ways from the cliff," Boris reminded him.

"That's the whole idea."

"But it would take months and months. Maybe even years."

"I would certainly hope so," Jack replied.

"Exactly what we need," Ivan agreed.

"Well, yes. Of course," the Professor said. "It might be fun, too. Especially if it was a joint effort amongst all the people here. At the least it would require cooperation."

"And inventiveness. Maybe we could find something to make wheels out of. And wheelbarrows."

"Maybe even some wagons."

"I'm certainly for it," Dean Whicomb said. "But what would it look like?"

"Anything, as long as it doesn't look like a government building or a religious artifact."

"With only rough stones to work with and no mortar it can't be very complicated or it will fall down."

"A pyramid," Deanna suggested. "Can you make a pyramid out of small stones?"

"We don't have any mortar," the Professor reminded them.

"Well, if we stack them carefully and keep narrowing the width like you would have to do anyway to make a pyramid, why not. We may be able to gather enough clay from that place on the western stream to help bind the sides together. Then the middle could be filled up with loose stones."

"Yeah, and if more people kill each other the dead bodies could be thrown in so they didn't have to be dragged clear down to the cove."

"Or burned like the Hindus still insist on doing and clouding up the atmosphere some more," Boris said with a very straight face. Then he began to chuckle. "I mean, after all, that's what pyramids were originally built for. Burial sites. Were they not?"

"But what will it symbolize? Shouldn't it symbolize something?" Dean Whitcomb asked after things settled down.

"Well, which side of human nature do you wish to dwell on," the Professor asked. "And really. Think of it. If we did put some bodies in there as we went along, that would certainly be symbolic of something. Wouldn't it?"

"Definitely. But so far we've seen much more bad than good. And we may be stuck here for the rest of our lives. I don't like to dwell on that."

"But it would still be nice to end on a note of hope," Ivan said, and with that he threw another stick of wood on the fire, making the sparks rise. Some of them landed on his newly woven shirt and he was forced to beat it out with his hands while others had begun to burn what remained of his beard. When it was over he laughed good heartedly.

Deanna laughed too and said, "Maybe you should have let it burn a little longer. I have never seen you with a completely bare face."

"Yeah," the Professor said. "Maybe she won't even like you. Then what?"

"Then nothing, she will only love me more," he said.

"My god," Dean Whitcomb said to Deanna. "Can you imagine what we would have done back home if these men had showed up in our offices one day looking like this?"

"Well, knowing us, we would have loved them anyway."

"Yes. I'm sure we would. And who are we to talk with our hairy, unshaven legs and ratty looking hair? No makeup or deoderant or decent clothing? Oh well," Dean Whitcomb sighed and was silent. Then she burst out with a monsterous smile. "That's it," she said joyfully. "Wow."

"What?" they all asked, almost in unison.

"Well. Maybe if everyone here looked a little more civilized, then they would begin to behave in more civilized ways. What do you think about that?"

"What are you talking about? What do you mean?"

"Look at Deanna's legs."

"Beautiful, aren't they?" Ivan said. "But don't get any ideas."

"Damned good point, Dean," Jack replied. "How come we didn't think of it sooner?"

"What?" some of the others still asked and looked at Jack and Dean Whitcome.

"We find more flint and make more razors. Then all the women can shave their legs and the men can get rid of their scraggly beards and cut off some of their long hair."

"And our armpits," one of the other women added with a laugh.

"And then if we look more civilized, we will begin to act more civilized," Ivan reiterated. "God, what a great idea. Sure as hell couldn't hurt."

And no sooner had he said it than Deanna turned to face him, gave him a quick kiss and said, "So, the moment of truth. Now I do get to see how you really look."

"But we don't have any mirrors," he replied in turn. "How am I going to shave without scraping off half my skin?"

"That's what you have me for, my husband," she said with a loving look. "I'll keep the fire going all night if I have to."

With that they all had a good laugh and it took a while but then the discussion came back to building a monument. Although not completely serious, Boris reiterated Ivan's remark about out how much of what had happened on the island had not exactly been an example of mankind's finest hour but agreed that there had to be something better than that to dedicate the monument to.

"You're right. We can't just build it and dedicate it to stupidity," Deanna said.

"It could be our own private joke, however," the Professor said. "What does it matter as long as we can get most everyone left on the island working on it."

"Exactly," Ivan added. "Besides, it will mean different things to different people anyway."

"If. If we can get everyone working on it. Or even half of them. And if it is ever completed. If we live that long. If, well...I'm tired," Dean Witcomb said as she got up. "Guess I'll sashay off in my new outfit and go get some rest."

"Well, thank you for the other idea. I think that's the best one of all," Deanne said.

"And with your permission, dear lady. Might I be so fortunate as to escort you home?" the Professor asked, seemingly out of character, even for himself, as he jumped to his feet from where they had been seated in a circle.

A bit surprised, Dean Whitcomb took a careful look at the man. Was this a joke? They were about the same age but the professor was at least two inches shorter than her and he seemed somewhat impish and even more disheveled than usual. But without all that hair on his face, well, who knows? And, who was she to complain? Besides, in any reality the Professor was still very intelligent and also often downright charming. With that she extended her arm.

"You want us to do what?" Ivan's men asked when they assembled in the morning.

"Volunterees only. If you have other priorities, by all means see to them."

"But gee, boss. We always had someone else to carry stones before. Can't you think of a better way to go about this?"

"There's a lot more to it than that."

"A stone is a stone. They are all heavy."

Ivan laughed. "True enough. But we also need a few people with brains. There are other things involved."

"Can you give us a for-instance?"

"Make some wheels."

"Wheels?"

"Go talk to Jack. Have him show you how to shape some of the flint. Make some sharp stone axes. Find some small trees you can bend into circles. Add some spokes, make some wheels. With wheels you can build wagons. With wagons you can haul stones easier than you can hand carry them. Then we need someone smart enough to find a large level spot and lay out a big square on the ground. And someone to experiment with using clay for mortar. Someone to make wooden shovels. And trowels. And a few more to organize and ..." he said as he rattled off a long list of other things that needed to be done.

They would need a lot of help from the rest of the people on the island also. A series of walls approximately eight feet thick and eight feet tall and more than three miles long, when pulled apart and reassembeled into the form of a pyramid, would make one tremendouly large pile of stones, regardless of what it might be a monument to or how long it took to build.

THAT'S CRAZY

It was mid December and the North American continent was undergoing a record breaking cold and snowy winter. "That's crazy," people were saying. "If global warming is making the planet hotter, how can that cause the winter to be colder?"

"Because we are only in the early stages of it. Warming the earth only one or two degrees doesn't sound very significant but if you calculate how much additional energy has been added to the system world wide in doing that, it's a staggering amount. The more energy, the more extreme the weather. Hurricanes and tornados are far more prevelant and severe. Warmer oceans create low pressure systems that suck up unusual amounts of moisture and high altitude jet streams move outside their normal flow patterns, pulling warm air and cold air and moist air and dry air into regions it usually doesn't go at certain times of the year. It creates extreme flooding and extreme drought that is highly abnormal for the areas involved. At the same time there are record breaking cold spells and warming trends that will only get worse as time passes. Difficult as it seems, we'd better get used to it."

That was now the prevailing school of thought in the scientific community. Others, however, still dismissed the whole idea in spite of all the evidence. But that was not unusual either. Some of the blindest, most closed minded people in the world call themselves scientists, having long forgotten the true meaning of the word. Some of them worked for the government or were heavily influenced by it and in their arrogance and self importance felt that, while they, themselves, could handle the bad news, the public could not, so, in order to prevent panic and upset, it was best to hide the truth. Others of course, were just dull minded and off course and thought that just because they had been away to college they were somehow qualified to make judgements without having to review the facts. Regardless, one thing was still true. The weather was taking its toll.

Night time temperatures had been hanging right at the zero mark on the fahrenheit scale for more than a month, clear across the upper band of states from coast to coast. Daytime temperatures rose somewhat, only to bring more snow every fourth or fifth day as fierce, howling winds followed out of the north and west to drive it around and pile it up, higher and higher, making it nearly impossible to even keep key roads open. Worse, thanks in part to the greedy speculation of Wall Street commodities brokers, the supply of heating oil was at the shortest it had ever been since the oil burning furnace had been invented. The supply of propane was little better and natural gas was at an all time, almost unaffordable, premium. To simply survive, people were moving in with each other, from houses without fireplaces to those with them and there was a joint effort to gather fuel. Trees closest to houses were chopped down first, and then they worked their way outward, but the wood was green and did not burn well. Elderly people without nearby families or friends froze to death in droves in their beds, trying to stay warm. Once it was known that they were gone, neighbors raided the houses for food supplies and then carried off the furniture to put in their own fireplaces. Then, as the cold dragged on, they began tearing off porches and knocking down garages. Eventually, they attacked the main structures themselves.

The cold worked its way down the eastern side of the Rockies, dropping clear into New Mexico and Texas and eastward almost to Florida and hung there for more record breaking amounts of time. But again, maybe the elderly were the lucky ones. They died peacefully, frozen in their sleep as infant mortality also rose to unprecedented heights. Other people agonizingly starved to death.

In the cities armed gangs roamed and raided, making food difficult to come by. The rural areas of the north east and the midwest faired somewhat better because of an over abundant deer population, which, because of the deep snow, made its way to farms and into small towns in search of food where the animals were easy targets. But even at that it was a lopsided diet without fruit or vegetables and had it's own long term affect on people's health. Before it was over the death toll in Canada and the United States combined was estimated at more than a million and once the snow had all melted the residential areas of towns and cities looked like a war zone. In big cities, where high density population was the rule and structures were made of stone or brick or concrete, the entire interior of buildings had been completely gutted of furniture and flooring and cabinetry and stairs and anything else that would burn and would now cost more to repair than they would if they were torn down and started over. But by that time nobody cared, so the empty hulks stood as a grim reminder to the tragedy.

When it finally began to warm, the people of the United States, the meager five percent of the global population that was responsible for dumping over sixty five percent of the greenhouse pollutants into the atmosphere to begin with, sent out a cry of frustration and anger. "Why the hell didn't they tell us this would happen? I could have bought a smaller car. And I probably could have done without most of those energy consuming toys and they could have turned off about ninety five percent of the lights in Las Vegas and Atlantic City and we could have still found our way from casino to casino."

In northern Europe it was even worse. The land warming Gulf Stream had changed course and plunged the Scandinavian countries into record breaking, artic cold while in north eastern Russia and Siberia the opposite was true. The snow had all completely melted by the end of March and by mid April a vast profusion of wildflowers had taken over the otherwise barren landscape, transforming it into a paradise so beautiful it nearly wrenched the heart out of the few husky souls who actually lived there.

At the same time, as the snow still fell in the northern plains of the US and the wind howled violently across the vast open spaces, deep underground, crews of dedicated men worked devotedly for a new cause. Key leaders had disappeared world wide but only leaders down to certain levels. In the military, officers with the equivalent rank of Army Captain or below remained behind. They were not in charge of military bases or flight squadrons or naval vessels, did not make policy decisions or directly promote war. Regardless, world wide, nations still had standing armies and air forces and navies, losely held together without over all guidance or supervision.

The result was that the remaining, lower level officers were now in control. They made their own decisions, sometimes in cooperation with other units of the same military and sometimes in total conflict with them. Scattered throughout the isolated areas of Montana and North Dakota there still remained underground complexes of nuclear tipped, intercontinental ballistic missiles which had never been deactivated. There were forty eight individual missiles in all, each one deeply buried in a protective hole in the ground, almost completely invulnerable except for a direct hit from another nuclear bomb. And they were all still operational. The only problem was, there was no one left that had the right set of keys and the right launch code settings to initiate a firing. For the ranking officers left behind in the cold wasteland of the northern United States that was a problem of great concern. What if, with everything else that was going wrong around the world, some other nation had not been so cautious and had not instituted the same set of safeguards. What if some American hating group was able to get their hands on some nations nuclear arsenal? What then? It was a question that plagued the officers badly and they spoke of it often when they were together. Then, one day their concern was overheard by a certain Lieutenant Stevenson. Stevenson was anything but an ordinary US Air Force officer, however. Instead, he was an overly brilliant but somewhat irresponsible engineer with an advanced degree in electronics who had joined the service simply to get away from a woman he had gotten pregnant at his last place of employment back in civilian life.

"By pass it," was the response he gave to his Captain.

"By pass it?" the Captain said. "What does that mean?"

"By pass the damned controls and reactivate all the missiles."

"You can't do that. It can't be done. The system is fool proof," the Captain stated with assurance, about to reprimand Stevenson for not saying, Sir, when he spoke to a superior. Stevenson had already spent a week in the brig for failure to properly acknowledge the commanding General before he disappeared and had continued to ignore such regulations ever since. Maybe another week in lockup would do him good.

"I doubt it," Stevenson responded, before the captain could

throw it at him. "What one bunch of engineers can put together some other engineer can take apart and change. Ultimately, no matter how complicated one makes all the button pushing, in the end the signal still goes to each individual silo and each individual missile. Ultimately, behind some panel somewhere in each silo is a single set of wires which ignites the rocket motor. You already know how to get the silo doors open. And unless you want to do inflight target redesignation, all major targets are pre programmed. So... By pass all the security, install a new button, open the doors and go."

"You're not serious. It can't be that simple," the Captain replied. But he was hooked on the notion and the idea of sending Stevenson to the brig slipped away.

"It is."

"I don't believe it. Why would they make it that easy?"

"I didn't say easy. I said simple. It still takes the right tools and the right people."

"We have the best equipment available. You know that. But where do we get the right people?"

"You have me."

"You? Is this some kind of joke."

"Not at all. I could do it."

"By yourself?"

"Me and a few technicians to do the dirty work."

Dumbfounded, the Captain stared at him. Brig hell. Under normal conditions he would have recomended Stevenson for a Section Eight medical discharge. But he kept looking and Stevenson's gaze never faultered. "Okay, assuming that can be done," the Captain said, backing off again, "which I doubt. You still can't have a control button down in each silo because the operator would be killed in the blast."

"So... where would you like to have the control button? All the silos are interconnected with both hard wiring, optical links, radio links and microwave links and they all run to the missile complex control center. More than enough circuits, just do a little rewiring. I could give you one button that would launch them all simultaneously or forty eight separate buttons so you could fire them each individually."

At first the Captain stood aghast, his eyes big as cue balls. He still did not believe what he was being told. On the other hand, geez? From what he personally knew of the system it seemed to

231

make some sense. Didn't it? Maybe. Maybe not. Stevenson was known to be a bit eccentric in his ways but he was still regarded as being very clever.

"Are you sure? How long would it take to do such a thing?" he asked, squinting hard, determined not to show his eagerness.

"I don't know," Stevenson said. "I'd have to get down in one of the silos and tear into some of the electronic bays first."

"But that stuff is supposed to be tamper proof," the Captain said with more scepticism.

"Nothing is tamper proof. If somebody put it together, I can take it apart. And, rebuild it."

"Hmm. We'll.. frankly Stevenson. I think you're full of crap. But you have my permission to try."

"Hot damn," Stevenson said with a caustic smile and snapped off a quick salute. "Thank you, Sir," he said sarcastically and was gone.

Eight days later Stevenson knew exactly what had to be done and how to do it. As he modified the control system in silo fourteen he also wrote out a set of detailed instructions that could be followed by any good technician. At that point he again asked the crucial question. "Where do you want the new master control station?"

"How about that concrete bunker over by silo eleven. There's lots of phone lines in there. Do you think that would work?"

"Don't worry about it," Stevenson said. "I haven't had so much fun in years."

Another month went by. Half the silos looked like disaster areas with bays of electronic panels ripped apart but at last Stevenson's efforts came together. At the unveiling of the new command center he showed his Captain and all the other officers of the missile complex his creation. The top off of a recent issue metal desk had been bolted to the north interior wall of the building at a forty five degree angle, making it readily accessible. On it were six rows of eight each, shiny new red buttons. Below each button was attached a piece of label maker tape with the number of each silo embossed on it, numbers one through forty eight. At the top of the large panel were two master arming switches, one at each side, away from each other to make any accidental activation difficult. Then, when everyone was admiring his handiwork and complimenting him he said, "There's only one thing wrong with it."

"After all this you're telling us there's something wrong with it? Is this some kind of joke?"

"Not at all," he said. "Here you have this brand new control system and you can now launch any missile you want, but, and it's a big but, you don't have a clue as to what any of the missiles are targeted for. Which one goes to Moscow? Which one to Tehran? If anyone ever pushes a button you may be blowing up the wrong city."

"My God," was the general reaction. "All that information is locked away in the Pentagon or the White House or underground in Colorado or Nevada or who knows where. Now we have something on our hands that's even more dangerous than ever. Anyone can set it off and destroy half the planet. Damnit Stevenson. We really ought to court martial you. What the hell do we do now? Maybe we'd better disable the entire thing and really fix it so it can't ever be put back together."

"Do what you want," Stevenson said. "I just told you what was still wrong with it. I didn't say we couldn't solve that problem, too. Most of it, anyway."

"Damnit Stevenson. Will you stop jerking us around? What does that mean?"

"It means I can fix it. You wanted control of the missiles, I gave you control. If you now want to know what the designated targets are for the missiles which I gave you control of, I can work it out. At least for most of them."

"How? Do you think someone wrote all that information on the shit house wall somewhere?"

"Knowing our government, damn right. But it would take longer to track it down than it would to do it with logically applied technical expertise."

"Whose? Yours?"

"Who else."

"Damn you, Stevenson. I'm going to bust your butt clear down to private. Er... Airman."

"Not if you want me to finish my assignment. Sir."

"All right. I'm listening. Lieutenant."

"Well, there are thirty seven of those birds out there that have the fused quartz windows in the side with the light beam from the autocollimator shining in. They all still have an inertial guidance system. Not as accurate as the later GPS units but what's a couple hundred feet when the bombs have a kill radius of up to twenty miles? Anyway, your people always have to recheck the autocollimator alignment periodically using the North Star as reference so you have all the data on hand you need for every site. The autocollimator is locked onto a small mirror on the inertial guidance platform and is coupled to the azimuth axis of the guidance system with an optical angle encoder. All we have to do is locate the conductors in the umbilical cable that contain the readouts of the encoder. From that we can find the angular heading for each missile. Then, with a good global map and some arithmetic we can find what potential major target lies along that line. If there is more than one, which is highly unlikely, I'll have to pick around in the cable some more and see if I can find what elevation angle is stored in the on board computer."

"What about the Multiple Insertion Re entry Vehicles."

"There are only three of them and the individual warheads are much smaller. I can still find the major heading and one of the possible targets will still be on that azimuth. With that we can pretty well guess what the associated targets are."

"That seems pretty far out to me," one of the other officers said. "How do you know all this stuff, anyway? You didn't learn it in the service, that's for damn sure."

"No, I didn't. But back in civilian life I was systems design engineer for the prime contractor who built the missile guidance."

"Really," they said and took another look at him. "If you're that smart how come you're only a Lieutenant?"

"Don't know," he said. "Guess I'm short on leadership skills."

"Well, stop being a smart ass," his own Captain said. "Just tell us your guess on the additional effort. How long?"

"Couple more weeks on my part. Maybe less. Then you'll need some good cartographers to finish."

Three weeks later there was another unveiling. The same basic master control panel was still in place but now it contained some major embellishments. Adjacent to the right and left side safety control switches were red lights that would come on once these switches were activated. They, however, could only be energized by a keyed switch in the middle of the panel. Under each of the other separate, forty eight missile launch switches there was both a green light and a red light. Also under each switch was another label in addition to the silo number. Thirty seven switches were clearly identified with the names of cities. There were twelve in China, three in North Korea, four in Iran, two each in Syria, India and Pakistan, five in Russia, one each in Libya, Turkey, the Ukraine and

Venezuela, and three in Saudi Arabia. The remaining eleven labels, however, had large question marks on them because as yet Stevenson had been unable to unravel the pre programmed targets of the on board guidance units. Thirty seven nuclear tipped missiles was still a lot of fire power, however. No matter how you looked at it.

"Looks like the Pentagon was completely paranoid, doesn't it?" Stevenson pointed out. "They didn't trust anybody. And who knows where those other eleven would go if we pushed the button."

"You're sure this all works, Lieutenant?" asked one Captain Limboust.

"Give it a try," Stevenson said and handed the Captain the key to the master switch. Just don't push any of these individual silo buttons"

"Hmm," said the Captain, intrigued with the awesome power he held in his hand. Slowly he inserted the key in the switch and turned it. Then he pushed the button that was the left hand safety switch and its red light came on. After that he pushed the one on the right. Not only did its red light come on but all the green indicator lights under each of the separate missile launch switches came on.

"These green lights show that each particular silo is now on line and ready for launch," Stevenson said as he pointed to one of them. "Push the button underneath, the green light stays on and the red light comes on also. That initiates the entire firing sequence. First, the silo door opens. As you know that takes less than a minute. Once the door is open the green light goes out, the red stays on and about thirty seconds later the missile rocket motor ignites and you have a launch."

"What if the silo door doesn't open? We've had some problems there due to the bad weather."

"That's something I can keep working on, but, for right now, once you push the button the damned thing is going to go, one way or the other."

"But once somebody pushes an individual firing button there is still about sixty seconds before the thing ignites. If the safety switches or the keyed switch is turned off during that time, will it shut down?"

"I could have added such a feature but I figured that if someone does push a button, they are going to do it for a good reason, right? So, why bother?"

"Yes. I see your point, Lieutenant. That's a very clever piece of work you've done. If there were still some higher ranking Officers around I'd seriously recommend you for a promotion. And, by the way. Who do you think should have the master key?"

"I don't know. That you'll have to figure out for yourselves."

"But you don't need one, right? You built it so you can bypass it, if it comes to that. Nothing is completely tamper proof, isn't that what you said? How do we keep you honest?"

"First, the bunker door is always locked and I don't have the keys to that. Second, there are around the clock armed sentries on duty. And last, if I had wanted to do it I could have sent them all flying a month ago," was Stevenson's reply. As an individual, he loved problem solving and technical challenge and while there would be little recognition for what he had accomplished, it was still the highlight of his career. Nor had he spent much time moralizing about the issues. All he had wanted to prove was that the wizards who had conceived this lethal system weren't half as smart as they thought they were in being able to protect it from miss-use. The mistake was in building the damned things in the first place. Put the fate of millions of people in the hands of a few and there was bound to be serious trouble, sooner or later. It would be interesting to see how this small group of men handled the earth destroying power that had been given to them so quickly and easily. In the larger scheme of things, however, he too, had not been completely honest. There was still one small technical detail he had withheld. Crude as it was, it was his own idea of checks and balances.

When the President had still been with them the whole world clearly knew the wrath-of-god power he held. That was always one of the main attractions of the job and it was a primary reason why that power always wound up in the hands of egomaniacs. Relocate that power to a small bunch of more ordinary men living out in the barren wasteland of North Dakota, however, and their own egos would quickly begin to muddy the dynamics of the situation. When power is held, someone else needs to be made aware of it. It demands to be recognized on some level, large or small, whether it be publicly or behind the scenes.

One of the officers had an extremely nagging wife.

"What the hell are we doing in this God forsaken place," she always wanted to know. "There's a whole world out there with interesting people and places to go and things to do. And most of them are a hell of a lot warmer than this damned hell hole. How did you ever get yourself dead ended here? Couldn't you have managed your career a little better than this? God, why did I ever marry you."

"But dear," he always said, and went on to try and convince her that it was an important assignment, vital to the future safety of their great nation.

"Garbage," was her usual response, followed by her usual threat. "If we don't get out of here soon, I'm leaving you anyway."

It was almost as if the cycle of her complaints and bad humor were etched onto a calendar somewhere and the Captain knew when he left for home one evening that it was about due so he had already steeled himself against the onslaught before he opened the front door. Sure as could be, it began halfway through dinner. He thought he was prepared as ever but he had over looked five little things. The importance of his own ego and the power of the four shots of Jack Daniels he had imbibed to fortify himself. Her tirade was too much and at last he blew.

"You can be such a bitch," he threw back at her. "Maybe you should leave. But before you do I want you to know that you are in the company of one of the most powerful men in the whole world."

At first she was so dumbfounded she couldn't even laugh. Then, when she had recovered, she thought better of it. Maybe she had better be careful. For sure he had finally lost his sanity and maybe he was dangerous. It might be best to change tactics and not push him any further.

"Oh, really," she said, instead, pretending an honest curiosity. "Please tell me about it."

It was too late. His male pride took over and he blurted the whole thing out. At first his wife was incredulous. It just wasn't possible. But still, he had related everything in great detail and even though she didn't understand the technical jargon, what he said sounded so plausible. Wow, she thought. What if it were really true. There was nothing left to do but share the story with one of the other officer's wives who was also unhappy about her forced stay in this Siberian section of the country. Then, within days, all the officers wives had heard the story and when they confronted their own husbands, none of them would outwardly deny it. Soon the non commissioned officers knew about it and all the enlisted men below them.

Then the local paper in Bismarck published the story. After that the Chicago Tribune picked it up but that newspaper wrote a very derisive article instead, claiming the whole thing to be a master hoax. That was soon followed by a TV news commentary where two major scientists in the field of rocketry and electronic security systems came up with a list of seventeen different reasons why it was impossible to do such a thing. First on the list was the statement that there was no one in that branch of the service bright enough to re engineer a whole missile control system, let alone that the system had been designed by experts of great caliber to begin with, like themselves, who had made the whole thing tamper proof and inviolate.

After the program had aired, the wives back on base all became extremely furious. They been manipulated and duped. It was all a subterfuge to keep them there.

"Tell all the stories you want," they said. "We don't believe a word of it."

"But it's true," the husbands still insisted.

"Well, then, dammit," the wives replied. "Why don't you show us."

That was the final straw. The officers would throw a party. They would have in it in the bunker. There would be wine and hors de oeuvres and music and another unveiling of Lieutenant Stevenson's handcrafted Master Control Panel. If they weren't convinced after that, then let them all leave and go back to LA, or Atlanta, or West by God Nowhere to their mothers. They, the officers were duty bound and burdened with the fate of the world. They would never leave their posts.

The party was on a, colder-than-hell-as-usual, Thursday night but the bunker was all warm and cozy and decorated with red, white and blue crepe paper ribbons taped to the walls and strung overhead. The CD player was loaded with music from the nineteen fifties and some of the men took the liberty of dancing with each other's wives. There was no caviar or gourmet crackers but someone had found some smoked herring in their pantry which was served with Melba Toast and wine instead. There were about seventy people in all and about eighty bottles of wine, ten full cases of beer, five gallons of vodka, three gallons of scotch and fifteen liters of ginger ale.

Stevenson, himself, was there, but not to take an active part in it because he didn't have a spouse he needed to impress. He was there because, true to form, he had been having an intermittent affair with the young wife of one of the Captains and he came to get another look at her, maybe even to dance with her, say some suggestive things in her ear and set up another rendezvous.

An hour went by and a lot of empty liquor bottles and beer

cans went into the trash barrel before he was able to get her alone for a brief moment and say what he had to say. She, in turn, was responsive to his suggestions and they were discussing the next where and when, when they were loudly interrupted. The Captain who had the special honor of carrying the keys that kept the fate of the world in balance was banging on a beer bottle with a table knife.

"A toast," he shouted. "To our wives," he said and raised the nearly full bottle of beer and downed the entire thing in a single gulp.

"To our wives," all the married men shouted in return, and finished their own drinks.

"The moment we have been waiting for," said the Captain and turned to the master control panel which had been draped over with an Air Force blue, standard issue, wool blanket.

"This, ladies and gentlemen, is what may save us from total destruction if things keep getting worse," he stated as he pulled back the cover.

A few people said, "Wow."

Most of the rest just stared at it, however, not fully understanding the ramifications of what they were seeing.

"At last," said his wife, who was by his side. "It looks complicated. How does it work?"

"Well, first you have to have the key," he said and proudly reached in his pocket to retrieve it. "Then, the key goes in the master switch like this. Turn it on, this red light comes on. See. Then flip this safety switch up here on the left like this and that red light comes. Then you flip this one on the right and it's red light comes on. But look what else happened. All the green lights came on under each of these individual red buttons where each one is labeled with both the silo number and the target the missile is aimed for. Except for those there with the question marks whose lights didn't come on. We haven't figured out what their designated targets are yet but once we do, we'll activate then also. Then, if and when such a terrible time may come, and we feel we have no recourse, we simply push the appropriate red buttons and those birds will exit their silos and seek out their pre programmed targets. Heaven help us if it should really come to that."

"I'm proud of you, Bill," the Captains wife said half drunkenly. "You're my hero again and I'm sorry I said all those harsh things to you."

"Well, thank you dear," the Captain replied as he turned off the safety switches and turned the key in the master control switch to the off position.

"I'll try and make it up to you," his wife continued and then gave him a hot kiss right in front of everybody. "Let's go dance," she said as she snuggled up close. "Then we can go home and have some real fun."

"Let's dance," the Captain shouted to the crowd and motioned to the center of the floor.

As he did so, most everyone turned their backs on the control panel and went on with their drinking and trivial small talk. Only one couple remained behind. It was an Airman Third Class and his wife of less than a year.

"Do you really believe this thing works?" the wife asked. "It doesn't look half complicated enough to be able to really launch a bunch of missiles."

"Who knows," the Airman said. "It could just be more morale boosting BS to keep us here a little longer. That wouldn't surprise me a bit."

"Well, suppose it was the real thing and you had control. Who do you hate the most in the world?"

"The North Koreans, I guess. My grandfather was killed in action in the Korean war."

"Hmm," she said, looking over the panel. "There it is. There's three Korean targets. Silos thirty six, seven and eight."

"Gee," said the Airman. "Those are in the Montana complex. No way they could be tied into here. They're over two hundred miles away. That's ridiculous."

Meanwhile, way over in Montana the winter had been even harsher. Not only was the snow deeper, there had been ice storms to freeze it all in place. It was so thick and unmanageable that the routine maintenance of clearing the areas around the almost impenetrable, eighty ton reinforced steel and concrete doors protecting the missiles, and the railroad tracks they were meant to move on, went undone, waiting for an early thaw, if and when it should come about.

"What's the big deal?" everyone on the base said. "Who the hell is going to attack us at a time like this, what with everything else going on? And now that all the top brass is gone no one is checking the maintenance logs anymore and besides, in spite of those rumors we've heard about how the Dakota complex has gained control, we don't believe it for a moment. And if nobody knows how to launch the damned things, what the hell good are they and why bother chopping all that ice away from the silo doors?"

"Well, you know that Lieutenant Stevenson and his techs were down in all the holes picking through the cables and making changes in the equipment bays."

"Sure, and so what? What does some lowly Lieutenant know about something as complicated as all this stuff is. If he were that smart he wouldn't be in the Air Force to begin with."

So there it was. They were just as skeptical as everyone else that wasn't directly involved. As a result, on the same fateful Thursday night as the Dakota party was under way, the Wyoming non-coms were embroiled in a heated, nickel ante, no limit poker game while most of their superiors were at the Officers Club doing there own drinking and hustling each others wives on the sly. They had no idea what was about to happen next.

"Oh, look," the Airman's wife back at the bunker said. "He forgot to take the key out of that main switch there."

"Damn. You're right. I'd better give it to him."

"Wait, dear. Before you do, couldn't you just turn it on so I can see all those pretty lights again. That won't hurt anything."

"I'd better not mess with it."

"Well, just turn the lights on. Everyone else is so drunk they won't notice. And if that's all you do it wouldn't hurt anything, would it?"

"Probably not," the Airman said. "But if I get caught I could lose my stripes."

"Go ahead. Please. Just once. Nobody will know if you're quick about it. You can turn it right off again."

"Well, I don't know. Maybe," he said, frightened but still intrigued with the idea as he scanned the room to see if anyone was looking and then, irresistibly, he turned the key.

"Now do those other two switches so all the other little lights come on."

"All right. But then, off it goes."

"Now, look," said the wife. "All those Korea lights are just as green as all the rest. Why don't I just push the buttons under them."

"God no, woman. You can't do that."

"Well, you said you hated the Koreans and you said all those missiles are way over in Montana and they couldn't possibly be controlled from here. So, if that's true, let's have a little fun and play

241

pretend. How often do you get such a realistic chance to blow up your enemies?"

"I don't know, Eunice. I could be wrong, you know."

"But sweetie, I've never known you to be wrong yet, so what the heck," she said and pushed all three buttons before he could stop her.

Immediately the three corresponding red lights came on. There was also an almost inaudible beep that most people were unaware of. The buzzer that made the beep hadn't added anything to the actual function of the system. It was just a small, personal touch Stevenson had included for his own amusement. But now, for his own sake, it was a good thing he had. Halfway across the bunker he still recognized it instantaneously and turned around. The Captain in charge of the keys heard it also and even though he was uninformed and didn't know the why of it, the sound triggered something in his fogged brain.

"Oh, oh," he said, feeling the empty pocket where the keys should have been and quickly headed back. Stevenson was already there.

"Oh my God," said the Captain as he stared at the three glowing red lights. "Oh my God," he said again. "What the hell are we going to do now?"

"There's only one thing left to do," Stevenson said. "Push this center button here right under the master switch with the question mark under it."

"But you don't know what it's for," the Captain said.

"Of course I do. I built the damned thing, didn't I?"

"Well, what is it then?"

"I call it the, just-in-case button."

"Will that fix it?"

"Of course," Stevenson assured him and reached over and pushed the button. Once it's red light came on he shut down the panel, took out the master key, handed it back to the Captain.

"What is it? Some kind of master over ride or something?"

"No. I reprogrammed that particular missile's guidance system. And, I just launched it. It will head out over the Pacific about four thousand miles, then turn around and come straight back here. This bunker is ground zero. You have almost an hour if you want to get your wife and head out."

The Captain laughed, half drunk as he was. "Stevenson, you are something else. What a wild story. I'm not sure I ever believed any of it, to tell you the truth. It's all too damned impossible."

"Then why did you come back to get the key you left in the master switch?"

"Just in case. Who knows. We certainly want to thank you for getting our wives to pay a little more attention to us, however."

"Last chance," Stevenson said.

"No, hell, I need another drink," the Captain said instead.

"Okay. But before you go, let me have the keys to your Humvie. I had a large chocolate cake made and I forgot to bring it. Maybe you could ask Captain Amhurst if I could borrow his wife for a little to help me carry it?"

"Of course," the Captain replied in amusement, as he handed over the keys to his official vehicle.

"How did you ever manage that?" Mrs. Amhurst, Stevenson's sometimes playmate asked.

"It was actually quite easy," he replied. "And I'll bet your husband doesn't even know you're gone."

"I doubt it. He always has to try and out drink his buddies when they're together."

"He's a damned fool. If you were my wife I'd treat you a hell of a lot better than he does," Stevenson confessed, suddenly realizing how much he had actually begun to care for this woman.

"Well, if we ever get out of this horrible place I'm going to get a divorce. I don't know where you'll be but if you want to get together after that, I'd like it."

"After tonight you won't have to worry about a divorce anymore."

"Why not? What do you mean?"

Stevenson quickly reiterated what he had told the Captain. "But he didn't believe me," he said. "Maybe you don't either but there's only about fifty minutes left. Even with the snow, we can be thirty miles away by then. That should be safe enough. Please, for God's sake. Come with me."

At first she was helpless to speak. Then she embraced him and gave him the most desperate kiss he had every received in his life. When he released her, she opened the door of the vehicle and got out. She didn't immediately go back inside, however, but stood there in the light from the fixture on the side of the building and watched him. Then she gave him a sad little wave and motioned for him to leave. He waited, but she shook her head so he started out, slowly at first, then quickly, without looking back, leaving her behind, leaving himself with an ache in his heart that he now knew would never go away. Three different times he stopped and wasted precious seconds, almost turning around, but in the end he kept going.

By this time back in Wyoming, however, several serious things had already happened. The missiles were all powered by solid fuel rockets. They do not throw out vast amounts of flame and heat and vapor and slowly rise off the pad and into the air. Once the electrical ignition pulse reached the igniter, the rest was practically instantaneous and there sure as hell had better be nothing in the way. The missile would breach the silo rim and be almost completely out of sight within less than thirty seconds. As the first and second rocket stages burned out, they would drop away. Eventually, all that would be left was the warhead, silently moving through space, arcing it's way over the horizon, arming itself at the proper distance down range, waiting until it had dropped back into the lower reaches of the atmosphere to where the proximity fuse would set off a small explosion. This, in turn, would heat and slam the critical masses of enriched plutonium into each other, converting mass into energy in a proportion of billions to one. First would be a wave of gamma rays and x-rays spreading out at the speed of light, followed by an extremely powerful electromagnetic wave which in turn would be followed by waves of neutrons, protons, electrons and other sub atomic particles, all accompanied by newly created radioactive streams of heavier material. Then comes the heat wave and the shock wave, everything spreading out from above, flattening, pulverizing, melting. Not one living thing would survive that was less than twenty miles away, even in the deep interior basements of tall buildings. Further away there was a chance, if someone were lucky enough, but even then they might not live very long if they had a high enough dose of radiation. And it would be one of the most horrible ways to die that humans had yet invented.

This was an accurate description of the missile that left silo thirty six. It cleanly and faultlessly left the one hundred foot deep, highly protected hole in the ground that was its home and headed straight and true for Pyongyang in North Korea. Things in silos thirty seven and thirty eight, however, did not go as smoothly. It was the fault of the weather and the extreme build up of snow and ice, the fault of the maintenance crews who had failed to remove it and the fault of failed electronic components that erroneously signaled that the silo doors were both completely open, when they were not. Had the units failed completely and the missiles fired with the doors closed, the rocket motors would have been powerful enough to lift the eighty ton masses up and over. In doing so, however, several other things could have resulted. In the delay the motors could have generated so much heat down in the silo that the missile would have blown up and destroyed itself. Or, had it lifted the door and exited the silo, the upper stages would have been so badly compressed that the guidance system would be destroyed and the missile would have lifted, floundered and fallen back to the ground to burn itself out. Missile thirty seven was a version of this.

Instead of remaining totally closed, however, the door of that silo had partially opened before it jammed against the ice and stopped, ramming the frozen sheet behind it into the limit sensors which triggered and told the system that the door was fully open. With that, the missile fired. When it did, the nose cone and first stage made it past the door's edge but the entire side of the wider second and third stages were scraped away in passing. Badly damaged, it drifted far off course and when it's second stage motor failed to ignite, it dropped into the Gulf of Alaska, as yet unarmed, and disappeared.

The launch sequence for missile thirty eight was nearly identical with the exception that the door was a few more inches farther open when the missile left the silo. As a result, less damage was done to the outside of the missile as it scraped its way past, but, there were still some serious problems. The shudder and shock of concrete ripping away on the aluminum alloy exterior had transmitted itself inward to the guidance platform. This caused the rotor of the main gyro, which just happened to be a few micro inches out of tolerance in sphericity to begin with, to briefly rub against the housing, which was also slightly out of tolerance, creating a thinner than necessary air bearing gap at one point. Although both surfaces were highly polished and extremely hard, the rotor, spinning at thousands of revolution per second, still ground off enough atoms of material to bind up. Once this occurred the guidance computer was without pitch and yaw information. This, combined with the effect of mangled sheet metal on the outside of the missile that altered its aerodynamics, caused the huge projectile to take a much different path through the atmosphere than was designated. Instead of dropping down in pitch and heading due westward like number thirty six, it continued almost straight up where, finally lacking in thrust, it tipped over and came back towards earth. But it did not come straight down. Helped along by the high altitude jet stream, it veered east and slightly south, the warhead arming itself along the way. But again, there was another peculiar operational failure.

The warhead should have detonated at a thousand feet above the surface but somehow it delayed and the missile nose cone drove itself into that great inland body of fresh water located between the United States and Canada, Lake Erie, and almost at the exact geographical center. Then, only after it was nearly one hundred feet below the surface, did it explode. When it did, millions of gallons of lake water were instantaneously vaporized and lifted in a huge, miles wide and many miles high cloud.

American Airlines flight 221, Toronto to Chicago with 261 passengers aboard, was over head at the time, cruising at thirty four thousand feet. So was Delta 197, headed east at thirty one thousand feet, and Midwest Air 311 at twenty eight thousand feet, along with two other commercial flights headed elsewhere across the lake. Total passenger count for the involved flights was nine hundred and twenty three, plus flight crews. The blast tore the wings off all the planes, lifted the battered fuselages upward as much as a mile higher in the sky and tumbled and spun them until they were totally disintegrated before allowing the pieces to fall back to the surface of the earth.

Meantime, back in the lake another law of physics came into play. Since water is a nearly incompressible substance, what was not vaporized by the horrific blast could only be displaced. The first underwater effect was a shock wave that expanded radially at extreme velocity, crushing and killing every living thing in the lake from fish to frogs to eels to turtles, from one end to the other. At the same time, billions of gallons of water were forced outward in every direction, away from the center of the blast, with literally nowhere to go except up onto the shoreline. It was an ocean sized tsunami occurring in the basin of an inland lake. A big lake, to be sure, two hundred fifty five miles long and sixty miles wide, but, very small in terms of the energy of the bomb.

Thirty story buildings in Cleveland toppled like match sticks as the monstrous wave of water washed up and over the shoreline, devastating everything in its path, in some places reaching inland ten, twelve, fifteen miles. Rushing eastward the wave rolled across Buffalo, New York and over Niagara Falls, taking out the hydro electric plant built deep in the rocky canyon walls and rolled on, up the waterway and over the land into Lake Ontario and clear into the St Lawrence waterway, almost to the outskirts of Montreal before it finally ended.

On the other end of the lake, Sandusky and Port Clinton were washed away, along with every other town and out post along the waterfront. Toledo was gone, but Detroit, somewhat shielded by the Windsor Peninsula, only lost half of its population. The total body count could only be estimated. Two million, three million, five, more or less.

And then there was Lt. Stevenson's own answer to stupidity. The little red button in the center of the control panel with the hand painted little question mark under it. His own little just-in-case button where ground zero was exactly where he had said it was. The bunker with the control panel where the party was being held. The bunker the woman he had finally realized he was in love with, the one who had gone back to to be with her husband. Twenty nine and a half miles away at detonation, he was still headed south at the fateful moment. A much more sparsely populated part of the country, the death toll was at least an order of magnitude less. Maybe more, but just as dead as all the rest. And yet, in spite of it all, Stevenson, the one person who had made it all possible, had managed to survive. And for what? Now he must somehow learn to live with his own contribution to the disaster. How would he manage? Was it just another, not too big, not too small tragedy when compared to some of the other atrocious things that man has done to man over the years. The English had starved a million Irish to death in recent history. Pol Pot killed two million of his own people in Cambodia. Stalin deliberately took the lives of thirty million Russians. Mao's Great Step Forward Policy killed thirty million while the entire Chinese Communist regime was responsible for seventy two million deaths. And what about Hitler? Yes, and what about the Americans? He was an American, wasn't he? Lieutenant Stevenson, United States Air Force. Yes, Sir.

How many millions of Native Americans were slaughtered in the great push westward across North America? How many Americans killed each other in the Civil war? How many Vietnamese did they butcher, how many innocent Iraqis were written off as collateral damage and how many more millions were deprived of life around the world out of greed and manipulation and how many thousands of assassinations were committed with the blessings of the occupants of the White House over the years. How many other poor souls had marched off in a religious fervor down through the ages, never to return home again? How much blood had he, Lieutenant Stevenson, actually been responsible for? How much blood was there on the ground anyway, and who had been more violent than who? If the life of one small child is important, how important are the lives of a million people? Or, is it true what Stalin had said, Stevenson asked himself. The loss of a single life is a tragedy but the loss of millions is only a statistic. One small push of a little red button in a cold and windy, remote place in North Dakota, by now, also disappeared, melted and turned to glass or vaporized and blown away, and out of it all he only saw but one face. The one face he would never see again but would never be able to put to rest.

TOWN SQUARE

"What are you doing?" Jed asked his oldest daughter, Mary, who was scurrying around in a semi disoriented way, gathering things together, two pieces of partially filled luggage on the bed.

"They're coming," she said. "I have to get out of here and I'm taken Janice with me."

"Calm down, girl. What are talking about? What's wrong?"

"They're coming to town and they're supposed to be here on Thursday. God, I hope that old car of mine will get me there without breaking down."

"All right. All right. Stop a minute and tell me what this is all about, will you please. Who's coming? And where a you going, anyway?"

"Up to Heber and stay with Aunt Jane. Oh, wow. Sorry dad. Guess I'm feeling a little panicky. It's the Hells Handoffs. They're coming here."

"That murdering motorcycle gang? God help us! How do you know? And why here, of all places?"

"Remember Bobby Markle? That kid I dated in High School for a while?"

"Of course. The guy who took you to the senior prom. What's he got to do with it? You haven't seen him in years."

"I know, but somehow he tracked me down. He's now part of the gang but I guess he still had enough decency to warn me about what's going on. He said I should take Janice and tell all my girl friends and leave for at least a month. Maybe you'd better come too."

"Those sons-a-bitches. Damnit," he cursed and let out a string of other strong explicatives. "Why Prescott, for god's sake?" he ended with.

"Cause it's what they do. The town is ripe for picking."

"But it's not big enough to put up any fight. Is that what the bastards are thinking? They can do any damned thing they want and we won't be able to defend ourselves? Damn them."

"Well, they're probably right, Dad, and you know it. That's why we need to leave."

"But what about everyone else? Lots of people don't have cars anymore. Or anywhere to go. What about them?"

"I see your point. But what can we do? We still have three days to get out before they get here."

They weren't handoffs from hell at all. Hell would never have left them get close enough for that. Most all of them were from somewhere far beyond. Twisted and mangled, they were a malignant growth with an insatiable appetite that sucked the life out of every place they had ever landed in. All except Bobby Markle, but he was getting there. Another six months and he, too, would be beyond help. But for now, Mary was still the love of his wayward life. She had been his one moment of sweetness and light in all the darkness and evil that had surrounded him. It had been six or seven years but he still thought of her with purity and it was pure anguish to think that any harm might come to her. It was not her fault the relationship had come to a bad end.

He'd already killed for the gang, too. There was nothing to be done about that either, but his pleading thoughts of Mary were both his last fading strand of sanity and the source of his growing madness and great depression, for she represented everything he could have had and might have done with his life, but stupidly threw away and turned his back on. Almost daily anymore, it churned painfully away in his mind, riling the anger that seared his crippled brain, the anger he felt against himself but could never admit to, and made him project it viscously out onto the world around him.

Oh, God! He cursed himself for his weakness and felt no hope. Drugs helped. Drugs and alcohol combined eased it a little more but nothing ever completely kept it at bay. Surprisingly, however, his disloyalty to the gang in calling Mary to warn her was a drop of secret pride for him at first. But it barely lasted. A spurious strand of reflected light into the darkness of his own degenerate soul, it vanished as quickly as he was able to wipe the oil off the old forty five automatic he had just cleaned. That done, he slipped it into the holster on his belt and went off to check over the battered and road weary, big black Harley that had carried him down far too many lonesome highways.

The booming thunder of their unmufflered exhausts could be heard for miles as they roared south on Arizona 93, five or six abreast like an attacking army, hogging both sides of the highway in the rising morning sunlight. Behind them lay the decimated ruins of Kingman. Thirty three dead bodies, another three dozen maimed for life, four new young women hanging onto the their new owners on the back of the big choppers, heads down in shame, hiding from the wind and the violation they were the victims of.

At highway 87 the quarter mile long, strung out mechanized snake of bandits turned northeast, then veered onto 96 and blasted through Hillside and Kirkland and Skull Valley and Iron springs without even slowing down and rolled the last five miles into Prescott with an eager vengeance, just as the clock on the old courthouse in the town square stuck twelve noon.

It was a perfect October day in the mile high town. Languid, almost loving in its way. Lulling, misleadingly at odds with their purpose for being there. But there was no hurry. They had another month before they needed to be in Mexico, away from the oncoming cold of winter. But they were hungry and thirsty from the long ride and always desperate for confrontation. That was what it was all about. Confrontation validated their meaningless existences as nothing else ever could. It was their faded glory. Without that, there was nothing. Without that they had no idea who they really were at all. Without that, *they* were nothing. Nothing at all, and far too proud and stubborn and stupid to realize it.

Nearly three hundreds cycles in all, pulled into the curb space around the square. A few last big revs of over sized engines. Then, as the sounds died, leather jackets and black boots moved out onto the grassy area surrounding the old library and the now abandoned old court house with the boarded up windows. They hadn't expected much of a reception. There never were but a few brave enough or dumb enough to be out and about once they realized a marauding band of slimy backed grease balls was in town. That was normal but somehow today seemed a little different. Of all people, Bobby Markle was the first to feel the hint of it. His own bike was already backed up onto its kickstand when his methamphetamine damaged brain kicked in a little and he stopped and took a deep breath of the higher altitude air and looked around. But before anything could have clicked he caught sight of the old corner tavern over across Montezuma Street where he had had his first ever taste of whiskey and he stomped across the pavement. He was up the steps and reaching for the door before he finally realized that his old hangout now had security bars on all the windows and an oversized padlock on the door. This was not right at all, he said to himself. How dare they do such a thing. He bent over, shielding his eyes against the glass and looked inside. It was still the same old place, just as he had remembered, with bar stools and pool tables and a well stocked back bar lined with bottles. Damnit. This was the place where it had all begun and again he thought of Mary.

Sweet Mary. He had started drinking right out of high school and she had always chastised him and pleaded with him about it, but all to no avail. Too weak to make the right choice, his drinking had driven her away. Then that thought was soon gone also, but still he hesitated, feeling confused.

"What's the matter?" a big voice bellowed at him from behind, that of a bulky, bearded fellow member of the gang still out in the street. It was enough to bring him back to the moment and make him realize he couldn't just walk away from this, old home town or not, and in an instant he was angry as hell. Who did these damned people think they were, anyway? Everyone knew that the only people that gangs always left alone were the barkeepers. As long as the booze kept flowing and they didn't complain too loudly over a few broken tables and a little blood on the floor from smashed noses, everything was just fine. What the hell.

But here he was out in front of all his associates, faced down by a locked door. This would never do. With a new certainty of purpose, he hunched up his shoulders, pulled out the monster forty five, cocked an oversized round into the chamber, aimed carefully and fired, blowing a hole through the lock and the door both. He smiled, put the safety on and holstered the weapon. That was the moment when everything changed.

From somewhere up high to the north, over on the far side of Gurley Street, a highly amplified, harsh voice boomed out and echoed off the walls of all the buildings ringing the square.

"That's as far as it goes, boys," it came in ominous tones, straight out of the old west. "Back away from the door and the whole damned bunch of you get on your machines and ride out of here if you want to stay alive."

Immediately, all heads turned towards the direction of the loud voice and a war cry went up as men who weren't already packing scrambled back to their vehicles to retrieve their own weapons. It couldn't have been better. They hadn't been in a major clash for weeks. "Yahooo," they screamed as Bobby scanned the second story windows that looked down on them.

Certain that he had seen a face in what was probably an apartment over the old furniture store on the corner, he grabbed his gun, flicked the safety back off, raised it, a let go a round.

It was hard to say which projectile arrived first. The one that Bobby had fired or the one that had left the barrel of a relic of an old hunting rifle, big as an elephant gun, with its much higher muzzle velocity. Bobby Markle, the hopeless shell of a man who had unwittingly warned the town. Bobby Markle, the man who had voiced his own unspoken death wish when he had slugged down his first taste of whiskey and heated that first small little crystal and injected himself. Such a long time ago. So many dark and ghoulish, ghost filled paths, his own lost and miscreant behavior, all erased in a microsecond, his ultimate wish at last fulfilled. He was dead before he even hit the ground, his brains splattered across the door he so desperately felt he had to breach. The rest was history in the making.

The sound of the shots and the rifles which appeared from out of nowhere all had zero affect on the mob. They never lost a step in their haste to do battle with this unseen enemy. As for the locals, while they were sorely offended by the idea of a bunch of lowlifes trying to take over their town and abusing their women, they hadn't intended to be completely merciless when they started out. The plan had been to wait, just as they had done, but to draw a hard line in the sand at the first provocation. Give the bastards a chance, little as they deserved it. But they were not about to be fired upon themselves, no matter what. Regardless, and decently enough, the first thing they did was to aim for the gas tanks on all the cycles.

Within seconds the air was full of explosions and gasoline fed flames and screaming hoodlums who had been too close. Unfortunately, it was not enough. Gang members mistakenly dived for cover, thinking they were safe because they were shielded from the north, and began returning fire. It was a serious error. The entire square was ringed with local gunmen and they had something more powerful and far more accurate than handguns. They weren't a bunch of card dealing wimps from the Lake Havasu casinos or a bunch of shoe salesmen. These guys were small town rednecks living in the high desert and the tall pines and they could pick the eye out of a coyote heading off in a dead run more than two hundred yards away. They could also knock down a deer or an elk with a single shot from even further. If they had the notion.

At the most it might have lasted two minutes and, except for the smoke and the crackling sounds of burning cycle tires, it was all too soon over and silence prevailed. Cautiously, the town defenders made their way down from their vantage points and entered the square. The only survivors were women. They were all alive but for two and those two had guns and had been shooting back. Then, out of curiosity, someone else walked back over to the bar to look at the first offender, the one who started the tragic chain of events. The face was gone so he dug around in the dead man's pockets for identification.

"My god," he said. "That's the weirdest thing I ever seen in my life. I don't believe it."

"What's wrong?" Mary's father asked. Mary's father, Jed. The man who had become livid with rage at the thought of motorcycle bums getting their hands on his beloved daughters. The man who had organized the resistance, the man who had stewed and cursed for three days prior, hatred building, now drawn back to the scene of the first casualty, now feeling weak in the knees, for he had been the one who had held the big rifle that had made that first fatal shot, now able to look more closely at the consequences of what he had done. He had never been in the military. He had never killed a man before.

"He's a home town boy," he was told. "One of our own till he ran off with this crazy bunch of bastards."

"Who?" Mary's father asked fearfully, not so sure he really want to know.

"That Markle kid, Bobby. Jeez, didn't he used to go with your daughter way back when?"

Mary's father dropped his rifle, his knees giving way under him and he came to rest against the building, unable to speak. He had killed the very man who's one lost moment of sentiment had saved the town from destruction. Then he swore.

"Son-of-a-bitch," he said, as he pulled himself together, looked at the blood and brains splattered against the wall and spat on the sidewalk.

In the end, what to do with all the burned out hulks of the motorcycles was easy. They were trucked to the city landfill. What to do with all the bodies was something else. Nobody seemed to want to claim them. And so it was that Prescott, Arizona soon had its own modern day boot hill, but it was way out on the very edge of the town limits, adjacent to the same land fill the machines had all gone in. It might have been a necessary happening, but it was hardly a proud one, and for the time being the burial grounds went unmarked. But none of it was forgotten. In the bigger American scheme of things it was an event of serious dimensions. A historical, turning point moment in time that helped changed the course of things in the post disappearance world. Citizens groups around the country began to organize and practiced shooting at simulated human targets on a ritualistic basis, saved their shell casings, reloaded them and fitted them with lead formed in home built casting molds. Then they started a tracking network. Within six months from the vigilante massacre in the Prescott town square no one ever rode into any town, anywhere, in a group with more than three or four people in it. And the bikes all had mufflers on them and they did it quietly. And they also made damned sure they never violated a locked bar room door or broke up any bar room furniture while they were there. Or ever laid a hand on some other man's daughter without her express permission.

RETURN

"Howard. This is Herb. Sorry to bother you at home but can you come down to the plant. Yeah, the sooner the better," one of Howard's former supervisors, who was now one of the employee owners of the company, said to him over the phone.

"What's going on?" Howard asked. "Did the power go out again?"

"No, nothing like that. There's a really ratty looking bum sitting in your old office behind the desk with his feet up on it, looking out the window. Hasn't had a shave or a decent haircut in a long time. He's wearing this weird set of clothes that is worse than hand made and he doesn't smell all that great either but says he won't leave until he gets to see you. Should we throw him out?"

At first Howard was silent, then it was, "God no. Get him a cup of coffee and make him comfortable. I'll be down just as fast as I can."

"I would have stopped at a barber shop for a trim but I forgot my wallet," Jack said, after Howard had arrived.

Howard laughed and gave Jack a monstrous hug, something he had never done before in his life and blinked a few times to keep the tears away. Then he wrinkled his nose and said, "Well, I guess we know where you came from."

"No kidding. We never did get around to inventing soap. Just as well, though. None of the men here ever got close enough to recognize me," Jack laughed.

Howard laughed again, too. Then took a closer look. "But where did you ever get those clothes?"

"Made them myself," Jack said proudly. "Wouldn't work for the spring ball but they kept me from dying of hypothermia."

"Hypothermia? On the island? What are you talking about?" Howard asked, puzzled, since it had been tropical when he was there.

"I know," Jack said. "Hard to believe but winter was setting in."

"Sounds like we have a lot to talk about," Howard said.

"You have no idea," Jack replied. "But plenty of time for that later. Any chance you have a real pair of scissors around so I can whack off more of this fur and clean up a bit before we go anywhere? I never did get around to a good shave back there."

"Margaret won't mind. Mine was much longer when I returned and I probably smelled worse than you do."

"That's hard to believe."

By now at least a dozen men from the plant had gathered in the office. Once they got over the initial shock and they realized who Jack was, they began hitting him with a barrage of questions. Then, when they saw that Howard had brought his camera with him, they all wanted their pictures taken with Jack.

"No way," Jack said. "Not looking like this."

"Just for the record," Howard stated and they all pleaded with him to concede.

"Okay. What the hell," he consented at last. "No one will believe it anyway."

Once the photos had all been snapped Jack again asked for some scissors.

"Better yet, I brought a pair of clippers," Howard told him. "Unless you want to stop for a formal shave and haircut."

"I bathed in the creek this morning but I still doubt if they'd let me in."

"You're right," Howard said. "I certainly wouldn't."

By the time they were done the wastebasket was full of matted hair. "Wow," Jack said. "There's enough wool in there to make half a dozen sweaters."

"No kidding," Howard agreed. "And I brought you some clothes, too. And in case you forgot, there's still a shower in my old office. But don't throw those old ones away. They belong in a museum."

Some twenty minutes later Jack felt presentable enough to face the world he had come home to.

"Okay," Howard said. "We'd better get you up to the house. Margaret is making steak and eggs."

"Unbelievable," Jack said, after he had wiped his plate clean and was on his third cup of coffee.

"That's what I said, too," Howard replied, "but I wasn't gone half as long as you were. Never understood why they, it, that, whatever, took you away to begin with. You weren't really running anything, anyway."

"No, but like I said when we were on the island. There had always been a powerful curiosity about the bigger truth of it. Sometimes I think I simply willed myself into disappearing just so I could have the experience. Does that seem possible?"

"No, but then what does? And what about coming back? Do you think you willed that too?"

"Hard to tell. But one night about a month ago I damned well decided I'd had enough. Wasn't sure it was a two way street because there was no way to tell if you had made it back but I decided I had to find out. So... Who knows. Of course there is a big flaw in that kind of thinking."

"There is. It would be hard to argue that all those people wanted to end up on that island. Let alone, that those who made it back, willed it to happen. Including me."

"I know. It's complicated."

"Without a doubt. But now that you've been there and back how do you feel about it?"

"Once was enough. As for the rest of it, I don't know. That's probably going to take a while. I'm damned glad I'm here, though. I can tell you that. Especially after how crazy it got toward the end."

"Just like coming back from the war."

"Equally as bad. And then there are still all the remaining questions. I'm convinced it wasn't just some far out dream. We have my hand tailored suit to verify that. But what about all the people who lost their lives over there. Are they really dead or will they just show up one day, too? And what about Katherine? If she's here I'd sure like to see her again. If she's still available, or interested or anything."

256

"You have no idea. She's been down here several times and we usually talk once a week. She doesn't ask anymore because she's probably too worried that maybe you wouldn't make it back but I know you are always on her mind. As far as people returning, there have been very few. Or maybe they are just like Katherine and I were. Just so damned glad to be back that we didn't even want to talk about it. Not to the media, anyway. Of course, if some public figure like the President had shown up, I'm sure it would have made the news big time."

"Well, if dead is dead, he and a lot of other formerly important people won't be returning. But we can talk about that later, too. Right now I need a little sleep. We were up all night keeping the fire going, and speaking of fire, that is another story you may want to hear sometime."

"No problem. But don't be surprised if you don't sleep very well in a bed. It's too comfortable."

"Yes," Margaret said, laughing. "Would you believe it. He slept on the floor for more than a month."

"I was kind of looking at that big tree out in the back yard, myself," Jack said. "The grass looks pretty inviting under it. If the bed doesn't work, I'll try that."

"Katherine, look!" Jack said in a subdued voice and motioned. Regal rack of horns lifted, a huge bull elk not more than thirty yards away looked directly at them and sniffed the air. They froze in their tracks and waited.

"My god. He's beautiful," Katherine stated, keeping her voice down also.

Patiently, they remained motionless for what felt like minutes as the beast studied them. Then it put its head down and began feeding on the vegetation that surrounded it. Mouth full, the head came up again as the animal watched and chewed. When the head went down again, Katherine and Jack slowly backed away. Then, moving cautiously, they circled around and upwards until they found a vantage point above the big bull. By this time he was not alone. Five females and two calves had also entered the clearing and were feeding nearby. One spindly legged calf was trying hard to hang on and nurse as his mother moved from place to place tearing up green shoots from the ground for herself. The other calf tottered around sniffing and bumping into the rest of the small herd.

Their backpacks removed, the two humans sat together in the warm sun, leaned into each other and continued watching. There had been a few bear, some bighorn sheep and other high country inhabitants but it was the first elk they had seen thus far. Without benefit of promises or vows, they had been out tramping around in the mountains for nearly two weeks now and were still about twenty miles from where they began. The cabin they had borrowed had gone almost unused. Perched high on a ridge overlooking a long, lush valley and meandering, trout filled river below, it would have made a great honeymoon haven all by itself.

The days had been balmy, the nights cool and precious. But what fool would want to sleep indoors under those circumstances? They had opted for extended, days long hikes instead, cooking over a campfire and sleeping bundled together in a double sleeping bag on the ground. It was a very large sleeping bag and, in addition to being an ideal place to star gaze from, it was more than roomy enough for other sorts of activity also. And if they happened to stop along the way to rest during the day and decided it wasn't rest that they wanted and there was no grass around, it served that purpose quite well too.

Half an hour later the elk had moved on.

"Forget the fine dining and the satin sheets," Katherine said. "That is what I missed the most. Except for you, of course, even though I hadn't even met you yet."

"You mean the animals."

"Yes. It wouldn't have had to be elk. If there had just been one little chipmunk sitting on a rock chewing on a seed or one little bird singing some happy little song. Can you imagine what it would be like living here on earth without them. The island was bad enough but think what a lonely place the planet would be, even for city people, without pets at home or squirrels and birds in Central Park or a zoo with live animals."

"I missed them too. I was always looking for deer. Some life in the ocean would have been nice, too."

"It's really comforting to have them here with us now. Did anyone else ever comment about it back there?"

"Very few. I think there were a lot of people there who would have just considered them to be a nuisance. A lot more would have been frightened to death sleeping outside, worrying about some creature showing up in the middle of the night. And then they got so caught up in their other silly games. I doubt if most of them even noticed that the only thing on the island was humans."

"Do you think it was something more than coincidence that there was no other life there?"

"I don't think any of it was coincidence. That would have been much too simple. There was a hidden message in everything about the place, I'm sure of that. The problem in living there, though, was that it was almost impossible not to get caught up in the craziness. And once that started it was all about the day to day struggle of just trying to stay alive. Other than our own small group, I met very few people who spent much time asking serious questions about the bigger meaning of it all. They never questioned much of anything else, either."

"Just like back here."

Seconds later their discussion was rudely interrupted by deep, distant rumblings in the sky.

"Looks like we'd better get the tarp up," Jack stated, and started digging through his backpack. Heavy at times, the rain lasted for nearly two hours and by then there was little time before dark. Katherine dug under the brush in the deeper grass looking for tinder as Jack went in search of wood dry enough to burn. They soon had a fire going and water was being heated for their powdered rations. There were enough supplies for two more days. That meant ten miles of hike both days. They would be heading back towards the cabin in the morning.

"I think the island setting was also a strong forewarning," Jack was saying as they moved through the tall pines, heading east, continuing their conversation from the previous day.

"How so?"

"The sea, for one thing."

"I remember the sea as being quite beautiful. From a distance. But up close it was so stark. Not just the absence of marine life. It was almost eerie, somehow. Did you feel it too?"

"Not that. But it was very strange. I used to have to wade out in the water at low tide to get around Ivan's wall in the beginning. I tasted it a few times to see if it was salty like the ocean here and it was. More so. Really salty. It also had a foul taste. Tainted, is the only way I can describe it. As though it were polluted, or had been at one time. Maybe that explains the rest.

"What?"

"Not what was there. But, what wasn't."

"In the sea? No fish. But.... of course. There wasn't any sea weed. Was there? No kelp or anything. No creature life in the sea. And no plant life. I remember. That bothered me almost as much as the rest. There weren't any coral reefs out there either, now that I think of it. And in that setting there should have been. Shouldn't there?"

"Probably. How did you know?"

"I used to sit up on the back side of the mountain and scan the water with Howard's binoculars all the time, just hoping I would see something out there. Guess I was too obsessed with finding another island off in the distance, or a ship or most anything indicative of other people. But I've been to the south Pacific. There should have been some coral out there."

"No doubt. But in that water ....."

"What else do you think we missed? You have an idea about it. Don't you?"

"Just a theory. A pretty wild one."

"Tell me."

"I don't want to be all doom and gloom, but seriously, consider the what-ifs. What will happen to the earth if more of the ozone layer is lost, if global warming continues, if people continue to over fish the oceans, if oil spills contaminate the waters and people keep using them as their city dump? No algae, no plankton, no krill. Nothing at the bottom of the food chain. That ends up meaning no food fish, no dolphins or whales, no sea turtles, sea lions, penguins, nothing. Not even coral because that's a living thing also. A dead sea.. Of course most people had already heard that scenario long before the disappearance, even if they wern't willing to help."

"But still just like the sea around the island."

"The same."

"But what's the connection?"

"Maybe there isn't one. On the other hand, if you were the one sending all the leaders off to some isolated island, putting them face to face so they were forced to deal directly with each other, how would you pick the place? If you're going to do that, why not also send them off into the future? Give them a hard look at the consequences of their actions further down the road if, in addition to everything else, they don't make some major environmental policy shifts."

"Yes, but if they all went there and got themselves killed, then nothing was accomplished."

"But that's the point. They weren't supposed to get themselves killed. That was their choice. If some of us made it back that means it wasn't a one way street at all. It means they could have all gone there, paid attention, learned a few things and returned. Sounds pretty harsh but what's so different? Life has always been a challenge. Behave stupidly, pay the price. Not in some second hand way far down the road like what's been going on back here but immediate and personal."

"Yes. And we don't have the luxury of ignoring it here any longer either. A few more nuclear bombs and that's it. There won't be people or animals. Do you think we'll ever know what really happened in North Dakota and Lake Erie?"

"Probably not," Jack had to admit after a moment.

"I wonder if there are any safe havens left."

"Not any more. It's all in jeopardy. Even this up here."

Having covered nearly five miles, they trekked on in silence. Half an hour later they stopped for a break. The day had been clear and warm, no rain in sight. They found a place in the sun and sat on an old dead log.

"But the good thing is we're together," Jack stated without prelude after they had dumped their heavy packs on the ground. "And that is a tremendous blessing for me," he told her truthfully, "because seriously, I was getting rather depressed just before I returned."

He was facing her, giving her a serious look, studying her face. He had gone from an almost bottomless pit of despair after his wife had died to a tempestuous, all too brief emotional incursion with Katherine on the island, to more than a years worth of being alone to try and sort through the myriad psychological perturbations. Even today he still sometimes felt a thin wisp of guilt pass over him when he looked at Katherine or thought about her and had to remind himself that he was no longer married. Yet he also knew that death was not necessarily a final separation. Still, it had to be dealt with and he knew he had every right to also be in love with Katherine. It was not a violation of what had gone before.

She returned the look and touched his cheek with the back of her hand.

"And because of you, life still has meaning and vitality. It more than keeps my hope alive," Katherine said, also feeling blessed and still often overwhelmed at the impact he had on her. Never had she dreamed she could have ever become so involved with another human being.

"Thank you," he said. "And at times I believe that maybe we could spend the rest of our lives just like this, up here in the mountains, letting it all go by."

"Sometimes, yes. Me, too. But then we both know there's

more to it than that, don't we?"

"There is. And it does gnaw away there in the background," Jack replied as he dug in his pack for some trail mix.

Several handfuls later and a drink of water, Katherine asked, "So the question is, where do we go from here?"

"There doesn't seem to be a lot of options, does there? The two of us certainly aren't going to save the world all by ourselves. But, as you say, there is no safe place to hide, either. So, what do you think we could do?"

"Well, we have been on the island so we've seen the other side of this. And since very few people have had that experience, maybe we have something of value to pass on. What do you think?"

"Might be interesting," Jack said. "Any feelings as to how we would go about it?"

"Not at the moment. But the next time I'm alone I'll give it some thought."

"And what does that mean?"

"That means your presence still overwhelms me."

"Really?" Jack said. "I thought that was my line?"

"I can't help it if I feel the same way."

"Even with your clothes on?" he chided.

"Ha, I can see where you're going," she said mischievously and started unbuttoning her blouse.

"Don't do that," Jack said. "That's my job."

"And vice versa," she giggled as Jack hurriedly untied the sleeping bag from the top of the pack and spread it out on the forest floor.

A very long time later they were up and dressed again. The day was nearing its end. "Well, looks like we'll just have to hike a little further tomorrow," Jack said.

"Who's complaining," she replied.

Still holding each other, there were no more words. There was only the sun sinking in the west, seeking the horizon, painting the scattered clouds, enhancing, stirring, changing the hues and textures, and the two people high on their overlook, far too awed by the beauty of the sky and their own connection to try and describe it, or even to comment about it. It was also in almost every respect like the one and only night they had spent together back on the island. But what was so unusual about that? For some reason, all of their nights together seemed to be that way.

DRAGONS

As the sun set over the western mountains it was still only two thirty in the afternoon at latitude sixteen degrees north and longitude one hundred and sixty eight degrees east where the sun was still high in the sky. At the time, however, none of the officers and crew aboard SSBN 734, an Ohio class, ballistic missile carrying submarine named Sea Lion, could see it because the vessel was at full stop, three hundred and fifty fathoms below the surface of the Pacific Ocean, far too deep for even the slightest trace of sunlight to filter through. Also, at the time, the officers were far too concerned with bigger issues. Secluded in the Ready Room, they had split into two sharply divided factions and a heated argument was taking place.

"I already know I don't have the authority to make that kind of decision," the Commander stated, "but there is no one left who does. And, since it's pretty clear by now that the North Koreans attacked the US mainland with two strikes and disabled our ability to retaliate after we only got one missile off, I don't feel we have any alternative but to finish things. That is precisely why this vessel was commissioned in the first place, and you all know that. We have no idea what residual capability the Koreans have, but, underestimating that capability could cost us Los Angeles or Chicago or even Washington DC. Now that we are within striking range, we must not hesitate."

"But Sir. There is no satellite imagery to support the claim that the Koreans were responsible at all. No radar data, no optical data and no visual data. We may be killing more innocent people," his second in command tried to point out.

"Maybe so, but be logical. None of the middle eastern countries, not even India, has powerful enough boosters to reach the North American continent. Even over the pole. We are not in conflict with England or France, so, with the exception of the Chinese, they are the only ones who could have done it."

The arguments continued but the opposition was dwindling because none of them could ever have imagined that it was all caused by one Lieutenant Stevenson back home in the United States. At that point the Commander gave the order for battle stations, followed by the order to proceed to standard launch depth.

"And bring Trident tubes, six, seven and eight on line and lay in target coordinates," he commanded as they all broke and headed for their separate stations.

Meanwhile, over in China, the Chinese were engaged in their own activities. Under normal circumstances before the Disappearance, they never would have directly attacked the United States except in the crucial instance of self defense. No. They had a far better plan and it had been working marvelously well. Having the largest and one of the cheapest labor pools on the planet, they had used it wisely, playing directly upon the excessive greed of American business, pumping out mass produced, marginal quality consumer goods. That was one thing. Of greater importance, however, was the technological transplant necessary to achieve it. More than willingly, the Americans shared their design secrets, trained the Chinese workers, provided precision tooling, metallurgical know how and proprietary electronic expertise, all in the name of profit. What they gave away was not only gainful employment for their own people but also balance of payments. Not only was the Chinese businessman becoming wealthy, so was the Chinese government. As a result, large shares of that money were, in turn, funneled back into their own research and development and the continuing education of their own brighter students. Building on American technology, rather than having to rediscover it, was a tremendous advantage, especially since the American economy had also provided the funding.

Ultimately, of course, even that had it's limitations. Eventually, American short term thinking would catch up with it's consequences and they would bankrupt themselves. Who knew what would happen then. Furthermore, Americans loved to meddle in the affairs of others, especially before upcoming elections, trying to impress the gullible public. Therefore, as a matter of simple prudence, the Chinese government had expended considerable effort in surveillance technology and weapons development and in some specific areas had even advanced themselves beyond the Americans. Therefore, even with the Disappearance, they were not nearly as handicapped as the American military might have supposed.

It was common knowledge that they already had nuclear capability but what was not known was their ability to detect and track potential dangers, not only in the atmosphere, but in the depths of the ocean. This ability was not limited to the East and South Seas of China, the Bay of Bengal and the Philippine Sea, but extended well out into the western Pacific as well. It had been achieved by salting the waters with extremely sensitive listening devices that could relay information back to the mainland over a newly discovered, narrow band, high frequency channel which, up until it's discovery by a student studying the behavior of gray dolphins, was considered to be theoretically impossible. As a result, not only had the Chinese tracked the American submarine all the way in from the Samoan Islands, they were aware of the two occasions when the sub extended its antennas above water and communicated with their military satellite in synchronous orbit over the mid Pacific. Their cryptographers had also successfully decoded all the transmissions. Then, based on heading and their own knowledge of the sub's capability, the intent became quite clear. It was a mission that must not be allowed to complete itself.

It was true that the American bomb that hit Korean had caught them unaware but they had been on, round the clock, full alert every since. They also had one other advantage over the Americans. While their military and governmental leaders had disappeared along with all the rest, certain key individuals had returned. Wisely enough, however, they had turned their backs on their old positions of authority and walked away. But, before doing so, they had given up the secrets they held. As a result, the lower echelon personal did not have to dismantle and re engineer all the missile control systems, they were simply handed launch codes and keys and everything else they needed to make their weapons systems fully operational.

"Do what you want," they were told. "Just know you are responsible for the consequences."

Additionally and of great importance regarding their decisions with respect to the Americans was the fact that while the prevailing winds would normally have carried most of the fallout from the Korean bomb westward over Japan, there had been a large storm system hanging over the Yellow Sea at the time and it had pushed radioactive waste inland and northward as far as Beijing and, above all, they were not about to let it happen again.

"Any change in the American's position?" one of the Chinese officers asked the lead tech at the monitoring station in the control center.

"Still dead in the water at three hundred fifty fathoms. Lot's of loud voice coming from amidships. I think they are arguing.. But it's too garbled to make out."

"Be ready when they stop. That may be the time."

The Chinese didn't tag their missiles with names like Triton or

Atlas or Minuteman. They were called Dragons instead. Depending on their warhead size and target range they were labeled Fire Dragons or Water Dragons or Earth Dragons or any one of a number of other categorizing titles. At the moment they had Air Dragons on line. They were inertially guided, medium range, nuclear tipped weapons of high accuracy and extreme velocity.

"Dragon One ready," the launch technician informed the group. "Dragon two is in backup."

"The sub just sounded the general alarm for battle stations," the surveillance tech stated as he watched his monitors and listened intently to his earphones. "Now they're blowing ballast, getting ready to surface."

"Any change in lateral position?"

"No. They are coming straight up."

"Maintain ready," the launch tech was told.

"Green light on both units."

"Are you sure this is the correct thing to do?" one of the junior officers asked. "What if we are mistaken?"

"If we are to preempt their launch we must do it now."

"But, Sir."

"Fire one," the lead officer said to the launch tech who quickly flipped the last switch in the sequence and pushed the appropriate button.

"Dragon one away," he said.

"Ready the interceptors," he was told, "in case we don't reach it in time. And continue to monitor the sub."

Then he turned to the junior officer who had questioned his judgment. "How long does it take an Air dragon to travel five thousand miles?"

Making a quick mental calculation, the officer replied. "About twelve minutes, Sir."

"And how long does it take a submarine to blow its tanks and come up three hundred fathoms?"

"I, uhh. I'm not sure, Sir."

"About the same. And if they come straight up, what do you think is their intent? And if we are wrong, what are our options?"

The junior officer blushed with embarrassment. "Sorry, Sir. I was out of line."

"Good that you see it that way. But you are here to learn, so pay attention."

"Two hundred fathoms," came the call out. "No lateral

movement."

"Estimate to reach launch depth?"

"Nine minutes."

"And the status of Dragon One?"

"Clean away and on course. ETA is ten minutes forty two seconds."

"Damn. It's going to be close. Now we'll see just how efficient they are."

"Depth one fifty. All engines are quiet. Still coming straight up. Looks like we were right."

"Good enough."

"Depth one hundred fathoms. Three minutes elapsed," the tech stated as they waited and time went by.

"Seventy five fathoms and slowing ascent. Passing fifty at six minutes in, slower still. Ten fathoms is the mark. Looks like that's where they're coming to. And twenty five, and twenty, almost stopped. Fifteen and, full stop. Nine minutes, forty four seconds."

Back on the submarine the American tech called out, "Launch depth achieved and steady."

"Tubes one through four," the Commander ordered. "Blow the hatches."

"Hatches open," came the quick reply.

"Launch one," came the command as the five hundred and sixty foot long, eighteen thousand ton vessel shuddered.

"One away," the launch control officer reported.

"Launch two," the commander stated crisply.

Again the vessel shuddered. "Two away," came the follow up call.

The Commander paused briefly and took a deep breath, wishing it were over. He still had to give the order to fire two more missiles. "Launch...." was all he got from his mouth, however, as the full force of Dragon One exploded less than a hundred feet over his head, crushing the huge submarine like a giant stepping on an empty beer can.

"Two birds got off successfully, sir" the Chinese tech stated. "But that's it. Dragon One must have made a direct hit. Blew out all our sounding sensors in the area."

"Good. But we still have to deal with the ones they were able to fire. Launch interceptors one and two."

"Interceptors away," the tech said as he pushed the appropriate buttons. "And as soon as the booster drops off, the on board cameras will come on. Intersect, approximately three minutes."

Together they waited, all huddled around the viewing monitors. Interceptors three and four were armed and ready and fingers were already on the buttons just in case one and two failed to bring down the incoming warheads. If all went well, however, the smaller, faster killer birds should reach the American bombs in the vicinity of Iwo Jima, long before they had fully armed themselves. And, if the strikes were successful, the bombs would fall harmlessly in the ocean. The incoming warheads were much too small and far too fast to be able to be seen directly on the monitors, however, but when the predicted time to target was up, there was a bright flash on monitor one and the screen went blank."

"Direct hit on one," several voices said in unison.

"Interceptor two must have missed. It's past its ETA," the tracking station tech said loud and clear.

"Launch three and four," was the shout. "Then send the command to have number two self destruct."

"Three and four away."

"Damn. Again we wait. What's the new intercept point?"

"Some where over the Ryukan Islands."

"Will the warhead be armed by then?"

"Possibly. If it's on course and trajectory."

"That's not good. There's half a million inhabitants on those islands."

The Americans may have lost their land based, missile launch capability but they still had ten additional ballistic missile submarines and every one had twenty four long range missiles on board. Then there were the four SSGN subs with one hundred fifty four Tactical Tomahawk missiles apiece, some with the Block II, nuclear variant version warheads and more than three dozen smaller attack submarines all loaded with Cruise missiles. They also had by far the most extensive, world wide military surveillance satellite system and they were now fully aware of the final fate of SSBN 734, the USS Tennessee. The impossible question to answer, however, was how? How had the Chinese known the vessel was there to begin with, obviously long before the final sequence of events began? It was a complete mystery. Within an hour the full channel alert went out.

"If you are within five thousand miles of the Chinese

mainland, we recommend that you move away with all due haste and stand back until we have a better idea of how the Sea Lion location and intent was managed."

It was an extremely critical moment in earth history. One more wrong decision at this point and the entire planet could be rendered almost lifeless.

THE PLAN

"Inside or out?" Katherine asked the first evening home from the mountains. Her house, while large in proportion, with high ceilings and openness in design, still felt confining and claustrophobic to Jack. Much of the time they slept on the screened in porch but occasionally there was need to stay out on the back lawn. Five acres of land, high walls and lots of mature shrubs and trees made for complete privacy. A good thing. Katherine still liked being topless. Jack also liked Katherine being topless. He wondered if he would ever get used to it. He hoped not. So did she.

On the practical side, the first task Jack set for himself was to find out as much as he could about everything that had happened here at home while he was on the island. It was an immensely depressing job. Awesomely so, the magnitude of the tragedy that had befallen earth was almost beyond comprehension.

But, in spite of all the disruption, the New York Times and the Washington Post were still publishing daily editions more than two years after the Disappearance. But their compilations were only available by Internet subscription. Paper and ink were difficult to obtain in consistent quantities and machine parts for equipment maintenance were nearly impossible to come by but they went on publishing electronically, almost as if the lives of the remaining workers demanded it. Quite reliably, elsewhere around the world, other people also felt compelled to report the ongoing situation in their own areas, again as if the record needed to be kept, as if there might still be some day of accounting and everything must be there, every last detail.

Perhaps it was a secret but growing fear that the world would soon self destruct and something must be left behind for survivors, should there be any. Or maybe for the day when some far off race of other beings finally came to earth and found the empty cities and towns. They would certainly need to know what happened. And if there was no record, then it would be as if there had been no living beings and then all those human lives would have been totally meaningless. Perhaps they were, anyway. The way things were deteriorating, it certainly seemed so. But regardless, the Times and the Post were still excellent sources of information, along with a multitude of other web sites from around the world.

Of all the continents, Africa was in the most trouble. But not by much. Prior to the Disappearance, Aids and Ebola had been the most devastating in spite of a growing degree of outside support, both medically and educationally. But now, no one else could afford to care. They were all far too busy with their own catastrophes, trying to save themselves, so the epidemics raged, fed by superstition, ignorance and misunderstanding. Helped by poverty, lack of focus and coordination and the unavailability of something so simple as protective latex sheaths and better information. If the rate of continued infection and the death rates were conservatively extrapolated, seventy five percent of that continents population would be gone within another ten years and, as the dying continued, the conspiracy advocates revived all the documentation from three decades earlier which blamed the whole thing on the World Health Organization. It was a sinister plot to rid the earth of the black population so the whites could pirate Africa's resources. Oil, gold and silver. Zirconium, iridium, molybdenum, diamonds and other precious minerals. Who knew for sure. Stranger things had happened. But never on such a monstrous scale.

The Aids epidemic was also raging throughout India and Vietnam. And Cambodia and Malaysia and New Guinea and the Philippines and up into China. Accurate statistics were unavailable but by all estimates that disease alone had already killed far more people than all the wars and havoc of the twentieth century. Worse, there was as yet no hope in sight. But in the end who was really to blame? The virus was not only communicable and deadly, there was also no easy cure. Everyone knew that, so what was the problem? Did they need leaders to tell them to abstain, or, to at least practice safe sex? Was that it? Or was it their own fault that they couldn't take individual responsibility? Of course not.

"And it's just the beginning of things in Europe," Katherine said to Jack as they shared information. "The Gulf Stream monitors all indicate more drop in water temperature. The revised death toll is now ninety million due to weather related problems. Norwegians, Swedes and Finlanders are migrating south in even greater numbers. They are just moving into abandoned houses wherever they find them," she ended, leaning back in her chair and sighing heavily. Of course there was a lot more to that story also.

Had Mother Nature suddenly turned capricious and malicious or had the leaders of the industrialized countries, the United States in particular, with considerable recent help from China and India, created the problem because they had refused to participate in any serious efforts to reduce greenhouse gas emissions? But what could governments do? As long as the average citizen would rather have a new automobile than breath clean air, well... Humvies had still been legal, too. So why not buy one? It made suburbanites look important when they pulled into the grocery store parking lot to buy a pack of cigarettes or when the wife picked up the kids from school, even though it was only two blocks away. And they had definitely needed all those useless gadgets and over sized TVs and the kids never would have grown up to be normal if parents hadn't bought them all those tons of plastic toys when they were little and others wouldn't have been able to lead a satisfying life if they hadn't chopped down all the trees to build over sized houses and what value would life have if people had stopped breeding like rabbits, and.....

But it was too late to talk about those aspects of it. That was before. This was now. Now it was too late. And while there were no new cars being produced as yet and gasoline was not easily available in many parts of the world so auto emissions were at all time low, it made no difference. The atmosphere was already so over polluted it would be decades before mother nature would be able to make a serious dent in the problem.

It was depressing stuff. They weren't completely sure exactly what they would do with all the information but it seemed important to have the facts straight before choosing a direction. Or was it?

"My god," Katherine said one morning shortly after turning on her computer. "I can't do this anymore."

Jack stopped what he was doing, swiveled around in his chair and looked at her, something he never tired of doing. Her face was always alive and full of expression, her eyes always intelligent and bright with color changes that reflected her mood. And today she had her long, blond hair haphazardly piled on top of her head as she often did so beautifully. He resisted the urge to touch her, to kiss her on the back of the neck, to stop what they were doing and slip his hands under the loose fitting old sweat shirt which she still favored. Then his eyes connected with hers. They were deep blue now, and bothered. "Need a break?" he asked.

"Need more than that. Need a hug," she said as she got up.

Jack rose, wrapped his arms around her and held her tight. "Enough research for awhile?"

"For a lifetime. All this doom and gloom. Maybe we made a mistake. What were our reasons for doing this again?"

"Good question. Guess we thought something might come of it."

"It's so damned dismal and depressing, Maybe we should go back up in the mountains. Just stay there for the rest of our lives and to hell with it. What do you think?"

"Wouldn't work. If we don't start getting involved in doing something positive, we're really going to get depressed."

"Yeah. But where do we start?"

"With you."

"What does that mean?"

"Don't you find it interesting that in all this time no one in the whole country has ever been publicly reported as having returned from the Disappearance except for you," Jack said. "And you went into such deep isolation most people have forgotten about it."

"Or didn't believe it to begin with. So?"

"Maybe it's time to start talking about what actually happened."

"Everybody knows what happened."

"They haven't been on the island. They don't know what happened there."

"Yes. You may be right. But we'll have to do more than just point out that a lot of people probably aren't coming back."

"True. But the fact that some people returned means that the potential was there in the beginning for all of them to do the same. That's an important part of it. And, it wasn't all bad. We met there."

Katherine looked at him and her mood mellowed. "We did. And tough as the rest of it was, I would never trade any of it away, good or bad. Other people might not see it that way, however."

"Probably won't. But the island was a place where every human trait became intensely more visible and exaggerated. I think that needs to be discussed. Maybe if enough people finally give up their ideas about leaders returning and saving them, they will begin looking for serious solutions to the problems we are faced with."

"Are you making a commitment?"

"I will, yes. Why not. You're absolutely right. We need to get turned around a bit. Stop focusing on the negative. There must be some good happening, too. At least on a smaller scale. Maybe we need to find it and start passing that on also."

Katherine hesitated before responding. "Maybe we could co author a book. Except that would take far too long, wouldn't it? And how would we ever be able to get it published? Or distributed, unless we did the whole project by ourselves. And by then, who knows what else may have happened?"

"Well, that decides it then."

"What?"

"As an ex Governor, I'm sure you've done some public speaking."

"Yes. But I've been out of the public eye for almost three years now."

"They'll love you anyway?"

"You're can't be serious," Howard said.

"Why not?" Jack asked.

"Driving to L A is one thing. Going there in that is another."

"It was one of the last Cadillacs ever built and it's in excellent condition. Only twenty thousand miles. What's wrong with that?"

"Everything. Still brand new. You could have just driven it off the show room floor. Every small time hood in the whole country will try to take it away from you. It's still not very safe to be out on the highway under most conditions but that would really be inviting trouble."

"Okay, I know you're right but we do have some weapons and I found that Katherine is really very good with a handgun. Besides, it's all we've got. You know how hard it is to find something that even runs anymore. Let along hang together long enough to get us where we want to go."

"You could change your minds and stay here. Or you might try renting a small plane."

"We already checked on aircraft and couldn't find anything. Besides, we'd really like to have the first hand experience of stopping at places along the way."

"Okay. I just thought I'd ask. So, come with me around back."

Behind the administration building of Howard's, now employee owned business sat a twelve year old windowless, full sized van.

"I'll trade you for the Cadillac," Howard said. "Temporarily, of course."

"Good grief," Jack replied after his first glance at it. There were scratches and dents everywhere, the paint was badly faded and randomly sprayed over with gray primer, the front bumper was twisted and there was a crack in the windshield. But, bad as it appeared, he knew Howard wasn't one to joke about such things so he went over and opened the hood. After a careful inspection he bent over and looked underneath the vehicle, then he opened the door and got in as Howard handed him the ignition key. It started immediately.

"Sounds damned good," Jack acknowledged. "Can I kick the tires?"

"Rebuilt it myself," Howard replied. "End to end. Except for the dents. Didn't want anyone to get too tempted. Six good tires, too. And a fifty five gallon auxiliary fuel tank. Overdrive. Should be able to do at least a thousand miles on a complete fill. That's also a modified vortex engine. Runs on almost anything you can pump into the tanks. Gasoline, diesel, methanol, corn oil."

"Good for some serious off road stuff, too," Jack stated as he also noted the four wheel drive, all terrain tires and big husky winch under the front bumper.

"Yeah, I hoped to do a little back country exploring this summer. You can even sleep in it."

"Are you sure you want to do this?"

"Well, I am kind of fond of it so try and get some of it back home with you when you're done."

Jack was silent, then he walked around the vehicle one more time and said. "Do you have any steel diamond plate?"

"What do you have in mind?"

"Since we're at it, might as well go all the way. What do you think? Would your guys mind if I ran it in the shop and borrowed an arc welder?"

"Good idea. I'll help you."

It certainly was not the Cadillac with all the amenities. No beepers, buzzers or manufactured voices telling you a door wasn't completely closed or climate control or plush upholstery or supreme quiet and comfort but it still hummed along, eating up the miles just as quickly, and Katherine was enjoying it. She liked sitting high up off the road with a good view over such obstacles as guard railings and ordinary automobiles as they swung south off of west bound I-70 onto I-15. Not only was the countryside somewhat desolate, traffic was extremely light in both directions but they were both in a good mood, happy to be headed down the road and at the rate they were going they would be in Las Vegas before dark.

"I know he'd never agree," she said with conviction. "But I'd trade Howard the Cadillac for this thing any day. Even if it does look like an army tank."

"Maybe we can build our own when we get back."

"We could probably start a business doing that. This is what, the third year since there have been any new vehicles produced?"

"They're not building trucks but there are people out there who have already started recycling cars. Instead of dumping them in the crusher to salvage the steel, however, they're putting Buick engines in Fords and Toyoto rear axles in Hondas and all kinds of things like that. Whatever it takes to keep them running."

"What's going to happen in another five years?"

"Good question."

"Well, there certainly isn't much traffic. We've only seen three cars in the last hour and they were going the other way."

"Not a great place to be stranded."

"I sure hope we don't break down out here."

"I don't think you have to worry. We have two spare tires, a full set of tools and a whole box of critical spare parts, thanks to Howard."

"Speaking of being stranded, is that a car way up there on the side of the road?"

"Yes, but I don't see anyone. Looks abandoned."

"Are you going to stop?"

"Maybe. Just take a quick look to be sure," Jack said as he started slowing well in advance, only to be interrupted by the sharp, metallic clang of something ricocheting off the steel plate he had welded onto the bumper out in front of the radiator.

"My god. What was that?" Katherine asked.

"Trouble, I'm afraid. Get your head down," he told her as he put on the brakes and screeched to a stop still more than the length of a two football fields away from the vehicle sitting alone on the graveled shoulder of the road.

"Where did we put the binoculars?" He asked as he put it in reverse and backed up at least another hundred yards further before stopping.

"They're behind my seat," Katherine said. "What's going on, Jack?"

"That was a small caliber rifle shot. Great way to stop a car. Put a hole through the radiator and you're soon stranded. Then a bunch of bullies move in and it's all over."

"Why not shoot out a tire? That would be quicker."

"They probably want the vehicle and all. A radiator is easy to replace. A blown tire might cause a rollover or something."

"Would they just leave us out here unharmed?"

"I wouldn't count on it."

"And I thought you were being silly for welding so many steel plates over everything," she said as she handed him the binoculars, keeping her head down the whole time.

"As near as I can tell, there are only two of them hiding behind the front of the car," he said after a close look.

"What do we do now?"

"Depends. What do feel up to?"

"I don't know. But I certainly resent the idea of being shot at.."

"It is kind of irritating, isn't it. Why don't you find your revolver and I'll see if I can reach Howard's deer rifle. But stay down," he said as crawled into the rear of the van. "Okay, got it. Stay put. I'm going out the back."

Seconds later Jack was standing on the rear bumper peering through the bars of the roof rack, looking down the road through the four power scope of the big rifle.

"Get ready," he shouted so Katherine could hear him. "This thing has one hell of a bark to it," and with that he squeezed off a round that destroyed the left rear tire of the vehicle.

It was one big gun and the noise shook Katherine badly. She trembled a bit and keep her hands over her ears as the passenger side front door of the parked car burst open and another man jumped out and ran around to the front and ducked down. Okay, Jack said to himself. Anyone else in there? He waited a little longer, then placed another round into right side tire and waited again. Nothing. Then he placed a shot that tore a hole through the trunk lid and down into the left wheel well and then repeated the act on the other side. Well, that was it. Anyone who wasn't convinced by now that it wasn't safe to remain inside the vehicle would have to suffer the consequences. But, just in case, he waited another minute, letting the deadly silence fill the air. Okay, he told himself and started to take his final aim when there was the crack of another rifle in the distance from out in front of the roadside vehicle. In the instant that he saw the flash, he heard the bullet punch a hole in the windshield. And, with nothing else left to stop it since the rear door of the van was open and the path was clear, he felt the slug embed itself in his left leg. It almost knocked him off the bumper where he had been standing but he caught himself and held on.

"Jack," he heard Katherine cry out. "Jack, are you okay?"

Thank god, he thought as the pain began. At least she was all right.

"I'm okay," he lied. "Just keep your head down. Do you understand? Keep your head down."

"Okay, you bastards," he said out loud. "That did it." And with a great effort he balanced himself on his one good leg and quickly zeroed in.

Ka-boom, the rifle spoke one last time as Katherine flinched again. Then in almost instantaneous sequence, there was another explosion in the distance when the gas tank blew and lifted the rear of the full sized car several feet off the ground. Immediately, three wild looking men were running like frightened rabbits down the shoulder of the road, away from the burning vehicle. With that Jack eased himself to the ground and checked his wound. Though extremely painful, he was able to stand. No bone damage, no arteriole damage, he would recover. It was in the muscle. He shut the rear door of the van, hobbled around to the front, placed his rifle between the seats and pulled himself in. Obviously Katherine was frightened but otherwise okay.

"You can look now," he told her.

At first Katherine was mesmerized by the dense black smoke and the lashing flames that rose fifty feet into the air, unable to look away. Then at last she found her voice.

"Was anyone in there?" she asked meekly, as though she might begin to cry. But then, with a determined effort, she pulled herself together. "What do we do now? Do they still have their guns," she said, turning to him, wondering. He seemed a little pale and he was grimacing badly.

"Jack, are you all right?" she asked, looking closer. "Jack! What's wrong?" Then she saw the blood oozing from around the hand he had pressed against his thigh. "God, Jack. You're hurt."

"I'll be okay. Just a flesh wound. It didn't go all the way through. Just give me a minute."

"We need to get to a hospital, Jack. Can we turn back and find another way around?"

"That would take much too long. And I'll be damned if we're going to just leave them out here so they can hunt down someone else," he said and ripped a hole in his pant leg. "The first aid kit is under your seat. See if there is any gauze in it," he told her and ripped more cloth away from the wound site. Within seconds he had a compress over the area, strapped down with a loop of surgical

277

tape.

"That's better," he reassured her as he started the engine. "Are you ready for this?"

"I think so. But what are we going to do? We can't just gun them down."

"You're right. There might be some justice in that but I think we have another option," he said as he looked down the road and scanned the area ahead through the binoculars. "But we'd better hurry."

The men had stopped their panic stricken running but were still moving at a fast paced walk. Less than another quarter mile father down there was a deep ditch running perpendicular to the road. From the looks of it there was probably a large culvert there, crossing under the highway. He couldn't let them reach it first.

"What are you going to do?"

"Let's see if a little more intimidation works," he said, as he stepped on the accelerator. "But just in case, remember that they would have probably killed us in the end so you still have be ready to use that thing if it comes to it."

"I know," she replied with more resolve, admitting it was true.

By the time they reached the burning vehicle the men were still walking rapidly away but when one of them looked over his shoulder and saw the van coming their way, they picked up the pace, almost stumbling over each other in their haste to be the one out in front. Jack pulled up as close as possible to the flaming wreck and quickly looked it over.

"Just wanted to make sure," he said as he started forward again, convinced no one else had been left inside. With about twenty yards to go he pulled the shift down into second gear to increase the noise of the big engine.

"Get back down on the floor," he instructed Katherine as he picked up speed and turned out onto the shoulder. With a roar he went on past them, purposely swerving as close as possible to frighten them, continued another hundred feet, cranked the steering wheel hard over and swung the van around, directly facing them.

The van stopped. The men stopped. Bad leg or not, Jack was outside in a split second, taking cover behind his open door, the deer rifle resting on the window frame, fully loaded and aimed. Slowly the men started to move apart. Blam. Jack placed a shot right between the feet of the one closest to the ditch, the big one. The biggest and meanest looking one of the bunch. The man stopped and swore as the one in the middle raised his own rifle and cocked it. But much too late. Jack's second shot went through his upper arm. The rifle flew off into the dirt. The man screamed and cursed.

Damn, Jack muttered to himself as he manually pumped another round into the chamber of the bolt action weapon. The 30-06 might knock down a full grown moose but it wasn't much for combat. Too damned slow. Wasted milliseconds could cost them their lives. Both the big man near the ditch and the one on the road had handguns. Heavy stuff. Looked like forty fives. Not very accurate at that range but they weren't standing still, closing the distance, their complete attention on Jack. And he had made a serious mistake. The thin sheet metal of the door would never stop slugs of that size. He needed to be back inside behind that thick steel plate welded to the front bumper. But, too late for that. All he could do now was to swing his sights around onto the closest one. Not half as ugly looking as that big son-of-a-bitch coming up behind, he thought.

But ugly enough and just as dangerous.

Following Jack's orders and scared to death, Katherine had kept out of sight the whole time. But she had hung onto the revolver with a desperate grip and now she had to know. Was she about to die? She took a quick peek up over the dash. Oh my god, she thought. They were awfully close. Blindly she put her hand out the window and pointed the gun without aiming. No idea if she would hit anything or not, she grimaced and pulled the trigger. It went completely wild, but still served its purpose. Caught by surprise, their attention momentarily diverted, Jack was able to shoot his chosen target in the leg and knock him down.

"Don't even think about it," he yelled at the other one, the big one, belligerent as hell, shouting obscenities back at him. The warning was useless. Before Jack could react the man started forward like an enraged bull, his hand gun swinging upward, letting out a volley of shots that swept across the van.

Some of them rang off the steel plate welded to the front bumper. One went through the windshield right above Katherine, bringing the glass crashing down on her. Several went straight up into the air because by now Jack had hit the man in the chest and spun him around where he fell, still firing wildly. Two rounds went into the ground, the last ripped his own leg apart.

"Do you think he will live?" Katherine asked as they tried to stop the bleeding, the man layed out on the shoulder of the highway, still fully conscious and being everything but cooperative, swearing vehemently about how he was going to kill them both and constantly trying to roll over and get up.

"He might. If he doesn't bleed to death. But not if he keeps this up. Christ. This is ridiculous," Jack stated as he undid the mans belt, pulled it loose and tied it around his ankles to keep him from kicking at them with his good leg. The man swore at him again.

"Okay, you son of a bitch. You're the dumb bastard who shot himself in the leg. The way your pumping blood you'll be dead in another ten minutes if you don't let us help you. Make up your damned mind!"

"What the hell," the man said. "I'll still kill you, even if you do save me. After I have my way with your woman here."

Jack was immediately down on his knees along side the man. "I hope this works," he said. "They used to do it in the movies." And with that he doubled up his fist and landed a ferocious punch on the man's jaw, rendering him silent.

"Damn," he said as he shook his hand. "That hurt." Then he looked at the wound. It was still spurting badly so he obviously hadn't killed him. Not yet, anyway. Quickly, he removed the man's belt from around his feet, wrapped it around the leg above the wound and pulled it tight. The bleeding slowed, then stopped. "Now for this one," he said as he ripped open the man's scruffy shirt and exposed the second, less serious wound on his chest. Katherine was ready with the gauze and tape.

"Jesus. What's wrong with people like this?" she asked as she jammed the sterile cloth into the bullet hole, plugging it up.

"Hard to tell," Jack said as he looked the man over. "Now if we can just get him in the back with the other two, we may have time. As long as he doesn't come to and get out of control. If I have to stop and hit him again, it might cost him his life."

CITY OF ANGELS

The Los Angeles Sports Arena was nearly packed. Over five thousand people had come to hear them speak. Jack had prepared a map of the two islands that was shown on large screen monitors throughout the auditorium as they gave their presentation, working as a duo. They spoke for two hours. Then, highly unprecedented in so large a group, they took questions from the audience as volunteers carried microphones back and forth. "We'll stay all night,

280

if necessary," they naively told the crowd.

It was a wildly mixed reaction. Once they opened the way for audience participation, they quickly lost control. Many people had been extremely shocked. The President, the Vice President and the Secretary of State were all dead? And the Pope, killed by a Cardinal while Reverend Billy Boxer committed suicide over some problems with the Arabs? Impossible, some extremely vociferous individuals said. They didn't wait to be recognized or for the microphone, either. They jumped to their feet and began shouting. What they were told couldn't be true. It was too ridiculous and incomprehensible. It was irresponsible, outrageous blasphemy. How dare they invent such a horrible story!

Others in turn, stood up and shouted them down as the conflict escalated. There were not enough security people in the building to handle the situation. The police were called, but long before they arrived another man came running down the isle shouting and shaking his fists. Even though there were no direct stairs from the floor onto the stage from where they had made their presentation, the man still managed the four feet difference in height and made his way toward them, eyes glazed, screaming almost incoherently.

"Get behind the curtains," Jack yelled at Katherine. "We'll go out the back way."

She hesitated, the man running towards Jack with fire in his eyes. Thank god he doesn't have a gun, she noted. He was also alone. No one else was coming their way, either. She backed away, still determined to help if need be.

Geez, he was getting tired of dealing with lunatics, Jack said to himself, summing the guy up. Suit and tie, shiny shoes, it seemed so grossly out of character. Too much flab hanging over the belt to be picking a fight for one thing. But here he came anyway, raging like a bull. Whatever the problem might be, this was not going to be a civilized discussion because, arms flailing and out of control he was already half way across the stage, a security guard following but way too far behind.

Geez, Jack mumbled to himself, again. His wounded left leg was hurting badly from having to be on his feet the last two hours. It had only been three days since the bullet was removed and he felt stiff and slow and he was already in enough pain and that made him suddenly angry. The adrenaline kicked in and two seconds later he had the man face down on the floor, his foot in the middle of the guys back, the wind knocked out of him. But quick as that was over, other things were happening.

"There's more," Katherine shouted.

At least another half a dozen, some coming down both isles, but none at the stage as yet, their voices merging into a bizarre battle cry. Quickly Jack took Katherine by the arm and they disappeared behind the curtains, looking for the fire escape door.

"There," he pointed. "Go," he said, detouring slightly to pick up a folding chair leaning against the back wall. Finally outside, he rammed the chair tightly against the door.

"This way," Katherine shouted, having located the stairway down to the parking garage.

"My God," Katherine said once they were safely away. "What the hell was that all about?"

"Guess we pushed a few buttons."

"No kidding."

"Maybe we just made a big mistake."

The morning broadcast of the news was even worse. Little was said about the content of the presentation but the reporters did an exceptional job of describing the aftermath. Several fights had broken out, seven people had been hospitalized with severe injuries. One had even been stabbed with a pocket knife and the speakers had been forced off the stage. As for the cause of it all? It was a result of a bizarre talk about the Disappearance given by the former woman governor of Colorado and her male friend who was once on the Presidential advisory staff. Quite possibly pure fiction, was the final comment.

"Well, where do we go from here?" Katherine asked in the hotel coffee shop where a large screen television took the place of unavailable newspapers. They sat in an out of the way booth hoping no one would recognize them because there were some shots of their faces being shown also.

"We could just say to hell with it," Jack said as he put sugar in his coffee. "Or, we could go back east and try again. If we drive it will give us a chance to see how things are across the rest of country."

"I don't know. That was pretty scary. Maybe we should reconsider writing that book instead. We could put it out on the Internet."

"You don't like dealing with people face to face?" Jack asked, trying to be cute about it.

"Not when they behave like that," she scowled.

282

"Yeah," he said seriously.

She looked at him. "Oh my," she asked as it came to her. "How's your leg this morning?"

"Still hurts," he stated, but with a grin.

She put her hand on top of his. "Sorry. Guess I shouldn't have jumped you like that."

"You don't look very sorry." Now he was smiling broadly.

"Are you?" she asked, realizing he had been teasing.

"You were doing most of the work."

"Want to go back upstairs?"

"Too late," he said as the waitress brought their orders.

"Well," Katherine said after a bit. "Driving cross country might be interesting. As long as we don't have to put any more dumb ass highway hoodlums in the hospital."

"Yeah. Sorry about that. Shooting people is not my idea of a good time. I didn't know things would be that bad or I wouldn't have put you in danger."

"It was my idea, too."

"Well. We don't have to do it again."

"Says who? We agreed we aren't going to run off and hide."

"Yeah, but.... geez, Katherine"

"Only thing we need is to find a place out in the desert where I can target practice. And find some ear plugs. My head is still ringing."

"Sounds good. If we can find a new windshield and a semi automatic rifle."

"What about hand grenades?"

They finished breakfast in silence. Then Katherine added one more thought.

"Next time we give a presentation we need a lot more security and no questions from the audience."

"Or maybe just written questions and we get to pick the ones we choose to answer."

"And maybe not such a large group. Say, ten people and ten security guards."

Jack laughed.

The first place it happened was in Torrance, California. It was a matter of public necessity. Forgetting the fact that the oil refinery located there was the property of a very large but leaderless public corporation, the employees took over its operation within a matter of days after the Disappearance and ran it in spite of the protests and lawsuits from remaining stockholders that followed. Without gasoline and diesel fuel, far worse things would have happened to Americans than dropping bombs on them. Dependency on the automobile and the truck was absolute and without alternatives. Although their deaths would be much slower, the inability to transport food and supplies would make the deaths of ordinary people just as certain as if a bomb was to have been dropped on them. Especially in the metropolitan areas. Realizing this, the far sighted employees of the complex formed a management committee and went back to work. Ultimately, even though they tripled their own salaries, the price of fuel at the pump dropped dramatically in the areas which they were able to supply. Without the burden of multi million dollar executives and hordes of greedy stockholders, they were able to cut the cost to the consumer by more than fifty percent. And, with the leaders of Mexico and Venezuela gone, there was a readily available supply of crude oil relatively close at hand. Sufficient at least to keep the refinery running at full production around the clock.

The only other source of fuel at the time was from a family owned refining company with their own oil wells back in Montana who had been giving the giants of the industry some reasonable competition for over forty years. It was business as usual for them the whole time. The only problem was location. They were still great distances from major demand areas but with their own fleet of tanker trucks they were able to service locations as far away as Seattle, San Francisco and down through the San Jaoquin Valley, some of the most vital food producing farmland in the entire nation. But it was nowhere even half as easy as before. Hijacking of delivery vehicles was rampant at first. Soon, however, another tactic derived from the old west was put into play. Just like on an old stagecoach line, someone rode shotgun in the cab of the truck. There was also an armed lead vehicle and an armed follower.

This west coast example and the Montana example were eventually followed by refineries across the country. This bold action did more to save the nation from total collapse than any one other single thing that had happened thus far. In the south, along the gulf coast, the transition was far too slow and hundreds of thousands of people suffered or died as a result. Eventually, however, in spite of everything else that was falling apart in the system, trucks rolled. And because they could get their product to market, farmers began broadening their outputs to include more food stuffs and started discontinuing what had formerly been raised strictly for export before the disappearance.

Tragedy also played a significant role. Between the direct destruction by the two nuclear blasts and the downwind radioactive fallout, more than thirty five million people had perished from North Dakota to the State of Maine, from the Canadian border as far south as Kentucky. An additional five million deaths were attributed to the extreme cold and shortage of fuel during the first winter of the disappearance, while the biggest toll of all, another forty million or so, died in large cities in the early days before the transportation system was up and running again. Although the problem was far from over, fewer people to feed meant more hope for the rest. Something much too sinister and guilt producing to ever be openly acknowledged.

Before leaving the Los Angeles area, Katherine and Jack stopped at the Torrance refinery and interviewed a number of the men handling operations.

"Actually, I was at the Sports Arena when you spoke," one of them confided. "And I thought it was one of the most fascinating things I've ever been to in my life. To hell with what the media said, I wish you'd stick around and give us a repeat. God knows we need to hear it."

"Thank you," they said. "Maybe we'll come back again. Right now we're really interested in how you're doing running this company."

The man summarized what had happened. The challenges and the difficulties, the stockholder outrage, the threat of legal action and all the rest. "But, product wise, it has been successful and most of the opposition has backed off because too many people see the absolute necessity of keeping the place running. We have come to terms with many of the stockholders and they have agreed to let us buy them out. At a greatly reduced price, of course. But they shouldn't complain. If the company were left to collapse, it would be totally worthless. So, once we get unanimous approval and the stock, we'll split it up amongst us employees, keeping some reserve for the future. The more responsible the job, the harder you work, the more stock you get. We think it will work."

"But you don't have anyone in an overall management position, like a president or CEO?"

"No. No one wants to try that again. Too many problems if that person were to disappear. Besides, I think we have already proved that kind of organization isn't necessary. We have what we like to call, shared responsibility. But obviously, that's not the whole answer either cause I know of one major exception to the rule."

"What's that?"

"Well, we have a supplier over in Nevada that must have discovered something important also. This is a big company, mind you. At least a couple thousand employees. Manufactures tanker trucks and steel pipe, drilling equipment and a whole periphery of associated items. One guy at the top and he's been there for more than six months so he must be doing something right."

"Looks like we need to stop in Nevada," Katherine said.

"I was the major stockholder before the Disappearance, completely inactive, however. Didn't even vote my stock unless there was some problem. So I took over afterward to keep the place from going under. Good thing I did, too. Or the country would be in even bigger trouble."

"So, you are the CEO and you are running the place in a conventional, corporate manner. How do you account for the fact that you haven't disappeared also?"

"I can't. Except for the fact that's there's nothing conventional about the way I run things. If you have the time I'd be happy to tell you about it. Might be of some interest, what with you both having been over there on the other side of things.

PROGRESS

They were given a tour of the entire company, top to bottom, and were allowed to talk to as many employees as they wished, along with having spent nearly a full day alone with the owner. Although it was a complex operation in many respects, there was an underlying commonality running through it.

"What I have is a system based entirely on merit. One hundred percent. There is no union or employee bargaining organization. I do not believe in mediocrity or ineptitude and I do not tolerate it for a moment. I believe in teaching the employees everything they want to know and letting them work as hard as they want, provided they meet the minimum standards I have set for the job. I try to provide them with challenges and I always sit down and listen when they have ideas and concerns. Believe it or not, some of the best suggestions for improving the place have come from some of the workers who were at or near the bottom. I listen, I evaluate and

I implement. That is my primary function here. Every person in a position of authority has to learn to share that authority with his workers and is required to have trained at least one other person to replace him if necessary. If they don't I tell them not to expect to ever be promoted. That includes me. I keep the upper echelon fully informed, the books are always open and there are at least two individuals who could step in if something did happen to me. Why not? I'm not on a power trip and I still like to travel and do some fishing."

"We don't care about related background, psychological profiling or any of that when we hire new people, either. A new employee is judged solely on the basis of willingness to work and the desire to excel at what they are doing. Honesty and integrity are paramount. Everyone is given a fair chance but incompetence and laziness are absolutely not tolerated. Well..... I guess that kind of sums it up. Time will tell, of course. And, oh yes. I recently heard there is another company somewhere in Tennessee, I believe, that has a similar kind of operation going. Not oil and gas equipment. Household products, processed food items, stuff of that nature."

With the simple exception that it was a wayward son instead of a stockholder who had taken control of his father's company when the older man disappeared, it was a strikingly similar story.

"Never did agree with the way the old man ran things," the son said. "The organization was full of stalled out, entrenched power playing incompetent executives, thieving employees, conniving accountants and bored to death, uncaring workers. I tried working for him for a while when I was younger but he wouldn't give me any responsibility and refused to see what was going on, so I left. Worked my way around the world doing everything from washing dishes to driving a bulldozer. I was back, thinking about starting my own business when the Disappearance happened but my mother wouldn't allow me to step in until it was almost to late to save things. Well.... that's about it."

"Sounds like a lot to us. So what did you do to fix it?"

"Started over. Ripped it apart from end to end. Got the best heads together and started a team. Threw away all the job descriptions and titles and broadened everyone's responsibility to include the whole company. Some guy gets too protective of his little empire, he's gone. So, shared responsibility kind of says it best."

"Any further plans?" Katherine asked.

"There haven't been any new cars built in three years now. That might be a real challenge. Pass this company on and start on that. Something really basic, however, and environmentally friendly and resource conserving for a change. Forget the chrome and the ten speaker stereo system and the GPS. The power seats and windows and radio antenna and all the buzzers, bells and whistles. Two models. A sedan and a pickup with all metal bumpers and enough simplicity and room under the hood so that backyard mechanics can keep it running by themselves. Lightweight and high mileage with some ongoing research into alternate fuels and power systems."

"Have any qualms about disappearing?" Jack asked.

"Not really. But, what the heck. Never got a chance to say goodbye to the old man."

"What's his name?"

"Arthur. And Branson, like me. Arthur Branson. Why?"

"Around sixty. Medium height, Bald on top. Maybe thirty pounds over weight?" Jack asked.

"Did you know him? You said you were there with the ones who disappeared. Do you think he might make it back, too?"

"Don't recall seeing him there but I think I met him at a business conference once before it happened. Maybe Washington," Jack lied. He didn't want to tell the son that his father was an early casualty of the fighting and wouldn't be coming home.

"Well, he'd be shocked as hell about what I've done to his old pride and joy," he said with a smile, meaning the company he was obviously so proud of.

"You said you weren't concerned about disappearing," Katherine said, returning to one of his previous comments. "Why is that? You have all these other plans."

"Because I think I'm in the safe zone."

"Safe zone? What do you mean by that?"

Two weeks, countless hours on the Internet and a lot of additional miles on the highway to interview other business leaders verified what the young Mr. Branson had only suspected.

"Seems pretty clear, doesn't it." Katherine said. "There probably is a safe zone after all."

"It wasn't about organizational size at all. Or at least it was never that simple, I'm happy to say."

"It's certainly intellectually more appealing."

"And now that we see it, it's amazingly clear."

"And hopeful. And something else we need to tell people about."

POLITICS

It was a shabby little bar around the corner off 6th Street in the capital city that would seem to be totally out of character for a group of over the hill politicians such as these five. But they showed up nevertheless, every week or so, and laid claim to a large round booth back in the far corner out of the way, somewhere around mid afternoon where they drank and haggled over personal concerns for three or four hours that they wouldn't dare discuss elsewhere. At first the proprietor wasn't sure he even wanted them in the place but they were borderline alcoholics who always drank top shelf booze in prodigious amounts, didn't try to impress the working class regulars, ignored the hookers who wandered in and out and left a lot of extra change on the table when they left, so, why not?

Senators all, physically in various degrees of disintegration due to lifestyle and age, it had been another tough day on the Capital Hill. Jowly Joe Clumsteder with the bushy eyebrows from Texas was especially annoyed with the way things were going.

"We need to pass a law doing away with all congressional elections," he stated to his contemporaries.

"Why would you want to do that?" Trad Primley of Kansas wanted to know as he slugged down his second tall scotch and water, spilled some of it on his shirt front and waved for the waitress. "We're senators. We have the most overpaid, cushiest jobs in the country."

"And I want it to stay that way. So do you, dammit. So does the rest of the bunch. The congressmen all want to keep their jobs, too. Who the hell wouldn't?"

"I don't know," old Pat Nugent from Pennsylvania grumbled as he unbuttoned his jacket and loosened his tie. "What with all the business failures and with employees taking over the rest, all the lobbyists are disappearing and the easy money is drying up. Along with the free trips and all of the rest of it. Jeeez, the wife is mad as hell. She wanted to go to Thailand this year and then on to Rio. Not that I personally give a damn. I was going to send her off with her sister, anyway. But what really hurts is that I had to give up that sweet little pumpkin I had stashed away over in Georgetown. A pharmaceutical lobby was picking up the tab on the rent. All I had to do was flowers and the lease payments on her Mercedes and now

I can't even afford that."

"Probably just as well. I heard she was doing half the guys in the Hoover Building on the side."

"Well, as long as she wasn't doing you," Pat said with a raunchy smile. "And I always got what I wanted."

"What with your stamina, it still left her with a hell of a lot of free time on her hands."

"Yeah, Pat. There was ass enough there for twenty guys and you were trying to hog it all. You should have worked out a time share arrangement with the rest of them and split the tab. Then you'd still be getting a piece of the pie," chided big bellied old Rufton Burke from Florida.

"What I never understood was why weren't you hustling that chubby secretary of yours, instead?" put in Clumsteder, who favored women with some meat on their bones. "There was a hell of a lot more bounce to the ounce there than with that pro. Would have been a lot cheaper, too."

Joe groaned and gave them all a nasty look. "Why do you guys always keep doing that?

Damnit!"

"What?"

"Missing the point, dammit."

"What's your point? You expect some, for hire bimbo to feel sorry for you and give you free blow jobs?" staid old Burk put in, the only true conservative in the group.

"Hell no. Where's the fun in that? It's a question of entitlement. The point is I used to be able to afford such folly and I should be able to go on affording it, just like all the rest of you, but now after twenty seven years on the job, I can't. And that is downright criminal."

"Well, yeah. Now that you put it that way, I'd have to agree. My old lady hasn't been able to redecorate in two years. And we haven't had a catered party in months."

"You think that's bad? I had to give up my beach front in Malibu but what has that to do with what Joe is talking about?"

"I don't know. What were you talking about, Joe? You want to put an end to congressional elections? Jesus. Then we'd really be up the stinky creek."

"No, no. You got it all wrong. What I mean is we need to pass a new law. We need a law that does away with elections and limits on terms in office. We make ourselves a permanently appointed body like the Supreme Court where we are in office for life."

"Well, damn me to hell. That is one great idea."

"Damn sure is."

"Yeah, Joe. That's great. Let me get the next round."

"Okay," said skeptical Ted Primley with raised eyebrows. "Sounds good on the surface but how would we ever pull it off? Doesn't seem possible to me."

"I don't know yet," Joe agreed. "But it's critical. There's a movement afoot in my state to do away with elections and institute some other sort of selection process."

"What's the difference? An election is already a selection process. If you can buy an election, you can always buy enough influence to get selected."

"I know that. That's not the point. Give me a chance to finish."

"Good. Finish. But we need another round, first," Senator Dugan said as Joe grimaced, but still slugged down the rest of his own and slid the glass to the edge of the table.

"Make mine a double," he told the girl when she came. "And he's buying," he said, pointing to Primley.

"Likewise."

"Me too."

"Look like doubles all around," she said as she picked up the fifty dollar bill Primley had peeled off his roll and thrown on the table.

"Okay. Election or selection process," old Pat said after he took a swallow of his new drink. "What's the difference?"

"Essentially none, as you have already pointed out. The kicker, however, is that these reformers want to limit us to no more than two terms max. Period. And anyone who has already held the office that long is automatically eliminated. Like us and everyone else presently in office. Even worse, they only get to come to Washington twice a year for a month. The rest of the time must be spent in the home state close to the constituency where they are accessible."

"Jesus, Joe. That's the most dismal thing I've heard in my whole life."

"Damned right. Tell me about it."

"But crap. Are they crazy? How can they ever expect anyone to get any work done with those kinds of restraints. It's bad enough the way it is."

"Video and computer networking."

"What about it?"

"That's the way they expect the new congress to work

291

together."

"On camera and with a damned computer. You're kidding," Rufton scoffed loudly.

"Like hell I am. I've never been more serious in my life."

"Jesus. What rabble rousing, unpatriotic bunch of anarchists thought this one up?" Rufton came back. He was getting angry now, looking as though he might pop a vein at any moment.

"Doesn't matter. The wheels are in motion and I understand there are already five other states headed down the path."

"Good god. Why didn't you say something sooner?"

"If you'd spend a little more time inside the beltway, I could have. I wanted to get together two weeks ago."

"Well, damn. Okay. I wish I had known. So, what do we do about it? We can't just permanently elect ourselves. Can we?" asked Dugan with a skeptical look. "They'd never let us get away with it. Especially without a bona fide President to sign it."

"So that's where we start. We get the Congress to elect a new Speaker of the House. But in name only. No powers, so they don't disappear. Then we can legally make that person the President per the Constitution, but again we strip the office of all its power. No more Commander in Chief and all that crap. Figurehead only. Our own little rubber stamp. Then we set ourselves up and the rest is history."

"Right. Then we give ourselves another raise in salary to make up for all the lost money from the lobbyists and the special interest groups."

"But quickly, damn it. Quickly, before the whole country falls apart."

"What does that mean? It's already fallen."

"I mean, while there's still a country left. Haven't you heard what going on in California, Arizona, Nevada and New Mexico?"

"Who cares. Nothing out there but queers and cowboys."

"You'd better care. Pretty soon there won't be enough of a United States left to even matter."

"What?"

"Well, look at the numbers. We lost nine entire states to nuclear bombs and radioactive fallout. Alaska and Hawaii have refused to participate and have gone their own way right from the beginning. Now these other four are making noises about seceeding from the union. The rumors are that Utah, Colorado, Oregon and Washington may be joining them. Then there are seven or eight southern states still grumbling about losing the Civil War and claiming they have been under the control of an occupational army every since. This whole thing might revive some bad thinking on their part, too."

"Let's see... Geez, we'd be down to less than half ."

"Yeah. And what about you, Clumsteder? Are you sure you're on top of things down there in Texas? You haven't even been back there for two years."

"Yeah, for sure. If we lost Texas and Oklahoma, what the hell would we do for oil?"

Clumsteder didn't answer but his face grew wane.

With that they nursed their drinks and contemplated in silence. It was still much too early in the afternoon and none of them wanted to put in an appearance at home just yet. Dugan was about to suggest that they adjourn, grab a cab and head on over to the topless bar across town where they could shoot a few games of pool before calling it quits when Primley spoke up.\

"Did any of you happen to see the flyer that was posted around town? There was one on the grocery store bulletin board. I should have grabbed it."

"What were you doing in a grocery store, for god's sake? You still have a maid to do the shopping like the rest of us. Or don't you trust her?"

"Of course I do. But I ran out of cigars and I was passing by."

"Okay. But what could you possibly see that was of any interest on a grocery store bulletin board? A used washing machine?"

"No, you putz. A bowling ball. Jesus," Primley stated. "But seriously, it was about a symposium at the Symphonic Hall auditorium and I believe some of us should go."

"Really, Ted? What could we possibly get out of that?"

"You probably don't remember him but there was this special advisor of President Druckus'. Jack Briggs. Him and the ex lady Governor Beaumont of Colorado are speaking there this weekend."

"Okay. So? What's so special about that? What would they have to talk about?" Ruftan Burk wanted to know.

"Wait a minute," Senator Dugan said. "Beaumont? How could that be? All the Governors disappeared as I remember things. And who would ever forget her. She was one luscious hunk of female."

"Exactly," Ted replied. "It's a matter of record. She did disappear. So did Briggs. And now they're back."

"Holy Christ. That's not possible. Is it? No one's every done that before. My god. If it's true, think of the ramifications."

"Awesome!"

"Holy hell."

"Damned right."

"Sure, but there's one hell of a downside to it, also. What if President Druckus showed up and demanded his old job back? What then? The office is still vacant."

"And then the rest of the world's leaders also showed up?"

"Boggles the mind. Let's not even think about it."

"That's exactly why some of us have to attend. We have to find out what Briggs and Beaumont know."

"Why in hell didn't you bring this up earlier. Our whole future depends on it."

"So does staying in office. Besides, I didn't believe it right off. Thought it might be a hoax."

"Pretty clever hoax, if you ask me."

"Yes, but I know Briggs didn't disappear at first. Remember, he used to come to the congressional meetings with old Jenson Wilson before that nut case shot him and that was at least three or four months after the initial disappearance. As for the Governor, maybe she's just been hiding out somewhere. Word was she and the husband were having some serious problems. Maybe she just wanted to get away from the bastard."

"Okay. So all we can do is speculate at this time. Which makes it imperative that we find out. Even if we have to kidnap the two of them."

REUNION

"Jack! Oh my, it's really you," Deanna said as first she hugged him, then backed off to look again. "Without the beard and all the hair. But just as handsome as always."

"And what about you," Jack said in return as he looked at the chicly dressed and very stunning looking woman before him.

"And Dean Whitcomb. Absolutely amazing. My God, it's good to see you two again. We have a lot to catch up on. But first, this is my, much more than dear friend, Katherine. You never met her but she was on the island for over six months, too."

"But we did meet," Katherine said, after looking at Deanna more closely. "On that very first day as a matter of fact. You were sitting on a rock waiting for your group to return from the President's first meeting. I was with Jack's brother and I passed on a man's suit coat someone gave to me."

"Oh, of course. I do remember. If only I had been wise enough to come with you at the time. What a horrible mistake that was. But I'm sure Jack has told you the rest of the story."

"He did. But somehow I never connected that with you being the same person. Welcome home."

"Thank you. It's nice to be in clean clothes and have ham and eggs for breakfast," she said, trying to be cheerful. But, there was still a trace of sadness in her face she couldn't completely hide because, given a choice, she would rather have been on back on the island with Ivan than back home without him. Maybe some other time, however. She wouldn't speak of it tonight. "And eat something besides fruit all the time."

"That's for sure." Katherine said. "I especially love clean clothes after having worn the that same old pair of pajamas all that time. Well, most of the time, anyway," she continued, smiling back at him who was also smiling, still remembering the look on his face when he first saw her topless.

"Yes, but I'll bet Jack will never forget how horrible I looked when we first met," Deanna added. "I hadn't bathed for more than two months. And you should have seen the rest of me."

"I hardly noticed," Jack said with a smile.

"The heck you didn't. Fortunately, all those men I was forced to live with did, too, and being disgusting worked for a long time. But, if it hadn't been for Jack, well......," she said, looking at him with gratitude. "I might not even be here."

Dean Whitcomb had seen the notices posted around town and contacted Deanna. Unaware of his now having Katherine in his life, they came early to greet Jack. But there she was. And though they had never crossed paths with her on the island except for the one very brief encounter of Katherine's and Deanna's, the fact that she had been there still made it an instant connection.

"What about Ivan?" Jack asked after a bit, full of hope but immediately realizing it might not be an appropriate question. Depending, it might also be a very painful one for Deanna. Ivan might not have returned. He might never return. The thought of that added a somber note to the conversation and he was embarrassed.

"I haven't heard from him," Deanna stated quietly, her eyes down, not looking at anyone.

Damnit, Jack thought. He could think of nothing more to say. But before he could change the subject Deanna continued with a sudden burst of confidence that seemed real enough.

"But as you know, Russia has been much more devastated than

here. The phone system is still out, half the rail system is down and..... but.... he's tough and I'm sure he'll be back. And then he'll make his way here somehow or other."

"Knowing Ivan, I'm sure he will," Jack said with encouragement, meaning it sincerely. "Even if he has to swim."

It was the right answer. As if Ivan's return was now a given, she looked at Jack with a different concern in her eyes.

"Do you think we'll still be as crazy about each other in our new environment?" she queried.

"Even more so," he said with assurance. At least Ivan would, he knew that. This woman was not only beautiful, she was strong, realistic and exceptionally well grounded. Elegant and feminine, there was no other answer to her question. And that is what Jack told her.

"Again, thanks to you, Jack. You're the one who brought us together."

"Yes, but it was only because of the way Ivan felt about you. That's the bottom line. He's the one. I was only trying to do him a favor."

"I know. But I also know that if you had become aware of my situation you would have rescued me anyway. Either way, you saved my life. I owe you a lot."

"And so do I," Dean Whitcomb added. "Along with all the people you helped separate from the rest of our mad American contingent."\

"Well..," Jack said, and shrugged his shoulders, dismissing it with a change of subject.

"If I thought the audience would behave, I'd ask you to join us on stage." he said instead.

The two women looked at him as if they didn't understand.

"Are you expecting trouble?" Deanna asked.

"Hard to tell. We seemed to have had a problem with that back on the west coast."

"Yes. We certainly did, didn't we?" Katherine added with a wry smile.

"What happened?"

They explained. Then Jack added that they had taken more precautions this time. Smaller audience, more security, only written questions from the audience, if they even decided to allow them.

"Yes, and Jack's leg is now healed," Katherine pointed out. "And we know exactly where the back door is this time."

"Guess we missed all the fun," Dean Whitcomb said. "But if

there is any way we can help..."

"That goes for me too," Deanna said.

"Good. You could certainly add some extra credibility to our stories if you want."

Amongst the four of them they spoke for nearly three hours, taking turns, each covering the different aspects of their experience on the island. Katherine was the first to speak. Jack thought she had never looked more radiant or beautiful. Poised, intelligent, full of energy and in control, she spoke with confidence and vitality. Since she had, for the most part, led a somewhat secluded existence on the island Katherine spent most of her time describing the geography of the place, the initial weather conditions, food situation and other physical aspects of the location, as well as her own thoughts, feelings and emotions from having been there. What she had learned personally and what realizations she had come to that might have been responsible for her return in the end. She also pointed out the dangers that resulted from being there and related the personal encounter that could easily have led to her own death.

Dean Whitcomb was second and elaborated in detail about what had transpired in the American sector. The entrenched power structure and politics, the intrigue, the conniving manipulation and the bizarreness of all that went on, from a White House made of sticks to the fanaticism of zealots. All of it was done in a polite and respectful way, a simply exposition of the facts as she saw them, without blame.

Deanna, in turn, spoke from her perspective, both as a captor amongst her own people and as a person living with the Russians and having control over the food supply, the significance of the wall of stones and how at last it was being torn down to build an even higher pile of stones, a monument to something as yet unspecified at the time she returned home.

Lastly, Jack spoke. Since he was the only one who happened to have had his picture taken when they returned, he first showed some slides of himself with his hand made suit of clothes, shaggy hair and beard. Then, because of his language skills and widely ranging encounters with people from all over the island, he filled in other gaps, described the barbaric battles, the fate of the President, of Reverend Billy and the Pope. The witch burning and body burning and all the sad and sordid details in between. But in the end, however, he purposely said nothing that was overtly inflammatory and tried to summarize and leave the story on a note of hope. Far too many people had died unnecessarily but many other people had also learned from the experience and in spite of the growing hardships caused by the weather changes, they had coped and persevered. The island had been a challenge and an opportunity to learn. There was a good chance that more of the disappearees would also be coming home. And that was the end of it.

There would be no questions from the audience this time, Jack and Katherine had finally decided, not wanting to risk another major disruption. Especially with the other two woman there. A quiet exit was the best they hoped for. Prepared as they were for the worst, however, they were completely surprised again, in a totally unpredictable way. Nothing happened. At first the audience was almost deathly silent. Not even a murmur. Then, one man seated about ten rows back stood up and began clapping. But he clapped alone. Then he stood up, made his way to the isle and started forward.

"Who is that?" Katherine asked Jack as she studied the well dressed, clean shaven older man.

"I don't know," he said, looking closely. Whoever he was he didn't look like much of a threat. Still, with three women by his side and only himself, there was some anxiety after what had happened in Los Angeles.

"I don't recognize him," he said at first, but then he felt both surprise and relief.

"Wait a minute. Could it be...? Of course. I never saw him without his beard and in a decent set of clothes....."

"Who is it?" Katherine asked again.

"You never met him," Jack said. "But Dean Whitcomb and Deanna have."

"Are you sure?" the Dean asked as she looked more closely. Then she beamed happily as the man began climbing the steps up to the stage.

"It's the Professor," she stated.

Regardless of the interruption, the audience remained frozen in their seats. It was only after the Professor had made his way onto the stage, hugged Dean Whitcomb and Deanna and Jack and was introduced to Katherine, however, that people slowly began to rise in little groups here and there and leave the auditorium as Jack and Katherine both kept a wary watch.

"Doctor Blumford Yates at your service," he said to the

women and squeezed their hands gently. Eventually the building emptied, except for one other man who remained far in the rear. Then, he too, started down the isle, but those on stage were so busy reuniting that they didn't notice until he was almost beside them.

Deanna saw him first but she could only stare. Then she put out her arms and said, "Ohhhh, wow," as her eyes filled with tears. By the time the others had turned their attention to the newcomer, she was in his arms and he was kissing her desperately.

"My God," Jack exclaimed. "It's Ivan."

Together, the six of them went to the hotel dining room where Jack and Katherine were staying and had a late dinner. Full of exuberance at being together again, they seemed radically out of place in the otherwise somber atmosphere of the times and location they were in. While Deanna and Ivan were almost totally engrossed in each other they still participated in the conversation between touches and kisses.

"Well, Professor," Dean Whitcomb said after dessert was served. "I thought sure you'd be carrying paper and pencil around, taking notes. Are you working on that book you wanted to write?"

"Absolutely. But it's a laptop computer out in my car. It goes everywhere I go."

"I'd like to have a copy when it's done," she said.

"And I would like more input from each of you," the Professor stated, scanning his eyes around the group. "But I wonder if I might get you to be the first volunteer for an interview," he said, looking ardently at the Dean. He had been watching her closely all evening and it was now quite clear he had a deeper interest in her, something that had been only superficially obvious on the island. But there it was, no doubt about it now. Katherine smiled as she watched the two of them. It was also obvious that the Dean was flattered by the attention and that their feelings might be mutual.

"And please call me Blum," he said to all of them. "Dumb name but it's all I've got."

"Well, I think it's cute," Deanna said. "But tell us what you did with that monster business conglomerate you had that was responsible for your disappearance?"

"Oh, that," he sighed. "Thank god that's over. I did keep a house in the Bahamas, however, and one in Malibu, one on the Mediterranean and another here on the Virginia coast, along with my privately owned bank to keep me in cash, of course. The rest I gave to the employees and so much for that. Oh, and a small publishing company so when I get my book written I can put it out there. I've never been so happy in my life. Now if I just had someone to share it with."

Dean Whitcomb blushed deeply and turned her attention to adding more sugar to her tea as the Professor continued, "but looking back I wouldn't change a thing. The island was the most stimulating educational experience of my life. Better yet, without it I never would have met any of you."

"I'll drink to that," Jack said, looking at Katherine.

"And I," Ivan repeated, taking Deanna's hand in his.

There was a moment of silence, then Jack asked one of the things he still wondered about.

"The first thing I want to know," he said, looking at Ivan. "Is did you ever get the monument finished?"

"The pile of stones on the cliff over the ocean? Not completely, but just as well. There were still several hundred people left there to work on it. I'd guess it's well over half done and half as tall as that big pyramid in Egypt. The Giza one. Bigger. I'm sure it's bigger than half. And after we had woven enough clothing for everyone from the grass, we took all the old rags and made a monster flag out of them and kept it on the top. Too bad there weren't really any ships on that ocean. It could have been seen for miles."

"Too bad we didn't have cameras. Nothing like more pictures to back up our story," Deanna said.

"Maybe the audience would have had an easier time believing us."

"What do think that was all about tonight?" Katherine finally asked, now that the subject had come up. "It was downright spooky with everyone so silent. Almost as if they were all in shock."

"Exactly," the Professor said. "I think that is precisely what happened."

"Really? But why?" Deanna asked.

"Having been in the audience with them," the Professor said, "I think the truth of it finally came home. I think they believed you implicitly and most of them were quite overwhelmed. I mean, all those people who had been highly important back here, now dead, and mostly because of their own doing. That would be quite shocking the first time you heard it, I think. And it certainly isn't something you'd stand up and start clapping about. Not from their perspective. The reason I started clapping was because I thought you all did such an exemplary job of presenting the story and I was so proud of all your forthright candor. It was a brave thing to do."

"I would have to agree," Ivan stated.

"Thank you," Katherine said, looking at Jack. "But do you think that's good? Maybe we over did it. Maybe we should have toned it down or let them ask questions, or something."

"Frankly, I don't think you could have hoped for more."

"Well, questions might be worth considering. I'm sure lots of people had them," the Professor said.

"I don't know. I guess you didn't hear about what happened on the west coast," Katherine stated and told him about it when he asked for specifics.

"Oh, my," he said. "That's terrible. Well. I don't know what to say. The people out there tonight all seemed so interested and well behaved."

"I'm sure having Deanna and the Dean helped," Jack said and let it go at that.

Again there was a period of silence but it was comfortable and warm, being in each other's company as they were. Then Katherine asked Deanna if she ever missed the Island, confessing that sometimes she, herself, did. But in an odd, strange sort of way."

"Of course I was there while things were still moderately peaceful and the rest of you went through something much more difficult."

"Actually," Deanna also admitted. "I do, now and then. Desperate and dangerous as things had become in the end, it had a different dimension to it. It was far less complex than the world here and, in its own way, manageable, I suppose, although that's not a very good word. And once I met Ivan," she said and leaned towards him, "and was able to get away from the Americans, I have to honestly say I never felt more valued in my whole life, regardless of all the things going on around us."

Ivan dropped his head in modesty while she spoke, then he looked up and into her eyes.

"And you certainly made it all worthwhile," he told her.

Then there was another brief pause before Katherine in turn asked Dean Whitcomb the same question.

"It was demanding," the Dean said. "No doubt about that. But seriously, I agree with Deanna. There was a certainty to it, depressing as it was most of the time. There were very few gray areas, very few open questions. The contrasts were so all intense and clear and so was the reason for all of us being there. At least I thought so. But in the end it was an immense tragedy, so extreme it is almost incomprehensible. But I was also very much alive. Every day it was right in front of me. Staying alive. And in the end so horribly sad, all those people dying for no good reason at all. I still don't have a handle on that. But then as a culture, I think Americans have always been so terribly spoiled. But as for people in other places of the world, where entire generations of people have never known anything except the horror of war? What must that be like? I have no idea how they are able to deal with it. And I have no idea why some of us complain so badly. And now, if people will just stop dropping bombs on each other, the worst is probably over. The only hope is to learn what we can from the rest of it and try not repeat the mistakes. I don't think there is anything else."

"True enough," Ivan agreed, "but I'm still a bit of a skeptic. Are people really capable of doing that?"

"Let's hope so," Katherine stated. "Humans can be absolutely amazing sometimes, even under the most desperate of situations. But..."

"And a big but it is," Jack said and turned to the professor.

"So," he asked. "As a student of history, do you think the human race is evolving, simply repeating itself or actually degenerating?"

"That's a difficult question. I would say it all has something to do with pain."

"Pain?"

"Yes, pain. Unfortunately, without direct experience, the anguish of pain itself cannot be passed on. Either from person to person or from generation to generation. Death is soon forgotten or pushed aside. Especially the deaths of strangers, no matter how great the numbers. And always new disasters quickly replace the old. So if new generations are not wise enough to heed what their elders have experienced and related to them, it starts all over again. Sometimes the best that can be hoped for is that the involved generation brings about new laws and ways of enforcing them so that the more horrific mistakes are not allowed to continue. Hopefully then, successive generations will see the wisdom of what has been accomplished and honor it. So, to answer the question more directly, I believe there has been progress but it is exceedingly slow, with many failures and fallbacks."

"But when it comes to the Disappearance, do you think the human race is better or worse off as a result?" was Dean Whitcomb's question.

"So far, worse. If you just look at the casualties. What do you think, Jack?"

"Definitely worse. No doubt about it. But there have been some good signs and the potential for developing into something much better than before is there. Once people fully accept the fact that the world is not going to be put back together through some outside force or that their leaders are not coming back and no one else is going to drop out of the sky and rescue them, then we should begin to see some real progress."

"You think they are still in denial after all this time? It's been three years."

"That seems to be a basic human trait in today's world. Maybe it is has always been. If it weren't, I don't think the world would ever have become such a corrupt place to begin with."

"You see the world as corrupt?"

"Well, maybe not completely. Bad choice of words. I see it as a place where it is easy for a few corrupt hoodlums to gain control, simply because the masses of people have always been too willing to give up their individual power. That's also a bit of an over simplification but still basically true. Another factor is just the inability to cope. As for the disappearance, the event was too big, too all encompassing and horribly frightening. It's hard to even get it in perspective, let alone know what to do about it or even where to start. Too many people sit back and wait. They don't want to make decisions because they don't trust their ability to do so. Some of them can't wait so they pray for someone else to take charge and tell them what to do. They even insist on it. For them, that's what governments and religious leaders are for. To take charge. But now, with the Disappearance, there is no one to give up their power to. Or, to take it away from them. So, in many respects, we're still in a stalemate, still having to learn to accept complete responsibility for ourselves on a one to one basis. And as difficult as that might be for a lot of people, that still has to be of some value."

"And maybe that's the way we can be of some real value," Katherine said. "It's not much, but hopefully, that's what we did by talking about what happened on the island."

"I think you are correct," Ivan agreed. "Presenting that to the public is a good idea. Is there anything we can do to help?"

"Absolutely. That would be marvelous," Katherine said. "We'll take all the help we can get."

"And as soon as the Professor finishes his book he can bring it along so people can get copies if they want," Jack added. "It's always nice to see things in print and it would certainly provide a source of reference."

"Blum," the Professor said. "And I would be delighted to be included. As for the books, I can well afford to give them away if you think that would be all right."

"Even if you charged for it, I think it will become the most widely read book ever published," Dean Whitcomb said. "And I'm available, too. If you need me."

"Sorry," Jack said to her. "I didn't mean not to ask. I just assumed that after tonight you would always be a part of the team. All six of us."

"The six of us, then," the Dean replied.

"The six of us," they all said in unison.

With that as a final toast, Ivan and Deanna left, eager to be alone together, with the Dean and the Professor quickly following.

"Well," Jack said after the others had all left. "That was some reunion."

He was about to continue when two older men approached their table. Taking hold of the back of one of the now vacant chairs as if to pull it out, the heavier one in the wrinkled suit said, "Mr. Briggs. Mind if we buy you another drink?"

The voice was smooth enough. Nothing sinister about that. At least they weren't cops, Jack decided. Except for their fleshy faces and fat little hands, they looked more like second rate hoodlums instead.

"Depends," Jack said, leaning back in his chair, looking them over, not at all sure he wanted to share the space with them.

Katherine was having the same reaction. She was also aware that the two of them had already had more than a couple of drinks and probably didn't need another. Her eyebrows went up and she made a face at Jack which clearly stated her reaction of, good grief. But, before she could add her own comment the first one spoke again.

"My apologies," he said, seriously back tracking. "I should have introduced us. I'm Senator Dugan from Iowa and this is Pat Nugent from Pennsylvania. We were at your symposium tonight and I have to say we were both quite fascinated with what you had to say."

It sounded a bit slick to them and neither Katherine or Jack were impressed but, what the heck. It was still early yet. Jack made a gesture for them to sit, always willing to be helpful.

"Just coffee for me," Katherine stated when the waitress came.

"Me, too," said Jack.

"Well, hmm," said Dugan, a bit flustered. How could they have a serious discussion without something alcoholic. But he sensed he had already made a poor impression so he agreed to coffee also.

"Right. Sounds good," said Nugent. "Any chance... uh, would I be out of line," he said, looking at Katherine and Jack. "Do you have any apple pie?" he asked the waitress. "And can you make it ala mode?"

The coffee came, the pie came and there was more coffee. Nugent concentrated on his pie and a series of stolen glances at Katherine while Dugan pointed out that he had been a friend of old Jenson Wilson and went on to described how he remembered Jack's accompanying Wilson to the joint congressional meetings and made an attempt to praise him. By then Nugent, meanwhile, had decided that if he had had a woman like Katherine in his life when he had been younger he could have spent an entire lifetime without ever looking at another female and when he got the chance he even tried flattering her, stating that in spite of the extreme distress of having been caught up in the disappearance, she still looked absolutely marvelous.

With that Dugan kicked him under the table and scowled at him, then did his best to get back on track, pursuing a more detailed explanation and confirmation of events back on the island. Half an hour later the two senators left, looking somewhat relieved. They were not half as relieved as Katherine and Jack.

"Sorry," he said. "I should never have left them sit down."

"Yeah. What was that all about?"

Jack shrugged. "Was a little weird, wasn't it? Hope you weren't too offended by old Nugent's compulsive staring at you."

"Actually, it was rather entertaining the way he couldn't keep his pie on his fork. I think there was as much on his lap as in his mouth. But why all the concern about the about the President, V P and Speaker of the House?"

"Hard to tell, but there seemed to a lot of concern about whether or not they were actually dead."

"Do you think they liked the answer?"

"I think they were pleased as hell. Whatever that's all about. Who knows. They're senators. That always raises a red flag. Dugan, anyway. Nugent, however, didn't hear a word we said. His focus was locked on something else," Jack said and gave Katherine a buzz on the cheek.

"Poor old guy. He looked lonesome. I hope you didn't take offense."

Jack ran his hand down her back, grinned at her and kissed her on the neck.

"I'm glad we have a king sized bed tonight." she replied in a soft, seductive voice.

"Should have been there half an hour ago. And now we seem to have another problem. Jeez."

"Really? What? Did you lose our room key?"

"No. But look over to your right and back a little. The guy sitting there. The one in the light blue jacket. He's been watching us every since we got here. He was also in the front row back at the auditorium."

Katherine stole a quick glance.

"I don't know. Are you sure? Maybe. What's going on? Do you think he's a problem? He looks kinda out of it."

"Well, we don't want him following us upstairs,." he said as he caught the man's eyes and waved him over.

The man simply stared back at first, then lowered his eyes and slowly got up. When he made it to their table he just stood there, seemingly very embarrassed by what had happened.

"How can we help you?" Jack asked as Katherine studied the face.

Somewhere in his thirties, he seemed tired and wasted. A bit unkempt. But it was the eyes that held her attention. Empty, haunted eyes, fearful and doubting that twisted at something inside her. Whatever it was, she wasn't sure she wanted to hear it. But here he was so would he please just say what he needed to and then go away.

"Sit down," Jack said with a bit of impatience.

"Please," he said with a motion towards the empty chair across from them.

The poor man sat, then raised his eyes to them.

"Sorry," he said. "I... I didn't mean to bother you."

"You were at the presentation tonight."

"I was. Yes, I... that was, ah, my god. It's all so horrible. So horrible. I'm...oh god. What I did...I......"

Pathetic, Jack thought, but there was no smell of alcohol nor any hint of anything drug induced.

"Would you like something? Coffee? A drink?"

"No... no, I don't drink. I'm just having a... a... ah, maybe I should go. I'm sorry," he said and slid back his chair, rising slightly.

"Okay," Katherine said. "But can you at least tell us who you are and what this is all about first?"

The man lowered himself back down and glanced from one to the other.

"Stevenson. William Stevenson. Lieutenant, US Air Force. Now absent without leave. But nobody knows. No one left to know. Or to care, either." The voice was weak and raspy, depleted.

"Okay. Whatever that means. So what's the problem? What does that have to do with us?"

"Nothing, really," he went on, going slowly. "Except you two have been through a lot. Saw all those people die back on the island. Probably lost some family and friends from the bombs. Tremendous amount of tragedy for everyone. Tremendous," he said and stared into the distance.

They left him like that, giving him time. Then he came back, looking first at Katherine, then at Jack.

"How do you deal with it?" he asked.

"What?"

"All of it. The tragedy, the...I don't know. All of it," he ended with a wave of his hand.

"Like everyone else, I guess," Jack replied after a reflective pause. "What about you? You don't seem to be doing too well."

"Oh, yeah... well. Nothing I can do now. Not a damned thing. I'm beyond redemption. Way beyond," he said with a sigh and a sick laugh, going inward again.

"Didn't have the guts to shoot myself. Drinking didn't help. Not even drugs. No matter what I do, the horror still always win out. So, I just stay sober. Damn. Maybe a train will hit me if I'm lucky. I should die. I should be dead. But I don't want to be even though I can't live with it."

He moved his head back and forth as if trying to shake the disturbing thoughts loose. Then, half sigh and half moan, he went on. "Guess hell will catch up with me soon enough. Hell, I guess it already has."

Katherine raised her eyebrows at Jack and made a face that said, good grief. He nodded and shrugged.

Stevenson lapsed back into silence, clinging to the desperate edge of his life as they sat waiting, knowing he would undoubtedly tell them the rest if they let him.

"I was in North Dakota," Stevenson began again. "At the missile complex there. You know... The one that got blown up..." he said, looking at them for their reaction.

"Yes, but you obviously weren't there when the bomb went off or you wouldn't be here now. Lots of speculation but nobody seems to know for sure where it was launched from, or why. Except that that it wasn't a missile that blew up in its own silo because it was an above-ground blast."

"I do."

"You do? What?"

"Yes, me. I know. Every day. Every day. Over and over. God help me."

"What are you talking about?" Katherine asked with a touch of irritation, now becoming impatient.

"Stupidity, ego, always trying to prove something. Me, and the rest of those damned fools. Damnit. God dammit."

"Okay," Jack said. "Enough. What the hell are you talking about? If you have something to say, get to it. Otherwise it's late and we'd like to get some sleep."

"I will," Stevenson said. And he did. The whole story. Even the part about the Captain's wife he finally realized he had fallen in love with. And driving away in the night leaving her behind. It took nearly an hour in all. Then, without another word, he got up, walked out the restaurant door and disappeared.

Boston and New York City were totally devoid of life. The radioactive fallout had reached that far east, leaving only empty buildings behind. The same was true of Philadelphia and that is why they held their next gathering in Richmond, Virginia, where all six of them participated in the presentation. The audience was a mix of men and women in nearly equal proportion. Many couples, but also singles and groups of singles. There were almost no elderly in the crowd, the great majority in their twenties to fifties, with a smattering of young here and there. Not a suit and tie or a pair of designer jeans in the entire auditorium, either. Lots of mended garments instead. Some well worn and threadbare but everyone quite neat and clean in spite of the hardships they had suffered. A sincere group who appeared like they had come to listen. To test audience reaction further, they had a short intermission about two thirds of the way through. Since everyone had been orderly up to that point, they decided to allow questions when they were done. Instead of direct, open microphone, verbal questions, however, they had paper and pencils passed out during the break, all collected near the end of their talks. Ivan and the Professor would then collate the questions and determine those most asked. The other four would divide them up and take turns answering them.

"What about the tough ones?" Deanna asked while they discussed it, waiting for the break to be over. "What about religion or other controversial things? How do you handle those?"

"I don't know," Jack told her. "In Los Angeles we called it like we saw it and like we said, there were a few problems. On the other hand what's the point if we can't be truthful?"

"And I agree," Katherine said. "What do you think?" she asked, looking at all of them in turn for a response.

"Well, it does seem silly not to be truthful," Dean Whitcomb said. "But of course I didn't have to run for my life like you two did."

Katherine smiled. "That was L.A.. This has a different feel to it. What do you think, Jack?"

"Let's wait and see what kind of questions we get. This is also a much smaller crowd and they seem more stable. We also have more security and you all know where the rear exit is. Right?"

"Right."

Jack had been the last to speak. When he was done there was a smattering of applause from the audience that slowly gained in strength, until at last, it seemed that everyone was clapping. After it subsided, Jack thanked them. Then he had a very brief huddle with Ivan and the Professor. "What kind of questions did we get?" he asked.

"Always the few," the Ivan said. "How did you manage without television, hamburgers or beer? A couple of perverted questions about sex but the rest are pretty serious."

"Heavy on religious and political issues," the Professor said. "Lot's of concerns about the future, some philosophical stuff."

"Still want to do this?" Jack asked as the three women.

"Absolutely. Who do you want to go first?"

"How about the Dean?" Jack said and moved back to the podium and spoke to the audience.

"We have looked over the written questions that were collected and there are at least a hundred different ones so we will not be able to answer them all. As a result we have selected those asked by the largest numbers of people regardless of content. But please remember one thing. Since you asked the questions we can only assume you want truthful answers. In that regard we will do our best to respond as candidly as possible. Dr. Whitcomb will be first.

Dean Whitcomb came forward and spoke directly into the mike attached to the podium. "The two questions I hope to answer are closely related," she began slowly, trying to remain serious. In any other situation she probably would have shook her head in dismay and laughed at some of them but she continued. Since there were at least three dozen similarly worded questions, maybe they needed to be answered anyway.

"The questions are; Is the disappearance a sign that God is watching over us and punishing us for some reason, and, Why did God do this to us? Is this finally a clear sign of the Second coming of Christ?" She paused again, seeking a place to begin that would seem unbiased and intelligent, all the while wondering if that were even possible. But she had volunteered so she was stuck with it. After what they had previously discussed she hoped her answers weren't the ones to start a riot.

"Well," she said, clearing her throat. "Let's first consider the fact that the Disappearance was a world wide event. It cut across all lines of power and structure without discrimination. All business, political and religious leaders were involved. No one was spared. The same was true on the island. No one, no outside force or power interceded to protect any one individual or group from themselves or from harm from others. Therefore, we can only conclude that if God was somehow involved, he, she, God, did not take sides. That, I think, automatically rules out the possibility that this has something to do with the second coming of Christ, if indeed such a thing will every happen."

Good going, she told herself. You're on the right track. Keep it up.

"Somehow it should be clear by now that there is no chosen race. It should also be quite clear that there is also no chosen religion. There is no chosen group. There are no chosen individuals. Whether or not you agree, that is exactly what everything that has happened to the world has made very clear thus far. The bottom line is, we are all in this together, without preferential treatment for any one. And while that is almost impossible to deny, it is still true that belief systems seem to depend on a different set of rules. Therefore, some of you may still see things differently. And since we agreed to be completely frank with our answers, that, in my opinion, may be part of the ongoing problem. How can we ever expect things to get better until we first accept them as they are? The situation must be acknowledged for what it is. It is difficult. Maybe even worse than difficult. But it far from hopeless. Please do not forget that. It is far from hopeless. That is the starting point. We can work together to make things better. And as for the part about, is God punishing us for some reason, doesn't it seem possible that we have been punishing ourselves when we were being dogmatic, arrogant, self centered, over indulgent and unwilling to protect our home, the planet we live on, and embrace each other equally as human beings?"

The auditorium was not nearly as silent as before. Some people seemed to be shifting uncomfortably in their seats in resistance to some of what she had said. Dean Whitcomb, however, stood there quietly looking out at the audience until everyone was still again. Then she passed the mike to Deanna and sat down in one of the chairs off to the side. Deanna also waited for a long moment before beginning, slightly intimidated by so many serious faces staring back at her. Then, purposely speaking softly, she began.

"The next question asked is, If what you say is true about the island being such a tropical place with all the necessities, why did so many people have to die there?"

"I don't think the answer is very complicated but the only way I can answer it is to also be extremely blunt. Remember, there were no contagious diseases, no wild animals, no tornadoes or earthquakes, no automobiles, no drugs and no guns. There weren't even mosquitoes or flies. So, bottom line, every single person who died there did it either by there own hand or at the hands of another. Some, but very few, died innocently enough. The rest just made bad choices. Brutal as it must sound, it was that simple. Fear drove many hundreds to suicide. Arrogance, ego, stubbornness, even madness, drove the rest to kill each other. Nothing else. It was a complete failure on the part of far too many of the people there to assess, evaluate and adapt to the situation they were faced with. Instead, they rigidly insisted on keeping the old power structure alive. They also refused to give up their old prejudices and hatreds and insisted on imposing all their own distorted standards on everyone else around them in spite of the fact that they were all placed in a completely new and radically different environment from the ones they came from. A situation that was totally conducive to achieving far better human relationships than ever before. Old rivals were not oceans apart. Everyone was within reasonable walking distance of everyone else and there was every opportunity for them to sit down together and discuss things. Far too many refused to take advantage of that fact, however. As a result, the experiment, or whatever else it was, failed miserably in that respect. And that occurred almost without exception for every nation represented on the island, including our own. You may not want to hear it, it may be totally unacceptable to you personally, but it is true, nonetheless."

"The next two questions are, 'Since you have seen both sides of the Disappearance, was it some weird, random event or do you think it had a purpose? And, second, 'What caused it?'

"Okay," Deanna continued. "Let's look at it. The Disappearance was anything but random and in the mathematical sense it was far from chaotic. If it had been, there would have been absolutely no connection between those who disappeared, if you will, and those who did not. It was a very, very specific, selective, ordered and precise event. Can we, therefore, conclude that it had a purpose? I say, yes, and exactly for those same reasons. And, as a result, it behooves us to look for it."

"But how do we do that?.... Well, by looking carefully at the unusual aspects of it. Leaders were removed from the rest of society. They were placed in a remote location with abundant food and water where the climate was warm and comfortable day and night. The main island was small and easily inhabitable. When we arrived, there were more than abundant supplies of food and a far more than adequate supply of pure, fresh drinking water. And as Dean Whitcomb has already pointed out, there were no storms, no earthquakes, no wild animals, no communicable diseases of any kind. And, as I just said, all the worlds leaders were living together in the open, all within reasonable walking distance of each other. The Chinese were not thousands of miles away, or the Africans, or the Europeans. Accessibility and ease of communication could not have been made much easier and every bit of it could have been face to face."

"The President of the United States had no army to hide behind or to send off to war. Neither did anyone else. There was no technology or modern weapons to tip the balance in anyone's favor. Everyone was equal and in the same predicament. And there it is, *the same predicament.* A level playing field. Why? To me, that is beyond coincidence. It had to have been that way for a reason, but, unfortunately, most of the major leaders in their respective areas saw it as a handicap instead. Isn't that interesting? A handicap. And, instead of taking advantage of it, they made excuses and chose to go on hiding behind those who still acquiesced and allowed themselves to continue being subordinated. They did it in all the same old ways. Posturing, threatening, intimidating, conniving and deceiving. The tactics of thugs and criminals. All the same old things they had done back home."

"What they seemed to have missed entirely was the fact that the situation was a grand opportunity instead. It was a challenge, a test of humanitarian values and a chance to grow into something better, because, in a place like the island, there was only one thing of any real value. That one thing was personal integrity. All the rest was meaningless. But, as has already been said, far too many of them failed. They failed to make good decisions, to set aside their prejudices, their hang-ups, their small mindedness and their insecure need to hang onto a power structure which no longer existed for them in the context of the island environment. So, what that tells me and what that should tell all of us is that these people, these leaders should never have been in charge of anything to begin with when they were back here. Certainly not whole nations. Certainly not nations with armies and navies and air forces and nuclear weapons and self serving agendas. Is it any wonder the world was rushing headlong into self destruction? But if you think the leaders got a raw deal by being transported off to some lonely island and had no control over their own destinies, consider this. Not everyone died there. Some of us returned. To me that means that the rest of the people there had the same chance to have done so had they behaved in a civilized manner while they were there."

"Ultimately, however, bad as it may all seem, things are what they are. But also remember, many options are still open for the rest of us. Instead of complaining, we can try to be positive. And being positive we can say, what an opportunity. Why not take advantage of it. Without them we have a chance to see what a horrific mess they made of things. With our own help, of course. Every step of the way. And now that we have had a chance to think about it we can ask ourselves, why in God's name did we ever let them have so much power to begin with, when all they did was to abuse it so badly. And when we saw them commit those abuses, we did nothing to stop it. Often we didn't even question it, or, blindly turned our backs. Others, however, just as often openly supported them with indignant self righteousness because somehow what our leaders were doing helped support their own misguided agendas."

"Unquestionably,however, it is easy to dump all the blame on our leaders. But, who elected them to public office? And if not elected, who allowed them to come into power? Who helped them?

The blame can only be shared. Both sides are equally to blame. That, I think, was the purpose of the Disappearance. It was a harsh and extremely clear wake up call for the human race. And while it may seem totally unjustified and completely barbaric because of the way it turned out, you have to remember that it only turned out the way it did because of the individual choices people made under the circumstances. There were always other options, and, as I said before, every step of the way. There are always options, individually and en masse. They exist here as well as they existed back on the island. And if the Disappearance hadn't happened, what then? In the short term there might have been less tragedy. But in the long run, if things had not changed, it might eventually have been far worse. What with nuclear toys in the hands of morally deficient people there might well have been no planet left at all. Or, with the abusive destruction of the environment, other longer term, equally destructive consequences. A lifeless orb of barren rock circling the sun, or, a planet with human inhabitants thrown back into the stone age."

"So, here we are. The survivors. Still alive. Where we go from here is entirely up to us. No one is going to drop out of the sky and save us. We... are.. it. The door is still open, opportunity still exists. As for the, what caused it, part, who knows? Maybe we did it to ourselves. Thank you," Deanna concluded and stepped back so Katherine could be next.

"In the last month and a half Mr. Briggs and I have traveled across a major portion of the country and we know from first hand experience that even after three years, these are still desperate times," she started. "There is much distress and despair, far too many problems and far too few good ideas about what must be done to solve them. Regardless, however, nothing will ever change for the better unless, as Deanna has just stated, we are all willing to face the issues before us full on, and stop waiting to be rescued by some thing, some power, some magic occurrence that is just somehow going to happen. Likewise, it does no good to look for some thing or someone else to blame it all on, especially other people who do not think or believe like we do. Is it their fault and are we all just victims? If *THEY* would change and do the right thing is it true then that *WE* wouldn't have this problem? These are the types of questions that seem to be on many people's minds. One of them is stated this way; Do you think that if we could unite all the different religions in the world that we could get our leaders back and everything would be okay?'"

"Well, in response, I have some questions of my own. First, why are there so many different and so widely divergent kinds of religion to begin with? And then, why didn't they find some common ground and peacefully come together a long time ago? Additionally, if such a thing were even possible, if all the various religions were to be combined, what religion would get to be the supreme religion? Yours? Mine? Someone else's? And why? Everyone believes their own religion to be the divine one, yet, how can that be? If there were such a thing as that kind of divinity, don't you think God would have somehow made that quite clear in the beginning so as to put an end to all the bloodshed over such an issue? Then, too, what about all the people who do not embrace any one religion? What about the ones who don't embrace any religion at all, at least in the most popular sense of the word and who still seem to function quite well without it, sometimes much better than those who subscribe to it? Up until the Disappearance there were a lot of them. They may have actually been a silent majority in the US, with their numbers growing because many of them viewed organized religion either as wrong and unnecessary, or, as an outright failure. However, for the sake of argument, let's still consider the alternative proposed in the question asked."

"If, and it is a very, very big if. If you could somehow force religion onto everyone so that all of the world's people were of one religious mind set and under the authority of one individual, or small group of individuals, what would life on earth be like then? Would that erase everyone's fears, would it automatically take away greed and hatred and jealousy and small mindedness? Would it be the end of racial issues, gender issues, class issues, political issues, economic issues? Would it, or would it make humans into some sort of homogenized, non thinking, non questioning, gutless sheep? And who, pray tell, amongst all the humans alive today, who would in any way be truly qualified to be in charge of such an organization and who would be qualified to round out the upper echelons of that power structure? If the religious groups which are in existence at this time have been unable to rid themselves of corruption, abuse of power, abuse of their brethren, abuse of financial status and abuse of nearly everything that comes within their grasp, how could you ever expect a consolidation to be any better. Would it make us better human beings, would it bring us any closer to God?"

"The point is, like it or not, while a good many of the problems we are now faced with were directly caused by religious closed mindedness, ignorance and sometimes downright dementedness, none of these problems were ever, and can never be solved by looking to religion for answers. In that sense they are not about religion and they are not about God. If they were, God would have given humans better guidance to begin with. And, as I just said, God would have fixed it a long time ago. God would never have let it happen in the first place, God would have made it very clear about who is right and who is wrong. Yet misguided, power hungry people from every religious affiliation step forward every day and claim that God has spoken to them and chosen them to be his emissary. Even the President did that and the gullible then believed that somehow made that person infallible. And look where that led us. Into more disaster. Prove to me that there is such a thing as an infallible human being. It is a ridiculous concept. God will not save you. God will not save us. All God will do and has ever done, if the idea of God works for you, is to give each of us the power to save ourselves."

"Of course it is really not all that simple either, is it, because society is not that simple. There are other driving forces in action. Business, for example. Consumerism. When business becomes the source of ones livelihood and, at the same time, one's religion, that leads to another type of moral disintegration where only bottom line profit is sacred. All else is subject to sacrifice, even the welfare of other people. Why else, in one of the most prosperous nations of the world, did we have millions of homeless, millions of hungry children and millions of people without health care? Well, we could go on all night criticizing and blaming and still solve nothing. So, what do we do? Again, I could say something so trite and lofty as, only you can save yourself. And, only in combination with other human beings can we save the human race and the planet we live on. Both statements are true, however, but, so what? We are in a catastrophic situation. Where do we start? And that leads to the next two questions."

"These questions are, 'How can we survive without leaders?' and, 'There are too many people in the world to run things by committee, so what do we do if we are never able to have leaders?'"

"Once again I will start by answering questions with questions. As for surviving without the kinds of leaders we had before, my question would be, do we have any choice? It doesn't look like it, does it? At least not until we invent a better way of doing things. And, even though most of us may not be living at the same comfort and convenience level as before, people are surviving. Certainly there is tremendous fear and uncertainty about the future but in no way do I think it is a hopeless situation. None of us who have been to the island and returned do. Resourceful people will always survive. And, since we apparently cannot have national leaders or state leaders or corporate leaders or religious leaders operating in the fashion they did before, then, if we want things to be different than they have become, we had better keep trying to work something out. In the long run and, in my own opinion, we will eventually be better off without them because now we are forced to re evaluate every thing we have ever been led to believe about life in general and mankind's role in the bigger scheme of things. We must reinvent our relationship with the planet we live on, and, we must reinvent our relationship with the cosmos, our deities and with the entirety of Creation. And, most importantly, we must also reinvent our relationships with ourselves and our fellow human beings ."

"All is not doom and gloom,however. Far from it. There are many positive trends. One of them is the fact that you are all here tonight and you are interested in continuing with your lives and having a better future, the best of all starting points. And, quite likely, the only way that most of you have been able to do that is because kind and decent people know for a fact that the only way to survive is to cooperate and behave in humanistic ways. Without that, many millions of people world wide would not have survived the early days of the disappearance. Without that none of us would be here in this auditorium tonight. Furthermore, the world is still full of bright, creative, highly talented individuals who are also reinventing everything from food production to the concept of business management. There is good reason to believe some of these concepts might be applicable to political structuring as well. It's about communication, experimentation and willingness to keep trying. As an example and, as was also presented early, there is the campaign to reorganize the National Congress and bring all legislators back home so they are readily accessible to their constituents and away from the lobbyists and the special interest groups. There is no reason why they cannot effectively conduct their ordinary business by video net. Not only will it save the taxpayers multi millions of dollars, it will go a long ways toward cleaning up the corruption that is still so obviously present. So, that is where the opportunity lies. It lies in taking those kinds of ideas, expanding on them and moving forward."

"Other than that, there is also a tremendous amount of Internet

317

networking going on and there are flyers at all the exits with many of the important sites listed. Please pick up a copy when you leave. Additionally, as often happens after some great tragedy or natural disaster, responsible people come out of their houses and begin developing some newer level of community. And that is probably one of the most healthy things that has happened to this country in several decades. Still, I know that none of what I have said is as specific as you might like, but again, the only real advice I can give is, don't look to authority figures for solutions to your problems and don't rush to turn things over to someone else for resolution. Think it through for yourselves. Then come together and consult and compare, but always question. And last, trite as this may sound also, stay informed, stay involved."

"Thank you," Katherine said and Jack came forward.

As he adjusted the microphone, Jack looked out across the crowded auditorium. Even though they had already been there nearly three hours, the members of the audience still seemed attentive and he was eager to continue, regardless of the final outcome.

"Well, this should be interesting," he said when he was ready. "Especially since this first question was asked by well over a hundred people. It certainly surprised me and it may surprise some of you. Namely, Do you think there is such a thing as mass insanity? The second question asked almost as much was, Do you think war is inevitable? and the third is, Why did leaders disappear? Why not someone else? The fourth question is, Do people have a moral obligation to help others? And last, What do you think it 's going to take before things really begin to get better?"

Here Jack paused a moment and took a deep breath. Then he continued.

"Since I think the second question is by far the easiest to answer, let me begin there by saying that as long as human beings believe that war is inevitable, war will be inevitable. Once enough people accept the fact that there are always other options to war and that almost anything is better than war, then wars will begin to cease. It is that simple. Every act begins in the minds of men. Change the thinking, change the action. War begins in some tyrant's warped mind and is ultimately made possible by blind allegiance to that person or that cause, all of which is helped along by the immense profiteering opportunity given to the weapons industry. Instead of letting others manipulate our fears and allowing our paranoia to control our actions, let's let our good sense lead us to lock up the perpetrators, instead. Before things deteriorate to the point to where there is little other choice than war. And, speaking of insanity, blind allegiance is a form of insanity. Nationalistic, social or religious. It doesn't matter. Anytime anyone abdicates their thinking process and blindly follows another, they have given up their own freedom and become determined to take away everyone else's in the process."

"Hypocrisy also comes into play. How can a person be pro-life and pro-war at the same time? How can one be pro-life and support the death penalty? How can they be pro-life and wantonly destroy the beauty of nature and the other creatures who also call the planet home? Those contradictions are all extremely clear. And while some seem to need everything defined in terms of black and white, there are many areas that have many shades of gray. These demand that we not take the easy way out by subscribing to someone else's agenda but that we do our own thinking. Sometimes there is no alternative but to make choices that defy old customs and rules."

"In that regard, let me ask you this. Do you believe religious dogma has a divine origin? If so, can you show the rest of us that connection? It cannot be done either logically or through historical fact because, for one thing, dogma is full of arbitrary contradiction. For those who have taken the trouble to examine it, doesn't it seem clear that dogma is an invention of the human mind? And if one is willing to follow it far enough, doesn't it appear far more likely that dogma is created to limit human thinking and to gain control over other people than it is to bring them salvation and set them free? But maybe not. The fear of being wrong and going to hell is a powerful force in many people's lives. People's good common sense and their logic tell them one thing. The church plays upon their deepest fear and tells them something else. It's a tough position to be in. The easiest way out is to shut down the mind and keep putting money in the collection plate. Understandable, perhaps. But in a world whose very future is at risk, not a very brave response."

"However, if you are brave enough to allow me my opinion and hear me out, it is my contention that dogma is totally arbitrary and extremely dangerous. Let me give you one small example. A rigid, pro-life stance means no birth control and no abortion. A very clear statement without shades of gray. That might work in some perfect world somewhere, wherever that might be. But in our world there are few absolutes. Certainly not in this area. Intelligent choices can be very difficult because they are not always easy or spiritually satisfying in terms of prevailing religious rhetoric. In this case in particular, in the question of pro-life, there is no black and white, yes or no. It is not a single question at all. It is a series of questions as to what is more pro-life than what. For example, is it more pro-life to practice birth control and sometimes, early term abortions in select cases, or, is it more pro-life to over procreate on an extremely over populated planet where a large number of those excess births, those children, will only live long enough to starve to death or die of some horrible infectious disease or, given a few more years, be forced into slavery or destroyed in war. Which is more humane and pro-life than which? These are the questions we have not spent enough time on. And until we do, they need to remain open, with freedom of choice, and not be mandated by religion or power groups or the political or judicial system. And that leads us to question three."

"Why did our leaders disappear instead of some other class or group of individuals? A few people also wondered if this was the work of the Devil and seem seriously concerned about it," Jack said as he loosened his tie. He was completely into it by now, fully enjoying what he was doing and pleased with the answers which seemed to come to him from out of nowhere. On he went.

"As was said before, it is difficult to live in fear. There is a tremendous amount of uncertainty in the world. Probably more so than at any other time in the history of mankind. We would be fools if we weren't all a little bit afraid at times. Especially now. But to have to walk around believing that there is a source of evil at loose in the world is too much. To think that evil is a separate force somewhere out there in the dark, lurking around corners waiting to do us in has to be terrorizing. At the same time, however, when something goes wrong which no one wants to take responsibility for, it is very convenient to be able to place the blame elsewhere. It's the Devil's fault. Again, a simplistic, black and white concept that gets some people off the hook."

"So.... people of faith. Where is your faith? Is your all powerful, all loving God so weak and helpless he can't keep the devil in check? What a strange melodrama. But for those who are on the edge wondering about it, I say there is no such thing as a separate force of evil, in and of itself, in existence. There are only people who do evil things. Very few, really. The vast majority of people are basically of good intent or society would have totally self destructed long ago. Unfortunately, in times of crisis, good intent alone is not enough. Nothing comes of good intent if people of good intent do nothing but sit idly by while people of other intent proceed with ulterior motive. That is why a little evil goes a long way and must be dealt with in an appropriate manner. Hopefully, that is what laws and justice systems are for."

"As for the question, why did the leaders disappear? Well. Who else but leaders? Of course business men would have had their competitors disappear, criminals would have law enforcement disappear, nations would have their enemies disappear and on and on. Then what? After while there wouldn't be anyone left on the planet but a few small isolated groups. And, not too much longer after that, there wouldn't be anyone. Is that what you think this is all about? And, as for the, what it it's going to take before things really get better...., well, it all depends. On one hand it would be very easy to argue that the pendulum hasn't swung far enough in the wrong direction as yet. Bad as things are, maybe they have to get even worse before enough people are willing to make serious changes in their thinking and their attitudes on a broad enough scale to really do permanent good, and that is a dismal thing to say because I certainly don't want them to get worse any more than you do. But," he said, and shrugged to emphasize the point.

"And now, the question about mass insanity. Under the circumstances, with nuclear bombs blowing up the world, it does seem to be an appropriate thing to discuss. So, while a part of me would just like to say, yes, there is such a thing as mass insanity and let it go at that, it would seem that we need to go a little further. And, if we are going to discuss it, the other thing that needs to be considered is the difference between committing insane acts, and, being insane, in and of itself."

"Sigmund Freud, long dead now, but credited as the father of psychoanalysis, was one of the first people to raise the possibility that civilization may itself be psycho-pathological. That even the entire whole of mankind might have become neurotic. And again, in the same vein, the eminent psychoanalyst Erich Fromm said that just because millions of people may share the same form of mental illness does not make them sane. In other words, if the majority of the human race was crazy, they would still consider themselves sane and would go about locking up everyone else. Maybe that is why this whole experience is so extremely difficult for so many. Why it seems so unreal and at times, even insane. But maybe the human race was already so far off the track and didn't even realize what it was doing long before the Disappearance occurred. Doesn't it seem insane to pollute the water we drink and the air we breath and to over run and endanger the planet we have to live on so badly that our own future is in jeopardy? Doesn't it seem insane to spend multi billions of dollars on war and almost nothing to help the homeless, multi billions for new weapons research and nothing to provide health care for the needy, billions more on drugs and alcohol and gambling and nothing to feed the millions of children who go to bed hungry at night, even in our own country. And that was just the start. As a race of beings, we have been behaving in very insane ways. And because of our often complete blindness to it, maybe that means we were indeed insane."

"Number one, our home, this planet, our own little island in space, is in serious trouble. Air, land and ocean, it has been badly poisoned, polluted and grossly abused. It has been this way for a long time. While to a large extent most everyone still alive today inherited it that way we have also continued to add to the problem. The direct cause for most of it was our own life enhancing technology. Its creators were clever enough to greatly improve the standard of living for those who could afford all the conveniences but they were not clever enough to do that without all the life threatening side effects. The two major ones being global warming and upper atmosphere ozone layer depletion. Nothing new about that. That knowledge has been around for so long it seems barely worth repeating. But either one of these effects could still destroy most of the life forms on the planet, including humans. Unfortunately, even that still didn't seem to bother a lot of people because the ultimate tragedy was always still somewhere further along in the future and far too few were willing to give up anything to help solve the problem. Worse, no one in any position of power or in a position of profiteering ever wanted anyone to do so anyway because it would have been politically limiting and economically destructive. Society was corrupted, top to bottom. The Administration was corrupt, the Congress, the Judicial system, law enforcement and, worst of all, the corporate world. Economically, the only way the system could have kept on functioning was to make consumerism a way of life and self serving, pocket lining abusiveness a given. As a result, it became mandatory that the population keep increasing and that people keep on buying a tremendous amount of goods and services they did not really need and, for the most part, could have easily survived without. Things that wasted natural resources and required the consumption of energy to produce. Fossil based fuel energy, for the most part, with it's life threatening consequences because of the vast amounts necessary."

"Unfortunately, by the time society finally found itself in a situation where it had no choice but to admit that global warming was real, it was already too late. The critical point had already been reached and passed by. Things of such magnitude cannot be reversed overnight. There is still so much pollution in the atmosphere that, even if automobiles and power generation were banned completely, it will still take many decades for any significant improvement. Granted, there were some attempts made to slow the process. But even right up to the point of the Disappearance, I don't think enough people wanted to do the things that were necessary badly enough to solve the problems in any systematic way. Far too many didn't even care. The real consequences, the ones that would affect them directly, were just too distant."

"But, that was before the disappearance. Now, three years later, at best guess the planet has about a billion and a half fewer people on it. A damning statistic, but even with twenty percent fewer people none of the old problems have gone away. They have only been added to. Four major nuclear weapons have been detonated in the atmosphere that we know of. Not small yield atomic bombs of the variety used way back in World War Two but fusion bombs who total output was about ten thousand times more deadly. And, as you already know, everything in the northern United States and southern Canada from North Dakota eastward will be uninhabitable for hundreds of years to come. But it is not just a localized problem. Prevailing winds have also carried the fallout around the globe to parts of Europe and even into sections of Russia and China. People are still dying as a result. Sooner or later we must ask ourselves, are these just insane acts committed by otherwise sane people or are they an expression of insanity itself? Is a person who smokes too much, or drinks too much or does drugs, or escapes into perversion and denial actually insane, or, just committing self destructive, insane acts? To be sure, it is a fine line. But in the end, destructive is destructive and, to me, it is a cowardly breach of contract with oneself as to why we are all here in the first place."

"So, a failing planet, war, destructive behavior and loss of freedom; these are all symptoms of larger problems, maybe even symptomatic of mass insanity. If not, certainly a race of people badly off track. However, setting that aside, we could also argue quite equivocally, that the major root causes of the world problems we face today are but two. If these had not existed we would not be in jeopardy with the environment and serious war would be almost unheard of."

"First, there is gross over population. We have been reproducing ourselves into extinction. In terms of the by products of present technology, the planet has at least ten times too many people on it. Half a billion to a billion people could go on with their over consumption, wastefulness and polluting bad habits and the planet would probably still be able to absorb and re balance. But it absolutely cannot do so with seven billion. To double that again would create a disaster that might bring and end to it all. So, I ask you. Is having babies in far greater numbers than the planet can ever hope to support in a healthy manner an insane act, is it insanity, or is it just plain stupidity? One thing is for sure. It is not pro-life. Without a doubt, much of our population growth has been underhandedly encouraged by world leaders. Again, the economic system in place before the disappearance would not have been able to sustain itself if there had been zero population growth. And negative growth would have been complete economic disaster. But, what is worse than what? If world population keeps increasing, all the environmental problems will keep accelerating."

"If you think you have a hard time breathing now, what do you think would have happened if just China, for example, had at least one automobile for each household? What would happen if India and all the other third world countries acquired the same, so called, standard of living as the United States when the US, with about five percent of the world's people, was producing about sixty five percent of the pollution? Then, too, how much of the armed conflict in the world is about natural resources and oil in particular? What will happen when there are a couple more billion automobiles on the planet and the owners are all screaming for gasoline? Is this the best we can do, to keep going down the same old insane path until we have poisoned ourselves to death? Or to create such a demand and shortage of resources that we must go to war to sustain our own gluttony?"

Here Jack paused, took a drink of water and looked out over the audience. They were quiet, waiting, their attention still focused on him.

"Okay, question number four. Do we have a moral obligation

to help others? Well... I could say yes. Or, I could say no. Or, I could say, it depends. But, if I do, then I am lending some support to the word "moral," and I don't want to do that. Moral is a loaded concept with many connotations. It means entirely different things to different people. For far too many it means there is a higher law involved which emanates from some divine authority. The result is that when someone talks about moral duty, they are making pronouncements and invoking some, claimed to be, higher source as their right to do so. Additionally, invoking moral authority not only provides the proclaimer with an excuse for trying to coerce others into complying with their own personal agendas but it also gives them an excuse for not accepting responsibility for their own actions. But, let me remind you of this. So far this evening everything we have talked about thus far supports the fact that no such higher authority is out there making direct proclamations about who is ultimately right or wrong in any dispute or taking sides in any way whatsoever. And no higher authority is making direct statements about what you are, or are not, obligated to do under the circumstances. None of that exists in the conventional sense that has anything to do with the situation we find ourselves in."

"Regardless, the world still has its share of self proclaimed Messengers of God. There are those who tell you most adamantly that the only way you can save your soul is to embrace the ideologies they propound. The truth is, however, they don't want to save your soul, they want to own it. Once anyone accepts such bizarre ideas they are trapped, victims of the proclaimer, victims of their own gullibility. Another form of self destructive behavior. By default."

"So... with that as a starting point and getting back to the question about morality, let me offer you my own opinion, leaving the word, moral, out of it entirely. Do we have an obligation to help others?"

"Harsh as it may seem, the answer can only be, no. But...., and I say this with sincere conviction. When the opportunity arises and someone else is in need, I sincerely hope you consider the circumstances. And, if conditions are right, that you do reach out and lend a hand. That is just something decent people do and I believe that is clearly expressed by the fact that there are so many of you here tonight. The very fact that you are here seeking answers to human questions means you have concerns, not only for yourself but for those around you."

"But. And there is a very large but attached. There is no room in the present world for the freeloader. There is no room for anyone who would intentionally sit back and take advantage of other people's good will. Helping someone who is capable of helping themselves is not help at all. It is aiding and abetting. On the other hand, if someone needs help and is willing to make some reasonable contribution in exchange, even though it may be a future one, help them. If they need help because they are extremely ill or dying, and you can afford to do so time wise, energy wise or money wise, do so, for that kind of an attitude is an investment in your own future because the day may come when you are in the same situation. But if helping another places your own life in jeopardy, or a member of your immediate family in jeopardy, then the decision becomes extremely difficult. There is no black and white, no moral right or wrong answer. There is only your own conscience. Your love of those around you. Your own human decency."

Jack paused again, this time to look at last of the five pieces of paper he held that contained the questions he was answering.

"And now the last question for the evening. What do you think it's going to take before things really begin to get better? Not an easy question, that's for sure. And not an easy answer. But, to answer it honestly I must relate back to some of the most volatile of all the things we have talked about here tonight. The place where I, myself, may be exhibiting a touch of insanity by even bringing it up. Be that as it may, however, and ask yourselves this. What have some of the world's longest, bloodiest and cruelest battles been fought over? You already know the answer so now ask yourself, why? What did any of it have to do with God? How can anyone justify it in those terms? And what is that all about? Again, bullies and hoodlums, blind allegiance, a refusal to think and evaluate, simply accepting the statements of other mortals without question, blindly, *as in insane*, knowing full well in the back of our own minds that if ideological and theological differences exist, not everyone can be right. Indeed, there is a very good possibility that they may all be wrong instead."

"Some people, however, keep insisting that without religion the world would be a far worse place in which to live. But how could it get more horrible or self destructive than it already is? How many insane acts have been and are committed in the name of "Religion?" How many more insane acts must be committed before we really get the picture. Religion, as presently practiced on planet earth, is a mind numbing, mind destroying, insane practice almost totally divorced from human values. The world would not be worse without it, but better, because then we might all be more willing to accept ourselves for what we are and to be willing to work together to make things better. But, for many people, for religious and political leaders in particular, it is not in their best interest to do so. And surely, if you let them, they will lead us all straight into extinction. The choice is ours to make. Yours and mine."

HISTORICAL PRELUDE   OPTIONAL

The first time planet Earth divided into two separate parallel worlds was shortly after World War II. The atomic bomb been developed. It had also been used on two infamous occasions to exterminate thousands of people. Mankind was now capable of destroying the entire human race. And from many perspectives, that is exactly where it was headed. The Disappearance, as it was called at the time, was intended to be a wake up call. An extreme event, designed to shake the foundations of human thought.

From the men's point of view, all women and female children completely disappeared from their realm while, from the women's point of view, the opposite was true. The resulting chaos completely devastated both groups as turmoil raged, wars broke out and millions of people lost their lives.

Once it had happened, the disappearance seemed to be permanent. Additionally, without the opposite sex, there would be no future generations. When those still living had expired, humans would be extinct. For many, there was little reason to go on living and they had a difficult time of it.

Then, one day, exactly four years later, totally unexpected, the two worlds merged back into one. Most unfortunate, however, was the fact that when this happened, it did so in a way that would later prove to be valueless in terms of contributing to human wisdom. As an example, at the start a man was sitting at home looking out the window, watching his wife digging in the flowerbed. A moment later she was gone. Gone for four entire years during which time he struggled to stay alive. Their home had been partially destroyed, the neighborhood almost totally demolished and many lives lost. The world had gone crazy with mayhem, madness, perversity and murder. And then, suddenly, in the blink of an eye, she was back. But it was exactly as before. Every trace of disaster had disappeared in the process. The last charred piece of lumber and

327

every lost drop of blood. It was as though the intervening four years had never happened. There was no physical evidence, whatsoever, left over. Absolutely nothing remained for verification. There were no surviving newspaper accounts or television documentaries, no back issues of magazines, no amateur photographs or other evidentiary material. Even such devastation as caused by an airline pilot disappearing from the controls of a passenger plane in flight over Miami that crashed into a row of suburban houses was gone. The only evidence of anything having happened at all was strictly anecdotal.

Unfortunately and for the most part, the psychological disparity of the sum total was far too great for the average human mind to grasp. The shock of the original occurrence had been overwhelming enough but now that it had ended without any solid evidence of it ever having happened to begin with, the entire episode became impossible to reconcile. Many millions of people sank into extreme anxiety and post traumatic stress disorder but went without treatment, fearful that their sanity had come into question. Other millions retreated into denial and escaped into drugs and alcohol. Those few still willing to discuss the happening at all were soon driven into silence by the vast majority who were unable to deal with it. As a result the entire topic soon became publicly taboo. Most even refused to talk about it privately. Nor did they write about it. What was there to say without questioning one's own sanity. Even the calendars had changed back, leaving the intervening four years unrecorded. Whatever had occurred had happened outside of time during some hole in the temporal fabric. A hole which closed back up without visible trace, leaving the stupendous catastrophe impossible to integrate into clear consciousness. Even for those who had risked trading stories and agreed on the supposed events, there was still no way they could be sure they had been reconstructing the truth. And so it went. Denial and repression kept the world functional but the bigger questions about why the disappearance had occurred to begin with, went unexamined.

As a consequence the disappearance never made the official public registry anywhere formal records were kept and in the entirety of all civilized society there was only one individual, a man named Phillip Wylie, who had trusted his own mind well enough to sit down and relive the entire event. Helped by his brave wife who filled in the female perspective, he documented all the tragic details of that four year period in a book titled, The Disappearance. It was published in 1951. This book was later considered to be significant enough to have been republished by the University of Nebraska Press in 2004. In both cases, however, the book had been classified as fiction and there was never a way to prove differently.

Then, all too soon, eighty eight years went by. Ninety seven percent of those old enough to have had any memory trace of the event were deceased. Those of the remaining few left to talk about it were dismissed as senile.

Only in remote indigenous cultures in isolated areas of the world did the tribal storytellers add their view of the happening to their ongoing repertory because, without calendars, they saw it all as a single chain of events rather than time flawlessly patching itself back together. Additionally, living simply without all the technological encumbrances of the rest of civilization, the consequences of the disappearance had far less significance. Thus, in the end, without even a small paragraph in a history book somewhere to back them up, that was that for the civilized world. Any good that might have come from the event was rendered worthless. The intended wake up call for mankind was neutralized. Nothing learned. As for the future well being of the human race, that was even far more questionable than could ever have been imagined back then, when the first disappearance had occurred.

Kiloton atomic bombs had turned into megaton nuclear monsters more than a thousand times more destructive. The ability to manufacture lethal viruses and deadly poisons in the laboratory had also made it possible for almost any nation, no matter how small, to obtain enough virulent substance to wipe out whole continents of other people. Additionally, religious animosity and hatred had risen to heights never before seen in history and fanatical suicide bombers were volunteering for assignments faster than they could be put to use. To further compound the problem, world population had not only doubled, but tripled and kept on growing as the demand for resources erupted into open conflict. Insidiously adding to the problems was the irreversible, humanly created truth of global warming. All in all, if the world had been ten steps away from the brink of self annihilation after World War two, it was now perched right on the edge, toes hanging over into the void. It would take something far more drastic than lingering dreams or questionable mythology to shake humanity awake and resolve the problem this time. And so there was a second "Disappearance" but this time it happened differently.